"How old are you?"

"Thirty." Leslie had almost said her own age of twenty-eight.

"You don't look it."

"Is my age a problem?'

Pierce Gallagher shook his head. "I was merely making an observation. What I need is someone who'll be with us at least until Cory starts first grade a year from now. Could you commit to that amount of time?"

"Yes."

"There's no man you left behind who expects you to return to New Jersey sooner than that?"

An icy shiver raced through her body. "I was engaged to be married, but it didn't work out."

The ranger was silent for what seemed like a long while.

"You're certain it's over?" he said at last.

If he only knew.

"If a trail is to be blazed, send a ranger,
if an animal is floundering in the snow, send a ranger, if a bear
is in a hotel, send a ranger, if a fire threatens a forest, send a ranger,
and if someone needs to be saved, send a ranger."
—Stephen Mather, first director, National Park Service

Dear Reader,

The above quote sums up my feelings about the rangers in my latest Harlequin Supperromance novel, *Woman in Hiding*.

Years ago one of the guys in my neighborhood became a U.S. Park Ranger. He worked in Grand Teton National Park before transferring to one of the national parks in Alaska, where he now resides. His experiences and exploits fascinated me, and I found myself wanting to write a story about these intrepid, rugged heroes guarding our national treasures.

Like a paramedic, the rangers respond to an alarm never knowing what they're going to find. Each call is different, each situation unique. They have to be prepared for everything!

In this novel, Pierce Gallagher is the Chief Ranger of Grand Teton National Park. You can imagine that he's a *ranger's ranger*. The buck stops with him. He's number one. The ultimate, real live hero who puts his life on the line every day. It's no wonder Leslie Hopkins, my terrified heroine on the run for her life, loses her heart to him and his vulnerable six-year-old son, Cory.

Enjoy!

Rebecca Winters

Woman in Hiding
Rebecca Winters

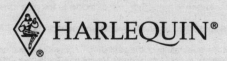

HARLEQUIN®

TORONTO • NEW YORK • LONDON
AMSTERDAM • PARIS • SYDNEY • HAMBURG
STOCKHOLM • ATHENS • TOKYO • MILAN • MADRID
PRAGUE • WARSAW • BUDAPEST • AUCKLAND

ISBN 0-373-71210-3

WOMAN IN HIDING

This edition published by arrangement with Harlequin Books S.A.

® and TM are trademarks of the publisher. Trademarks indicated with
® are registered in the United States Patent and Trademark Office, the
Canadian Trade Marks Office and in other countries.

www.eHarlequin.com

Printed in U.S.A.

This book is dedicated to Ralph—
a dear family friend and ranger's ranger.

CHAPTER ONE

"LESLIE? IT'S DIANA! Let me in!"

Leslie Hopkins raced to the door of her New York City apartment and opened it. Her married sister slipped inside. After locking it, Leslie grabbed her and clung.

"If I hadn't known you were coming any second, you wouldn't have found me here."

Diana looked at her in fresh alarm. "Why? What else has that demented ex-fiancé of yours done in the last twelve hours?"

"Take a look at what he left on the coffee table while I was at the pharmacy picking up the tint for my hair. He must have followed me there and knew he had time to break in."

Her sister marched into the living room, then came to an abrupt halt. "Black roses? Ed's not very original, is he."

"It gets worse. You should see what's in my bedroom."

"Worse than your own underwear showing up in the pizza you thought *I* had ordered to be delivered to you last week?"

"Yes."

She dashed down the hall to investigate. Leslie followed.

Two-dozen cut-up photographs of Leslie had been laid out on the quilt. He'd taped the portions with her head to the wall over her bed. A heart had been drawn around them in Leslie's lipstick, the one she'd discovered missing from her purse ten days ago.

Diana blanched. "I take back what I said."

"I don't understand how he got in here! The locks were changed yesterday morning for the fourth time."

"He probably forced a window open from the fire escape."

"I checked them. They're locked! There's no place I'm safe. I've taken every piece of advice the police have given me, but nothing has helped." She buried her face in her hands. "Ed knows every move I make."

"Not after today he won't!"

Leslie lifted a tear-ravaged face. "I don't think the plan we talked about is going to work. He has some kind of supernatural radar."

Diana took her by the shoulders and shook her. "No, he doesn't! It just seems that way because he has focused all his attention on you.

"Remember what Detective Santini told you? Former-partner stalkers have their entire sense of self-worth caught up in the 'she loves me' syndrome. Any evidence to the contrary is seen as an inconvenience to overcome."

"He's like an evil child," Leslie muttered.

"Exactly. Since he's not getting any response from you, he's acting out because even negative attention is better than none at all. Roger says Ed follows the typical profile, with his history of spousal abuse.

That's why we're going to get you away from him permanently.''

"I don't see how we can. He's already been here this morning and is lurking in some hallway right now working on a plan to get inside and kill me.''

"It's not going to happen, Leslie. Come on. I've brought everything you need to disappear where he'll never find you. First, let's get this rinse done, then I'll cut your hair.''

Within an hour, Leslie's long blond hair had been tinted light brown, and she wore it at chin length in a feather-cut like Diana's.

They stood side by side in front of the mirror. Leslie was five foot eight, an inch taller than her sister.

Diana nodded with satisfaction. "We may not be twins, but the resemblance is strong enough for you to use my driver's license and get away with it.''

She spoke the truth. With both of them hazel-eyed and slender, there were more similarities than differences.

Leslie hurried into the bedroom to put on the cotton top she planned to wear on the plane with her jeans. "Is Roger really okay about my impersonating you?''

"The logistics were all my husband's idea, and he's the attorney in the family. We both want you to get as far away from Ed as you can and make a new life for yourself. There's no reason it won't work. I'll get a duplicate license.''

"But your credit card—''

"We've been over this before. I don't need it.''

"I don't know where I should go! No destination sounds right. I can't make a decis—''

"Don't worry," Diana broke in. "Roger has made the arrangements."

"As long as it's light-years from here, I don't care where it is."

"A nonstop flight from Kennedy to Salt Lake City leaves in two-and-a-half hours. Your ticket's prepaid. All you have to do is check in."

Salt Lake? "I've never been there." She would never have thought of it.

"Neither have I, but Roger insists it's the perfect location. A flyover city. Not too big, the people are nice, the pace is slower. You'll be able to find an anonymous office job that will leave you free to explore the canyons on the weekends. We know how much you love getting out in nature."

Leslie couldn't imagine ever feeling free enough to do that. She shook her head. "He'll track me down, Diana. I know he will."

"Listen to me. When he finally figures out you're nowhere around, he won't have a clue where you've gone."

"He can always find me on the passenger list."

"Not right away. First of all he'll have to figure out *how* you left New York, and it'll take him a while before he realizes you got away using my name. Even if he eventually gets that information and follows you to Salt Lake, he won't know where to begin looking for you."

Diana could say that now...

"You're booked at the Scenic View motel, and you'll have to take a taxi from the airport. Roger said not to use a rental car unless you have to. They're too easy to trace.

"On the way to the motel, stop at the Fred Meyer store on Fourth South. They're open until midnight. You can buy a suitcase and some clothes and toiletries there."

Fred Meyer. "I'll remember." She tried to swallow but couldn't. "This has to work!"

Her sister's expression sobered. "I agree. Otherwise you'll be in and out of court for years. New York may have passed heavier penalties for stalking, but Roger says nothing will stop someone like Ed who's intent on ruining your every living moment. At least this way you have a fighting chance to get on with your life."

Another shudder passed through Leslie's body. She reached out to hug her sister. "What would I do without you and Roger? You're the only reason I haven't had a complete nervous breakdown."

"This past month has been a nightmare, but it's going to end the second you get on that plane."

"You promise?"

"Would your big sister lie to you?"

"No," Leslie whispered before reaching for her tote bag, which contained her laptop computer. She hadn't dared pack anything from her apartment that she wouldn't normally take or wear to work. If Ed discovered anything else missing the next time he broke in, like her camera, passport and suitcase, it would be a dead giveaway.

"I can't bear to leave Josh and Amy."

"It'll be harder on them. We'll explain you're busy and won't be able to come over for a while." Like forever? "Without specifics, they won't be able to give away information to anyone Ed might set up to call our house.''

''I don't know how to repay you guys.''

''You already have by being such a loving sister and aunt. Is your answering machine on?''

''Yes.''

''Good. As long as that psycho is able to keep leaving messages, he'll get his kicks out of believing you actually listen to them.''

''How did I ever fall for a man who's so sick?''

''That's easy. Besides being good-looking, he's a smooth charmer who fooled everyone. Just remember—you weren't his first victim.''

How could Leslie ever forget Maureen Strickland, a former off-Broadway actress who turned out to be Ed's ex-wife, a wife he'd never bothered to tell Leslie about.

Maureen had heard through a friend that Ed was engaged to a photographic journalist who worked at the *New York Chronicler,* too. Afraid for Leslie, she'd approached her outside the newspaper office while Ed was in Florida on assignment.

She'd come to warn Leslie to get away from him before their wedding could take place. According to Maureen, Ed was a psychopath with a history of domestic violence on public record.

Even if Leslie had acted on the other woman's warning that very day and had disappeared, she would still be living in fear he would eventually track her down.

''Don't dwell on the past,'' her sister urged. ''Here's the passport to your new life.''

She opened her purse and handed Leslie her

driver's license, a credit card and five thousand dollars in large bills. The money had come from Leslie's savings account. By phone she'd asked her bank manager to transfer her balance.

"From now on, *you* are Diana Farrow. Are you ready?"

"I don't know—this is like a terrible dream." She put everything in her wallet and closed her tote bag. "The last thing I want to do is leave all of you, but the alternative is no longer tenable. If I don't get away from here, I know I'll end up…dead."

"Don't ever say that again!" Diana chastised her. "Remember—phone calls are out, too easy to trace. No matter how far-fetched, he might get hold of our phone bills. They would lead him straight to you."

Leslie didn't need to be reminded that Ed was a savvy newspaper reporter with resources and instincts that made him a terrifying adversary. Guilt and pain assailed her. "I'm so sorry he's been harassing you and Roger. Heaven knows who else! Your lives are in danger, too."

"Nonsense. It's you he wants. Expect an e-mail from us after you get to your motel. That'll be about 10:00 p.m. Salt Lake time."

"I'll be living for it."

They stared at each other before Diana said, "Give me five minutes to do some reconnaissance work on my way out of the building. If I don't come back, then you'll know it's safe to carry on with the plan. I love you. God bless."

After another fierce embrace, her sister slipped out while Leslie stood there in a cold sweat. She kept an eye on her watch. When five minutes had passed and there was no sign of Diana, she grabbed her tote bag and left the apartment. There was a service elevator at the rear of the building. She hurried toward it, looking over her shoulder with every step.

The ride from the twentieth to the ground floor seemed to take forever. She jumped when the doors opened, expecting to find Ed standing there. Thankfully no one was around except a building security guard she'd never seen before. He sat on a chair reading a magazine.

His job was to prevent anyone from coming in without authorization, but Ed would know how to get past him. He had probably done so already by flashing his newspaper credentials and saying he was there on a big story.

Leslie walked straight to the door. She earned a nod from him, nothing else.

People and cars filled the alley outside. With her heart fluttering like a hummingbird's, she scanned the scene. No sign of Ed, but that didn't mean he wasn't in the crowd somewhere.

"Help me, God." She murmured the words over and over as she merged with the foot traffic. By the time she reached the corner of the next block she was able to hail a cab.

"Kennedy airport, as fast as possible, please."

"Okay, lady."

If Ed had spotted her, it was too late for him to prevent the driver from taking off. But he could grab the next cab and follow her.

She kept turning around. A few minutes later she said, "Can't you go any faster?"

"I could, lady, but nothin's worth losing my job over. Know what I mean?"

Once upon a time she did, but those days were over. She was a woman on the run now. If she was going to survive, she would have to live by her wits. When the detective had first told Leslie that, she hadn't wanted to believe him.

Her hand reached for the wallet in her purse. "Not even an extra forty dollars would induce you to get creative?" She leaned forward and dropped the bills next to him.

After a sideward glance he said, "I'll see what I can do."

Leslie couldn't fathom she was leaving New York, her job, her family. She adored her niece and nephew, tended them whenever the breaks in her work allowed.

During the six months she'd dated Ed Strickland, he hadn't seemed to mind spending time with the children. However, after he'd given her a diamond, he'd wanted her all to himself.

She'd chalked up his possessiveness to prewedding frustration due to the newspaper assignments that kept them apart. She should have realized something was wrong. But she'd been oblivious until Maureen had enlightened her with tales of being prevented from going to work. He'd kept her a virtual prisoner in their own home.

Even after being divorced eight years, Ed's ex-wife still had to keep moving around so he wouldn't find her.

When Leslie had first met Maureen, she'd thought the nervous woman was a lunatic and had related the incident to Ed when he got back in town. To her shock he admitted he'd been married before but it represented a dark period in his former life he preferred to forget had ever happened. He denied any abuse.

Confused and shaken by what she considered a serious sin of omission, Leslie had broken down to her sister. Roger checked out the woman's story. When it all came back true, the subsequent confrontation with Ed turned into a hellish situation.

Though she'd called off the wedding, he'd refused to believe they weren't getting married. For the last month he'd done a good job of destroying her life. She cringed to think what he would do to Maureen if he ever caught up with her again.

The other woman had been so courageous to intervene before Leslie had taken his name and met with a terrible fate. Some day Leslie wanted to thank her. That is, if either of them lived that long…

WHILE DIANA WAITED for the doorman of Leslie's apartment building to flag down a taxi for her, she heard a voice call her name. She looked over her shoulder. Through the busy noontime crowds she watched Ed Strickland work his way toward her.

His presence meant he'd seen Diana go in the building and had been waiting for her to come out again. Terrified as she was of him after the way he'd stalked their house in New Jersey in order to talk to her, she thanked God this plan had worked. Leslie had escaped without detection! By now she ought to be well on her way to the airport.

Diana forced herself to calm down. The last thing

she wanted to do was face her sister's tormentor, but if talking to him would give Leslie a few more minutes head start, it was worth it.

She had to admit that Ed'd proverbial guy-next-door good looks had first captured Leslie's heart. A dark blond with warm brown eyes—a man every eligible woman wanted to meet. Six feet tall, nice build. The clean-cut guy an editor liked on his payroll. The trustworthy type who got interviews with people others said would be impossible to reach.

No one passing by could imagine that Mr. Hyde lurked inside this charming Dr. Jekyll.

"Hi," he said with that easy smile. "I saw you go inside and have been waiting to talk to you. How's the family?"

He was so good at pretending there was no bad history between him and her sister, it was terrifying. When she thought of the black roses and those cut-off heads he'd left in Leslie's apartment as recently as a few hours ago...

How *had* he gotten in there?

Maybe he was a man with a true split personality. Was it possible the personality emerging right now honestly believed everything was all right? A chill seeped into her bones.

"We're fine."

"That's good, because I need your help with Leslie."

Diana shook her head. "We've been through this before, Ed. She had her reasons for giving you back the ring."

"I know, and I don't blame her for breaking it off with me. But it's been a month, and I was hoping she would agree to see me so I can explain my side of the story.''

"Leslie's not interested. You need to let it go and move on.'' Of course he wouldn't, but she didn't know what else to say to him.

''She's not being fair to me. She listened to Maureen without giving me my turn.''

"None of it matters now. It's over.''

A wounded look entered his eyes. "She would agree to a meeting if you were in the room, too. All I ask is ten minutes. That's it. Come on.'' He put his hand on her arm. "Please. I can't eat, sleep. I'm in pain, you know?'' His voice trembled.

She believed him. But it was a twisted, dark pain within his tortured psyche. A place where she doubted even the best psychiatrist could reach, let alone help. Roger would be upset if he knew she'd given Ed this much time.

''Not every relationship is meant to be.''

''Ours is.''

''Only in *your* mind, not Leslie's. I have to go. My taxi's here.''

It had drawn up to the curb, thank heaven. The doorman held the rear door open for her. She had to pull hard for Ed to let go of her arm. Tomorrow there would be a bruise.

A feeling of revulsion and horror swept through her to realize such deceptive strength had resulted in Maureen Strickland being beaten up and battered.

Fly far away, Leslie. Never come back.

Diana tipped the doorman, then climbed inside the cab without looking back.

WHEN LESLIE GOT OUT of the taxi at the Scenic View motel, it was almost 11:00 p.m. After stopping at Fred Meyer to shop for a suitcase and some necessities, she'd phoned for another taxi to bring her to this quiet residential area on the east side of Salt Lake.

Throughout both taxi rides she'd kept turning around to see if anyone was following her. In her gut she knew that as long as Ed was alive, she would always be looking over her shoulder.

After the humidity of a sweltering August in New York, the dry, balmy air over the Great Salt Lake Valley came as a welcome surprise. She paid the driver, then went inside the office to register. A sign on the wall said they served a continental breakfast in the lobby starting at six.

That was a relief. It would save her having to call for another taxi in the morning to find a place to eat. But the fear never left her that Ed could walk up to her at any time no matter where she was, flashing that easy smile that was supposed to heal all wounds.

It wasn't beyond the realm of possibility that he'd seen her leaving the apartment and had caught up to her at the airport. He might even have flown to Salt Lake on the same plane with her. The thought petrified her that he could be here where she had no safe house, no family. But if she continued to let fear paralyze her, she might as well have stayed in New York.

Until this nightmare had begun, Leslie had always had an adventurous spirit. Her career as a photographic journalist had sent her on assignments around the globe for the newspaper. In the last year she'd been to the Amazon, Malaysia and Australia for weeks at a time on a project covering the world's disappearing rain forests.

On her most recent trip to Madagascar, she'd been flown by helicopter into a deep valley with a team of research scientists to film one of the few known rain forests yet untouched by man. During the dangerous three-week expedition, their group had been isolated from the world.

After she'd returned with priceless footage, her boss Byron Howell, the science editor at the *New York Chronicler,* had called Leslie fearless and her work brilliant. Ecstatic over the filming she'd done, he'd given her the month off to get married. When she got back from her honeymoon, they'd talk about a new project.

Thrilled by her boss's praise, and excited to be able to concentrate on the last-minute details for her marriage to Ed, Leslie had hurried out of the building intent on picking up their engraved wedding invitations. She hadn't counted on being approached by Maureen Strickland.

In the horrendous weeks that followed, Leslie had learned the true meaning of fear. If her boss could see the shape she was in now—scared of her own shadow—he wouldn't believe the change in his formerly gutsy photographer.

Since Ed reported national news for the *New York Chronicler,* everyone at the paper who knew them would eventually realize something had gone wrong when their marriage didn't take place.

But both Detective Santini and Roger had warned Leslie not to tell her boss or co-workers anything. Word would get to Ed's boss. If Ed's job were threatened in any way, he could turn even more violent. Leslie's best plan of action would be to disappear.

Diana had promised to get in touch with Byron Howell and tell him her sister needed a few more weeks off from work to deal with a broken engagement. It would buy Leslie more time before Ed realized she was gone for good.

And when he did find out the truth?

She shuddered.

Ed had the clout and access to people who could trace anyone. At some point he would vet the apartment security staff and learn she'd left the building disguised as her sister. Leslie couldn't afford to let her guard down for an instant.

Certainly until Leslie had heard from Diana and could e-mail her back that so far everything had gone without a problem, she wouldn't be able to take a deep breath.

On her way out of the motel lobby, Leslie purchased a copy of the *Salt Lake Tribune*. Later she would read through the want ads. With it tucked under one, she grabbed her tote bag and suitcase and went in search of her motel room four doors down from the office.

When she let herself inside and locked the door, she was too apprehensive to do anything until she'd made an inspection of the closet and bathroom. Relieved to discover dowels in the locked windows, she opened her tote bag to get at her laptop.

Neither Diana nor Roger would go to bed until they'd heard from her. Since it was one o'clock in the morning New Jersey time, there wasn't a minute to lose.

As soon as she found the phone connection and electric outlet, she logged on to her Web mail account. Three weeks ago she'd changed servers and taken a new user name so Ed could no longer contact her. Except for her family, not one soul knew this address.

Warmth stole through her body to see a message in her Inbox. It represented home. She opened it.

Dear Leslie—If you're reading this, we're assuming you arrived in Salt Lake. Instant-message me the second you can. I have a lot to tell you.

Leslie typed a reply.

Thanks to you and Roger, I'm in my motel room. Fred Meyer had everything I needed. So far so good, but that doesn't mean Ed isn't far behind.

Her sister must have pasted something she'd prepared ahead of time because in the next moment Leslie received a lengthy letter.

Ed has no clue you've left New York!

Leslie couldn't have read sweeter words.

The reason I know is because he left another message on the answering machine a few minutes ago sounding angry with me because I refused to help him this morning. If he knew where you were, he wouldn't be harassing me!

The bands constricting Leslie's breathing loosened as she read the rest of the message, telling about Diana's conversation with Ed out in front of the apartment.

Leslie knew from the doorman that Ed hung out there part of every day, yet he still managed to do his newspaper work, too. It made her skin crawl to think

Ed had manhandled Diana no matter what benign face he'd put on initially to get in her good graces.

His only focus is you, Leslie. He's terrifying! The smartest thing we ever did was get you out of New York today.

We know the post office is forwarding your mail to our house because some of your bills came today, which we'll take care of. There were three letters from Ed among them. We've read them and they're the same ravings about forgiveness.

Just hearing that made Leslie feel sick to her stomach. Ed had grown up the only son of a minister and his wife, who'd done service in Africa and had died there in an epidemic of some kind. At eleven, Ed had been taken care of by a series of Christian missionary couples until he'd grown old enough to be on his own and return to the States.

He'd never liked to talk about his religious upbringing. With hindsight Leslie could see that losing his parents at that age had caused severe emotional damage, turning him into the unstable man he'd become.

Roger had said he would keep Ed's e-mails and letters as evidence against him in case she had to face him in court one day.

Don't worry about your boss. Next Friday I'll call him and tell him you need more time to get over your broken engagement. No matter what he says, I'll reassure him that at one point you'll contact him, but it will have to be on your timetable.

Leslie typed her reply.

Thanks, Diana. I hate doing this to Byron, but there's no other way.

In the next instant Roger said hello.

One day your boss will know the truth, and he'll understand. As for Ed, I don't want either of you girls having anything to do with him anymore. I'll handle everything from here on out. Glad you're there, kiddo. I imagine you're beyond exhausted and need sleep in the worst way. We'll talk to you tomorrow. Love you.

Tears smarted Leslie's eyes.

I love you, too. Thank you from the bottom of my heart for all you've done for me. Give the kids a hug and kiss from their aunt Leslie.

Diana came back on.

Will do. Go to bed and sleep in. Treat yourself to a few days' relaxation. After your month of terror, you need some downtime to relax.

Roger was in Salt Lake a few years ago and says Temple Square is a fabulous place to visit.

While he was there, he ate at a great French restaurant in an old French manor house surrounded by a vineyard that serves wonderful food. It's called La Caille at Quail Run. He insists it rivals anything in New York. You'll have to try it and tell us what you think.

So, dear sister, give yourself permission to enjoy your freedom, and dream happy dreams tonight.

That would be impossible. While they'd been instant-messaging each other, another thought had occurred to her. Ed could have left that last message on her sister's voice mail to make everyone believe he wasn't aware of her disappearance.

In reality, he could be hot on her trail right now. After his ability to come and go from her apartment at will, she didn't put anything past him. The thought filled her with fresh terror, but she kept it to herself.

I'd say the same to you guys, but I'm afraid there'll be no rest for you as long as Ed keeps phoning. I'm so sorry. I'll e-mail you tomorrow evening and let you know how my job search went. Good night.

Then the last message from Diana appeared on the screen. Night-night.

Those were the words her little three-year-old niece always said before going to sleep. Leslie suffered another sharp pang of homesickness.

She shut off her laptop and got ready for bed. Though her body seemed to move in slow motion, she felt emotionally wired. It wasn't like being away on a photographic assignment where she knew she'd be going home at the end of a shoot and could fall asleep without a problem.

This time Leslie couldn't go home....

CHAPTER TWO

"THE GRAND PRIZE WINNER of New York State's PTA Reflections contest goes to Leslie Hopkins, a ninth-grader at Cosgrove Junior High in Rochester. The original and captivating photographs depicting the birth and growth of her dog Marvel through its first nine months of life won a unanimous decision from the judges.

"She's receiving two prizes. Besides the one thousand dollars donated by the PTA, her photographic outlay will be published in the *National Pug Society Gazette* next spring. I have a check made out to Leslie from them for five hundred dollars. Leslie? If you'll come up on stage to receive your prizes, please."

"I knew you would win, honey!" her beaming father whispered. "Now you know you're on your way to becoming the great photographer you want to be one day." He squeezed her hand before letting her go.

Her mom and sister gave her a hard hug before she worked her way around her father's wheelchair at the end of the aisle.

After the presentation, the head of the PTA said, "Now the audience would like to hear a few words from you, Leslie."

Leslie approached the mike. "Thank you. I'm so

happy to have won, but I don't see how when there were so many other kids with great projects. I want to thank my dad, who runs a photography studio with my mom out of our home.

"He was a newspaper photographer during a civil war in Africa where he got shot and lost the use of his legs. He's the one who taught me how to take pictures. Some day I hope to be as good as he is.

"Thanks, Dad and Mom, for encouraging me in this project. I want to thank my sister, too. She helped me set up my shots by bribing Marvel with his favorite treats."

The PTA lady smiled. "It sounds like a real family affair. How lovely. What do you think you'll do with the money?"

"Give it to my father to buy a new camera he's been wanting."

On the way back home, her parents told her about the present they were giving her for winning. As soon as school was out, they were signing her up to join a teenage photography club that took numerous trips to the Catskills and Adirondacks to learn about filming birds and wildlife.

That night sealed her fate as a photographer. It led to other trips and opportunities. The next year she was able to film eagles in the Poconos of Pennsylvania. Later on that same summer she traveled to the Blue Ridge Mountains of North Carolina with a teenage hiking-and-photography club. She happened to catch a cougar on film.

As it turned out, the wildcat had been killing a lot of deer, and the rangers had posted a cash reward for anyone who got a picture of it. Leslie ended up with her picture in the paper along with her fabulous shots of the cougar. She returned home from that trip with money in her pocket.

Tragically, it was only a few months later that her father died of a blood clot to the lung. Before his death he told her he'd put the money she'd won from the Reflections contest in a savings account so that one day she could buy a really fabulous camera.

Leslie was sad that he never got to see the one she eventually bought before entering college. Nor did he live long enough to know that after she had freelanced for several years, she'd landed the plum job of working for one of the nation's great newspapers.

Memories of her beloved father and mother who'd made everything possible caused the tears to roll down Leslie's cheeks. But it was just as well they hadn't lived long enough to go through the trauma of watching Ed Strickland terrorize their daughter.

His determination to destroy her meant that as long as he was alive, she would never be able to use her fabulous camera to earn her living at the profession she adored.

Dear God, what *was* she going to do?

Roger and Diana had urged her to take a few days to relax and sightsee. As they pointed out, she had enough money to pamper herself. Now that she was free, there was no rush to do anything.

However, Leslie knew herself too well. Until she'd found a job and a place to live, she couldn't possibly relax the way they'd suggested.

Even if Ed didn't know where she was right this minute, it wouldn't be long before he realized she'd disappeared. The knowledge that she'd escaped would set him off in ways she couldn't bear to contemplate.

No. For sanity's sake, she had to get herself settled first. Then maybe on her days off from work she would feel brave enough to treat herself to dinner at La Caille or explore downtown Salt Lake.

Still jumping out of her skin every time thoughts of Ed intruded, she reached for the newspaper and turned to the want ads.

Get an anonymous office job, Roger had counseled her.

Her gaze went directly to the heading for Secretaries Wanted. She studied the long, boring list until she felt so claustrophobic, she couldn't breathe.

After a lifetime spent in the outdoors, after her jaunts around the world photographing nature, the prospect of working in some low-profile, innocuous office job where she'd be shut up inside all day sounded like prison to her.

But what else could she do? Ed would search for her in any field related to photography or journalism. She had to rule out positions in sales or big business, where she'd be forced to travel to the East Coast.

Frantic because no job looked appealing, she went to the beginning of the want ads and began working her way down the alphabet of listings. She wasn't accountant material. An advertising firm might be too much exposure for her.

Bakers, bartenders, bricklayers. All of the above were out. She kept on going until she came to Caregivers.

The word brought Leslie's mother to mind. Before she'd died of cancer last year, Leslie and Diana had taken turns nursing her over a nine-month period. It had been a very sad yet sweet time for the three of them.

Her gaze traveled to the first job advertised.

Nanny wanted. Three days/week. 9:00-3:00 p.m. References req. Two kids, ages 5 & 2. Call Brandy: 555-3600 or 555-2184.

Leslie's thoughts flew to her niece and nephew. She could do work like that! She loved children.

It would be low profile and she wouldn't have to stay cooped up indoors all the time. There were parks and zoos to visit, picnics to plan. But this particular position was only for three days a week. She needed a full-time job with benefits that offered a salary she could live on.

No doubt it was because she was missing Josh and Amy so badly that this section of the want ads attracted her attention. She was a hopeless case where the kids were concerned.

There were a dozen listings for nannies, and double that for caregivers for the elderly. None of them seemed quite right. Either the pay was too low, or there were no benefits, or some nursing skills were required, or the position was seasonal. Leslie was about to go on to the job descriptions in the Cashier category when the last listing piqued her interest.

Mature woman needed ASAP to live in year-round and care for a six-year-old boy.

Six? That was Josh's age.

Some light housekeeping, cooking and driving required. Pay and benefits negotiable. Refs required. Phone: 307-555-4668. Moose, Wyoming. Ask for Chief Ranger Gallagher.

Chief Ranger?

Intrigued, Leslie scrambled out of bed to go online again. She typed in Moose, Wyoming.

Her eyes widened when she discovered Moose was in Grand Teton National Park. Good heavens—the fabulous Tetons! She'd only seen them in pictures, but they were one range of mountains she'd always wanted to visit and film.

After doing a special photo shoot of the earth's unique volcanoes for *International Mountaineering Magazine,* her love of mountains had increased a hundredfold.

The spectacular pictures she'd captured after climbing the Volcan Licancabur in the Chilean Andes, with the help of guides, had captured Byron Howell's attention at the paper.

That particular shoot, which included her photographic layout of Mount Spurr in Alaska, plus the Ecuadorian Avenue of the Volcanoes, had given her the entrée she'd needed to join the ranks of the prestigious New York newspaper.

She read the ad again.

If she wanted to stay hidden from Ed, she couldn't imagine a safer, more glorious place. Besides offering a full-time job, benefits and a roof over her head, she would be living in a spectacular nature setting year-round.

Though New York City had its attractions, she'd been raised in Rochester and had never been a big-city girl. In that regard she was much more like her mother, who'd enjoyed being a homemaker.

But there was another side to that coin. She'd inherited her father's love for photography, too. It was the challenge of capturing photo essays in nature rather than the glamour of a job that sent her around the world that she loved.

Living in the Tetons would allow her and the boy to explore the mountains to their heart's content. It would be fun to show him how to take pictures, just like her father used to do with her. Being able to help a child develop a hobby like that would satisfy something at the very core of her being.

Leslie studied the rest of the information on the Web site. There were daily flights from Salt Lake to the airport in Jackson Hole, Wyoming, with shuttle and taxi services to the Tetons and Yellowstone. Moose was only about twelve miles from the airport. Perfect!

Once she got back in bed, she spent the next half hour reading through the rest of the want ads. She made check marks with her pen by the few jobs she might be able to stand.

One was for a waitress at a ski lodge in Park City that was open year-round. Another advertised for a maid at a ski lodge at Snowbird, also open twelve months of the year. Both offered benefits and housing. At least either job would be in the mountains where she wouldn't feel stifled.

But time and again her mind went back to the ranger's ad. Before she got too excited, she would phone first thing in the morning to find out if the job had been filled. She noticed the ad was almost a month old. That meant she was probably too late. Still…

"HEY, CHAMP. JANICE IS HERE. Got to go to work now."

"When are you going to help me put my racetrack together?"

"Tonight."

"Promise?"

"Yup. Be a good guy at kindergarten and clean up the toys in your room before you go. Okay?"

"Okay. Can Logan come over after school?"

"That's up to Janice, but it's fine with me. Give me a hug."

Pierce Gallagher's heart melted every time he felt Cory's arms go around his neck. So far the two of them were doing fine, but Pierce was worried because their life was about to change. All because his friend Jim Archer had been made chief ranger at Yellowstone Park.

It was a well-deserved promotion and Pierce was happy for him. But it meant that in a few days Jim and his wife Janice would be leaving Moose. Pierce hadn't found the courage to tell his son about the transfer yet. Cory would be forced to face another loss he wasn't ready for.

Pierce hadn't found a replacement for Janice and time was running out. It had been almost four weeks since he'd placed an ad in the major newspapers throughout Wyoming, Idaho, Utah and Montana.

He'd had a few bites, mostly widows in their late forties to sixties. But once they were given a chance to think about the isolation and long winters, they decided the job wasn't for them. At least they were honest about it, but that didn't solve his problem.

If he didn't find someone soon, he would have to

leave Moose and move to his hometown of Ashton, Wyoming, where he was certain of finding good day care for Cory.

They could live in his deceased parents' house, which he'd held on to as a rental property. It would mean taking a leave of absence and finding a temporary job with the forest service if it came to that. Rex Hollister, a fellow ranger, would be appointed acting chief ranger in his place. Rex was a good man, but the whole scenario left Pierce cold.

He'd only been chief ranger for two and a half years. There were a lot things he'd planned to accomplish in his job, but Cory's needs came first. He'd made that promise to Linda....

If their son wasn't happy and secure, then nothing else would ever be right.

He left the bedroom and headed for the kitchen, where Janice was cleaning up from the breakfast he'd made for them.

"Cory wants Logan to come over after school. Will that be all right with you?"

She smiled at him. "Sure. They play well together. Any luck finding a nanny?"

He shook his head.

"I'm so sorry, Pierce. I'd give anything to help you out. Jim and I have talked about it. For the next few months I could stay with you Mondays through Thursdays. You could probably find someone to help out on Fridays."

Pierce was touched by the offer. Janice's selflessness was one of her greatest qualities.

"I couldn't ask you to sacrifice that way. It's long past time Jim had his wife back on a full-time basis."

"I'm pregnant. He's had me," she teased.

Pierce smiled, envying the lucky couple. "I'll figure something out. You've done more for Cory and me than you'll ever know. I'll never be able to repay you, but I'll always remember you offered. See you at five."

He left the house and got into his truck. Though he didn't need to drive to the nearby headquarters, something always came up during the day that required his presence elsewhere in the park. It made sense to keep a vehicle close by. As he was about to enter his office, his secretary, Sally, looked up from her desk.

"'Morning, Pierce."

"'Morning, Sally. What's lined up for today?"

"Except for a phone call for you from Salt Lake, it's been a pretty quiet Tuesday morning so far."

His brow lifted. "Salt Lake? Did someone else answer my ad?" He'd all but given up hope.

"Yes. She said she'd call back in fifteen minutes." Just then the phone rang. "I bet that's her now."

Pierce waited to find out. When his secretary nodded he said, "I'll take it in my office. What's her name?"

She covered the mouthpiece with her palm. "Ms. Diana Farrow. You can tell she's an easterner."

He kept that in mind as he shut the door and reached for the phone on his desk. "Ms. Farrow? This is Pierce Gallagher. Sorry I wasn't here when you called earlier."

"No problem. I've been out west on vacation from New Jersey and like the area so much, I'm thinking of getting a good full-time job so I can stay here. Your ad sounds exactly what I'm looking for.

"I've had a lot of experience with children. I grew up in Rochester, New York, and I've been driving since I was sixteen. But before I begin my job search, I wanted to know if the position in question has already been filled."

The woman didn't sound in her fifties or anything close to it, but voices could be deceptive. "Not yet. In order to save you time, I'll be frank. Moose is in Grand Teton National Park."

"I know."

"Then you also know the winters are fierce. Couple that with long periods of isolation and you'll understand why the other applicants decided to look elsewhere for work."

"I can deal with all of that. Tell me about the boy. What relation is he to you?"

The question caught him off guard. "Cory's my son, of course."

"The ad didn't say. You could be his grandfather or uncle, even a stepparent who might just have been awarded custody."

She was right.

"I think you were wise not to give away too much information. You never know what kind of people you'll attract."

Her direct way of speaking was refreshing and disturbing at the same time. This was probably the most bizarre conversation he'd ever had, yet he was intrigued by the stranger's native intelligence.

"Due to my line of work, emergencies crop up. I need someone on a twenty-four-hour basis. Cory lost his mother eighteen months ago. Since then, a close friend has been coming in to take care of him during the day. But she'll be leaving at the end of the week.''

After a silence the woman replied, ''That's going to be very hard on your son. You must be dreading another change in his life so soon.''

Pierce was beginning to think a psychic had answered his ad. ''I am.'' He cleared his throat. ''Can you tell me about your previous job experience?''

''Following my graduation from college, my mother was diagnosed with cancer. She died after a long bout with the disease. My married sister Leslie and I took turns nursing her until the end. I tended Leslie and Roger's children when she was with Mother and other times as well, of course. Josh is six years old like your son, but he and Amy are their children, not mine.

''With Mom gone, I decided it was time to take a vacation and see a new part of the country. But I've discovered you can only travel so long. Now I'm at a loose end and need to be needed by someone again, but I have to earn an adequate living, too.''

Pierce's eyes closed tightly. He could relate.

''I have another reason for wanting to find work here. My sister's family deserves a break from me. I don't want them to start looking at me as a lifetime project they'll always have to worry about. When I reached Salt Lake yesterday, the first thing I did was buy a newspaper to search the want ads.''

''What references do you have?''

''My sister and her husband. That's probably not very helpful to you, but the three of us have been very close for the last six years. They live in New Jersey, too. Would you like her cell phone number?"

"Please. I also need her last name and the number you're calling from."

After she gave him the information he said, "I'll get back with you before the day is out."

"I can't ask for more than that. Thank you very much, Mr. Gallagher. Goodbye."

The second he heard the click, he phoned the New Jersey number. After three rings a voice answered that sounded as if it could have been Ms. Farrow herself.

"Hello. My name is Pierce Gallagher calling from Wyoming. Is this Leslie Hopkins?"

"Speaking."

"Your sister Diana Farrow gave me your name as a reference. She answered my ad for a nanny."

There was a prolonged silence.

"You're kidding—a nanny?"

Strange. "Is there something wrong?"

"No. No. Please don't misunderstand! When Roger and I spoke to her yesterday, she told us she'd decided to stay in Salt Lake and look for work. There was no talking her out of it. But she took care of our sick mom and has saved our lives doing a lot of baby-sitting. I guess I'd hoped she would want to try something different.

"Don't get me wrong. Josh and Amy adore her and she loves them. She would make the best nanny in the world, but there are other jobs out there. Of course if that's what she really wants to do..."

He got the distinct impression she didn't want him to hire her sister.

"I'm going to need help with my son for at least

a year. Do you know of any reason why that time frame might present a problem for her?''

''No, but I'm not privy to everything that goes on in Diana's mind, even if we are close.''

He refused to let her honest admission dampen his spirits. Ms. Farrow was her own person. She wouldn't have responded to his ad if the job hadn't appealed to her on some basic level.

''Thank you for being frank with me, Mrs. Hopkins. I appreciate it.''

''You're welcome. If you have more questions, feel free to call anytime.''

He had a lot of them. But he wanted to meet Diana Farrow before he decided what to do.

''I might do that. Goodbye.'' He clicked off.

There was no pressing park business for the moment, so Pierce decided to phone the Salt Lake number. It rang six times. He was about to hang up and try later when he heard a breathless voice say hello.

''Ms. Farrow? It's Pierce Gallagher.''

''Forgive me for taking so long to pick up.''

''No need to apologize. Your sister sounds like you over the phone.''

''You've already talked to Leslie?''

Why was she so surprised? ''You did tell me to call her.''

''Of course. I just thought—well, it doesn't matter.''

''If I'm moving too fast for you, perhaps it means you've changed your mind.''

''Not at all!'' she insisted with what sounded like unfeigned fervency. ''Knowing how busy you must be, I assumed you would have to fit in a phone call when you could. I didn't really expect to hear back from you today.''

His hand tightened on the receiver. "Finding a nanny is my top priority. Although, I don't believe your sister likes the idea of *you* becoming one."

"That's because she imagines I'll be a wife and mom one day, too, so why not find another kind of job right now. Maybe something secretarial in a challenging office atmosphere that doesn't involve taking care of children."

"She has a point."

"I suppose." More silence ensued before she asked, "Did she say something to put you off the idea of interviewing me?"

He detected undertones of surprise, even hurt.

"No. My reservations are my own."

"Then you're worried about your son's reaction to me. I'm afraid I'm worried about that, too. My heart aches for what he's going to have to go through again."

Pierce grimaced. The woman said all the right things—she sounded almost too good to be true. Lord, how he hated losing Janice. She'd been so good for Cory, he couldn't imagine another woman winning his son over in the same way.

"When could you be in Moose so we could meet?"

"Today."

Like he thought—too good to be true. Something serious had to be wrong. He just had to figure out what it was.

"It's a five-to-six-hour drive from Salt Lake."

"I'll be there at three."

Ask and ye shall receive.

"Good. I'll reimburse you for gas and meals. Come to park headquarters. Reception will show you where to go."

"Thank you for giving me this opportunity, Mr. Gallagher. See you this afternoon." There was a click.

He didn't doubt her sincerity, but he had reservations concerning her hidden agenda—because she had one!

Maybe she'd been passed over in the marriage department and was jealous of her sister's happiness. What was it she'd said to him?

But he and Amy are their children, not mine.

Her desire to be a nanny was beginning to make sense. The plan was old as time itself. Win the child over and the father would follow.

He grimaced. *Not this father.*

It was possible that Leslie Hopkins understood her sister's needy nature very well and had tried to warn him off in the most discreet way possible.

Ms. Farrow had asked up front about his relationship to Cory. In retrospect, he doubted their conversation would have gone any further if he'd told her he was his grandfather.

Then again maybe she was so desperate for a husband, any man was fair game.

He let go with a curse. That's when he realized the deep-seated anger he'd felt at Linda's death hadn't dissipated after all. It had only been percolating beneath the surface, waiting for a moment like this to consume him once more.

Pierce shot to his feet and stormed out of his office.

"Sally?"

Startled, she looked up from her desk. "Yes?"

"In case there's an emergency and you need to get in touch with me, I'm headed for Lizard Creek campground."

"Okay."

"The last early snowfall has made that area difficult for campers to access. It's time to close it down for the winter," he muttered.

She sent him a compassionate glance. "Did Ms. Farrow back out like all the others?"

"Not yet." He feared he understood the reason why. If she was husband hunting, he'd know it within an instant of meeting her. Then he'd send her packing. "She'll be here at three for an interview."

On that note he left headquarters and roared off in his truck. At ten to three he roared in again. This time the parking area was full of cars. Several were rentals. He spied one shuttle van from Jackson Airport.

When he passed reception, Mindy Carlson said, "Your three o'clock appointment just arrived. Sally's taking care of her."

"Thanks, Mindy."

He strode down the hall past his secretary's cubicle and entered his office.

One look at the stunning female wearing jeans and a cotton sweater, and he had to reassess everything he'd been thinking. With a willowy figure and classic bone structure like hers, she could have any man she wanted and several thousand she didn't.

She must have sensed his presence, because she turned from the park mural she'd been studying and looked in his direction. His body tautened. If she hadn't married yet, it was *her* choice.

CHIEF RANGER GALLAGHER WAS powerfully built and stood tall, at least six-two, six-three. With the lines on his rugged face, she put him somewhere in his mid-thirties. Leslie had been a photographer all her life and recognized some of those lines came from experience, others from grief.

He made a commanding figure in uniform. When he removed his ranger's hat, it revealed a head of fairly short-cropped hair, more black than brown. Eyes as blue as the sky above the Grand Tetons glinted beneath dark, well-shaped brows. The bronze of his skin attested to a life in the outdoors.

She felt negative tension emanating from him, separate and distinct from his natural curiosity about her. Why?

"Welcome to Teton Park, Ms. Farrow. Please sit down."

"Thank you." Leslie took a seat in one of the chairs opposite his desk. Her gaze fell on the five-by-seven photograph propped on his desk. "I presume that's Cory. May I see it?"

He leaned forward and handed it to her.

His son was a small, wiry-looking boy with straight blond hair, glasses and an endearing pixie face. It was apparent he resembled his mother, unless he'd been adopted.

The boy would have been four-and-a-half when he'd lost his mom, old enough to remember her. A pang of loss attacked Leslie just remembering how hard it had been to lose her own mother and father.

No child deserved to be without his mom so young. It was tragic. Leslie had been lucky to have her mother for twenty-seven years.

The idea of this man's son now having to say good-bye to the only other woman who'd been a mother figure to him tugged at Leslie's heart. Because Leslie knew what the pain had been like when her dad had died so unexpectedly, she wanted to help the boy if she could.

"He's adorable." She put the picture back on the desk.

"Cory's my flesh and blood, in case you were wondering."

She met his unsettling scrutiny. "He probably has your mannerisms and dozens of your characteristics that aren't apparent in a mere photo."

The ranger sat back in his swivel chair, studying her as if she were a species of park animal he hadn't come across before. Neither fish nor fowl? Something was bothering him.

"How old are you?"

"Thirty." She'd almost said her own age of twenty-eight.

"You don't look it."

"Is that a problem?"

He shook his head. "Merely an observation. What I need is someone who'll be with us at least until Cory starts first grade a year from now. Could you commit to that amount of time?"

"Yes."

"There's no man you left behind who expects you to return to New Jersey sooner than that?"

An icy shiver raced through her body. "I was engaged to be married, but it didn't work out."

The ranger was silent for what seemed like a long while.

"You're certain it's over?" he said at last.

If you only knew.

"I'll place my hand on a Bible and swear to it if necessary."

A grim expression stole over his striking features.

This man would be hard to convince of anything. He was one tough guy. A breed apart from most men. She supposed he had to be to run one of the major national parks on the North American continent.

"When could you start?"

"Right now." Sensing his reluctance, she said, "But before either of us were to commit, I'd like a chance to observe Cory's interaction with the woman who's been looking after him. You told me she was leaving at the end of the week.

"It would be a great help if I could witness his routine. She could tell me about him, and he could get used to having me around while she's still here. We would take it a day at a time. What do you think?"

He took a deep breath. "I think you're saying all the things I want to hear."

"But you don't trust me," she said in a quiet voice. He might not know her secret, but he sensed she was holding back something vital. Her guilt intensified.

"Did I say that?"

His tension seemed to grow.

"You didn't have to. Letting a total stranger into your life, entrusting that person to look after your precious son—it's a scary proposition for so many reasons that if I were in your shoes, I'm not sure I could do it.''

In fact Leslie *knew* she couldn't.

Cory's father needed her total honesty, something she couldn't give him.

She'd made a mistake applying for a nanny's job. It was a good thing she'd asked the shuttle driver to wait outside in the parking area for her. Though it was costing her plenty, it was worth it because this had to be the shortest job interview on record.

''Thank you for your time, Mr. Gallagher,'' she said, getting to her feet. ''After consideration, I've decided I'm not the woman you're looking for. I hope for your son's sake you'll be able to find the right person before long. No—please don't get up.''

The blank look on his face as she walked out of his office with her suitcase and tote bag lived with her for the first two miles of the drive to Jackson Hole. That's where she planned to spend the night.

Tomorrow she'd fly back to Salt Lake and pursue one of the other job options she'd marked in the want ads. But it was the last thing she wanted to do. Unfortunately her heart had been set on this job much more than she'd realized.

CHAPTER THREE

"Uh-oh."

The shuttle driver's remark jarred Leslie out of her thoughts and alerted her to the fact that a siren was wailing behind them. He pulled over to the side of the road and stopped. They were still inside the park boundaries and had been going the speed limit.

She looked over her shoulder. A white park patrol car with a green stripe had come to a stop behind them. A man in uniform climbed out and walked toward the driver's side of the van. What on earth?

A fit, attractive-looking guy around thirty leaned into the window. "Good afternoon, sir, ma'am." When he looked at her, his eyes lit up with male interest.

"Did I do something wrong?" the driver asked.

"Not a thing. Chief Ranger Gallagher asked me to find Ms. Farrow and escort her back to headquarters."

Leslie's heart thudded from a surfeit of guilt and other emotions she didn't have time to sort out now. "Why? I only went there for a job interview. I haven't done anything wrong."

"I have no idea. He gave me my orders."

And Pierce Gallagher's word was law in a federal park.

Heat crept into her face.

"Driver? Do you mind taking me back and waiting for me again? I promise it won't take long and I'll make it worth your while."

"Sure." He was probably so relieved he wouldn't be getting a ticket for something, he would have agreed to anything.

"It won't be necessary for you to escort us," she said to the ranger.

He smiled at her. "I'm going there, anyway."

In a few minutes she was back in the head man's office. Pierce Gallagher stood up when she walked in once more carrying her bags. Like déjà vu, he asked her to sit down.

"Your hasty departure told me you've got secrets you don't wish to share," he began in a neutral voice. "In all fairness, I have a few of my own which no doubt you picked up on."

He was clearly a shrewd judge of character. But Leslie knew in her case, he had no idea what kind of a secret she was keeping.

"Why don't we start this interview again, Ms. Farrow. You answered my ad because you need a job. I placed the ad because I need a nanny. If I haven't found one by the weekend, I'll have to take a year's leave of absence and move to Ashton, where there's guaranteed day care."

She bowed her head. The job he loved was on the line. But he loved his son more. Her admiration for him continued to grow.

"Taking each other at face value, shall we go from there?"

The olive branch had been extended.

"I'd like that," she replied, despite her conscience screaming at her.

"Good."

He was a courageous man, fighting against all odds to carve out the life he'd chosen for himself and Cory. That meant taking a risk with her, *if* he decided to hire her.

It was a risk, all right. If or when Ed traced her here, she'd be forced to tell Mr. Gallagher the truth. What if she had to leave in a hurry?

But when she weighed her fears against the opportunity to befriend a grieving boy and try to help him through this difficult period, her decision to accept the position won out.

"You haven't asked about the financial arrangements," he said. "I would provide room and board, insurance, and pay you a salary of eighteen hundred dollars a month. You would have Saturdays and Sundays off, the use of my car, plus two weeks paid vacation during the year. How does that sound?"

"Much more generous than I had imagined."

"And far lower than the going rate in New Jersey."

He was right. When she'd been reading the *Salt Lake Tribune* want ads, the difference between the types of jobs offered compared with those of the *Chronicler* had made for fascinating entertainment. The disparity between the higher wages paid on the East Coast and those proffered in the Salt Lake area was another revelation. It seemed the majority of the people here worked for peanuts.

She looked at him and saw the makings of a half smile. A first for him. Leslie reciprocated.

He handed her a form on a clipboard. "As soon as you fill that out, I'll drive you to the house to meet Cory and let you see where you'd be living."

Drive—

"Oh, no! I forgot! The shuttle driver from the airport is still outside waiting for me."

"Don't worry. He has been sent on his way."

"Unfortunately I didn't pay what I owed him."

"It's been taken care of." Judging by his authoritative demeanor, the matter was closed. "I would have run you back to the airport or Jackson Hole, if you're wondering. After all, I did offer to pay your expenses to get here." He studied her for a moment. "How come you didn't drive up from Salt Lake?"

She had to think fast. "I could have rented a car, but I was worried something might delay my getting here on time. The short flight from Salt Lake seemed the smartest thing to do."

With an unsteady hand she began filling in the blanks on the form, thereby committing herself to this critical trial period. Roger had advised her to tell the truth whenever she could. But without Diana's ID and social security number, getting a reputable job would have been impossible.

Cory's father took a phone call while she finished up. His terse, one-syllable questions alerted her there was some kind of emergency. If she worked for him, his directness was something she would have to get used to. The responsibility on his shoulders awed her.

"Keep me posted." He clicked off. "Ready?"

"If this isn't a good time—"

"A small brush fire broke out in the Signal Mountain area, but it's already eighty-percent contained.

Shall we go?'' He came around his desk and took the clipboard from her. On their way down the hall he set it on top of his secretary's monitor.

''A careless camper?''

''No. Dry lightning, one of the park's natural enemies.''

She wanted to know more, but would ask questions another time. Right now he seemed intent on ushering her past the front reception area and out of the building.

Instinct told her he was a private person, yet he lived in a fishbowl. Anything the chief ranger said or did would be news. Already Leslie detected the two female employees' growing curiosity about her. She supposed it was only natural since their boss had been advertising for a new nanny. They probably knew his boy well and were worried how everything would work out.

On the way to his truck, they passed the ranger who'd come after her. Though he was talking to some tourists, he tipped his hat to Leslie. As her host helped her into the cab, he said, ''That's our newest married ranger.''

The head man didn't miss much, and was letting her know he ran a tight ship.

For the first time since the nightmare had begun, plunging her into chaotic horror, she felt her life had some purpose again.

Please, God, let this feeling last.

They drove past the visitors-center complex to a cluster of about twenty-five older-looking ranch-style houses. Moose was its own little world in the cosmos, framed by the Tetons. The mountains were more magnificent than any pictures she'd seen of them. To capture them on film and do them justice presented the kind of challenge on which she thrived. Maybe one day...

There were two cars in the driveway, one behind the other. Pierce pulled the truck alongside them. She watched his hand move to the visor where a remote was attached. The garage door opened and they drove in.

Before Leslie had a chance to climb out, the door into the house opened. Two boys, one brunette, the other blond, appeared in the entry wearing SpongeBob T-shirts and sneakers.

"Daddy!" A world of love was reflected in that one word.

Pierce came around the end of the truck. "Hi, champ!"

His son hugged the life out of him. "Logan's playing with me." Both of the boys held dinosaurs in their hands.

"So I see. How are you, Logan?"

"Good. Who's that?"

The two boys had just noticed Leslie and were standing still, examining her. They stopped playing around.

"Guys? This is Diana Farrow. Diana, meet my son Cory and his friend Logan."

"Hi!" Leslie said, making no attempt to get out yet.

Cory wasn't wearing his glasses. He had blue eyes like his father, but they had a tendency to cross, thus the need for correction. Oh—he was so cute! She felt a sharp tug on her emotions.

He was looking at her the way his father had done when he'd started interviewing her in his office. As if he didn't know what to make of her. If Pierce Gallagher dated other women, she had an idea he didn't bring them home very often.

His son grabbed on to his father's arm and whispered something.

"No," Pierce murmured, "Diana's not a ranger. She's…a friend. I invited her home for dinner."

With that explanation, Cory and his buddy relaxed and started to play again. Pierce put a hand on his shoulder. "Say hello to her."

Cory craned his head and said hi before running off with Logan.

"Don't—" she whispered when Pierce turned to her with a bleak expression in his eyes. "I wouldn't have expected any other reaction. My nephew behaves the same way around strangers."

Pierce nodded. "Come inside. I'll introduce you to Janice."

In order not to alarm Cory, Leslie decided to leave her suitcase on the seat of the truck's cab before she got out.

She could smell a roast cooking when she entered the kitchen behind Pierce. It made her stomach rumble. Suddenly a dark-blond woman around Leslie's age joined them from another part of the house.

"Hello," she said in a friendly voice. With such a sunny smile, she won Leslie's immediate approval. "I was in Cory's bedroom straightening it up."

"He was supposed to help," Pierce muttered. "Janice Archer? Meet Diana Farrow."

"How do you do?" Leslie said. The two women shook hands.

"Diana answered my ad and flew to Jackson for an interview this afternoon. I brought her home so she could meet you and Cory, see the situation for herself."

"Does Cory know why she's here?"

"Not yet. I told him she was a friend."

"I see." Her amber eyes turned serious. "I wondered why you were home earlier than usual. Do you want me to leave so the three of you can have time alone? Logan's mom planned to come for him at five, but I'll run him home now if you want."

Pierce shook his head. "I'd rather you carried on as usual. Diana's here to observe."

"Maybe I could help you with dinner?" Leslie suggested.

"Sure. That's a good idea. Would you like to freshen up first?"

"Thank you."

"Come on. I'll show you around."

Pierce glanced at Leslie. "I promised Cory I'd help him put his racetrack together. It won't take long."

The traditional house had been furnished in earth tones with attractive accents of plum and sage-green throughout. An entrance hall ran past the kitchen and dining area to the living room. Another hall opened up to three bedrooms and a bathroom. Janice explained that the master bedroom had its own en suite bathroom.

Minutes later Leslie emerged from the guest bathroom. She could hear the boys' voices followed by

Pierce's deep laughter coming from one of the bedrooms.

For the moment he'd shed his ranger hat and had become a normal father. Being able to laugh like that meant he'd gotten past the worst of his grief. No doubt having a son to raise had forced him to get on with life sooner than he might have if he lived alone.

When Leslie's mother had been so ill, it had been wonderful to turn to the children for comfort. Josh had only been five and Amy two. Leslie had cuddled both of them for hours. It had helped offset the pain of watching her mom suffer. If she could be that comfort for Cory now, nothing would make her happier.

"What can I do to help?"

"Do you want to set the table? The dishes and glasses are in that cupboard over there. The cutlery is in the top drawer next to the stove. The napkins are in the second one down."

Leslie got busy. "I haven't had lamb roast in ages. It smells wonderful."

"Pierce is a meat-and-potatoes man like my husband Jim. Nothing fancy."

"My father was the same. One of his favorite meals was meat loaf."

"Pierce likes that, too."

"What does Cory like?"

"None of the above."

"Of course not." They both laughed.

"He's such a light eater you wonder how he survives. His taste runs to three items only. Peanut butter sandwiches, cheese pizza and chicken nuggets Pierce buys in bulk from the store."

"My nephew Josh is Cory's age. He's not so different. He likes canned spaghetti, sugary cereal and corn dogs. His little sister Amy is a much better eater.''

Janice smiled as she mashed the potatoes. ''Where are you from?''

''New Jersey, where my sister and her husband live.'' She was getting so good at her lies it was scary. ''Our mother was ill for a long time. After she died, I needed to get away and ended up in Salt Lake.

''I really like this part of the country and want to stay for a while, so I decided to look for a job. But I miss the kids so much, I suppose that's the reason I gravitated to Mr. Gallagher's ad.''

''I'm sure Pierce is glad you did.''

''He hasn't hired me yet. It all depends on his son's reaction to me.''

''Cory's a sweet boy, but a little shy. He likes to pretend he's tough like his dad.''

''Don't they all.''

''I don't know. I was an only child and never did do much baby-sitting. Cory's been my guinea pig. Jim and I are expecting our first baby in seven months.''

''How thrilling for you!''

''We're excited. But I've been worried about leaving Pierce. It's almost impossible to find child care when you live in the park.''

''Mr. Gallagher has been very fortunate to have a good friend like you to step in. He told me about your husband's new position. Congratulations.''

''Thank you. It's what he's been working for. Everything would be perfect except that I hate deserting Pierce and Cory. They've been through a lot,'' she said in a quiet tone.

"I can imagine. Cory's not going to take to anyone else for a long time."

As if saying his name conjured him up, he and Logan came running in the kitchen to get a drink. This time he had his glasses on, probably Pierce's doing. They both carried flashing plastic ray guns and goofed around while Janice accommodated them. Leslie might as well have been invisible.

"Tell your father dinner's ready."

"Let's go," Cory said to his friend.

Leslie watched them run off. "Do you and your husband eat dinner here?"

"No. Normally I get it started, then leave when Pierce comes home to take over. He's totally self-sufficient like Jim, but I know he appreciates walking through the door to a hot meal in the oven."

"I have to admit I did, too."

Janice smiled. "I come over every weekday morning when Pierce is ready to leave for work. I spend the mornings with Cory but now that school has started and he has to go to afternoon kindergarten, he's been getting harder to handle. I don't know why."

"He's probably afraid his daddy won't be here when he gets back."

The other woman stared at her. "You think *that's* the reason?"

"It's just a guess, but I remember how I fought going to school after my father died. Part of me feared that my mother wouldn't be there when I walked in the door."

If anyone understood a child's paralyzing fear, Leslie did. Not much had changed since she'd become an adult. The fear that Ed would show up no matter where she hid was just as immobilizing.

"I hadn't even thought of it," Janice murmured. "A bus arrives from Jackson at eleven-thirty to pick up the kids. So far he hasn't wanted to ride with the other kids so I've had to drive him."

"The poor little guy." Leslie finished pouring the water. With each task she was becoming better acquainted with the kitchen.

A horn honked outside.

"Logan?" Janice called out. "Your mom's here!"

"Coming!"

The boys raced down the front hall. They seemed to never walk anywhere, reminding her of Josh, who sort of darted around like an insect, zigging, zagging and giggling. On the surface Cory seemed a happy child.

But not for long. Not when he found out Janice was leaving...

From Leslie's vantage point in the kitchen she could see Pierce, who'd followed the boys to the entry. He waved to Logan's mom before shutting the door.

When he walked into the kitchen, the overhead light drew her attention to his hair. It was damp. He must have just come from the shower.

In place of his uniform he wore a plaid flannel shirt with long sleeves and a pair of Levi's that molded his powerful thighs. Even without his ranger's attire, he had an imposing presence that dominated the room.

Janice reached for Cory and gave him a quick hug. He wouldn't tolerate a long one, not even with the woman who'd been with him since his mother died.

"Did you tell your dad about your assignment for tomorrow?"

He shook his head.

"You need a computer to do it," she said to Pierce. "I'll see you in the morning."

Pierce walked her to the front door. Cory went with them, ignoring Leslie.

Though she could have all the concern in the world for this motherless boy, whose fears were as great as her own, it might not be enough to win him over.

Since discovering Ed's true nature, she was no stranger to fear. And now that she'd met Cory—now that she felt a strong urge to help him get over a seemingly insurmountable hurdle—she was beginning to find out there were different kinds of fear.

In this case her presence here was very tenuous. That's what was killing her. She'd managed to get out of New York without Ed's knowledge. Her new employer was decent and fair and, as far as she could tell, a wonderful man. It would be unbearable if this situation didn't work out. She wanted to be here—to stay put and do exactly what she was doing for as long as she was needed.

CORY CLUNG TO PIERCE after he closed the door. Pierce knew why. There was a strange woman in the house and his son didn't understand.

When Pierce had heard Logan whisper Diana's name to Cory, his son had kept playing as if he hadn't heard him. But the damage had been done. Cory would be confused until he learned the truth.

The moment Pierce had been dreading for weeks

was here. "Come on. Janice made us a delicious dinner. Let's eat."

"I'm not hungry."

"Even if you aren't, will you come and sit with me while I eat?"

"Is *she* going to be here?"

Before Pierce could answer, Leslie appeared with a plate of food in hand. "Do you two mind if I watch TV in the living room? I want to see what the weather's like in New Jersey."

"Go ahead," Pierce murmured, appreciating her diplomacy at such a critical moment. She moved past them while he headed into the kitchen. Cory stuck to him like glue.

"Hey, look at these—" Cory ran over to the table.

Pierce had already seen the napkins. They'd been folded next to the forks so they looked like birds ready to fly. Clever. Had she learned to do tricks like that waitressing? Did it mean anything? Nothing?

Janice had prepared a plate of chicken nuggets and sliced bananas for Cory. Pierce served himself a big portion of lamb and mashed potatoes, then poured on the gravy and tucked in. He could hear the TV, but it wasn't loud enough to make out words. "I bet Diana would show you how she made those."

Cory put his bird down. He was totally uninterested in his food. His earnest little face looked up at Pierce. "Is she your girlfriend?"

"No."

"Logan thought she was. Then how come she's here?"

The million-dollar question.

"Cory—" He put his fork down and turned to his

son. "There's something important I need to talk to you about. Will you sit there and listen?"

His son nodded, but his lips had gone tight. They always did that when he was nervous.

Pierce was nervous, too. Nervous as hell.

"Do you know how much I love my job?"

"A lot."

"That's right. But I love you more."

"I know."

Tears stung Pierce's eyes. "Here's the situation. Jim has been made chief ranger of Yellowstone Park."

"Just like you?"

"Yes. It means he and Janice have to move to their new home in the park this weekend."

Cory stared at him for a long time. Pierce could hear the wheels turning. "Is that lady going to tend me now?"

The quiver in his voice was almost Pierce's undoing.

"Only if you decide you like her."

The corners of his mouth fell. "I want Janice."

It felt like a giant hand was squeezing Pierce's heart.

"I know you do, but she has to go with her husband. I was hoping you would give Diana a chance. But if it doesn't work out, we have another choice."

"What is it?"

Pierce took a deep breath. "We could move to the house in Ashton where your grandparents used to live. You could go to day care part of the day with other kids who also attend kindergarten. If we do that, we won't need anyone to take care of you."

It took a long time before Cory said, "Will you still work here?"

"No. I'll find a job in Ashton so we can be together just like always."

"You won't be a ranger?"

"No."

Cory was pondering everything. "Will Janice come and see us sometimes?"

"Of course. And we'll go visit them."

"Could Logan come to school with me?"

"No. He has to stay here with his family. But you two could play on the weekends. We'd arrange for your other friends to come to our house, too."

"I wish Jim didn't have to move," he said in a croaky voice.

"I know exactly how you feel." Pierce pulled his boy into his arms and rocked him while he sobbed.

"It's going to be okay, Cory. We'll do whatever will make you happiest."

"I've got to go to the bathroom." He slipped away and ran out of the kitchen. Pierce went after him. He met Diana coming down the hall with her empty plate.

"I saw him run past the living room," she whispered. "I take it he knows everything."

Pierce nodded.

"Forget me and go be with him."

"Thanks for understanding."

He continued down the other hall. When he couldn't find Cory in the bathroom, he headed for his bedroom. His son had planted himself next to the racetrack. While he fiddled with one of the cars, Pierce hunkered down next to him.

"What did your teacher want you to do on the computer?"

"Stuff."

"What kind of stuff?"

"It's in my backpack."

Pierce reached inside and pulled out a printed sheet. After looking it over, he put it on the bed. "Shall we go over to headquarters and get it done now?"

"I don't want to."

"Come on. It'll be fun."

Cory let out a sigh. "Do I have to?"

"No, but you won't feel very good tomorrow when everyone else has their assignment done except you."

"My stomach hurts. I don't think I can go to school tomorrow."

Pierce had been waiting for that. "Do you want a ginger ale?"

His son nodded.

"Okay. I'll get you one. Be right back."

When Pierce reached the kitchen, Diana was scouring the sink. Everything had been put away and was in order. She'd made the room immaculate. He pulled a soda out of the fridge.

Her eyebrows lifted. "Tummy ache?"

"You got it. Can't do his homework."

"The one on the computer?"

"Normally he likes to play games on the one in my office."

"I guess that means he won't be able to go to school tomorrow, either."

In spite of his pain Pierce smiled. "I can see you've been around this block before."

"Josh has taken me around it many, many times when he didn't want to go to his little preschool. But in all fairness, Leslie and I used to pull the same stunt when we were in grade school. If one got sick, the other pretended. I honestly think Mom liked it, too. She made us treats and bought us coloring books. We had a perfectly marvelous time."

"I'm afraid my mother wasn't quite as compassionate."

The green flecks in her eyes lit up. "That's because she was raising you to be a ranger and knew you would have to be tough."

His pulse quickened for no good reason.

"My father was the tough one. She went along with him to keep the peace."

"My dad ruled the roost, too, but mom knew her way arou—"

"Daddy?" Cory called from the bedroom, cutting her off.

"Coming!"

"Wait—" she said as Pierce turned to go. "I have a laptop in my suitcase, but it's out in your truck. If you would bring it in, I could turn it on and Cory could do his assignment on it. That is if you can talk him into it."

What was she doing with a laptop? Did she have another job on the side she hadn't told him about?

The second he asked those questions, he chastised himself for his suspicious mind. Millions of people had laptops. It was none of his damn business. The fact that she'd offered it to help Cory was a gracious gesture. For some strange reason he kept waiting for her to make a mistake, but he couldn't help it. If he did end up hiring her, she was going to be a big part of Cory's life. That meant he needed to learn everything he could about her as soon as possible.

Face it, Gallagher. Diana Farrow has knocked you sideways.

And she kept on surprising him in all the right ways. Until she made a wrong move, it was time to get off her back.

"I'll bring it in now."

He put the soda on the counter and went out to the garage. The suitcase was not large. She traveled light. Had she been in such a big hurry to leave New Jersey she hadn't worried about a lot of clothes? He supposed she might have decided to buy more once she'd found a job.

Did that mean she received extra money from an undisclosed source? She'd marked down that she was single on the application form so she wasn't receiving alimony. Unless that was a lie...

Maybe her mother's death had brought her an inheritance. Maybe he was looking for trouble that wasn't there, but too many things about her weren't adding up.

"What are you doing?" Cory had come out of his room to discover what was taking so long.

"Getting this." He walked back in the kitchen with her suitcase. "Diana has a surprise."

Hoping to arouse Cory's curiosity, Pierce carried it over to the table. His eyes met Diana's before she unlocked it. When she opened the lid, he caught sight of some silky garments. After rummaging beneath them, she brought out the desired item and laid it down.

Cory frowned. "I've seen a laptop before. Can I have my drink now?"

Diana was closest to the counter and handed it to him. "Here you go. If you want to use my computer, just let me know."

Pierce was on the verge of telling his son to say thank you, but Diana shot him a glance that said to leave it alone.

"I'd like to e-mail my sister and let her know I'm here. Do you mind if I hook it into your phone line, or do you need to keep it free for emergency calls?"

The fact that she didn't have a cell phone sent up a red flag. It meant she didn't want anyone knowing where she was. E-mail was a good way to keep her whereabouts a secret.

"I have a cell phone for that. You're welcome to set up in here or the guest bedroom. It's the first one down the hall on your left."

"Thank you."

"Come on, Cory. If your stomach's hurting, you need an early night."

"Is she going to sleep here?" his son whispered once they'd left the kitchen.

"Yes."

"I wish she was staying someplace else."

"I know. It's only for a few days." With her around the house, Pierce could keep a better eye on her activities when he was home. He didn't have the luxury of weeks or months to decide if Diana Farrow was someone he could trust.

"As I said earlier, if you decide you'd rather live in Ashton, that's what we'll do."

"Can I use your bathroom?"

Cory, Cory. "Yes. Go get your toothbrush and pajamas."

His son darted into the bathroom for his things.

Six weeks ago Pierce had learned about Jim's new assignment. Some instinct had prompted him not to advertise for new renters after the old ones had moved out of his parents' home last month.

Obviously he'd been guided by an unseen hand, because the way things were going from bad to worse, he and Cory would be living in Ashton next week.

And Diana Farrow would move on to another job. Where? Why did he care?

His troubled thoughts shot ahead to Rex Hollister. The ranger didn't know it yet, but he'd be the one to replace Pierce if things didn't work out.

Don't think about any of it tonight, Gallagher. Just don't think.

Cory came running into Pierce's bedroom. "Can I sleep with you?" He'd brought his pillow.

Pierce caught his son up in his arms, toothbrush, soda and all. "What do you think?"

"I love you."

"I love you, too."

CHAPTER FOUR

DIANA KISSED HER CHILDREN good-night and hurried downstairs to the study to check her e-mail. Roger had slipped out to the drugstore for some more pain-killers. He'd been nursing a sore tooth all afternoon and probably needed a root canal.

It was a quarter to ten. That meant a quarter to eight in Salt Lake.

Ever since that phone call from Mr. Gallagher this morning, Diana had been going crazy waiting to make contact with Leslie.

She scanned her Inbox. Besides the half-dozen messages Ed had left on their answering machine in the last twelve hours, there were six new e-mails from him. He'd learned her address a long time ago.

It made her sick to her stomach to see them, but it meant he hadn't given up hope of gaining Diana's cooperation to talk to Leslie in person. As long as he was still harassing her, then he wasn't aware Leslie had left New York.

She would love to delete them, but Roger was tracking Ed's movements and storing the messages for evidence. That's why they hadn't changed their Web address or home phone number. Except for getting Diana a new cell phone number, they hadn't done anything that might set Ed off.

Still nothing from her sister yet. She typed her a message.

Leslie? Where are you? What are you up to? I'm sitting here at the computer. Answer as soon as you can.

While she waited for a reply, curiosity got the best of her and she opened Ed's last e-mail.

Diana? Today was supposed to be my wedding day to Leslie. You don't know the pain I'm in. I thought you of all people believed a person was innocent until proved guilty. My first marriage was a mistake. It happened ten years ago and only lasted six months. I found out Maureen had been unfaithful to me with one of her actor friends. She taunted me and I overreacted. But that's in the past now and has been for a long, long time. People can change. I've changed. You go to church and believe in the Bible. How can you treat me like this and go against your own beliefs? Have I ever done anything to you or Leslie or the kids or Roger that made you think I'm a bad person? You can't answer that, can you, and that's because I'm a different man than I was ten years ago. I'm a good journalist or I wouldn't be working for the *Chronicler*. I wouldn't be where I am today if I were as terrible as Maureen says I am. The biggest mistake of my life was not telling Leslie about Maureen. I know that now and I'm paying for it. Believe me. But I've got to talk to Leslie. Please. You're the only one she'll listen to right now. I know she's hurt, but she's in love with me, Diana. That's never going to go away. If ever two people were meant to be together, we are. Tell her I'll agree to anything she says as long as she'll let me see her again. Please answer. I'm feeling desperate.

What a great manipulator! He could have had Diana going if she didn't know his history and hadn't seen the decapitated photos. It was his desperation that made him so dangerous.

While she rubbed her arm where she could still feel the strength of his hand, the sound on the computer indicated an instant message from Leslie. Finally!

Diana— Would you believe I'm in the guest bedroom of the chief ranger's house in Grand Teton National Park? His name is Pierce Gallagher, the one you talked to on the phone. He lives in Moose, Wyoming, and has the most adorable six-year-old son named Cory, who has to wear glasses to correct his lazy eye.

Mr. Gallagher is losing the woman who has helped him since his wife died eighteen months ago. I saw his ad in the *Salt Lake Tribune* and phoned him.

Diana? Why did you try to dissuade him from hiring me?

Diana broke in.

Do you honestly need a reason, Leslie? Roger told you to find an anonymous office job and he was right! You can't afford to get emotionally involved with a child right now.

Her sister came right back.

It's too late. I already am emotionally involved. Cory is a dear little boy who has some major fears I totally understand. I want to help him.

Luckily you didn't succeed in getting Mr. Gallagher to change his mind. We had a three-o'clock meeting in Moose. I flew up to Jackson Hole, Wyoming, and took a shuttle from there.

Janice, the woman taking care of Cory, is married to the new chief ranger of Yellowstone Park, Jim Archer. They have to move to their headquarters in Yellowstone this coming weekend. Mr. Gallagher has been looking for someone ever since he found out he'd be losing Janice.

Diana interrupted.

Then let him find someone else! What's the rush? You're supposed to be taking this time to relax and get a feel for Salt Lake before you throw yourself into anything!

In the next breath Leslie was instant-messaging her again.

I told you Mr. Gallagher has to get someone by the weekend. Listen, Diana. This is the perfect job and the perfect place for me. But there is one catch, of course. It's Cory himself.

He fell apart tonight when he found out Janice was leaving. I'm only here on approval for the week. If things don't get better, I'll have to go back to Salt Lake and start over again. Say a prayer that Cory learns—

"Honey?"

"In the study!" Diana called to her husband.

Just a minute, Leslie!

"Anything from Leslie yet?"

"I'm afraid so." She was frightened to tell him. "Did you take a pill?"

"I took three."

"Oh, Roger. That's too many." She got up from the desk so he could sit.

"Not with this pain. Tell me what's going on with Leslie."

When she related what she'd learned so far, Roger exploded. "Chief ranger? He's the chief legal authority for the park. If he found out about her lies, he could charge her with a federal offense! She shouldn't have done it! Damn."

Diana swallowed hard. "The man's phone call shocked me, too, but I had no idea who he was. The thing is, you have to admit she sounds so happy for someone who left here terrified yesterday."

"Honey—" He looked up at her. "She may think she's found a safe haven, but we have to tell her to pack her bags and get out of there in the morning. Mr. Gallagher will have to find someone else. She was supposed to find an office job where she melted into the woodwork. Good grief—the chief ranger—

"What if she has to leave there on a moment's notice? It would be an emotional and physical disaster for the boy and his father, not to mention the fact that she could face charges that would earn her jail time. What was she thinking?"

Quick to defend her sister, she said, "Leslie's been too petrified to think clearly, Roger. You know what a soft heart she has for kids."

He shook his head. "She might as well have applied for a job with the head of the FBI! You and I are equally implicated in this, don't forget! I could be disbarred."

"You've convinced me." Diana's voice trembled. "Will you tell her?"

"Damn right I will."

He sat down at the computer. "I see you opened one of Ed's e-mails."

She nodded. "He's so sick, Roger."

"Tell me about it. My secretary took five calls from him today. At least he doesn't know Leslie's gone yet. When we don't hear from him anymore, that will tell us he figured it out and has gone hunting."

Diana shivered. "How's the tooth?"

"On a scale of one to ten, the pain is an eight."

"I'm so sorry." She massaged his shoulders while he sent a stinging message to Leslie. "You'll have to go to the dentist in the morning without an appointment. I'll call and tell them you're on your way." Just then Leslie's reply came up on the screen.

Dearest loved ones— If I've made a mistake, it's too late to back out. Perhaps I won't even have to if Cory doesn't warm up to me by the weekend.

I promise that if I'm caught in my lies, you two will never be implicated. I'll testify that I coerced you into helping me, but you had no idea I'd stolen your ID.

Mr. Gallagher knows that you were hesitant about me taking this job, Diana, so he won't blame you for anything.

If I go to jail, so be it. Ed will have a hard time reaching me in there.

Please understand that there's more here than meets the eye. If Mr. Gallagher doesn't find someone by the weekend, he will have to take a year's leave of absence and move to Ashton to put Cory in day care. You don't get to be chief ranger unless you're an exceptional man, which he is.

I want to look after Cory and help his father keep his job. The poor man has already lost his wife.

As for Cory, he's so frightened about losing his daddy, too, he can't even get on the school bus with the other kids. Since I understand that kind of fear, I want to see if I can help him get over his. How many chances does one get in life to do something that will really make a difference?

If Ed learns where I am, then I'll tell Mr. Gallagher everything and take the consequences. At least he'll know Ed is the reason why I lied. It isn't as if I've committed a crime and am trying to elude the police. I swear I won't let you take the blame for any of this.

Please tell me you understand and be happy for me. This place is absolute heaven. You should see the Tetons. They're indescribable!

Diana looked down at her husband, who'd put his head in his hands. Translated, it meant "I give up."

"Lord help her," he muttered.

Diana echoed his sentiments.

Yet Leslie didn't sound like the same person who'd been on the brink of a nervous breakdown yesterday morning. In the past twelve hours something profound had happened to her. She sounded more like the old Leslie, who was a fighter. That was a good thing, wasn't it?

"COME ON, CORY!" Janice called out. "It's time to leave for school."

Leslie knew the only reason he'd decided to go after all was because she was in the house and he didn't want to be there with her.

Earlier that morning after she'd helped Janice make breakfast for everyone, Pierce left for work and Cory went to his room. He never came out again. Janice played with him in there for part of the time, then joined Leslie in the living room.

They went over the school-year calendar. Janice gave her the information on Cory's next appointments with his doctors.

He was supposed to wear his glasses as often as possible. One day his eye would be corrected and the glasses wouldn't be necessary. He got the usual colds, but otherwise he was healthy and active.

There were four friends he liked to play with: Cameron, Tyler, Richie and Logan, who was his favorite. He loved orange jelly beans and Baker's semisweet cooking chocolate. Everything about him endeared him to Leslie a little more.

She waited in the kitchen for the two of them to pass through to the garage. Janice reached for her purse sitting on the counter. "After I run him to school, I've got errands to do. We won't be back until three-thirty, quarter to four."

"I'd like to do a little shopping, too. Cory, could I drive to town with you and Janice?"

"How come you don't have a car?"

"I don't own one. In New Jersey a lot of people ride the subways to get around." She'd always driven the family car until she'd moved to New York City, where she didn't need one.

"Oh" was all he said before heading for the garage ahead of Janice.

Perhaps Leslie shouldn't have asked to go along, but if she hoped to get on any kind of a footing with him, she needed to make all the headway she could while Janice was still here. The fact that the other woman hadn't signaled her to stay behind meant she thought this was a good idea, too.

"I brought our old truck today," Janice said as they all got in the blue Ford pickup, where Cory hugged her side. "Hope you don't mind."

Leslie smiled at her before shutting her door. "Of course not. I think trucks are fun. In fac—" She caught herself in time to change what she'd been about to reveal about her travel experiences related to work. "I'm sure this type of four-wheel drive is the only way to get around the park in winter."

"This one has never let us down yet."

During the twenty-five-minute drive into Jackson Hole, Leslie asked Janice questions about the animals living in the park. She hoped Cory might add something to the conversation. To her chagrin he didn't say a word. When they pulled up in front of his school, Janice got out so he could jump down.

"See you later, Cory," Leslie called to him, but he just kept walking with Janice.

"How come there weren't any kids outside?" she asked after Janice climbed back into the cab and they took off.

"I've been planning our arrival to coincide with the first bell. He's afraid for them to see me walk in with him."

"Of course. The kids would probably tease him."

Janice nodded. "I'm scared for what my baby's going to have to face when it comes time for school."

"You and I managed to survive."

"You're right. I'll have to remember that."

"However, Cory's problems are a little more complicated. So far he doesn't want anything to do with me."

"I have to admit I'm surprised. He's never been deliberately rude to anyone before."

"He's afraid, Janice." Leslie could weep for him. "After next week he knows you won't be here."

"But he knows I'll still see him sometimes," she reasoned.

"That's true." Leslie's spirits brightened at the thought. Cory wouldn't be losing her the way he'd lost his mother. "If he could phone you when he starts missing you, I'm sure it would be a big help."

"Of course."

As loving and kind as Janice was, she didn't understand what it was like to be truly terrified. When fear ruled a person's life, to be able to stay in constant contact with someone you loved was vital. In the past, her cell phone had been Leslie's lifeline to sanity. And now she felt the same about her laptop—her only connection to the people she loved.

Thinking about this gave her an idea.

"Janice—before you leave this evening, why don't you tell him he can call you in Yellowstone," Leslie suggested. "I have a feeling it will reassure him."

"I will. Which reminds me, when we get back from town I'll give you the keys to everything. You can use Pierce's Grand Cherokee to drive Cory to school and run errands. Fill it up at the gas station by the visitor's center. He has an account."

Janice talked as if it were a foregone conclusion Leslie would be taking her place. But in point of fact, nothing was certain.

When they reached the center of town, the two of them parted company for a couple of hours. It gave Leslie enough time to get acquainted with some of the stores in the small community of seven thousand people.

Though she couldn't forget for a second that Ed might have tracked her to Jackson Hole and was looking around for her, she girded up her courage long enough to buy groceries at the supermarket and make a few purchases, including two new cell phones.

When she'd paid cash for them, she'd given the salesclerk the name of Diana Farrow, whose home address was the old Hopkins family address in Rochester, New York.

As soon as she got back to Moose, she would e-mail her sister to tell her about giving out the address. Diana would understand that it had been a necessity so Ed would never be able to trace Leslie to the Tetons through the phones.

If Ed found out she was living in Wyoming, it would be because he'd found out she'd flown to Salt Lake using Diana's name and credit card.

Relief swamped her when she met Janice back at the truck at ten to three without incident.

The other woman had loaded the bed with empty boxes she needed for their move coming up on Saturday. She raised the toolbox lid and told Leslie to put her sacks in it so there'd be room up front for the drive back to Moose.

A few minutes later they pulled up in front of the school. The kids came pouring out of the building. Some walked off the grounds, some got in waiting cars and others boarded buses.

Leslie noticed Cory didn't make an appearance until the bus he was supposed to ride had driven away. It wrenched her heart to see his white, tear-stained face as he scrambled inside the cab from the driver's side.

"What's the matter?" Janice asked as soon as she'd gotten behind the wheel.

His head was bowed. "The teacher got mad," he said in a tiny voice.

"Why?"

Cory didn't offer an explanation.

The two women exchanged a private glance before Janice said, "Do you want me to talk to her?"

"No…"

"Then come with me and we'll do it together," Janice urged him.

"No." He burrowed against her side.

Leslie could appreciate what Janice was trying to do, but Cory was either too upset to listen to reason or something else was making him afraid.

"I have an idea," Leslie interjected. "Why don't you two wait here while I go in and have a little chat with her. Nobody knows me. Nobody would realize why I'm there. Would that be okay with you, Cory?"

He didn't answer her, but she thought he gave a slight nod.

"I'll be right back," she mouthed the words to Janice.

The other woman looked relieved. "It's room three to the right of the office."

Within minutes Leslie found the middle-aged teacher in question. She was alone, straightening up the room.

"Hello. I'm Diana Farrow. I wondered if I might speak to you for a moment. Cory Gallagher's father has hired me to be Cory's new nanny."

The other woman looked blank. "Yes?"

"Cory was very upset when he came out to the truck just now. Could you tell me what happened?"

"Cory?"

"Yes. He's blond. Wears glasses."

"Oh, yes. A couple of the boys kept teasing him at recess. When he wasn't prepared with his homework, one of them said that the chief ranger's son sure was stupid and a real pussy for not riding the bus."

Leslie flinched at the ugly word, which unfortunately the young kids always picked up from adults.

"I'm afraid that raised my blood pressure. We spent the last part of class making up rules of behavior, which I wrote on the board. It wasn't part of Mrs. Nixon's lesson plan, but I'm sure she'll understand when I tell her."

"Mrs. Nixon?"

"She's the regular teacher. I'm the substitute."

Now Leslie understood why the woman hadn't known Cory right off.

"Is she going to be out for a while?"

"No. She attended her niece's wedding today. She'll be back tomorrow."

Under the circumstances Leslie felt it wasn't necessary for the substitute to know Cory's history.

"Thank you for telling me what happened. Teasing is something all children have to deal with, but it always hurts."

"Isn't that the truth? You tell Cory he was one of

the best-behaved boys in class today. I should have told him myself, but the second the bell rang, he ran out of the room before I could catch him.''

Everything was making sense. Leslie wondered where he'd hidden until the kids got on the bus. She could imagine how awful those moments had been for him. Such cruelty mingled with his other fear made Leslie wonder how the boy even functioned. And the problem was going to be magnified when Janice left.

''Don't worry. I'll let him know. Maybe you could leave a little note saying as much to Mrs. Nixon so she might praise him in front of the others tomorrow?''

''I'll do it.''

''Thank you.'' At the door Leslie paused. ''Did you assign homework tonight?''

''No. I leave that to the regular teacher unless I'm called in to cover for several days at a time.''

''That's good to know. Thanks for talking to me. Now I have a better idea of how to help Cory.''

Deep in thought, she left the room and hurried out to the truck. Besides everything else wrong in Cory's life, he was a typical child who already understood that tattling on those boys would only make things worse for him.

Once inside the cab, Leslie passed on the teacher's compliment to Cory but didn't elaborate about anything else. Janice seemed to read between the lines and changed the subject by suggesting that maybe one of Cory's friends could come over to play before dinner.

When they walked into the kitchen, Leslie put her

bags on the counter and insisted on making dinner so Janice could play with Cory until his father got home.

Before Cory ran off, she said, "If you're thirsty, how would you like this?" From the grocery bag she pulled out one of the juice-in-a-box drinks she'd bought.

His gaze darted to it. She had an idea he wanted it, but he wasn't about to accept anything from her. Before she could blink he shook his head, then disappeared into the other part of the house to find Janice.

No overtures on Leslie's part seemed to be working. Deflated, she put the groceries away and started cooking. Once she'd stuffed the pork chops and put them in the oven to bake with the potatoes, she set the table.

Since there was time to spare, she e-mailed her sister and told her about Cory's problems at school and the phones, knowing Roger wouldn't be too happy when he found out she'd used a defunct address.

By the time the wall clock said ten after five, she turned off the computer to fix Cory's dinner. Pierce would be walking through the door any minute.

She'd prepared enough food to send a meal home with Janice, and had it ready to go. While she waited, she put ice in the glasses and poured the water.

"Diana?"

"Yes?"

Janice had come into the dining room.

"I just got a call on my cell phone from Sally, Pierce's secretary. He's out on an emergency and there's no telling when he'll get back. The problem is, I'm supposed to meet Jim at five-thirty with the truck.''

Uh-oh. ''Have you told Cory?''

''Yes. I assured him he could call me on my cell phone anytime tonight and in the future. He isn't happy about my leaving before Pierce gets home, but he hasn't gone into hysterics, either. I left him in his room playing with his Transformers. Too bad none of his friends could come over, but that's the way it goes.''

''Then I'll just stay in this part of the house and leave him alone. Here—'' She handed Janice the food she'd wrapped in foil and put in a plastic bag.

''Thanks, Diana. What a luxury not to have to cook tonight. Jim's always starving and can't wait to eat.''

''I look forward to meeting him.''

''We'll all get together on Saturday night.'' She drew closer. ''What did Cory's teacher have to say?''

''I'll tell you later,'' Leslie whispered.

Janice nodded. ''Good luck with him tonight.''

''I'm going to need it.''

''You'll be fine. I'll see you in the morning.''

Leslie walked Janice to the door. On cue Cory came running and went out to the truck with her. She'd had an idea he'd been eavesdropping.

''If you're hungry, I've fixed cheese pizza for you,'' she said when he came back in the house.

''I'm going to wait for Daddy.''

''Okay,'' she said to the empty air. He'd already disappeared down the front hall.

She had no choice but to put the food away. Nevertheless, she left the table set in case Pierce came in at some point ready to sit down to a meal.

The quiet was so pronounced she went into the living room and turned on the TV. With the remote in hand, she sat back against the cushions of the couch and started flipping channels. At the dinner hour most channels were broadcasting the news. She only half listened because she was preoccupied with thoughts of Cory. He was in pain, and she was helpless to do anything about it until she talked to his father.

Then her ear picked up the words "Snake River" and she turned up the volume.

"It's reported the mentally ill grandfather kidnapped the child and drove to Grand Teton National Park, where he apparently committed suicide in the river and took the eighteen-month-old boy with him.

"The child's shoes and blanket were found along the edge near the Jackson Lake campground. A massive effort by park rangers and search-and-rescue units is ongoing to find the bodies.

"The search is complicated by the coming nightfall, and the waters of the Snake are murky. We'll continue to give you live reports as information becomes available."

Dear God! Someone's helpless little child in the hands of a demented relative—

In her mind's eye she could see the faces of her niece and nephew, of Cory.

She turned off the TV and buried her face in her hands. How did Pierce stand it? How did any of the law enforcement people stand it, let alone the parents?

"How come you're crying?"

Cory—

She lifted her head and wiped her eyes. Knowing

how his mind worked, he was probably afraid something terrible had happened.

"Hi. I didn't know you were standing there."

He'd come halfway into the living room holding one of his monster toys. His little face looked frozen. "What's wrong?"

"I'm crying because I'm a long way from home, and I miss my niece and nephew tonight."

"What are their names?"

Leslie couldn't believe he was talking to her. Her spirits soared. "Amy and Josh. She's three and he's six."

He stared at her through his glasses for quite a while. "Why don't you go back?"

Was that a plea?

"Because I'd like to stay here in the park where it's so beautiful. I think you live in the most wonderful place in the world."

Cory moved closer and perched on the arm of the couch, ready to take flight at any minute. Still...

She sat forward. "Are you hungry yet?"

He shook his head.

"Do you want to know what I bought us in town today?" She wished his father had come home so she could have cleared this with him first. But the moment seemed to have been chosen for her because for once Cory was willing to give her the time of day.

Ten seconds must have passed before he said, "What?"

"It's in the sack on my bed. Why don't you bring it in here."

She could tell he didn't know what to think about her. When she'd all but given up hope of his being interested enough to get it, he slid off the end of the sofa and walked out of the living room.

Her heart pounded in anticipation of his return.

If he returned.

In another minute he reappeared with the sack in hand. He brought it to her, then stood there eyeing her soberly.

Praying for a little inspiration, she said, "Cory— when my father died, I didn't want to go to school anymore."

He blinked. "Your daddy died?"

"Yes. I cried a lot and I wanted to stay home with my mommy all the time. But I couldn't. I bet you wish you could stay home with your daddy every day."

Cory's lower lip quivered before he nodded.

Encouraged, she continued. "I know how you feel, so I bought you something that should make you a lot happier." She removed the box with his name on it and handed it to him. "Go ahead and open it."

He undid the lid and pulled out the new cell phone. "This looks like Daddy's."

"But it's not. It's *yours*. I bought one for me, too."

While she was wrestling with her conscience over giving this to Cory without talking it over with Pierce first, his blue eyes rounded in astonishment.

"You can keep it with you all the time. Whenever you want to talk to your daddy, all you have to do is call his cell phone and he'll answer."

"What if he doesn't?"

She'd been waiting for that question. "He will because your name will show up on the little screen every time."

A glimmer of excitement animated his features. Already the wheels were turning. "I could call him at recess."

"Yes, or at the bus stop."

The excitement spread to his eyes. "Does it work now?"

"Yes. Let me show you."

After giving him instructions, she told him to dial his own house phone number. He pushed each digit carefully. In a second, the phone rang in the kitchen.

A broad smile broke out on his face.

She hurried into the other room to answer it. "Gallagher residence. Diana speaking."

"Hi."

His bright voice warmed her heart. "Hi, Cory. Why don't you come in the kitchen where Janice has all the important phone numbers written down. We'll program your phone so you can call your daddy by only having to press one button."

Cory came running.

CHAPTER FIVE

BETWEEN THE RANGERS, FBI and police, the area cordoned off near the river resembled a war zone.

One of the veteran rangers coordinating the search-and-rescue-units' efforts to find the missing toddler and his grandfather walked over to Pierce. His grim expression said it all. *No bodies yet.*

"The divers can't do any more work tonight. We'll start again at first light."

As Pierce nodded a frowning Rex Hollister, his second in command, approached him. "As if things aren't bad enough, Lewis Fry from CBN cable wants a statement."

"Go ahead and give him the status quo while I find out how he got past the roadblocks. Who did you put in charge?"

"Cracroft." *Wrong choice.* "But I found out it was one of the younger rangers who let Fry through."

Not without Cracroft's approval, Pierce wagered. He would talk to him at his evaluation interview next week and learn the truth.

The younger, untried rangers had been doing excellent work this past summer. Pierce had few complaints. Yet they'd be intimidated by a seasoned heavyweight like Cracroft, who'd been hired as a Teton ranger at the same time as Pierce more than eleven years ago. If Cracroft gave his approval for Fry to pass freely, then the newer recruits wouldn't have questioned it.

They'd trained together. The man knew his job and did it well, but his people skills left a lot to be desired. He'd always been a loner and had a problem with authority.

The rangers functioned on the old Three Musketeers philosophy of "all for one and one for all." Except for Cracroft, whose behavior on occasion led Pierce to believe the other man didn't feel a particular allegiance to anything. Tonight was a case in point.

No doubt he got his kicks from letting Fry through. The newsman had a reputation for stirring up controversy, the uglier the better. Cracroft knew the drill. He had his orders to keep out everyone not involved with the crime scene, but Pierce had a hunch he'd knowingly defied the rule and would let the inexperienced rangers take the blame for it.

Cracroft reminded Pierce of a temperamental grizzly that could be calm one minute, then turn fuming mad the next, given the right provocation. That made Pierce nervous as hell. Since the man's divorce two years ago he'd become moody and unreadable.

Recently he'd harassed a female ranger who'd transferred to another park to avoid trouble. After writing the other man up, Pierce warned him that if another incident happened against any employee, male or female, he'd be out of a ranger's job perman—

Pierce's cell phone rang, interrupting his thoughts. He pulled it from his pocket and checked the ID, but he didn't believe what he was seeing.

Cory Gallagher? If this was someone's idea of a joke...

He clicked on. "Chief Gallagher speaking."

"Daddy?"

His son's voice. "Cory?"

"Hi! I'm calling you on my new phone." Pierce's dark brows furrowed. His new phone? "Diana bought it for me so I can call you wherever I am. When are you coming home?"

Pierce moved out of earshot of the other men standing around him. His mind reeled with questions only she could answer. "I'm leaving right now and should be there within twenty-five minutes."

"Okay. Hurry! I'm hungry."

It seemed the acquisition of his own cell phone had resurrected his appetite, too. "You haven't eaten yet?"

"No. I'm waiting for you. Diana fixed my phone so all I have to do is press number one to reach you. Do you want my number?"

"We'll discuss it when I get there. See you soon, champ."

"OK. Bye, Daddy. I love you."

"I love you, too."

Surprised and troubled by this development, he put the phone away and headed in Rex's direction. "I've got to go. Call me if you need me."

"Will do."

Pierce climbed into his truck and took off. Halfway to Moose he noticed Nick Kincaid's truck coming in the opposite direction. He slowed down to talk to the chief ranger in charge of biological wildlife research, who'd been his best friend for the past eight years.

Nick's thirteen-year-old daughter Jessica often tended Cory if an emergency cropped up on the weekends.

"You're supposed to be on vacation until tomorrow morning," Pierce called to him. "What are you doing out here?"

"The news about the murder-suicide was on every station as we drove in from Gillette. I dropped Jessica off at her girlfriend's house and came to help."

"There isn't anything to be done tonight. Go home and get your sleep."

"If you're sure."

"I am. Rex has it covered. You're not expected to report for duty until morning."

"You're the boss."

"I am, so mind me."

Nick chuckled. "Any luck finding a replacement for Janice while I've been gone?"

His friend knew all about the situation and commiserated with Pierce. Nick had raised Jessica from the time she was born and had been through many difficult years of finding the right caregivers for her.

"Yes," Pierce muttered. The picture of the stunning woman standing in his office where he'd first met her rarely left his mind.

"That's good!" came Nick's heartfelt response. "What's she like?"

Good question. "Her name's Diana Farrow. She applied for the job a couple of days ago, and is staying with us on a trial basis until the end of the week."

"You didn't answer my question," he replied, but like the close friend he was, he recognized Pierce didn't want to talk about it right now and left it alone.

"How did Cory react to the news that Janice was leaving?"

Pierce rubbed his eyes. "Until a few minutes ago, you wouldn't have wanted to know."

"That sounds cryptic."

"I didn't mean it to be."

Pierce had been getting several conflicting messages from his gut where Diana was concerned. So far he hadn't been able to sort them out, and this business of the cell phone had set off new alarm bells.

Nick leaned farther out his window. "Speaking as someone who has been there before, if your gut is telling you she's the wrong person for Cory, then don't keep her, no matter how desperate you are."

"I intend to take your advice, Nick. Glad you're back."

"Me, too. Jessica and I will be over on Saturday morning to help plan the goodbye party for Jim and Janice."

"Good. We can decide on the food then."

"You're on!"

After putting the truck in gear, Pierce continued down the highway. Through the rearview mirror he saw Nick turn around and follow him into Moose.

Two minutes from the house his cell phone rang again. A wry smile broke out on his face when he saw who it was.

"Hi, Cory."

"Hi, Daddy. Where are you?"

"If you'll walk out on the front porch, you'll see me drive in."

"Okay. Don't hang up."

He grinned. "I won't."

"This is fun."

"You think?"

"You're funny, Daddy." Cory actually laughed.

Pierce couldn't remember the last time his son had sounded this happy. How could his own cell phone have caused such a remarkable change in him?

Maybe Diana's nephew had one and this was her way of trying to be Cory's friend. But Pierce would never have thought of buying him one. Not until Cory was an older, responsible teen.

For Diana to have assumed it would be all right without checking with Pierce first led him to believe the situation wasn't going to work out. For one thing, Pierce didn't believe in giving children everything they wanted.

Some of Cory's friends had fancy computers with all kinds of games to play on them. Pierce could see how addicting they were and he hadn't yet buckled under the pressure to let his son have one. No matter how well meaning, he wouldn't allow Diana or anyone else to sabotage his efforts in guiding his son.

"Here I come!" He pulled into the driveway with the phone still to his ear.

Cory jumped off the steps and came running up to the driver's side of the truck. "You sure took a long time!" he spoke into his phone.

"Well, I'm home now. What do you say we hang up and give each other a hug?"

"Okay."

As Pierce got out and felt his son's arms tighten around his neck, he was reminded of the drowned toddler's distraught parents. They'd never be able to hug their child again. Fighting tears, Pierce picked up Cory and carried him into the house.

"Mmm. Something smells good."

Diana was busy putting food on the table. She looked up as they entered the kitchen. Their gazes met. "I had to warm everything up. I hope it tastes all right."

"I'm sure it will." Her eyes looked almost as green as the kelly-green sweater she was wearing with bleached denims. She had the kind of figure and feminine grace that made anything she wore look like she'd stepped out of the pages of *Vogue* magazine.

The woman had a sophistication that led him to believe she'd done a lot more in her life than nurse her dying mother. Yet she seemed at home in the kitchen, too.

He put Cory down. "I'll wash my hands and be right back."

Cory followed him through the house to the bedroom and waited while he went into the bathroom. The second he came back out Cory said, "I asked Diana to put more numbers in my phone, but she said I had to talk to you about that first."

What an enigma she was—buying Cory his own cell phone without consulting Pierce first, yet leaving it up to him to decide the limits of its use.

Diana Farrow didn't play by any rules Pierce knew of, but the woman definitely lit her own fires.

Until he'd had a chance to talk to her in private and hear her explanation, he wouldn't act on Nick's advice. At least not until after Cory had gone to bed.

IT WAS AFTER 10:00 p.m. before Pierce walked into the living room where Diana was watching TV. She used the remote to shut it off. In truth she'd been staring at the screen without taking in the content, except for the news about the missing child and grandfather, of course. Evidently there was still no news that they'd been found.

She had to give Pierce highest marks for dealing with that crisis *and* the cell phone issue as if nothing extraordinary had occurred today. Cory was blissfully unaware of any undercurrents. Before getting ready for bed he'd eaten three pieces of pizza and had drunk a full glass of milk, a first for him since she'd moved in.

Diana decided Pierce was a master at handling the unexpected, whether domestic or professional. Otherwise he wouldn't be the chief authority of Grand Teton National Park and such a superior father, too.

He stood in the center of the room in his soiled uniform, evidence of his participation in the treacherous search along the Snake. With his hands on his hips, he was the epitome of the quintessential rugged male. "That dinner was delicious, Diana," he began.

"But you're afraid the arrangement isn't working out," she said, reading his mind. "What I did today has given you every right to think I'm not the proper person to care for your son."

"One thing I can count on from you," he replied. "You don't mince words."

"Neither do you, and it's refreshing. Even when I explain why I bought him that phone—even if I can make you understand why—you'll probably harbor some residual concern over what I might do the next time I decide to act without your permission.

"Much as I would like this job, we both have to feel good about it, so I'll understand if you ask me to leave in the morning."

He put his head back and rubbed his neck. The gesture revealed a man who was physically and emotionally exhausted.

She cleared her throat. "Cory had an unpleasant experience at school today. I think he's probably had an unhappy experience every day since it started. But bad as the bullying is, I—"

"Bullying?" he whispered incredulously, cutting off the rest of her words.

"Yes." In a few minutes she'd explained everything that had happened.

Pierce looked stunned. "Are you telling me Janice doesn't know any of this has been going on?"

"No, and Cory didn't want her to find out. If I hadn't happened to go to town with them, I wouldn't have met the substitute teacher. We'd still be in the dark, because Cory isn't about to be labeled a snitch along with everything else. That's the word my nephew calls kids who tattle."

Lines shadowed his attractive face. "School's been going for nine days. I wonder why his teacher hasn't called me about the problem before now."

"Maybe it only happens out of her sight."

His eyes grew bleak.

"Pierce, I don't believe Cory is that bothered by the teasing. At least not yet. I think there's a much greater problem at the heart of things."

"What problem?"

"After my father died, I went through a period where I didn't want to leave the house because I was afraid I might come home and find out my mother was dead, too.''

Silence filled the room. ''I had no idea,'' he finally whispered.

She got to her feet. ''Hearing that Cory wouldn't ride the school bus reminded me of myself. That's when I got the idea of buying him a cell phone. I bought one for me at the same time so you could always reach me.

''I thought if Cory could call you whenever he got scared, just hearing your voice would reassure him you're still there and help him to overcome his fear. It's such a paralyzing emotion.''

Ed had frightened Leslie to the point that if she hadn't been able to phone her sister day or night for reassurance, she was convinced she wouldn't be alive now. But she couldn't tell Pierce that.

''I hadn't planned to give it to him without talking to you first, but after Janice left today Cory started talking to me, and one thing led to another.

''Just so you know, I didn't tell him anything I learned from the substitute about the kid's teasing. All I did was talk to him about my fears after my father died.

''When I asked him if he felt that same fear after he left for school every day, he nodded. So I told him to bring me the sack from Samuelson's on my bed because there was a present in it for him. He acted so relieved to think he could call you whenever he wanted, even at recess—''

''Good Lord.'' Pierce shook his head. ''I didn't know he'd been in this kind of agony. I thought it was because Janice was leaving....''

"I'm sure that's part of it. I bet if you told Cory you would program her number into his phone so he could call her whenever he wants to hear her voice, that would ease his anxiety in that department, too."

He looked at her strangely, but not unkindly. "When I was talking to you on the phone in Salt Lake, there were moments when I had the impression you were psychic. Are you one of those people?"

"No. Not at all. But I am acquainted with fear." She could hear the tremor in her voice and despised her own weakness. "I recognize it in Cory. Fear dominates his world right now. It's prevented him from doing his homework and a lot more.

"What I'm hoping is that being able to phone you when those moments of panic come will help him to calm down. In time he'll find the courage to ride the bus and be a normal boy. If he'll start doing those things, most of the bullying will stop."

Pierce inhaled deeply. "I'll call his teacher before class in the morning and get her permission for Cory to keep the phone on him. We'll have to establish some rules so it doesn't cause disruption, but I'm convinced you're on to something. When he called me a little while ago, he sounded like a different child."

Leslie's eyes smarted. "I'm so glad. Let's just hope this hasn't created a monster."

His lips twitched. "I can handle all the phone calls he wants to make to me."

That was because he was an exceptional father. "When you move to Ashton, it won't be as traumatic for him knowing he can ph—"

"Ashton—" he interrupted her. All amusement had vanished.

"Yes. Cory was happy I bought him a phone, but he doesn't like me. Maybe *like* is the wrong word," she said when his facial muscles tautened. "I don't register with him, do you know what I mean?

"I'm not part of his world, and I'm not so sure he's ever going to let me in. I'll find some way to keep busy this weekend so he won't think I'm hanging around him all the time."

"You've only been here a couple of days. That's hardly long enough to make any kind of judgment."

"Maybe."

"There's no maybe about it." The steel edge in his tone told her he would be an awesome adversary if he were ever crossed. Roger's warning sent a stab of anxiety through her. "We're not going to know much of anything until after Janice has been gone for a while."

"Even so—"

"Even so nothing."

She averted her eyes. "Thank you for being willing to trust me a little longer." Thank heaven he wasn't sending her away yet.

A palpable tension seemed to link them.

"From the beginning I thought you were too good to be true. Now I'm finding I have to eat those words. Good night, Diana."

"Good night."

She waited until she heard his bedroom door close before she put out the lights and went to her own room to e-mail her sister again. When she turned on the laptop, a new message was waiting for her, probably in response to the one she'd sent before dinner.

Yet every time Leslie started to open a message,

she was almost afraid to read it. What if Ed had found out she'd left New York? What if he had proof?

He seemed to have superhuman powers. There was no doubt in her mind he would come after her. But now she had the added concern of Pierce and Cory's welfare. For their sakes she already regretted not telling Pierce there was a madman out there—and she was his prey.

Dear God. What was she doing involving these decent, wonderful people in a situation where their lives could be in danger? If anything happened to them because of her...

Talk about paralyzing fear.

It took Leslie a good five minutes before she found the courage to read her sister's message.

Leslie? Your idea to get Cory a phone was brilliant! Who cares about the old address? That was smart thinking. I'm glad you got one for yourself, too. Now Cory'll be able to phone you if he can't reach his father.

I've got good news. You can relax about Ed for the time being. He showed up at Roger's office this afternoon and waited in the reception room two hours on the chance of catching him when he came back from court.

Roger's secretary alerted him to the problem. When he arrived, Ed pulled the same thing on Roger he pulled on me by trying to make him feel guilty for not giving him a chance to explain his side of the story.

My husband told him to get out of his office or he'd call the police and have the judge slap a restraining order on him. Ed realized he meant business and left, but there was a whole new slew of e-mails from him tonight with a different tone.

Now he's threatening suicide if we don't help him to see you. Neither of us buys his threat for a second. It's anyone's guess how long he can keep this up.

Roger and I have decided to take the children and fly to Maine to see his parents this weekend. I'll stay through the next week, then he'll come up and get us the following weekend. Josh will only miss a week of kindergarten. He's ecstatic about it.

Don't worry. I'll take Roger's laptop with me so we're in constant touch.

If you want to talk in the morning, e-mail me at nine my time. I'll have just come back from driving Josh to school. I can't wait to hear how the phone thing works out with Cory. Love you to pieces. Diana.

Thank heaven Diana approved of what Leslie had done. At least Cory hadn't refused her gift. It was a beginning of sorts....

Winning him over was of paramount importance because she recognized she'd become emotionally involved with him and his father. All the more reason to go to Pierce and tell him the truth about everything before they could be hurt, or worse...

After telling Diana to hug the kids for her, Leslie shut off the computer, relieved to know Ed was still in New York and that her sister planned to fly to Maine where they'd be free of his harassment for a while.

"DADDY? ARE YOU AWAKE?"

Pierce felt the mattress give as Cory sat down on

the bed next to him. He lifted his head from the pillow, surprised to discover his son was already dressed for school. The new cell phone was clutched in his hand.

"You're up early." It was only twenty after six in the morning. Pierce's alarm wouldn't be going off for another ten minutes.

"I want to call Logan and tell him I have my own phone."

It looked like the conversation about the phone rules couldn't wait until breakfast. Pierce sat up, rubbing his chest absently.

"Let me ask you a question, Cory. Who bought this cell phone for you?"

"Diana."

"Did she tell you why she bought you such a grown-up present?"

He nodded. "So I could call you whenever I wanted."

"That's right. Normally children aren't given cell phones, but in your case I think it's a terrific idea as long as you use your phone for what Diana intended."

Pierce could hear Cory's mind working. "You mean I can only call *you?*"

"No. She told me she thought you would want to phone Janice, too."

"Even when she moves to Yellowstone?"

"Yes."

A smile lifted the corners of his mouth. "Would you put her cell phone number in my phone?"

"Sure. Go find the box with the instructions."

Cory left the phone with him and dashed to his bedroom. He was back in a flash with the sack containing the empty box and the sales slip. It reminded him he would have to reimburse Diana.

After a brief look at the instructions, Pierce programmed it. "There. All you have to do is press number two."

"I'm going to call her right now."

Pierce's first instinct was to tell him no. It was too early in the morning. But if he did that, or told him someone had to pay for the calls, Cory might not feel as free to use it, which would defeat the whole purpose of the exercise.

"Hi! It's me." Cory nodded. "Yup. Diana bought me my own phone. Now I can call you and Daddy whenever I want. I'll show it to you when you get here." He nodded again. "Okay. Bye."

The face he presented to Pierce was glowing. "She'll be here in forty-five minutes."

"I bet she was surprised to see your name."

"She couldn't believe it!"

"I couldn't believe it, either." Pierce grinned. "I think there's one more number we ought to put in there."

"Whose?"

"Think real hard."

"Jessica's?"

"No. What if you got to school and discovered you'd forgotten something important you were supposed to take to class? Who could you call who would get right in the car and bring it to you?"

"Janice?" he said in a tentative voice.

"Not when she's in Yellowstone."

His son averted his eyes. He knew what Pierce was asking.

"When are we going to move to Ashton, Daddy?"

The question devastated Pierce. It was an effort not to react. "Is that what you've decided you want to do?"

It took a minute before Cory slowly nodded.

Well. That was that.

Last night Diana had insisted she wasn't psychic, but after this revelation Pierce knew otherwise.

"Tell you what, champ. We're going to have a party for Jim and Janice on Saturday night. On Sunday we'll drive to Ashton and take a good look around the house and neighborhood. I'll drive you past the school. If you still feel you'd be happier there than here in Moose, then we'll make plans to move."

After a minute Cory slid off the bed. "Do I have to give the phone back?"

Pierce frowned. "Of course not. It was a gift. Diana told you why she you gave it to you. She intends for you to keep it whether you want her to live with us or not. However, there is one thing I'm concerned about. Did you thank her for being so kind and generous?"

Cory's eyebrows arched like his wife's used to do, indicating he hadn't thought about it. "Maybe I did."

"You aren't sure?"

After a slight hesitation, "No."

"Then you can thank her this morning after you straighten up your room. While you do that, I'll get showered and dressed."

Feeling as if he'd just taken a lethal blow to the gut, Pierce headed for the bathroom on leaden legs.

He needed to make a call to the teacher out of Cory's hearing. Her cooperation was required, even if his son would only be attending school in Jackson for another week.

Another week. Then life as he'd known it was going to change.

A year and a half ago the pain had been so bad he couldn't have imagined being alive today. But for Cory's sake he'd forced himself to go on living.

For Cory's sake he would do it again.

It was going to be a wrench to put his career on hold…perhaps for good if fate had something else in store.

What really surprised him was how much he dreaded telling Diana he was going to have to let her go. Not only for her sake, but his own.

In just a few days she'd pinpointed Cory's problem, which turned out to be a crippling fear neither he nor Janice had picked up on in eighteen months.

He was convinced fear was the reason she'd bought herself a new phone after coming to work for him. That way she could control all incoming calls. No one did that unless they didn't want to be found. Who or what was she afraid of?

Diana had an intuitive nature he'd never come across in another woman, yet in some ways he felt she was as vulnerable as Cory. She had a secret that was eating her alive, otherwise she couldn't have spoken so convincingly about fear or sensed it in his son so quickly.

He grimaced. Every time Cory shut her out, something deep inside Pierce wanted to pull her back in.

CHAPTER SIX

LESLIE? ARE YOU THERE?

Leslie answered.

I'm here. I've been in bed for about a half hour with the laptop next to me, hoping you'd be able to contact me tonight.

Diana came right back.

Frank and Minnie picked us up at the airport an hour ago. It's so wonderful to be here! My in-laws are angels. The minute we walked in the house they took over the kids and are putting them to bed right now.

I'm so glad it's the weekend! Roger is downstairs raiding the kitchen. He's going to bring up some treats and a little wine for a midnight feast. I didn't realize how much we needed this time alone.

Guilt consumed Leslie. When she'd fled New York, she'd left her family to deal with Ed.

It isn't fair what you're being put through because of me.

Her sister responded with a question.

Was it fair that you had to drop everything years ago to take care of me and Josh for two months when I had such dreadful morning sickness with Amy?

Leslie's fingers flew over the keys.

You can't compare the two situations. Ed mustn't be allowed to go on torturing you.

She didn't have to wait long for a response.

He won't be bothering us here, so stop agonizing about it. Besides, I have wonderful news! I talked to your editor before we left the house. He thinks the world of you and told me to tell you to take all the time you need before coming back. I had no idea he was so nice. Somehow I expected him to ask a dozen questions and pry into the reason for your breakup, but he didn't.

Thank heaven.

Thank you for doing that for me, Diana. Byron's all bark. Did he give any clue that Ed had been bothering him?

Adrenaline surged through Leslie's veins while she waited for her sister's answer.

No, but I don't think he would have told me, anyway. Now, let's change the subject. Anything new with Cory?

Leslie's eyes closed tightly for a minute before responding.

Not really. He did thank me for the phone, but I know Pierce put him up to it.

She could have predicted what Diana would say next.

These are early days, Leslie. What are you going to do with your free weekend?

Good question.

Tomorrow evening Pierce is having a going-away party for Janice and her husband. Without saying it in so many words, Cory doesn't expect me to be around. Since Saturday and Sunday are my days off, I've decided to take a two-day tour of the park while the fabulous weather is still holding. I think I'll spend Saturday night on one of the privately owned ranches with tourist accommodations inside the park boundaries.

She planned to get away in Pierce's car while he and Cory were still asleep. He'd already given her permission to use it during her time off.

That sounds fantastic! When you get to that ranch tomorrow night, I expect a full report.

Leslie smiled as she typed her final message.

I promise not to ask for a full report of your midnight feast with Roger. Love to the children from me. I think I'll wait until Sunday night to talk to you, after you've taken Roger to the airport.

She logged off, leaving her sister and Roger alone. They deserved to forget the world for a few days.

How would it be to have a marriage like theirs? Not only were they more in love now than when they'd married, they *liked* each other.

While Leslie had been doing some housecleaning with Janice earlier in the day, the other woman had shown her the Gallagher's wedding album. One look at Linda Gallagher explained Cory.

His mother had been an adorable, five-foot-two blonde with brown eyes and those pixie features she'd bequeathed to her son. According to Janice, Linda and Pierce had been very much in love since college, where they'd met.

When a light plane crash took her life, Pierce had retreated within himself. Fortunately he had Cory. The boy needed him desperately, forcing him to get on with living sooner.

Janice confided that in the last six months he'd had the occasional dinner with a woman when he went to Ashton or Jackson, but Cory was always so upset, those dates had been few and far between.

That didn't surprise Leslie. It had taken only five days to learn that Cory was Pierce's raison d'être. Nothing was more important than loving his son and making him feel secure. Not even his career.

Cory had no idea how lucky he was. He would have to become a man before he could fully appreciate a parent like Pierce.

When Leslie had first started dating Ed, and had watched the way he'd interacted with Diana's children, she'd assumed he would be a loving husband and father, too. Once they decided to start a family, she'd planned to put her career on hold until their children were older. She'd also assumed Ed would make career concessions so he could be around to enjoy their children.

How could she have been so wrong about a person? Then again, he was mentally ill.

Was it because Ed had turned out to be disturbed that Leslie looked upon Pierce as someone exceptional? Of course he wasn't perfect, yet she couldn't help but admire his mature, intelligent, levelheaded way of handling problems without being overbearing.

She might have been living in Pierce's household for only five days, but that had been long enough to realize how controlling Ed had always been. Her fault had been to mistake that sick possessiveness for a desire on his part to take care of her.

Hindsight had taught Leslie that losing her father

in her teens had made her ripe for the kind of constant attention Ed had showered on her at the beginning.

Without Maureen's intervention, Leslie would have gone into a hellish marriage where Ed may have literally smothered the life out of her.

If he ever caught up to her, that was exactly what he'd do, and he wouldn't care if he had to get rid of Pierce and Cory in the process. At the thought of them coming to any harm because of her, shudder after shudder rocked her body. For their sake she didn't dare wait too much longer to tell Pierce everything.

A LOW WHINING SOUND brought Pierce out of a deep sleep. Someone had just opened his garage door. What the hell?

"Damn—" he muttered after stubbing his toe on his way over to the window. When he looked behind the curtain he saw Diana drive off in his Grand Cherokee.

He glanced down at his watch. It was only twenty after seven! Where did she think she was going at this unearthly hour? Saturday mornings were a time for everyone to sleep in!

Last night every available ranger had volunteered to help in the ongoing search for the missing grandfather and child. Nick had worked with Pierce in the chilling waters of the Snake. Finally they'd discovered the drowned body of the grandfather wedged between some boulders in the river. After that find there'd been a renewed effort to locate the missing toddler.

Using searchlights, all the rescue workers had assembled to look for the child in the same general vicinity. Around eleven o'clock it was one of the rangers, not the FBI or police, who spotted the little boy's lifeless form caught in a logjam farther downstream.

The mood among the rangers had been one of relief and sorrow. Pierce had sent Nick and the exhausted men of the search crew home, assuring them they would be receiving the governor's commendation for their untiring valor.

Pierce stayed at the site to finish up the rest of the investigation. As a result he hadn't rolled up the driveway until after midnight.

Craving his bed, he'd planned to sleep around the clock before getting things ready for the party. He still could, *if* he climbed back under the covers. Cory would watch cartoons and make himself a bowl of cereal until Pierce got up.

But for some reason he hadn't figured out yet, the sight of Diana stealing away before the sun's rays hit the front porch had disturbed him. The fact that his toe still throbbed didn't help his negative frame of mind any. He didn't think he'd be able to sleep now. Maybe she'd gone to the store for some necessity and would be right back.

He put on a T-shirt rather than the matching half of his pajama bottoms and headed for the kitchen. Halfway there he remembered a certain conversation with her.

The other day she'd said something about finding a way to keep busy this weekend so Cory couldn't accuse her of hanging around. Since technically she was free to do what she wanted with her days off, he couldn't fault her for leaving. He'd told her the car was at her disposal.

Even though it looked like he had his explanation, the knowledge depressed and concerned him. Yesterday he'd purposely run into Jackson to do a little detective work by speaking to the salesclerk who'd sold Diana the cell phones.

Pierce had an account at Samuelson's. He'd used that as the pretext to find out if his new nanny from New Jersey had charged the phones to him or had used a credit card, because he wanted to reimburse her.

He knew she'd paid cash, but she might have said something to the clerk during the transaction that would provide Pierce with additional information about her. Convinced she was hiding from someone or something, he was determined to get to the bottom of the mystery.

When the clerk checked his records, he told Pierce she'd paid cash, but had put down Rochester, New York, as her home address. Pierce quickly corrected himself, saying that he'd meant New York. After thanking the clerk, he left for headquarters.

During the job interview she'd told him she'd been raised in Rochester. Maybe she'd been willed her parents' home and was still hanging on to it. Whatever the explanation, she hadn't given the clerk her sister's address in New Jersey, where she said she'd been living before she came out west. More than ever Pierce had the feeling she didn't want someone from New Jersey to find her. Who? The man she'd once planned to marry?

If Pierce had been engaged to a woman like Diana,

he couldn't imagine what it would take for him to give her up.

Were they having a lover's quarrel? If so, it had to be the mother of all quarrels for her to go to these lengths not to be found.

"Hi, Daddy."

His son, dressed in his Pokémon pajamas, was planted on the floor in front of the TV watching *Scooby-Doo*.

"Morning, champ. How come you're not wearing your glasses?"

"Oh—" He put his fingers to his lips. "I forgot." He scurried out of the living room and returned in a shot wearing them perched on his nose.

"Did you see Diana leave?" Pierce asked after coming back in the living room with a large bowl of cereal and milk.

Cory nodded, too engrossed in the cartoon to answer.

"Did she say where she was going?"

When Cory didn't respond, Pierce prompted him. "Where did she go?"

His son hunched his shoulders, still glued to his favorite show. "I don't know."

Pierce frowned. "You mean she didn't say anything?"

"No."

"Not even when she'd be back?"

"I think tomorrow night."

Growing impatient, Pierce shut off the TV with the remote. Cory turned his head around in surprise.

"You only *think?*"

"Maybe she said I'll see you tomorrow night."

Damn. "Did she take her suitcase?"

Cory nodded.

"Why didn't you stop her? You knew we were having a party."

"'Cos she doesn't work on Saturdays and Sundays."

Out of the mouths of babes... Diana had been right. Cory hadn't wanted her around, so she'd gotten out of the way to accommodate him.

How strange to think that in only five days he'd become accustomed to her being here whenever he was home. Hell—he looked forward to seeing her when he walked in the kitchen after a tough day.

He liked the way she looked at him, as if his presence pleased her, too. He liked the way she moved on those long, shapely legs. He liked the fragrance of her freshly washed hair....

"Are you mad at me?"

"No. Of course not. I don't suppose you know her new cell phone number." Pierce had meant to get it from her.

Cory averted his eyes. "No."

One thing was obvious. His son really didn't care for Diana and there wasn't a thing Pierce could do about it. He tossed Cory the remote and went to the kitchen with his cereal still untouched.

Needing to channel his negative energy into something physical, he got dressed before asking Cory if he wanted to walk to the store with him for a newspaper. Pierce was curious to see how many distortions of the facts about the murder-suicide case had been reported.

"No. *Space Rangers* is going to be on."

"Okay. I'll only be gone a few minutes."

Once Pierce had locked the front door behind him, he broke into a run. It didn't take long until he came in sight of the gas station.

"Hey, Pierce!" the owner called out, waving him over.

Pierce slowed to a stop near one of the pumps where the man was refilling the paper towel dispenser. "What's up?"

"I was hoping you would tell me," he said with a grin.

Pierce squinted at him. "Come again?"

"You know," he drawled. "The beautiful babe driving your car. When she stopped for gas, I asked her how come she happened to be at the wheel. She said she was helping out with Cory. You lucky dog," he growled in a confiding voice. "How is it to have a total knockout like that living under your roof? If I weren't happily marr—"

"She's only here on a trial basis," Pierce broke in. He knew the other man didn't mean anything by his teasing. Normally Pierce could laugh off comments like these, but the situation with Diana was special. It wasn't like anything he'd ever experienced before. He wanted what went on in his home to be private.

"What's there not to like?" the owner persisted in an insinuating tone.

"Cory's having trouble letting Janice go." While he didn't mind offering this bit of the truth, Pierce had no intention of discussing the situation with Diana with any of the gossipy locals. He cut the conversation short. "See you later."

No sooner had Pierce started to walk away when

he spied a couple of the unmarried, seasonal rangers coming down the road in a park patrol car. They pulled up beside him and Pierce assumed they wanted to talk about last night's recovery of the two bodies.

The one driving leaned his head out the window. "Hi, Chief."

"Chief." His companion called from the passenger side of the car.

"We're glad we saw you."

They both looked a trifle sheepish. Pierce walked over to the driver's side. "What's wrong?"

"We made a mistake a little while ago and I guess you ought to know about it."

"Everyone makes mistakes. What happened?"

"While we were on patrol this morning, we saw your Grand Cherokee going down the highway at a pretty fast clip. A woman was driving it and she wasn't Mrs. Archer. So I stepped on it to catch up to her and find out what was going on.

"After I put on the siren, she pulled over. We asked to see her license. She told us some story about taking care of your son and having permission to drive your car. At that point I could see she had a suitcase with her, so we told her to step out of the vehicle."

Oh, Lord.

"She was telling you the truth," Pierce said through gritted teeth.

"We know that now, sir. We called your cell phone, but you didn't answer, so we called your house."

Never again would Pierce go anywhere without

taking his cell phone with him, not even for what was supposed to be a five-minute jaunt.

"You weren't there obviously, but everything Cory said checked out with her driver's license. He intimated she'd been sleeping there the last few nights. Sorry, sir. We were worried she might have stolen your car."

Pierce took a calming breath. "You did the right thing."

"Ms. Farrow was really nice about it. Do you mind if we drop by your house on Sunday when we're off duty and tell her we're sorry?"

From the glint in their eyes, Pierce knew exactly why they wanted to see her again. She had every male in the park in a tailspin. It gave him perverse pleasure to tell the guys she wouldn't be arriving back until late Sunday night.

Both faces fell. "Then we'll visit her sometime next week," one said, not willing to give up.

"Better check with me first. She's only working for me on a trial basis."

"If it doesn't work out, will she be going back to New Jersey?"

Pierce couldn't think that far ahead, not where Diana was concerned. Besides, it was none of their damn business. The information on her driver's license wasn't meant for public consumption. He grimaced to realize they knew anything at all about her.

"Probably," he said, not wanting to give them hope. "While you're out this morning, double check the latrines at Gros Ventre campground for signs of raccoons. We trapped a mother and five babies there last week. She'd gnawed her way through the back wall.

"Though we released them miles away and repaired the damage, there could be other families hanging around. Let me know what you find."

"Yes, sir," the rangers answered at the same time.

Pierce turned on his heel and started to sprint toward the store. Any more interruptions—any more men asking questions about Diana—and there wouldn't be a newspaper left!

Pierce walked into the store and greeted the son of the manager. "Hi, Scott."

"How you doing, Pierce?" Scott was all smiles, as if he knew a secret. The college kid had a cocky attitude that got under Pierce's skin. It was a shame because Pierce thought his parents were the salt of the earth.

His gaze flew to the end of the counter where the newspapers were kept. He saw a few copies of the *Rocky Mountain News* and nothing else. "No *Denver Post* or *Salt Lake Tribune?*"

"That's what the hot-looking chick who parked your Grand Cherokee out front a little while ago asked me. I told her they're late getting dropped off this morning." Scott's smile betrayed his lascivious thoughts. "How long has this been going on?"

The kid had just stepped over the line, kindling Pierce's anger. He put three dollars on the counter and took a copy of the *Rocky Mountain News* before giving the younger man a direct stare.

"Whatever's been going on couldn't possibly live up to that eighteen-year-old imagination of yours. I'm sure your folks were hoping college would help you grow up. Looks like it's still going to be a few years."

The smile vanished.

Pleased with his bull's-eye, Pierce left the store. But by the time he reached the house, he realized his behavior had been out of control all morning.

It had started when he'd seen Diana slip away. He had an idea she would spend most of her weekend studying the want ads.

Cory stood in the open doorway waiting for Pierce with an anxious look on his face.

"Daddy—"

"I know all about the phone call. The guys told me." He picked up Cory and hugged him before shutting the door.

"They thought Diana stole your car. That's funny."

Pierce wished he could laugh. Lord—why couldn't he?

"It probably wasn't funny to Diana," he said before lowering his son to the floor. Tossing the newspaper onto the hall table, he headed for the kitchen, needing a cup of coffee. Cory followed.

"Nick and Jessica are coming over to help us decorate for the party."

"When?"

"In a minute. He wanted to know what we're going to eat. I told him we're having manicotti."

That was news to Pierce. He doubted Cory even knew what the dish was. "Why did you say that? Did Janice tell you it's her favorite food?"

"No. Diana made them."

Diana? "I didn't see anything in the fridge."

"Last night after Janice left, she fixed a big pan and put them in the freezer in the garage. She made brownies, too."

In the next instant Pierce hurried out to the garage and lifted the freezer lid. Sure enough he saw two large pans covered in foil. His gaze darted to Cory's. "When were you going to tell me about this?"

"I forgot."

Pierce had reached his limit of tolerance. "On purpose?"

"No. I just forgot till Nick asked me."

Cory was probably telling him the truth.

"Well I'm glad you remembered." Pierce pulled out both pans and closed the lid. Diana was an excellent cook. As she'd been born on the East Coast, he imagined her manicotti would be authentic Italian.

"Did you help her?" he asked after bringing the pans into the kitchen and putting them on the counter to thaw. When the manicotti wasn't so icy, he'd find a place for it in the fridge.

"No."

Pierce fixed himself some instant coffee and put the mug in the microwave. "So what did you do while she was busy preparing something delicious for Janice and Jim?"

"Cameron came over because his parents had to go to the clinic."

"What was wrong?"

"His dad cut himself on the chain saw. His mom had to drive him."

"That doesn't sound good." Gary Morgan, Cameron's father, was one of the best rangers around.

"He's okay. He just cut his palm. I saw him when

they came back to get Cameron. His hand has a big bandage.''

"I'll bet." Pierce would have to bring Gary into the office for the month. Hand cuts took a long time to heal properly.

No sooner had he drained his coffee than they heard Nick's familiar rap on the front door.

"I'll get it!" Cory dashed off. Jessica was one of his favorite people. In truth, she was a favorite with Pierce, too.

The cute, short, enthusiastic thirteen-year-old had a mop of red-gold curls and eyes like the brilliant blue Alpine forget-me-nots growing at the highest elevations of the Tetons.

Pierce had only seen Jessica's mother in a picture Nick had given to his daughter. It had been taken in college. The strong resemblance between the women was as remarkable as Cory's resemblance to Linda.

Many times Nick and Pierce had chuckled over the fact that their offspring didn't look like them. Nick was tall like Pierce and had brown hair and gray eyes. Most people on a first meeting acted surprised that Pierce and Cory were father and son. But not Diana.

On several occasions she'd made the offhand comment that Cory was a dead ringer for Pierce. His mannerisms, the way he walked, and the unique way he had of concentrating on something important.

"Hi, Pierce!" Jessica called out, and waved to him from the doorway.

"Hi, Jess."

"Cory wants to show me something, then we'll start putting up the streamers.''

He grinned. "I was kind of hoping you'd take over that job."

"You and Dad are rangers. No one expects you to be decorators, too!"

"I take exception to that," Nick muttered.

"Sorry, Dad, but it's true. Who else but you would have picked out red, white and blue streamers at the store if I hadn't been along?"

"What's wrong with those colors?"

"This isn't the Fourth of July. They're going to have a baby! I've decided we'll give them a baby shower and do everything in pale blue and pink. Come on, Cory."

Both men chuckled as their children disappeared down the hall. Nick's gaze swerved to Pierce. "You know something? My daughter's right. Looks like I'm going to have to pick up a baby present along with the rest of the food and drinks."

"We'll all go to town to shop. Do you have any idea if they've bought a crib yet?"

"Nope."

"Jessica will know," Pierce said, and smiled.

They eyed each other in amusement before Nick said, "Where's Diana? I've been anxious to meet her."

Pierce turned sober. "Ask any ranger in the park except me and you'll have your answer."

A strange sound came from Nick's throat. "What is *that* supposed to mean?"

It was liberating for Pierce to be able to spill his guts. After he'd vented his deepest feelings, Nick was the one who looked devastated.

"You can't move to Ashton." The emotion in his voice spoke volumes to Pierce.

"Do you honestly think I want to leave? Hell, Nick. What am I supposed to do? Cory won't give Diana the time of day, yet she's every bit as terrific as Janice ever thought of being. In fact, in many ways she's even better, if that's possible. Her insights about Cory are nothing short of extraordinary."

Nick walked over to the doorway, looked around, then came back in the kitchen. "I'm pretty sure I know what the problem is," he whispered. "Jessica tended Logan after school yesterday. When his parents brought her home, she said something in passing, but I didn't realize how important it was until now."

Pierce's body surged with adrenaline. "Tell me."

"Apparently Logan overheard his parents talking about the possibility of you ending up marrying the nanny you hired. He told Jessica. I warned her not to repeat it to anyone because it was pure gossip.

"But the thought just occurred to me that Logan has probably discussed this with Cory at school. Maybe your son's afraid you'll love Diana more than him. I know Jessica gets nervous whenever I go out with a woman more than a couple of times."

Pierce had the gut feeling Nick was right. He'd been dealing with his daughter's fears a lot longer than Pierce.

Fear.

Diana had said Cory was dominated by it. So was she, and he had a strong hunch that it had something to do with the man she'd once planned to marry. Before long Pierce intended to get to the bottom of Diana's fears, but right now he had other problems.

The whole park was buzzing about the woman sleeping under Pierce's roof. With Logan's parents talking about it, too, it could have frightened Cory. And that was why he was so reluctant to warm up to Diana.

When Pierce thought about it, his son wouldn't have had the same problem with Janice, because she was already married to Jim and stayed in her own house at night.

No matter how innocent the situation, for a woman who looked like Diana to be living with Pierce on a twenty-four-hour basis wasn't the kind of behavior people expected from the chief ranger. Without meaning to, he'd set both of them up as a target for innuendo and that had impacted Cory.

Thanks to Nick's insight, Pierce had an idea. "On the way back from town, let's stop at Grayson's rental cabins on the other side of the river. I'm sure there's one available for Diana. When Cory asks me why, I'll tell him she was only staying at our house long enough to learn how to run things. From now on she's going to stay in the cabin at night and only come over during the weekdays."

"You've hit on the perfect solution!" Nick exclaimed. "It'll stop all the speculation and should relieve Cory of his fear. Tell you what—I'll clue Jessica in. Maybe she can help influence him to give Diana a chance."

Pierce nodded. "Pray it works, Nick."

"It's got to! I'm not about to lose my best friend."

CHAPTER SEVEN

WHEN LESLIE PULLED INTO the garage at seven o'clock on Sunday evening, Cory opened the door into the house and waited for her. Since she knew how he felt about her, she was surprised *his* was the first face she saw upon her return to the house.

There could only be one explanation for it. Pierce had told his son they were going to move to Ashton. With those words Cory could give himself permission to relax and be friendly toward her until she was out of their lives for good.

Under the circumstances he would probably accept the small, handheld electronic game she'd bought him for a goodbye present. After deciding to drive to West Yellowstone for part of her trip, she'd found it in a souvenir shop and hadn't been able to resist. She couldn't believe there was actually a game that featured a park ranger.

The fact that the larger-than-life hero on the box bore a superficial resemblance to Pierce in his green-and-gray uniform, even down to the gold badge with a bison on it, had nothing to do with her purchase.

She walked around the end of the car toward him. "How was the party, Cory?"

"Good." Clearly his mind was on something else. "We've been waiting for you to get back."

"I bet your father has missed his car."

"We went to Ashton in the truck."

Her heart plunged to her stomach. She'd been right in her assumption. "When did you do that?"

"Today."

She swallowed hard. "I see."

Cory followed her into the kitchen where she came face-to-face with Pierce, who was casually dressed in a gray pullover and thigh-molding jeans. While her pulse raced because of his powerful male sensuality, his eyes played over her features with a thoroughness she found so exhilarating it made her a little breathless.

"I'm glad you returned safely." His voice had a husky quality to it.

"Me, too." He was probably referring to a possible car accident. Leslie had been thinking about the possibility of Ed catching up with her and hurting them. Thank heaven neither eventuality had happened.

She put down her suitcase and turned to Cory. "This is for you. If you'd seen it in the store, you would have wanted it."

"What do you say?" Pierce prodded his son.

"Thank you."

For a boy who normally had a lot of energy, Cory seemed to be moving in slow motion. His father reached into the sack and pulled out the box. After studying it for a moment, his mouth curved into a smile, then he chuckled.

Pierce's eyes met hers. They were smiling, too. Her system flooded with warmth.

Cory reached for the box and opened it.

Leslie cleared her throat. "I have no idea what the

buttons do, but if your father will read you the instructions, I'm sure you'll be able to figure it out in no time. All I know is, Ranger Riley is hunting grizzlies so he can tag them. But they're hiding in logs, caves and under waterfalls. He has to face many dangers to reach them.''

"I always wanted to be a ranger,'' Pierce confessed. ''If I'd been given a gift like this at Cory's age, I would have thought I'd died and gone to heaven.''

His son looked up at him. ''After we take Diana to the cabin, will you show me how to play it?''

Pierce nodded.

The blood pounded in her ears. ''Cabin?''

''Daddy got it for you 'cause you're not going to live with us anymore.''

Dear God.

She fought not to show any emotion. ''I know, so I don't need a cab—''

''I still need you during the day for the next week,'' Pierce broke in. ''It'll take me that long to prepare for the move to Ashton. I hope you don't mind that I rented a furnished cabin for you. There are a group of them down the road about a mile.

''After you pack your things, we'll follow you in the truck and get you settled. You can keep the car to come back and forth.''

His eyes flicked to the paper next to the kitchen phone. ''If you'll write down your cell phone number, then I'll be able to reach you in case of an emergency.''

With those words, her hopes that Cory might have

learned to tolerate her presence had just been smashed to smithereens.

''I'll do it right now.'' She reached into her purse for a pen and walked over to the phone.

''Come on, Cory. While Diana gets her things together, let's go in the other room and learn how to play this game.''

Her hand trembled so much, she was thankful they were no longer standing there to witness her turmoil.

DIANA LOOKED THROUGH the rearview mirror for the dozenth time. Her body broke out in a cold sweat. She *was* being followed!

After a delicious seafood dinner with Roger in the Old Port district, she'd dropped him off at the Portland jetport before heading back to her in-laws in their car.

The weekend with her husband had turned into a mini honeymoon. They'd had trouble saying goodbye to each other. Yet at the turnoff a few miles away from the house, all the pleasure she'd been feeling drained out of her because a car traveling several car lengths behind her after she'd left the freeway was gaining on her and closing in fast.

Nothing like this had ever happened to her before. With her heart pounding, she pulled out her cell phone and called her in-laws. After three rings she heard Frank's voice.

''Dad? It's Diana! I could be wrong, but I think Ed Strickland might be following me in a blue compact car. I'll be at the house within two minutes. I can't find the remote, so please have the garage door open for me.''

"I'll do it right now."

Since the broken engagement, Roger's parents knew all about the nightmare Leslie and the rest of them had been living through. Roger had warned his parents it was possible Ed might come to Maine looking for Leslie. Since Ed had met the senior Farrows in New Jersey several months earlier, he knew where they lived.

By the time she turned into the driveway, the reassuring sight of Frank standing in the garage helped her pull herself together. The door closed behind her the second she parked next to Minnie's car.

She jumped out of the seat and into her father-in-law's arms, unable to stop shaking.

"I saw a blue car drive past the house as you pulled into the garage, honey. It was a man and he was alone. Let's go inside and call the police."

Diana couldn't bear to think this horror story had grown to encircle her in-law's lives, but Roger had predicted as much. Suddenly she knew what it was like to be in Leslie's skin. It was terrifying!

GRAYSON'S FURNISHED RENTALS turned out to be a small cluster of rustic cabins with white trim around the windows and doors. They sat in a meadow with the Tetons rising majestically behind them. Several tall trees provided a wind break.

The charming interior of her cabin contained a leather couch and chairs with red-and-green-plaid curtains. Various paintings of the Tetons hung on the walls.

She loved the fireplace and the old-fashioned rocker placed next to it. Braided oval rugs covered the floor of the kitchen-cum-living room, lending a cozy, homey touch.

The covers on the twin beds in the bedroom were made of the same plaid fabric as the curtains. An adjoining bathroom with a stall shower and forest-green towels looked neat as a pin.

After Pierce had seen to her comfort, he'd driven off with Cory. Leslie waited until she couldn't hear the sound of his truck, then she walked out on the little porch to breathe in the crisp air. The silhouette of the glorious Tetons dominated the landscape.

Over the weekend she'd stopped at the Jenny Lake campground to hear one of the rangers give a fascinating lecture on the famous mountains. Afterward he'd approached her because he'd noticed she was driving Pierce's red car and wanted to meet the new nanny the other rangers had been talking about.

When he learned that she intended to go hiking the next weekend, he invited her to have dinner with him on Monday night when he was off duty. He'd bring some maps and tell her where to go for the best scenic views. She'd accepted his invitation because he said he'd be happy to answer all her questions.

If she couldn't work for Pierce, she planned to buy a camera and get some shots of the Tetons before she went back to Salt Lake. This was too great an opportunity not to take advantage of it. The Grand Teton range was magnificent.

At its sixty-five-hundred-foot elevation, the thinner atmosphere revealed a clear sky studded with stars. She studied the heavens, awestruck by the beauty of the night, the chirping of crickets, the smell of honeysuckle from the bushes growing next to the cabin's walls.

The scent took her back to summers in Rochester where she and Diana had grown up carefree and innocent. But this heavenly view wasn't like anything she'd seen before. And she was a grown woman now, aware of a woman's feelings, like the curious ache she could feel even to the palms of her hands.

She knew what that ache was all about.

Pierce Gallagher.

A week ago she couldn't have imagined ever trusting another man again, aside from Roger. It shocked her to think that in so short a time she could feel this way about Pierce, despite her constant fear of Ed.

Nothing had changed in that department. She still expected him to be lurking around the next corner waiting for the opportunity to grab her and do whatever his twisted mind could invent. Despite this constant awareness, Leslie was compelled to care for Pierce. Her attraction to him continued to grow.

Tonight when his hard body had accidentally brushed against hers in the cabin doorway, she'd wondered if he'd felt the same jolt of electricity. Maybe, maybe not.

Since returning from her two-day jaunt an hour ago, Pierce had praised the food she'd made for the party, had thanked her for her thoughtful preparations, but he hadn't taken her aside to explain what was going on in his mind. He couldn't, not with his little shadow hanging on every word. Yet it was clear he expected Leslie to read between the lines and understand that his son's happiness had to come first.

Of course it did. From the outset Leslie had realized this first week had only been a trial run.

While it didn't matter what kind of a job she found next, as long as it met certain criteria, Pierce would have to give up the career he loved for at least a year. It had to be the second hardest thing for him to face after burying his wife.

The thought that in another week she would never see him or Cory again was so painful, it sent her back inside the cabin to e-mail her sister. If she couldn't unburden herself tonight, she knew she wouldn't get any sleep.

She'd plugged in her laptop in the bedroom, but to her disappointment there were no new messages from Diana. Leslie tried instant-messaging her. No response. Most likely her sister had been caught in traffic coming home from the airport.

Desperate for something to fill her time while she waited, Leslie took a shower and got ready for bed. Still no activity on the computer.

The temptation to simply call the senior Farrows' house had her reaching for the cell phone she'd put on the bedside table next to the cabin phone. But at the last second she remembered the promise she'd made to Roger and couldn't do it.

As she started to put it back, it rang.

A little thrill of excitement coursed through her veins, because only one person knew her number....

She moistened her lips, which had suddenly gone dry. "Hello?"

"That was fast," Pierce said. "Sounds like you were waiting for someone to call."

"I was hoping it was my sister," she lied.

"Are you sure you weren't hoping it was your ex-fiancé?"

A gasp escaped before Leslie could stop it. "Why would you say that?" Her voice shook.

"I didn't mean to upset you, Diana. When I first interviewed you, I noticed how emphatic you were about your relationship with him being over. At the time you seemed a little too emphatic, which led me to wonder if you weren't regretting your breakup. It would be understandable if you were hoping to hear from him again."

"No!" she cried. "Never!"

"I believe you," he said in a quiet voice. "Forgive me for having brought you any distress. If you want, I can call you back."

"No—please don't hang up. If my sister is trying to phone me right now, it doesn't matter. She'll e-mail me."

Leslie pressed a hand against her heart where it hurt from the throbbing. "Is there an emergency? Do you need me to drive over?"

"No, Diana. I need you to listen."

She bit her lip, still shaking in reaction. "All right."

"I didn't mean to sound rude. It's just that Cory has finally fallen asleep in my bed, but for the last few nights he has been restless. I can't assume he won't come walking in the kitchen any minute now, so I'm going to make this fast."

The clarification filled her with relief. "I understand."

"That's what's so amazing about you. Your understanding of the situation. What you don't know is that there has been talk about you sleeping under my roof. The gossip may have affected Cory."

"I don't doubt it." Everywhere she'd gone on her tour, people had recognized Pierce's car. She could imagine how it might have caused speculation. "You were wise to move me here. If I'd known there was a place like this within the park boundaries, I would have come here first."

"I'm afraid I wasn't thinking too clearly last week."

One of the things she admired about Pierce was his ability to admit a mistake. "Neither was I," she confessed in a tremulous voice.

"Maybe one day you'll be able to tell me why," came the low reply.

Since he knew she was hiding something from him, no amount of denial would change anything, so she didn't bother. If she could be assured that Cory liked her well enough to let her stay and be his nanny, she would tell Pierce the truth right now.

But as it stood, there was no point in alarming him tonight, not if she had to leave the Tetons next week and look for work elsewhere. Once she'd gone, he and Cory wouldn't be in danger.

"The bottom line is, I don't want to move to Ashton, Diana. I'm hoping that deep down Cory doesn't want to go, either. Therefore I'm counting on you to help us get through this next week, because anything could happen now that Janice has gone."

"I agree," Leslie said, attempting to keep the excitement out of her voice. He didn't want her to leave...

"When reality hits my son, and it will, who knows

what his reaction is going to be. We'll have to play it by ear, something you do instinctively. If I haven't told you before, I'm telling you now. I'm very grateful you didn't let what happened at the interview prevent you from giving this job a try.''

''I'm glad, too,'' she whispered. ''Cory's happiness has come to mean everything to me.'' *And yours...*

''Amen. I'll see you in the morning.''

''I'll be there at seven-thirty. Good night.''

She clicked off with the sure knowledge that her future lay in Cory's hands.

Her gaze darted to the screen of her laptop sitting next to her on the bed. Still no response from Diana. It was after midnight in Portland. Too late to expect to hear from her sister tonight.

Leslie typed a message that said she'd talk to her in the morning, then she put the laptop on the nightstand. After setting her watch alarm for seven o'clock, she turned off the light.

With images of Pierce filling her mind, sleep took a long time to come.

It wasn't until she awakened the next morning that she realized it was the first time in more than five weeks she hadn't been plagued by nightmares of Ed.

When she checked her e-mail and there was still no message from Diana, she started to get worried. Of course there could be half a dozen reasons why her sister hadn't found the time to go online.

Maybe one of the children was sick. Or maybe Roger had decided not to go back to New Jersey and they were sleeping in. Possibly the grandparents had taken Diana and the children on a little trip somewhere.

Yet always hovering beneath the surface was the fear that the silence had something to do with Ed.

For once Leslie would have to be patient.

She dressed in Levi's and a new turquoise T-shirt she'd bought at the same souvenir shop where she'd found the ranger game. The front looked like it had women's makeup all over it. The caption read "I Ran Into Tammy Faye." Leslie hadn't been able to resist it.

When she walked into Pierce's kitchen ten minutes later where he was fixing breakfast, he took one look at her chest and burst into full-bodied laughter, the kind that started in the belly. He actually had tears running down his cheeks.

Then she, too, broke into a laughing fit. At the height of their mirth, Cory came running into the kitchen still dressed in his pajamas.

He looked from one to the other. "Why are you laughing?"

Pierce wiped his eyes with his arm. "I don't think I can explain so you'll understand."

Afraid Cory would feel left out Leslie said, "There was a lady on television who always wore a lot of makeup on her face. Kind of like paint. It was gooey and shiny. See this mess on the front of my T-shirt?"

He studied it through his glasses before nodding.

"The words say, 'I ran into her.'"

Cory stood there blinking without comprehension.

"Diana's taller than the woman she's talking about," Pierce chimed in. "Can you see that if she bumped into Diana by accident, the makeup would get all over Diana's T-shirt?"

"Yes," he said at last. "Why does that lady wear all that stuff?"

"Because," Pierce explained as he carried the platter of eggs and bacon to the table, "if she'd been born with beautiful skin like Diana's, she wouldn't have to cover it up."

Leslie, with a little difficulty, followed with the plate of toast he'd made. After the compliment he'd just paid her, it felt like her legs had turned to an insubstantial mush.

"Some women feel more comfortable with a lot of makeup, Cory. Just like some men like to wear a beard and mustache."

They all sat down to breakfast, but judging by Cory's next question, it was obvious Leslie's remark had fueled his curiosity.

"Did you ever have a beard, Daddy?"

Pierce nodded.

"When?"

"In college. All the men in the forestry department grew one for a contest."

Leslie didn't dare look at him. He was a gorgeous male. With such black hair, a beard would have made him fascinating in a completely different kind of way.

"A contest? Did you win?"

His father chuckled. "No. After a week I hated it so much, I shaved it off. They itch."

Cory giggled. "Maybe I'll have a beard one day."

It surprised Leslie that Cory was in such good spirits. Maybe it was because he knew they were moving to Ashton. He seemed to have shed his anxiety over Janice being gone.

This was the first time she'd felt things were normal in the Gallagher household. Instead of running to his room, Cory stayed to eat breakfast and talk to both of them. The atmosphere was so pleasant, Leslie was in danger of believing it could always be like this.

She could almost believe Ed didn't exist.

No sooner had the thought entered her head than Pierce pushed himself away from the table. "I've got to go."

There wasn't a thing Leslie could do about his leaving. The man had a park to run, but she was so disappointed it was a real struggle to stifle her moan.

He walked around and kissed his son. "Have a good day at school." His eyes flicked to Leslie. When he'd been laughing earlier, they'd glowed a bright blue. Now they had darkened, indicating his light-hearted mood had changed. A stream of unspoken messages flowed between them before he said, "I'll see you tonight."

She nodded and started clearing the table.

Cory followed his dad out to the garage, then ran off to his room where Leslie imagined he would hibernate until lunch.

No one could have been more shocked than she was when he came back to the kitchen a few minutes later with his backpack. He plopped it on the table. Out came his cell phone followed by a scrunched-up piece of paper.

Leslie kept loading the dishwasher.

He walked over and handed it to her.

"What's this?" She smoothed it out so she could read it.

"Homework."

"For the computer?"

Cory nodded.

"You want me to help you with it?"

"Will you?"

This was a different child.

"Of course. Let me wipe off the counter, then I'll get the laptop out of my tote bag."

In a few minutes they sat side by side at the kitchen table, where she plugged it in.

"Let's see what you're supposed to do." She read the words aloud. "Goal—students will understand the significance of famous people and holidays. State the names of holidays of significant historical people. Identify various historical figures.

"Specific computer assignment—look up the name of the president of the U.S., identify what he does and where he works, look up the name of the governor of the state of Wyoming, identify what he does and where he works."

"I know who the governor is already!"

"You do?"

"Yup. He and Daddy are friends."

Leslie smiled. "Then you know more than I do. Let's look it up on the computer, anyway, so I can see where he works."

Cory did a nice job of printing the letters of the names and places needed for his assignment. She praised him for it. After they'd finished, she clicked on to Rodent's Revenge, a computer game that had already been installed when she'd bought her laptop.

He'd obviously played the same game installed on his dad's computer at work. The little monkey was good at it once he'd figured out how to use the laptop's mouse pad.

When it came her turn, she couldn't erect the boxes fast enough to stop the mice infiltrating from every direction. Cory kept telling her what to do, but she was too slow.

At this point he stood next to her, laughing and jumping up and down. It was so much fun to be interacting with him like this, she never wanted it to stop.

In the middle of the next game she heard the little sound that an e-mail had just come in. Thank goodness.

Cory turned his blond head toward her. "What was that?"

"It looks like I have a message from my sister."

"In New Jersey?"

"Yes."

"Do you have to read it now?"

She made an instant decision. "No. Let's keep playing."

Following a few more rounds of Rodent's Revenge, they played his electronic ranger game until it was time for lunch. Once he'd finished half a peanut butter sandwich and a glass of milk, he dashed to his bedroom to get dressed for school.

She wanted to help him but didn't dare push her luck. Instead, she put everything in his backpack and had it ready when he returned a few minutes later wearing jeans and a T-shirt.

"Maybe you should comb your hair. What do you think?"

"I forgot."

He ran to the bathroom. A second later he came

back not looking that much different, but she had to give him points for trying.

"Shall we go?" She reached for her tote bag.

He shook his head. "I called Logan. We're going to ride the bus together."

At that revelation, Leslie was so excited she could hardly breathe. He must have phoned his buddy from Pierce's bedroom.

She followed him to the front door. "Do you think you'll ride the bus home, too?"

"Yes." But he didn't sound as certain.

"I'll be there at the end of school just in case."

"No! I don't want you to come!"

His negative reaction after this morning's break-through was like a shot in the heart at close range. Here she'd been thinking they'd made so much progress. Not true.

Cory was counting on her being gone by the end of the week. Therefore he'd decided to be nice to her as long as no one else knew about it.

Was he afraid that if the kids saw him with her, he might have to endure a lot more teasing? In light of what Pierce had said about the gossip, it would make sense Cory was willing to ride the bus.

"Tell you what. Give me your phone and I'll store my cell phone number in it. Then if you change your mind, you can call me at recess. All you have to do is press number three. How does that sound?"

After a long hesitation he reached into his backpack and handed it to her. She programmed it and put it back for him. "There. You're all set and even have your homework."

"Yup."

More than anything in the world she wanted to wrap her arms around him and hug him tight, take away his every fear. Yet all she could do was stand there and watch through the crack in the door as he ran toward his friend, who'd just appeared in the driveway.

Once they were out of sight she closed the door, wondering if at the last second Cory wouldn't be able to get on the bus after all.

She waited in the hall for a good six or seven minutes. Evidently his fear of being seen with her was greater than his other fear at the moment.

Her heart aching, Leslie walked back to the kitchen. She needed a good, long talk with her sister.

CHAPTER EIGHT

"PIERCE? RANGER CRACROFT is here for his interview."

"I'm almost through, Sally. Tell him to wait five minutes, then send him in."

"Yes, sir."

Pierce turned to Bill Shiffers, head of the Teton Grizzly Bear Study Project. "Sorry about the interruption."

"No problem. We're ready to work with some rangers on that new tracking study you and I discussed. As you know, there are forty to fifty radio-collared grizzlies currently loose in the Yellowstone ecosystem, which includes the northern part of the Tetons. They need to be monitored."

Pierce nodded. "How many rangers do you need?"

"Four from you would be terrific, but we could manage with two."

"I'm afraid I can only spare two at the moment. Maybe more later on down the road. Give me a couple of days and I'll get back to you."

"Excellent." As Bill stood up to shake hands, Pierce's cell phone rang. He glanced at the ID. It was Cory.

Since coming to work, Pierce had been half listening for his son's call. It was almost eleven-thirty.

Time for Diana to be driving him to school. Something told him Cory wasn't cooperating with her.

He nodded goodbye to Bill, then clicked on with a feeling of dread. "Hi, champ. How are things going?"

"Hi, Daddy. I'm at the bus stop with Logan."

Pierce sat back down. His breath had caught in his lungs. How had Diana managed that? "It ought to be fun to ride the bus to school. I used to love it when I was your age."

"Logan says it's okay. Here it comes, Daddy. I'll call you when I get there."

"I'll be waiting."

As soon as he heard the click on Cory's end, he hung up.

Elated at this much progress, Pierce decided to phone Diana and find out what she'd done to accomplish such a miracle. The truth was, he wanted an excuse to hear her voice.

Their conversation over the phone last night had convinced him she was no longer in love with her ex-fiancé. That was the best news he'd heard in a long time. But her denial didn't mean her ex was finished with her.

Maybe he was one of those types who couldn't handle rejection and refused to leave her alone....

"Pierce?"

Dave Cracroft had just entered his office. Pierce had forgotten all about him. The call to Diana would have to wait.

"Sit down, Dave."

The sandy-haired ranger eyed him suspiciously. "I already know I'm in the doghouse about the other night, so go ahead and write me up. What else is new?''

Pierce sat back in his chair. ''Let's get something straight, Dave. I don't have it in for any ranger. But since it's my job to call the shots, I expect everyone to obey orders. On several occasions in the past you've chosen to ignore them.''

''Maybe it's because you've screwed me and made it look like things were my fault one too many times.''

''Be specific.''

''We both know you had a thing for Gilly, so you turned her against me by telling her I was the reason my marriage failed. Then you had her transferred out of here.''

Cracroft was delusional. ''She asked to be transferred.''

Dave's light complexion tended to get red when he was angry. Pierce noticed red blotches starting to appear on the man's face and neck.

''Like I said. You screwed me. When Fry asked me if you were as tough a bastard to deal with as other members of the press had reported, I told him yes. When he asked for a reason, I told him the truth—that you were a frustrated widower who'd had trouble with one of the female rangers and it made you hot-tempered. So what are you going to do? Demote me again?''

It stunned Pierce that Dave would intentionally bait him, knowing he could be thrown out on Pierce's say-so.

There were times like now when he wondered if Dave didn't have a chemical imbalance. If he put him on medical leave and recommended that he see a psychiatrist, a thorough evaluation might explain why he flared up at unexpected times and carried such a big chip on his shoulder.

Or Pierce could skip that, write him up for insubordination and be done with him for good.

Pierce considered the possibility that Dave's wife leaving him had made him go a little crazy. The loss of a spouse was painful, no matter the reason. Pierce could relate.

Dave was also one of the best outdoorsman around, which made it hard for Pierce to think about ending the man's career at thirty-seven. Being a ranger was all he knew. All he had going for him.

To fire him would be like kicking him while he was already down. Maybe what Dave needed to get his act together was to feel important. Something told Pierce that when the other man was growing up, no one had ever told him he was special.

He leaned forward. "No. What I'm going to do is take you off campground duty and put you in charge of a new job to do with the Teton Grizzly Bear Study Project. There'll be some training involved."

Because Dave had been expecting the worst, the astonished expression on his face was almost comical.

"It requires someone seasoned, someone who knows the back country inside and out. That's you. You'll take your orders from Bill Shiffers. No doubt you saw him leave my office on your way in. Pick any ranger you can work well with who isn't in charge of an assignment. What he doesn't know, you can teach him."

Dave's eyes narrowed. "You're putting *me* in charge…"

"Yes."

"Why?"

It was truth time. "Because this is a vital, dangerous job best suited for a loner who doesn't like to be around a lot of people. It's a job where you'll have to operate on your instincts most of the time.

"You grew up in Jackson Hole. Your grandpa taught you everything about hunting and survival. You know these mountains as well as any man living. Nobody has better instincts than you. That's the kind of man Bill needs. Do you want the job or not?"

A long silence ensued. "Does Rex know about this?"

Rex Hollister was Dave's immediate superior. "Not yet. I thought I'd feel you out before I cleared it with him."

"Yeah." He nodded. "I'd like the job."

"I'm glad. Do a good one. Don't force me to let you go."

There was a strange glitter coming from Dave's light brown eyes. "I'll keep that in mind."

The second he went out the door Pierce buzzed his secretary. "Sally, hold my calls. I'm going out for lunch." Actually, he was headed home to talk to Diana, but he had no intention of broadcasting that information to everyone in hearing distance.

He took off in his truck. A few minutes later he pulled into the garage alongside his car and shut off the motor. He started to get out when his cell phone rang. After glancing at the caller ID he clicked on. "How was the ride, Cory?"

"Fine, but the driver got mad at some of the kids for yelling out the windows."

"I'll bet. Where are you now?"

"In front of the school. The bell rang. I have to go in."

"All right. I'll see you when you get home from school."

"Okay. I love you."

"I love you, too."

In Pierce's opinion, the step Cory had just made was more remarkable than Neil Armstrong's first step on the moon. Overjoyed, he rushed inside the house. "Diana?"

Her laptop sat on the table, still turned on. Where was she? He started down the hall. "Diana?"

"I'm in Cory's room."

Pierce didn't know exactly what he expected to find, but when he caught a glimpse of her haunted green eyes in that white, tear-stained face, he felt like an ice ax had just been planted in his abdomen. She reminded him of a frightened, quivering forest creature caught in a snare.

"I didn't know you were coming home for lunch. I would have had it ready if you'd phoned first."

"Forget food and tell me what's wrong."

She looked ill. In fact she was so changed from the beautiful woman who'd laughed with him earlier in the morning, he had a hard time believing they were the same person.

"It's a hormone thing I get once a month. I'm totally embarrassed you had to walk in and find me like this."

She was lying through her teeth, but he had no right to demand anything of her.

In the next breath she said, "Did you know Cory took the bus this morning?"

"Yes. He called me twice. That's why I came home, to find out what you did that got him to go to school on his own."

Diana shook her head. "I didn't do anything." She confided her theory that Cory was probably afraid to be teased by the kids if they saw him come to school with the woman who'd been living at their house.

Pierce didn't know what to believe. "Wherever the true explanation lies, he *did* overcome his fear enough to get on that bus. What I'm concerned about at the moment is *your* fear. Has there been bad news from home? Do you need to leave, but you're afraid to ask me?"

"No!" she cried. If anything, her face went whiter. "No," she murmured again before averting her eyes.

He followed her out of the bedroom.

The urge to take her in his arms and force a confession out of her made him realize how emotionally involved he'd become with her, without being completely aware of it.

"How can I help?"

When they reached the living room she wheeled around. "You helped me when you hired me. I'm so grateful, you'll never know."

The tremor in her voice resonated to the depths of his being. Pierce took a ragged breath. "Whoever or whatever it is that you're afraid of, when you want to talk about it, you know where to find me."

THE SECOND LESLIE HEARD Pierce drive off, she ran to the kitchen and pulled her cell phone from her purse to call Roger at his law office.

She was still reeling from the news that Ed had been stalking Diana at her in-laws. It had upset Roger's mother and now the whole Farrow household was in a state of chaos.

This situation couldn't be allowed to continue. Leslie punched the digits, no longer caring that Roger had advised her not to call him, or her sister.

"You've reached the offices of Pirelli, Mason and Farrow. If you know the extension, you may dial it at any time. If—"

Leslie pressed the numbers and waited.

"Mr. Farrow's office. May I help you?"

"Yes. This is Roger's sister-in-law, Leslie. I have to speak to him now! Is he there?"

"Yes. Just a minute."

Perspiration beaded her brow while she waited.

"Leslie?"

"Roger? Please don't lecture me. Diana e-mailed me a little while ago and I've been sick ever since."

"I told my wife not to say anything, but I should have known she wouldn't listen to me."

"That's because this has grown out of control!" she cried. "Now Ed's holding your entire family hostage. I can't let this go on any longer. The way things are looking, Pierce will be moving to Ashton with Cory at the end of the week. Then I'm coming home to deal with Ed myself!"

"No, you're not!" Roger thundered in the most savage voice she'd ever heard. "Diana's on her way home with the children as we speak. That'll bring Ed back to New York.''

''Poor Diana!'' Leslie's voice shook.

''Your sister's tough. It's Mom who got upset, but she has Dad, so stop worrying about it.''

''I'm so sorry to have brought this on your family.''

''You didn't bring on anything. These things happen to decent people more often than we know. I've spoken to the detective on your case. He gave me the name of a good P.I. Stalking cases are her specialty. She works with a couple of backup people.''

''I bet she's expensive.''

''It's worth it. This morning I hired her to keep track of Ed's movements. She'll document everything. In time we'll be able to throw the book at him. The point is, Ed has found out we're not hiding you, my parents aren't hiding you and you no longer live in your apartment.

''By now he realizes you've flown the coop, especially because you haven't shown up for work in a while. Our harassment is going to stop because he'll start looking elsewhere for you.

''As the detective reminded me this morning, if Ed had wanted to injure any of us, he would have done it by now. It's you he's after. That's exactly why you *can't* come home. I want you to stay where you're safe. Keep using your laptop to communicate. Do you hear me?''

''Yes.'' She wiped the tears off her cheeks. ''I love you and Diana so much, Roger. If he hurts you or the children—''

''He hasn't. He won't! We love you, Leslie. With

the help of the P.I., this nightmare's going to end. Now I've got to run. Promise me you'll stay put?''

"I'll promise for now," she said. "But if Ed does one more thing to terrorize you, I'm coming home."

"Fair enough. We'll talk later."

He clicked off.

Leslie walked over to the sink and rinsed her face. She prayed Roger was right, that Ed was looking elsewhere for her now and would leave the family alone.

The news that her brother-in-law had hired a P.I. came as a relief to Leslie if only because it meant Roger no longer had to carry the burden of this alone. She planned to pay him back whenever she could. Which reminded her, it remained to be seen if she still had a job with Pierce when the week was over.

Because of her, he'd left the house without eating lunch. She feared he'd gone back to work not bothering to stop and eat somewhere else. That meant he would be starving when he returned tonight.

Without wasting precious time, she got started on her mom's homemade cinnamon rolls. Even Cory would like those. Later on she would put a beef tenderloin roast in the oven.

For the rest of the day she kept busy cleaning and doing laundry. So far no phone call from Cory. At three-thirty she opened the front door to watch for him. When it got to be four o'clock and there was still no sign of him, she was alarmed and called Logan's mom to find out if the bus had been late. Unfortunately she got voice mail.

While she was looking for Cameron's number on the list by the phone, she heard voices in the foyer.

Suddenly she saw Cory walk in the kitchen with a cute, redheaded teenager.

Leslie straightened. "You must be Jessica Kincaid. I've heard a lot of nice things about you. I'm Diana Farrow."

The girl stared up at her with flattering interest. They shook hands. "I've heard nice things about you, too."

Leslie glanced at Cory. "I'm glad you're home. I was just going to call one of your friends to find out where you were."

"That's my fault. I'm sorry," Jessica spoke up. "My bus pulled up behind Cory's. When I saw him get off, I invited him to my house. But then I realized you would be worried, so we came straight over."

"I appreciate that." Her gaze settled on Cory once more. "Did you like riding the bus?"

He nodded, but he appeared distracted. "What's that smell?"

"Roast and cinnamon rolls. I'll be taking the first batch out of the oven in about three minutes. Can you stay and have one with us, Jessica?"

"I'd love it!"

"Good."

"Can she play Rodent's Revenge with me?"

"Sure. The laptop's still on."

"My dad needs to see your T-shirt," Jessica commented. "He'd crack up."

Leslie chuckled. "So you know who Tammy Faye is?"

"No, but I have a teacher at school who wears enough makeup to sink a battleship. At least that's what Dad said after we got home from back-to-school night a couple of weeks ago.''

"Come on, Jessica."

"I'm coming."

"What grade are you in?" Leslie asked the girl, who sat down at the table next to Cory.

"Ninth."

"That's the grade I was in when I got my first dog."

Cory's head swung around. "What kind?"

"A toy pug."

When those big blue eyes looked at her through his glasses, her heart melted. "You mean he wasn't real?"

Jessica laughed. "A toy dog means a little dog, Cory."

"Would you like to see one?" Leslie asked.

He nodded.

"Jessica? Have you ever used a laptop?"

"All the time. Dad carries one around with him."

"Then why don't you look up pugs on the Internet for Cory while I get the rolls out of the oven?"

"Cool."

Leslie smiled to herself as the precocious teen got busy. Soon the three of them were munching on hot rolls while they viewed a Web site with dozens of photos of adorable pugs.

"Their faces look smashed!"

"That's the way they were bred," Leslie explained. "My pug looked like that black one."

"It's so cute," Jessica said. "What was his name?"

"Marvel."

"I wish I had a dog," Cory remarked.

"What kind do you want?"

"One like in *Dexter*."

Leslie knew that cartoon. Josh watched it all the time. "You mean a basset hound."

"They're so funny." Jessica did a search and pretty soon a darling basset hound popped up on the screen.

Cory jumped up and down. "I wish I had him."

"If you weren't moving to Ashton, you could ask your dad for one."

He frowned at Jessica. "How come?"

"Because nobody will be home all day," spoke a deep male voice directly behind them.

Pierce!

Leslie whirled around. "I didn't hear your truck."

"It needs a new fan belt, so I left it at the station and walked the rest of the way. Hi, Jess." He tousled her curls before reaching for a cinnamon roll. After biting into it he made a sound of approval. "These are out of this world."

"Thank you," Leslie replied.

"Daddy? Could I have a dog like that?"

Pierce put a hand on Cory's shoulder while he munched. "You heard Jess. With you at day care and kindergarten and me working a new job, it wouldn't be fair. Dogs get lonely."

His face fell. "Diana had one when she was little."

"That's true, Cory, but my parents worked at home and took care of Marvel while I was at school."

"You were lucky," Jessica murmured in a wistful tone.

"I was. In fact I was spoiled rotten."

Jessica smiled. "How come your parents stayed home?"

"Dad was a photographer. He and my mom ran a portrait studio in the front of the house."

"I wish you could be home all day, Daddy."

What child wouldn't want his father home all day? Leslie thought she'd better explain.

"Cory, my father didn't work at home because he wanted to."

She could hear him thinking. "How come?" It was his favorite question.

"He was a photojournalist who traveled around the world. While he was covering a civil war in Africa, he got shot and ended up in a wheelchair. No matter how much I loved it that he was home, I knew he'd give anything to be able to walk again and do the job he once did."

Cory's expression sobered. "Oh…"

Leslie had revealed more than she'd meant to. It was time to go.

She unplugged the laptop and put it in her tote bag. "Jessica? It's been a pleasure meeting you. Maybe we'll see each other again."

"I hope so."

"Bye, Cory. Dinner's ready whenever you want to eat. I'll see you in the morning."

"Okay."

Her gaze flicked to Pierce. "Do you want to run me home so you'll have a car?"

"That won't be necessary. My truck'll be fixed by the time the station closes. I'll walk you out."

Pierce followed her to the garage. When he helped her into the car, her heart thudded loud enough she feared he could hear it. She put the window down to thank him. The action created a certain intimacy with their faces so close.

His eyes searched hers. "Are you feeling better than you did at lunch?"

"Much, thank you."

"I'm glad. What are your plans for this evening?"

The question surprised her because she'd assumed he'd wanted to talk about Cory.

"I was asked to meet someone for dinner at Jenny Lake Lodge, but since your truck is being worked on, I won't go. You might need the car before it's ready."

A palpable tension emanated from him. "Is it a ranger?"

She supposed he had a good reason for asking. "Yes. Since I work for you, would you prefer I didn't accept the invitation?"

His jaw hardened. "I have no right to tell you what to do on your free time."

"You do if you feel it compromises your position in some way."

"No. I don't think that," he said in a thick tone. "I trust in your discretion."

"Thank you, but you still didn't answer my other question."

He breathed deeply. "If I need transportation, a patrol car could be here within a minute."

She averted her eyes. "Still, I'll keep my cell phone handy. If something should come up and you need me to stay with Cory, all you have to do is call."

A long silence ensued. "Have a good evening, Diana."

"You, too," she whispered, sensing his emotional

as well as physical retreat before he disappeared inside the house in a few swift strides.

Halfway back to her cabin, she drew out her cell phone and called the number the ranger had given her when they'd exchanged phone numbers. After three rings he answered. "This is Dave Cracroft."

"Hello, Dave? It's Diana Farrow."

"I know. I saw your name on my caller ID. I've been looking forward to this evening ever since we talked."

Unfortunately she wasn't interested in him the way she feared he was in her. "I've been anticipating it, too, but something important has come up and I'm afraid I can't make it. Could I take a rain check?"

She heard his hesitation before he said, "Sure. There's the monthly party for the park employees and their families at the Teepee in Moose this Saturday night. It's potluck and starts at seven. Would you like to go?"

Not with him, but she hated turning him down again. Maybe it would be a good idea to go. There'd be a lot of people around. Everyone including Cory would see that she and Pierce weren't an item. Of course if she didn't have a job after Friday, it wouldn't matter, anyway. Still...

"Since I don't know what my circumstances will be, could we tentatively agree for me to meet you there? I'll call you if I can't make it."

"I guess I'll have to say yes if I hope to spend an evening with you."

"Thanks for being so nice about this."

"Just don't disappoint me again." For a moment he sounded a lot like Ed. Not so much in his voice as in the intensity of his words. "I'm only teasing, Diana," he added when she didn't say anything back.

But was he?

Stop it, Leslie. You're so paranoid, you imagine every man is like Ed.

"I know that. See you Saturday night."

"I'll be watching for you. Every colleague of mine will be jealous." He clicked off.

No doubt his flattery was meant to reassure her. Ed had flattered her in the same way.

She put down the phone and drove the rest of the distance to her cabin, wishing she could throw off the bad vibes. It wasn't fair to a man she'd only met one time in a crowd of vacationers.

Before getting out of the car she phoned Pierce. He answered almost immediately. "Diana?"

Maybe it was her imagination, but it seemed like there was a wealth of emotion in his voice.

"Sorry to bother you."

"You never bother me. I'm glad you called. You outdid yourself on dinner tonight."

His compliment chased away the chill from her body. "When you left the house without eating lunch I got worried. I'm glad if it tasted good." She paused to catch her breath. "I'm calling to let you know I canceled my dinner date. If you need the car or a baby-sitter later, I'm available."

"You didn't have to do that."

"I know, but as long as I'm working for you, I've decided to make myself available for Cory during the weeknights. You did hire me to live in. The fact that I don't shouldn't change our original agreement."

She had a ton of literature to absorb about the park. It would keep her nights occupied. "Enjoy the evening with your son. Good night."

"Good night."

CHAPTER NINE

WHEN THURSDAY EVENING rolled around, Pierce could no longer put off what needed to be done. On the way out of his office he stopped by his secretary's desk.

"Sally? Would you locate Rex and ask him to meet me here at eight-thirty in the morning? Tell him it's important."

"Will do."

"Thanks."

All week Pierce had hoped Cory would tell him he'd changed his mind about wanting to move to Ashton. His son's troubling silence was killing him.

Diana continued to do her part like a Trojan. It was getting harder and harder for Pierce to watch her leave the house every evening the minute he walked in from work. No matter how busy his job kept him, thoughts of her never left his mind.

The desire to spend time alone with her had grown into a burning need. But knowing how Cory felt about Diana, Pierce hadn't crossed that line yet. Lord, from the look of things he'd never be able to.

It had been hard enough to consider putting his career on hold for a year. Little did he know Diana's entrance into his life would cause sensations he'd thought dead and buried to spring to dizzying life, catching him totally off guard. The thought of a future without her in it was anathema to him now.

The situation had become impossible. It was time to face the facts, including that Diana would be soon leaving the park to find work somewhere else. The rational part of him recognized it would be for the best if he never saw her again.

Beyond the fact that Cory didn't like her, she had a secret. One Pierce probably didn't want to know about. He sensed in his gut she was attracted to him, yet she was fighting it with extraordinary determination. Her admirable strength of will was only one of the things increasing his desire to get her alone in his arms.

But giving in to that desire would only create more pain for everyone involved if Cory felt threatened, and it looked like he did....

When he pulled into the garage, Diana was there at the door with her bag in hand ready to go back to her cabin. If he didn't miss his guess she, too, was ready to crack from the tension.

"Hi!" she greeted him, bright as ever, but it maddened him that her eyes avoided his. "Your meat loaf and scalloped potatoes are in the oven. Cory's in his bedroom playing with Logan. His mom said she'd be available to tend to him if you had an emergency."

"Where's the fire?" She'd already gotten in his car.

"I have an appointment at the hairdresser's in Jackson."

He didn't like the sound of that. When she'd canceled her date on Monday night with one of the rangers, she'd probably made plans to go out with him on the weekend coming up.

Pierce had a hunch it was one of the two rangers who'd pulled her over that first day who was now making his move on her.

The idea of her being with another man, let alone one of those hormone-riddled guys, filled Pierce with a kind of rage he didn't know himself capable of. Yet there wasn't a damn thing he could do about it.

She flashed him a brief glance. "See you in the morning." On that final note, she backed out of the garage and took off.

Normally the smell of meat loaf would have enticed him, but he'd lost his appetite. He walked through the house to Cory's bedroom, where the boys were playing with his race car track.

"Hi, guys."

"Hi, Daddy!"

"How would you two like a job? I'll pay you."

Cory looked up. "What is it?"

"I've got a bunch of boxes in the back of the truck. If you'll help me bring them in, we can start packing up your stuff for the move."

"I think it's dumb you're going to live in Ashton," Logan grumbled.

So do I, Logan. So do I.

"Come on, guys. You can play after."

He headed back to the garage and climbed into the truck bed. By the time the boys had joined him, he'd emptied it. Logan carried two of the boxes into the house, but Cory just stood there staring up at Pierce through his glasses.

"Are we really going to move?"

Alert to the odd inflection in his son's voice, Pierce schooled himself not to react. "Isn't that what you wanted?" He picked up some boxes and started into the house.

"I don't think I want to move."

Cory—

Pierce's heart leaped. He pivoted around. "How come?" He asked the question his son always asked.

"'Cos I just don't. Do you?"

"No, I don't. What about Diana?" Pierce's world teetered waiting for his son's next response.

"Jessica likes her."

And so do you, Cory.

"Does that mean it's okay if she takes care of you?"

He nodded.

Dropping the boxes, Pierce reached for his son and hugged him.

"Daddy—I can't breathe."

"How come you two are hugging?"

"Because we've decided we're not going to move to Ashton after all," Pierce declared.

"Yippee!" Logan cried. "I'll go get the boxes." He ran off making whooping sounds.

In a few minutes Pierce had put all of them back in the truck. He turned around with his hands on his hips. "I've got an idea. Let's drive to Jackson for hamburgers and French fries."

Cory's smiling face turned to Logan. "Give me five!"

"While I lock up, you guys get in the truck."

Pierce's hands literally shook with excitement as

he put the food away in the fridge. He would eat it tomorrow.

Before going out to the garage he called Logan's mother to tell her the news and get her permission to take Logan with them.

Her first response was to break down in happy tears. It turned out she and her husband had been dreading the day Cory moved from Moose. She didn't know the half of it!

With the assurance that he'd have Logan home in a couple of hours, he joined the boys. The three of them laughed and giggled all the way into Jackson. The lighthearted ring in Cory's voice spoke volumes.

As for Pierce, he was too intent on trying to spot his Cherokee to keep pace with the boys' conversation. It had to be parked somewhere in the center of town. *If* she'd told him the truth…

"Hey—there's our Cherokee, Daddy!" Cory's eagle eye had spotted it right away.

"Yup." He pulled into the empty parking space next to it. "Diana's getting her hair done. I'm just going to pop in and see if she wants to meet us for dinner. I'll be right back."

He levered himself from the cab. The second he entered the small beauty parlor, his gaze fused with Diana's in the mirror. He could have sworn she gasped.

One look around the claustrophobic room revealed she was the last client in the shop for the night. The well-endowed stylist in the tight-fitting jeans blow-drying Diana's hair flashed Pierce an inviting smile.

"Hi, there. What can I do for you?"

"He's waiting for me," Diana spoke up with a ring

that sounded possessive to his ears. But maybe Pierce only thought that because he wanted to believe she was equally excited to see him.

"Lucky you," the other woman said, still smiling at Pierce. "I've never seen a ranger in here before."

Pierce stayed where he was near the door. "This is a first, all right."

The stylist might be irritating, but he couldn't fault the way she'd fixed Diana's light brown hair. The feathered style framing her gorgeous face looked natural, the way she always wore it.

"Okay." The woman turned off the switch. "You're done." She untied the drape and brushed off the back of Diana's neck. Pierce would have liked to have done those honors himself.

"How much does she owe you?"

"That's all right," Diana said, attempting to dissuade him from his intentions.

"Fifty dollars."

For that much money Diana must have had more done than a shampoo and haircut. He pulled some bills out of his wallet and laid them on the counter.

By now she'd gotten out of the chair and was ready to go. He couldn't take his eyes off her.

"It looks good."

She looked good all over, as a matter of fact. Those long, slender legs of hers had been a weakness of his since day one.

"I'll take that as a compliment," the stylist said.

"You do nice work. Shall we go?" He stared pointedly at Diana.

He heard her thank the other woman before they

left the shop. Once the door closed behind them, Pierce gripped her arm.

Diana turned dazed eyes to him. "Is something wrong with Cory? Is that why you came to find me?"

There was no way she could fake a look like that. She truly cared about his son.

"If you'll glance at the truck, you'll see he and Logan are just fine."

He heard her draw in a labored breath. "Then what are you doing here?"

"I thought you might like to join us for dinner."

She bit her lip. "Didn't you want meat loaf? Janice said you liked it."

It thrilled Pierce that Diana was always trying to please him.

"I love it, but tonight the boys and I are in the mood to celebrate. I'm afraid their idea of party food runs along the line of hamburgers and shakes. If you'll follow me, we'll drive to Shivers."

There was a stunned expression on her face. "Are you sure Cory won't mind me coming along?"

"Not this time."

A hand went to her throat. "What's so different about tonight?"

It was cruel to keep her in suspense any longer, especially knowing how vulnerable she was.

"When I took the boxes in the house to start packing up his room, he decided he preferred to live in Moose after all."

Diana didn't move, didn't breathe. Only her eyes spoke. The hazel irises ignited into glittering sparks.

"Even if it means I'll be taking care of him?" she whispered at last.

"Yes."

"Pierce—"

Her eyes filled before she hurriedly dashed the moisture away with her hand.

"Daddy? How long are you going to take? We're hungry!"

"YOUR STALKER HAS BEEN a busy boy this week, Mr. Farrow. My team has videotape on him flashing a picture of your sister-in-law to every airline ticketing agent at La Guardia, Kennedy and Newark. Yesterday they followed him on his rounds of the agents manning the bus and train station counters."

Roger gripped the phone tighter. Talking to Private Investigator Rita Cardenas was a bit stressful, no matter how much of a help she was being. "If he's been checking the trains and buses, it means he hasn't discovered that Leslie flew out of Kennedy using my wife's ID."

"Not yet, anyway."

It was the "not yet" that hit him in the gut. "Where is he now?"

"Still in his apartment. I'll be tailing him today. We'll see where he goes this weekend."

"You're doing great work. Stay on him. If he ever figures it out and traces Leslie to Salt Lake, then I'll alert her. Until then there's no point in saying something that's going to frighten her even more than she is."

"We'll do our best."

After they'd clicked off, he went downstairs. He could hear the TV on in the family room. Josh and Amy were watching their favorite Saturday cartoons.

"Honey?"

"In the kitchen. Your breakfast's ready!"

He found her putting eggs and toast on the table. "I just got off the phone with the P.I."

Her head lifted abruptly. "What did she say?"

"Ed's on the prowl. That's why we haven't had any more e-mails or phone calls."

She shuddered. "I *knew* it. We'd better warn Leslie."

"No, honey. We're not going to upset her unless we know he has followed her to Salt Lake."

"Then you believe it's only a matter of time."

"I don't honestly know."

"Why can't we have him arrested?"

"On what charge?"

"Breaking and entering her apartment! Stalking your parents' house! Jamming our machines with his sick messages! Lurking outside buildings and driveways! Terrifying the children!"

"Easy, honey. So far the police have never been able to catch him in the act. That's why this business is so damned difficult. But the P.I.'s in contact with the detective on Leslie's case. If she sees anything the police can get Ed on, she'll summon them. That's part of what we're paying her for."

He watched his wife toy with her eggs. "I don't think I can stand much more of this."

Roger got up from the table and went around to hug her. "One day he's going to make a mistake, Diana. Then we'll nab him."

Her tear-filled eyes stared up at him. "You have that much faith in the P.I.?"

"Yes." It wasn't a lie. The real question lay in how brilliant and resourceful a psychopath Ed truly was....

Sniffing, Diana moved out of his arms. "I didn't hear anything from Leslie yesterday. Maybe she has written something while I've been cooking."

With a deep sigh he followed his wife into the study. She sat down at the computer and clicked on to the e-mail. Roger stood behind her.

"There's a message!"

He leaned over her shoulder to read it with her.

Dearest family, the most wonderful thing happened on Thursday night. Cory decided he didn't want to move to Ashton! You've never seen a happier man than Pierce. Of course, I'm so happy I think I'm going to burst! I now have a permanent job in the most glorious place on earth!

"Oh, Roger— She's *too* happy."

"I agree," he mumbled.

Before you take me to task, let me assure you I'm going to tell Pierce about Ed. In fact I plan to tell him this weekend when he's not on duty.

"She's really going to do it, Roger!"

Tonight I have a date of sorts with a ranger named Dave whom I met on my tour last weekend. He's going to meet me at a potluck dinner for the park employees and their families. It's held here in Moose once a month.

He's a walking encyclopedia of information about the Tetons. (So is Pierce, of course. But the situation with Cory precludes me spending any time alone with him). I've decided to pick Dave's brain. I'm hoping he'll be able to tell me about the best places to photograph. I can't wait to go hiking in the mountains and start taking pictures. I've got a whole lay-out planned in my mind.

What I'd give to have my camera with me, but since that isn't possible, I'm driving into Jackson to buy one today. Something semidecent that isn't too expensive. Don't worry. I'll be careful not to give myself away. I'm hoping to interest Cory in photography.

Did I tell you Pierce is going to buy him a dog? Remember when I won that Reflections contest taking pictures of Marvel? I'd love to teach Cory how to set up good shots. In fact, I'm so full of ideas I can hardly contain myself.

Got to run now. Talk to you tomorrow morning. All my love, Leslie.

"No, no, no—" Roger blurted. "Instant-message her, honey. Tell her that if she's going to buy a camera, she needs to find a souvenir shop where tourists can pick one up for under fifty dollars. If by any chance Ed should make it to Jackson one day, he'll visit every camera outlet and trace her right to the park."

"I'm doing it now." His wife's fingers flew over the keyboard. After she sent it, they waited.

Five minutes went by. "I don't think Leslie's there."

Roger groaned.

PIERCE HEARD HIS NAME called above the sound of the local band's rendition of a popular Latin American number. "Over here!"

He turned to the side and saw Nick waving his hands. Jessica sat next to him at one of the tables set up inside the tepee for the employees' monthly get-together.

"Come on, Cory. They've saved us a place."

"Cameron asked me to sit with him. He wants to see my ranger game."

"Let's get our dinner first, then you can eat with him and his family if you want."

Pierce put the shrimp pasta salad on the buffet table. Diana had made it for the party the day before. "The Gallaghers' contribution," she'd murmured near his ear on her way out to the car last evening.

Her breath on his cheek had invaded every atom of his sensitized body. Needless to say, he'd spent a restless night imagining the taste of her mouth and flawless skin....

In danger of forgetting where he was, he found plates for himself and Cory, then served himself a heaping portion of the pasta before it disappeared. Diana's cooking was unsurpassed. If he kept overindulging on her food, he'd be ten pounds heavier in another week!

The only thing that would have made this night perfect was if she could have come with them. But he didn't dare push anything with Cory. By some miracle his son had accepted Diana as Janice's replacement. But that didn't mean his son wanted her along once Pierce was home at the end of the day, or on weekends.

In the months to come he intended to change that situation. For the moment he had to bide his time. As he was finding out, patience was not his strong suit. He didn't want to think where Diana might be tonight, or that she might be with a man. If he started down that track, it would tear him apart.

"Daddy? Are you going to eat the whole bowl?"

Pierce had been so immersed in thought he hadn't realized how much pasta he'd piled on his plate. He grinned. "Guess I'm hungry. Don't you want anything else except pizza?"

"No. Can I go sit with Cameron now?"

"Okay, but you guys come and see me later."

"We will."

A feeling of gratitude swept through him that he and Cory were here in Moose tonight instead of Ashton. To see his son responding to the crowd of friends and associates who made him feel so welcome brought a lump to Pierce's throat. This was where they belonged.

Somewhere in Cory's psyche he must have known that their house, these people, this *place,* was their home. Otherwise he wouldn't have changed his mind.

Pierce was proud of his son. He'd made huge strides in the last few weeks. Most of the success went to Diana, though she refused to take any credit.

She'd developed the art of knowing when and when not to exert her influence around Cory. In a gradual process she was gaining his trust. The cell phone had been pure genius. He'd ridden the bus to and from school all week. There'd been no more tummy aches. That was progress.

Experiencing a peace he hadn't felt for a long time, he threaded his way through the tables nodding to everyone until he reached Nick's table. "There's a full house tonight."

His friend nodded. "Summer's over. Everyone's back."

"Where's Diana?"

He sat next to Jessica and smiled at her. "I have no idea. Her weekends are her own."

"But—"

"You heard Pierce," Nick cautioned his daughter.

Pierce winked at her. "How's the prettiest redhead this side of the Continental Divide?"

"You always say that."

"Because it's true," he said before tucking into the salad and barbecued ribs.

"That's a fact," Nick remarked.

"You always say that, too," she accused her father. Both men laughed.

"I thought Amanda would be with you tonight."

"She'll be here in a little while. We're going to have a sleepover at my house with Jenny and Sandra."

He darted an amused glance toward Nick. "That sounds fun."

His friend groaned. "You just wait!"

"No rest for the wicked, eh?"

Nick leaned back in his chair. "You got that right."

"Jessica? Before Amanda gets here, I want to thank you for your help in getting Cory to change his mind about moving."

"All I did was tell him how cool Diana is. She's awesome."

Tell me something I don't already know.

"That was powerful coming from you. I appreciate it more than you know. Thank you."

A becoming blush filled her cheeks. "You're welcome. I'm glad you're staying. It's a relief to see Dad in a good mood for a change."

"It hasn't exactly been the best two months for me, either," Pierce confessed. Just then Cory ran up to him. Cameron and Logan trailed. "Hi, champ. Come and sit with us."

"We just want to walk around and stuff." He leaned closer and whispered in Pierce's ear. "Diana's here."

Pierce's heart gave a fierce kick. Diana had come to the party? He didn't dare turn around to look.

"Did she see you?"

"No."

"Why don't you ask her to come and sit with us so she won't be alone."

His son drew near once more. "She's with a ranger."

The same one she'd canceled on before? "Which one?"

"Dave," he whispered.

"Come on, Cory, let's go outside," Logan urged.

The boys ran off, but Pierce was oblivious. In a matter of seconds a blackness had engulfed him with such intensity he felt dizzy. He gripped the edge of the table for support.

Nick sat forward eyeing him with concern. "What in the hell did Cory say to you? You look like you've seen a ghost."

"I'll call you later and tell you all about it. Right now I've got to go."

He shoved himself away from the table and stood up. His gaze swept the crowd until it lit on Diana.

Cracroft.

He was all over her. In a minute he'd get her on the dance floor and then he'd be touching her.

This was one of those moments Pierce didn't ask if what he was about to do was right or wrong.

Cracroft saw him coming and smiled.

No one else might detect the challenging glint in his eyes, but Pierce was blinded by it.

"Diana?"

Her head swerved around in surprise. "Pierce—" Was it relief he heard in her voice? Or pure wishful thinking on his part?

"I've got an emergency and need you at home now. Did you bring the car?"

"Yes."

"Good." That meant Cracroft hadn't picked her up. "I'll see you at the house as soon as you can get there. Dave—" He nodded to the man before heading for the entrance to the tepee. The boys were running around in front.

"Cory?"

"What is it?"

"We've got to go home."

"How come?"

"An emergency."

"Okay. See you guys."

Once they were in the truck, Pierce said, "Do you want to know a secret?"

Cory's head jerked around. "What?"

"Promise you won't tell a single soul?"

He crossed his heart.

"There's no emergency."

"There isn't?"

"No. But I told Diana there was so she would come to our house to tend you."

His son stared at him. "Why did you do that?"

"Can you keep another secret?"

"Yes."

"I think Dave Cracroft is too unhappy a person for Diana to be around. You know that boy in your class at school? Kenny? The one who lives in Jackson?"

"Yes. He's mean. Sometimes he tries to punch me in my private parts and he calls me a pussy."

"That's because he's jealous of you. Sometimes that happens when you're kids, and sometimes it happens when you're a grown-up."

"Is Dave mean to you?"

"Yes. That's why I didn't want Diana with him. She doesn't know him the way I do. I want to protect her."

"Would he be mean to her?"

"I don't know. Dave used to be married, but his wife left him and no one knows why."

"Maybe he was mean to her."

"Maybe."

Cory was quiet for the rest of the drive home. When they pulled in the garage he turned to Pierce. "I'm glad you told Diana to come home."

His emotions brimming over, Pierce tousled his son's hair. "I'm glad you told me Diana was at the party. Part of a man's job is to protect a woman. You do good work."

CHAPTER TEN

LESLIE COULD TELL DAVE Cracroft was not a happy ranger.

This was the second time his attempt to spend an evening with her had been thwarted.

"I'm sorry," she said on her swift walk to the car. "This is the first emergency to crop up since I started taking care of Cory."

"Does the chief expect you to be on call twenty-four hours a day?"

"In a way, yes. He advertised for a live-in nanny. I knew what he expected of me when I accepted the job. Luckily you're a ranger, so you would understand better than anyone."

She unlocked the door and climbed behind the wheel, anxious to get going.

"I do, but I won't pretend I like the situation. Good night, Diana. I'll give you a ring next week."

Leslie nodded before he shut the door. She started up the motor and drove off without delay. Halfway to the house she remembered the pasta bowl, but it was too late to go back for it now. She'd put some masking tape on the bottom with the name Gallagher on it. Someone cleaning up after the party would call the house about it.

The garage door was already open when she pulled

into the driveway. She drove all the way in and parked the car next to the truck. The next thing she knew the garage door closed behind her.

Surprised, she looked in the direction of the doorway and saw Pierce standing there with Cory. If he wasn't taking his truck, then one of the rangers was probably coming by to get him.

She got out of the car and followed them into the kitchen. "I came as fast as I could. Why don't you get that Operation game out, Cory? I saw it in your closet. Bring it to the table and I'll play with you. We'll have a contest to see who has the steadiest hand."

"Okay."

He dashed off.

Pierce still hadn't left. She put her tote bag on the counter before looking at him. "Are you being picked up?"

"No. I'm staying home."

Her eyes widened. "Did the emergency turn out to be nothing after all?"

He was looking at her so strangely. "Let's just say one was averted."

"I'm sure you're relieved."

"That's putting it mildly."

Of course she was glad of the news for his sake, but it meant she would have to go home now, which was the last thing she wanted to do.

Ever since he'd come over to the table where she'd been sitting with Dave, wishing she'd never talked to him in the first place, Leslie had been counting on spending the evening with Cory. *And* seeing Pierce again whenever he came home.

It was up to her to leave.

She rubbed her palms against the sides of her hips in a gesture he followed with his eyes. "Well, then, I'll say good-night and see you on Monday morning."

"You can't disappoint Cory now." At those words her heart skipped a beat. "Unless of course you're anxious to be with Dave. It's not too late to call him."

"No!" she cried. "I mean, I don't want to do that. I only agreed to meet him at the party because he knows so much about the Tetons. We met after I heard him give a nature talk last week.

"Naturally I would prefer asking you questions, but an opportunity hasn't presented itself yet. Since I'd like to do some exploring before the heavy snow comes, I thought his information would be useful." Heavens—she was babbling like an idiot. "You really think Cory wants me to stay even though you're here?"

Pierce cocked his head. "He knew I wasn't going anywhere, yet he ran to get his game to play with you. I'd say you have your answer."

The joy of hearing those words translated to a smile she couldn't hide. Pierce reciprocated, filling every dark place in her soul with light.

"I found it!" Cory ran back in the kitchen and set everything up.

Pierce walked over to the table to help him. "Can I play, too?"

For the next couple of hours the three of them laughed their way through half a dozen of Cory's games. Pierce turned out to be a fierce competitor, which came as no surprise. Leslie and Cory found themselves doing everything they could to beat him, without success.

When he declared it was Cory's bedtime, she said, "Does your daddy always win?"

"No," Pierce said flat out. "Tonight I got lucky." He stood up and stretched. Leslie couldn't help but notice the play of muscles across his back and arms. "Come on, champ." He lifted him onto his broad shoulders. "Let's get your teeth brushed."

"Do I have to? This was fun."

"Tell you what. If you go to bed now, we'll do it again tomorrow after church. It's over at one."

Cory looked down at Leslie. "Can you come?"

Oh, Cory— "There's nothing I'd love more than to be given a chance to beat your daddy at one game at least!"

Pierce's gaze trapped hers. "You can try…" Her heart turned over. "Cory and I will do the cooking for a change."

"I can't wait!" She walked over to the counter to get her tote bag.

"See you tomorrow." It was the first time Cory had ever said that to her.

"Call us on Cory's cell phone when you're safely locked inside the cabin so we'll know you're all right."

"Do you know my number?"

She tore her eyes from Pierce to glance at his son. "I have it stored in my phone, Cory. Good night."

"Good night," they both said at the same time.

All the way to the cabin she had the sensation of floating. But when she approached the door and saw a rolled-up sheet of paper wedged between it and the screen door, she let out a frightened cry.

It was happening again.

She stood there trembling as she relived a flashback of those first few days after she'd broken up with Ed. After coming home from her sister's, she'd found a dozen different notes taped to her apartment door.

While she was still standing there immobilized, her cell phone rang.

Pierce. He would be calling to find out why she hadn't phoned them yet. Her hands were shaking so badly it was hard to get the cell phone out of her purse to answer it.

"Hello?"

"Hi. I'm glad you answered so fast."

Oh, no. It was Dave.

She should never *never* have given him her number! But at the time he was simply a ranger who worked under Pierce. Something was definitely wrong with her that she couldn't read men better.

All she'd wanted was information. She hadn't been attracted to him. Her biggest mistake was agreeing to meet him at the party tonight.

"It's awfully late, Dave."

"I realize that, but I have work up by the Grassy Creek Road tomorrow and thought you might like to go with me. If you want to see unparalleled scenery, that's the place. I left a note in the screen door of your cabin inviting you. Then I realized that if you were stuck at the chief's all night, you might not see it until too late."

Dave had left that note? She'd never told him where she lived! But with gossip running rampant, she supposed everyone knew she'd moved out of Pierce's house to Grayson's.

"I'm afraid tomorrow is out for m—"

"Diana?" At the sound of Pierce's voice she swung around in time to watch him striding toward her from the truck. Beyond his shoulder she could see the top of Cory's head in the cab. "What are you doing out here in the dark on the phone?"

"Dave? I'm afraid I have to go. Pierce has just come home. As I was saying, I have other plans tomorrow."

"I get it. You can't talk in front of him. I'll call you in a couple of days." The line went dead.

"Good Lord," Pierce whispered when he saw her face. "You look like you did the other day when I came home for lunch. What's wrong? And don't tell me it's hormones. When you left the house a little while ago you were perfectly fine!" His voice sounded ragged, as if he'd been running a long distance.

She put the phone back in her purse. "I made a mistake in judgment. Now I'm paying for it."

He seemed to be looking beyond her to the cabin. "Who's been playing mailman at your door tonight?"

"No—" she cried out as he made a move to grab the paper. "I-it's all right," she stammered. "I know who left the note."

Pierce grimaced. "Stop trying to protect Cracroft. The man's a menace."

Hearing Pierce's opinion only made her angrier at herself for ever having said one word to the other ranger.

"Come on. Let's get you inside."

He cupped her elbow and walked her to the porch of the cabin. While she rummaged for her key, he plucked the note from its resting place.

"What about Cory?"

"We'll leave the door open so I can keep an eye on him."

Once they'd gained entrance, Pierce turned on the overhead light to read Dave's message. Despite the bright light, his features appeared even more chiseled than before.

"Is Dave in trouble with you for this?"

When Pierce had finished, he folded it up and put it in the front pocket of his jeans. "Don't you worry about it."

She buried her face in her hands.

In the next instant a pair of strong arms slid around her and pulled her slender body against him. One of his hands cupped the back of her head where she could feel his fingers twine in her hair.

"Cory saw you with Dave before I did. His protective feelings came out and he alerted me."

"Dear Cory—"

"I had to avert disaster with my only weapon at hand, so I invented that emergency to get you out of there."

His explanation caused her to nestle instinctively closer. "Thank you," she whispered against his throat, where she could detect the clean scent of the soap he used.

"I want your promise you'll nev—"

"You've got it!" she cried before he'd even finished. "The moment I canceled that first date with him, I realized he was a man with too many problems. But when he asked me to attend the employees' party, I hated to be mean and turn him down again, a-and I thought it would stop the gossip about you and me.''

''No power on earth could do that.''

''You're right. What a fool I was to give him an inch.''

''Forget him, Diana. He won't be troubling you anymore.''

That's what she'd thought after she'd given Ed back his ring. A shudder of terror rocked her body to consider, even for a millisecond, that Dave might be anywhere near as mentally ill as her ex-fiancé.

''I'm sure every eligible female park employee has known to stay clear.''

''Not every woman. Certainly not his ex-wife.''

Leslie gasped and tried to pull away from him. Pierce was too strong and kept a firm grip on her upper arms.

''What in God's name has upset you so much?'' he demanded.

She felt ill. ''Dave didn't say anything about having been married before.''

''Some men are embarrassed to admit their first marriage failed.''

A half sob escaped her throat. ''Not healthy men!''

''Agreed. Is that why you broke up with your fiancé? Because he lied to you about a past marriage?''

Dear God.

''Answer me, Diana.'' He shook her gently.

''Yes, he lied,'' she blurted. ''If his ex-wife hadn't introduced herself to me the day before the wedding invitations went out, I'd be married to a very sick man right now.''

He inhaled sharply. "How long ago did this happen?"

You don't want to know.

"Pierce—you'd better hurry out to the truck or Cory will start to worry."

"How long?" he prodded, still holding her.

"I don't know exactly. About seven weeks now."

"Lord—" His hands moved up her shoulders to her flushed cheeks. "All this time you've been helping me with Cory, you've been in intense pain. Yet you never said a word." The compassion in his beautiful blue eyes moved her to her very soul.

"Taking care of your son has been a joy that has saved my sanity."

"And mine." His voice throbbed with emotion. "I'm indebted to you, Diana." He lowered his dark head and kissed her forehead with infinite tenderness.

Then he looked her in the eye and said, "Pack your bag. You'll be living at my house until I've resolved the situation with Dave. It could take a week or more. At this point I don't give a damn what anyone else thinks or says."

"Are you sure?" she asked, almost giddy with relief that she didn't have to stay another night alone. Somehow he knew she was frightened of Dave. "Won't Cory be upset?"

"We had a talk about Cracroft earlier tonight. My son's as anxious to protect you as I am. Come on. I want to get you and Cory settled, then I've got to run over to headquarters to take care of a little business."

She was sure that business had everything to do with Dave Cracroft.

Grateful and happy as she was to hear those words, the incident with Dave had brought the reality of the situation with Ed to the fore once more.

In the next few days she would have to tell Pierce about him, but it would have to be when they were alone and there was no chance of Cory overhearing them. Maybe while he was playing at Logan's or Cameron's...

"NICK?"

"I was hoping I'd hear from you."

"Sorry it's so late."

"With the all-night party going on here, you don't need to worry about that."

"Thanks." He sat back in his office swivel chair. "I need to talk."

"That doesn't surprise me. I swear I've never seen you look like you did tonight except on one other occasion."

Pierce knew his friend was referring to the day he'd received word his wife had died. The memory no longer hurt as badly as it once did. It proved he'd come a long way out of yesterday.

"Do you want to drive over and bring Cory? He can sleep in the guest bedroom. The girls have occupied the living room."

"I'd take you up on it if Diana weren't asleep in *my* guest bedroom."

"Say that again?"

"You might well ask. Oh, hell, where to begin..."

"Just start talking and don't stop till you're through."

Pierce could always count on his friend. For the next ten minutes he unloaded. It felt good.

"I don't envy you having to deal with Cracroft," Nick said when Pierce had finished. "Being a scientist, I've tended to look at Dave as one of the 'unstable elements.'"

"A perfect description. The other day I gave him a last chance to prove himself, but after reading his note to her, it's obvious he doesn't think the rules apply to him. I'm going to have to let him go."

"Agreed. However you do it, be careful. He's jealous of you. Always has been."

"I know."

"I got my first look at Diana when you walked over to her table tonight. She's a knockout. Talk about adding fuel to the fire—"

Pierce's eyes closed tightly for a minute. "She was vulnerable enough without Dave being added to the mix."

"I hear you. Having just come out of a broken engagement, her emotions can't help but be fragile."

"The day she came to Moose to apply for the job I sensed she was holding something back."

"You were wise to move her from Grayson's. You'll be her best protection until he's gone for good."

"Thanks, Nick. Hearing your take on everything has helped."

"All I've done is listen."

"That's the best help there is. I owe you."

"After the years you've had to put up with me

going on and on about Jessica's mother, I'll be in your debt forever.''

He made a grunting sound in response. ''Talk to you later.''

They both clicked off. Now that he'd posted a couple of his best rangers to keep an around-the-clock watch on Dave, Pierce could go home.

All was quiet when he entered the house. He almost gave in to the temptation to knock on her door. By some miracle he withstood it and reached his own bedroom. Once he was ready for bed he lay back against the pillows with his hands clasped behind his head. His body was so alive with feelings, there was no way he was going to fall asleep anytime soon.

Now that he'd held Diana in the name of comfort, it wasn't enough. Whether she was emotionally ready or not, the next time he touched her there was going to be a conflagration.

He groaned and buried his face in the pillow. Eventually oblivion took over. When he awoke, it was to the sound of someone backing out of the driveway.

Diana hadn't decided to take off again, had she? He raced to the window and looked out to see the Morgans' Pathfinder drive off. Relief filled his system.

At this point he was wide awake and headed for the shower. Ten minutes later he walked through the house to the kitchen where he could hear voices.

''Hi, Daddy! I'm making the pancakes for breakfast.'' Cory stood at the table stirring batter.

''So I see.''

His gaze flicked to Diana frying bacon at the stove. She looked incredibly beautiful in anything she wore.

This morning she was wearing a navy T-shirt and jeans.

"What was Liz Morgan doing here?"

Diana glanced over at him. "She was on the cleanup committee for the party and brought back the pasta bowl."

"That was nice of her."

Cory ran over to him. "She invited me to Cameron's birthday party on Friday. It's going to be after school and it's supposed to be a surprise."

"Sounds exciting, champ."

"Can we buy him a ranger game? He always wants to play with mine."

Cory's question gave Pierce an idea. "Tell you what. After breakfast why don't the three of us get in the car and drive the Wyoming Centennial Scenic Byway to Yellowstone. We'll make a day of it and take a long hike. On the way home we'll stop in West Yellowstone where Diana bought your game. Maybe Jim and Janice can meet us there for dinner."

Pure joy broke out on his son's face. He grabbed Pierce around the waist. "I love you, Daddy."

"I love you, too." As he raised his head, he discovered Diana's misty gaze studying them.

"What do you say?" he asked her quietly. "I'm yours for a whole day. You can ask me all the questions you want about the Tetons."

Her eyes ignited an intense gold. "I bought a little minirecorder and journal in Jackson. Would you let me get you on tape so I can write it all down later?"

That was an interesting and provocative question. Why would she go to that much trouble?

Cory turned around excitedly. "Will you let me

talk into your recorder?'' he asked before Pierce could respond.

She smiled. ''I'll bring a special tape just for you. It will be something to keep for posterity.''

''What's posterity?''

Pierce couldn't wait to hear her answer. Everything Diana said or did delighted him.

''Well—one day when you're a daddy, and your little girl or boy asks you what you were like when you were young, you can give them the tape to listen to.

''Sometimes I think it's better than a video, because there's a quality in the voice when you're speaking naturally that brings out the personality. Your children will love hearing you talk and finding out what you sounded like when you were six.

''Before my father died, my mom interviewed him on tape. He had a wonderful, distinctive voice. After the funeral when I was feeling sad, I'd go to bed and listen to that tape in the dark over and over because it made me feel like he hadn't gone to heaven yet.''

By now Pierce's throat had almost closed up from emotion.

Cory jerked around and stared up at him. ''Do you have a tape of when you were little like me?''

''No.''

''I wish you did.''

''We needed Diana around to give my parents ideas.''

''You're funny, Daddy. Diana wasn't born when you were little.''

''I didn't know your daddy was so old,'' she teased.

"Yup." Cory nodded. "He's thirty…"

"Five." Pierce helped him with the answer.

"That's pretty old, all right," she said, sending Pierce a wicked grin. "Probably too old to eat all these pancakes we made."

"Want to make a bet?" he fired back.

She bit her lip. "After losing every game last night, maybe I'd better not."

Diana—

"MOMMY? I'M GOING TO BE sick again." Josh ran to the bathroom.

"It's okay," Diana assured him. "I'm right here."

Monday morning had started off with a bang. Roger had left for his office at the crack of dawn to get ready for a big court case at nine. Now Josh had a bug and couldn't go to school.

Amy wasn't up yet. Who knew if she would awaken with a sick stomach, too. It looked like it was going to be one of those weeks.

Though the harassment had stopped, Diana lived with a different kind of dread. Every time the phone rang she feared it would be Rita Cardenas telling them Ed had stumbled onto a clue.

"Do you think Aunt Leslie could come over to-day?" Josh's face looked pale against the pillow.

"I wish she could, sweetie. I miss her as much as you do." That was the understatement of the century. Especially after seeing the last of her series of photographs on the world's disappearing rain forests in the newspaper yesterday. The shots were breathtaking and spectacular.

"Why can't she come?"

''Because she's so busy working.''

''Can I talk to her on the phone?''

''I'll e-mail her and ask her to call if she gets a minute.'' Leslie had contacted Roger on her new cell phone. There was no reason she couldn't phone to chat with Josh for a few minutes. Ed wouldn't have a clue about it.

''Will you do it *now?* Tell her I'm sick.''

''I have to go downstairs to use the computer. Will it be okay if I leave you that long?''

''Yes.''

''I'll hurry.''

Still no sound from Amy's bedroom. She hurried to the study and sent Leslie a message.

It was only eighty-thirty, which meant six-thirty in Moose. Her sister probably wouldn't get up to check her e-mail for another half hour at least. But in case Diana was wrong, she waited a few more minutes for a response.

When there was none, she filled Josh's SpongeBob water bottle with some ginger ale and went back upstairs. His doctor had recommended it the last time Josh was sick. It had stayed down better than anything else.

By now Amy was wandering around looking for her. Diana swept her into her arms. ''Good morning, sweetie pie. How's my big girl?''

''Fine.''

Hallelujah! ''Shall we go see your brother? He doesn't feel good today.'' She'd almost reached his bedroom when the phone rang.

''Mommy?'' Josh called to her. ''Maybe that's Aunt Leslie.''

Maybe it was.

Diana made a detour to the master bedroom. She put the bottle on the nightstand and picked up the receiver of the cordless phone to check the caller ID. It was out of area. Please, God, don't let it be Ed starting up again.

Amy squirmed to get down. Diana let her go while she waited with a thudding heart to hear the message on the answering machine.

"Hello, Mrs. Farrow? Mr. Farrow? This is Leslie's boss from the *New York Chronicler.* If Leslie hasn't seen yesterday's Sunday edition of the paper yet, she should. In a word, her photo essay of the Madagascar rain forest is superb. I know she's in pain, but she has a special gift. The sooner she gets back on the job, the sooner she'll be able to put the past behind her. Tell her I'm anxious to talk over an exciting new project with her. I'd like her to contact me as soon as possible."

After almost seven weeks of no-show on Leslie's part, even her boss's patience was running thin. If Ed had been harassing him for information, he wasn't letting on out of sensitivity to her pain.

"Mom—is it Aunt Leslie?"

She grabbed the bottle and hurried into his room. Amy had gotten into his toy chest and was emptying it. "Not yet, sweetie, but I'm sure she'll phone as soon as she can."

"Heck."

Leslie, Leslie. We need to talk!

WHEN LESLIE OVERHEARD Pierce saying goodbye to Cory in the hall outside her door, she opened her eyes to check her watch. It was only seven o'clock in the morning. She had no idea he was going to leave for work this early.

They hadn't pulled into the garage from their trip until eleven o'clock the previous night. Pierce had carried his dead-to-the-world son to the bedroom without Cory stirring. She'd assumed Pierce would get up at his normal time so she could fix his breakfast.

She threw on her terry-cloth bathrobe over her nightgown and hurried through the house in time to see Pierce opening the door to the garage.

"Pierce?"

He wheeled around. The sight of him in uniform, freshly shaven and smelling wonderful, rendered her speechless.

Like a desert wind, his intimate gaze created instant heat as it started at her bare feet and traveled over every line and curve of her body till it reached her eyes.

She could hardly breathe. "If I'd known, I would have fixed you something to eat."

"That's why I didn't say anything. What I have to do this Monday morning is better done on an empty stomach." He'd said something about an early appointment having to do with Dave Cracroft. "I'll see you this evening." He opened the door, then glanced back at her.

"Did I tell you I like your hair that way?"

She let out a distressed cry. "I just got out of bed!"

"I know," he whispered.

Long after he'd backed out of the garage and

driven off, she stood there trembling like a newborn being given its first bath.

"Diana?"

She swung around. "Good morning."

"Hi. Can I call Logan and ask him to come over? I want to show him the water-jet gun Janice bought me in West Yellowstone."

"It's a little early. Maybe his mom and baby sister are still asleep. Why don't I fix your breakfast first? After you've finished, then you can phone him."

"Okay."

While he darted into the living room to watch cartoons, she fixed juice and toast. He loved cereal, too, so she poured him a bowl and put some sliced bananas on top. To make the table more interesting, she folded their napkins to look like turkeys.

"Come and get it!"

Cory stormed the kitchen like a member of a SWAT team, brandishing his new gun.

"Ugh...you got me!" She faked a collapse on the floor. It sent him into peals of laughter until he saw the napkins and recovered.

"Hey—" He put the gun on the counter and ran over to examine his. "Will you show me how to make one of these?"

"I'll do it while we eat."

She grabbed a fresh paper napkin from the drawer. Between bites of food she demonstrated the trick to a very attentive boy. It took six or seven napkins before he got the hang of it.

"See? Now yours is perfect. You can impress all your friends."

His smile of satisfaction was worth everything. He looked over at her. "Who taught you?"

"A waiter on a ship."

"You've been on a ship?" His eyes looked huge behind his glasses.

She started to tell him she'd been on several, but caught herself before she revealed anything else. "It was a long time ago."

"I wish I could go on one."

"Maybe you will when you're older. Do you want another piece of toast?"

He shook his head. "Can I phone Logan now and ask him to come over?"

"Go ahead."

He dashed off. It gave her time to get her laptop from the bedroom. She had so much to tell Diana about the glorious day spent with Pierce and Cory yesterday while they'd hiked and she'd taken pictures.

She'd insisted the scenery was always more interesting with people in it. But she could tell by the way Pierce smiled at her from time to time that he knew she wanted souvenirs of their day together. Almost as if they were a family.

As always when she discovered a message waiting for her, the happiness she experienced was overshadowed by the specter of Ed's presence in their lives. But this time the news was about Josh. He was home with the stomach flu and wanted his aunt Leslie.

Diana didn't have to ask Leslie to phone. She dashed to the bedroom a second time for her cell phone and made the call. It was hard not to cry while she told her nephew how much she loved him. But she controlled herself until her sister came back on the line. Then she broke down completely.

"This is agony, you know?" The phone got all wet. She kept wiping her eyes. "Part of me has never been so happy in my life! Then reality hits, and I can't believe I live in the same world with a lunatic like Ed.

"I'd give anything for you and Roger to bring the kids and come out to the Tetons. You'd both love Pierce and Cory. We could all have such an amazing time together. I love this place, Diana. I can't even begin to describe how I feel."

"You don't have to," her sister murmured. "It's all there in your voice. Dare I bring you down off that cloud long enough to tell you about the message your boss left on our answering machine this morning?"

Leslie got up from the bed and started pacing. "I knew he wouldn't be patient forever. It isn't fair to him or the paper."

"What are you going to do?"

"The only thing I can do. Phone him and tell him my broken engagement has affected every aspect of my life. I'm giving up my career as a photojournalist to do other work."

"Oh, honey—"

"It's all right. Honestly! I love taking care of Cory and plan to stay with Pierce as long as he needs me. Tonight I'm going to tell him about Ed. It terrifies me just thinking about his reaction, but it terrifies me more to imagine what Ed could do to him and Cory if Ed finds me first," she added in a shaky voice.

"I'm glad you're going to be honest with Pierce.

And it's my opinion Ed's *not* going to find you!'' Diana declared.

"One more thing, Leslie. If you can track down a copy of yesterday's edition of the newspaper, your Madagascar photo essay was in it. The photographs are absolutely incredible. We've had a dozen phone calls from our close friends about it already. I'm so proud of you. If the folks were alive, especially Dad…''

Once more Leslie dissolved. So did Diana.

"I'll phone my boss this afternoon after Cory leaves for school,'' she said at last. "Finally I can make a decision about this. Now I won't have to feel any more guilt about putting him off.''

"I'm glad if you're glad. Leslie? I've got to go. Josh is sick again.''

"Go. I'll e-mail you in the morning and tell you if Pierce wants me to pack up and leave.''

"If he's the man you say he is, he would never do that.''

"He's wonderful, but what I've done is unforgivable.''

"Surely not unforgivable, honey.''

"I pray he forgives me, Diana.''

"I'll pray, too.''

"Give Amy a squeeze for me.''

"I will. Love you.''

"Love you.''

The rest of the morning Leslie kept busy cleaning. She interacted with the boys once Logan came over to play. After lunch they left for the school bus. Alone at last, she phoned her boss. It did her good to hear his voice and talk shop.

Though he regaled her with the news that her work had been nominated for this year's Pulitzer Prize in the photo-feature category, he couldn't talk her out of leaving the newspaper.

Of course it thrilled her that her name had been put forward for the coveted award with other photo-essay journalists from the *Los Angeles Times,* the *Boston Globe* and the *Washington Post.* But she wasn't the same woman anymore.

A terrifying man named Ed Strickland had changed her world for all time, setting her feet on a different path. God willing, he would never find her.

After saying goodbye, Leslie drove into Jackson and approached the clerk in the Valley Bookstore. She was anxious to see the newspaper. "Do you have a copy of yesterday's *New York Chronicler?*"

"I believe we do. Look on the middle rack against the far wall."

After a brief search, she found one left. Without wasting a second she took it to the counter to pay for it, then left the store eager to read it when she had time later.

Right now she was more excited to greet Cory, who would be getting off the bus soon. She loved it when he came running into the kitchen to greet her. One day maybe he would reach out his arms to her. Leslie was living for it.

CHAPTER ELEVEN

PIERCE HAD BEEN FORCED to wait until early afternoon to locate Dave, who'd gone off early that morning to train with the new group of recruits above the Grassy Creek Road.

The transitional portion of the old Indian route between Yellowstone and the northern portion of Grand Teton National Park was a favorite location of the grizzlies, who needed a large area to forage.

He found Dave eating lunch in his truck parked along the side of the road away from everyone else. Pierce pulled to a stop behind him and got out of the cab. This critical meeting had been coming for a long time.

Cracroft sat at the steering wheel, staring at Pierce in the side mirror as he approached. Any other ranger would have climbed out to greet him by now. But Dave wasn't like the others and never would be.

"Do you want to put your window down?" When the other man made no move to oblige, Pierce said, "That's okay with me." He pulled out the note Dave had written to Diana and held it up for his perusal.

"By inviting a tourist to this particular location when you knew you would be on duty, you not only broke a cardinal rule, you broke the most important one of all—knowingly putting a visitor to the park in mortal danger.''

Dave's eyes narrowed to slits. Pierce put the note back in his pocket.

''I'm relieving you of your duty immediately, and placing you on medical leave for a period of two months while you're evaluated at University Hospital in Salt Lake City. You'll continue to be paid your full salary plus a food and lodging allowance. Nothing will be decided until the testing is complete. At that time the superintendent and I will meet with you to discuss your case.

''I'll inform your new boss of the change in your status without revealing the reason for your medical leave.

''Come by the office in the morning with your uniforms, badge and all paraphernalia belonging to the job. Sally will have the paperwork ready for you. It will give you the name, address and phone number of the doctor, and suggestions where you can find affordable accommodations while you're undergoing evaluation.

''There are storage facilities in Jackson Hole. You have twenty-four hours to vacate your cabin and the park. If you're found anywhere on the premises after that, you'll be arrested.''

Pierce walked back to his truck and climbed in the cab. As soon as he'd made contact with Bill Shiffers, he phoned one of the rangers to find out how the rescue mission was proceeding for a climber who'd slipped from a ledge at Teepee Pillar below the east face of the Grand Teton.

As he listened to the man's report, Cracroft finally

started up his truck and took off down the road. A minute later he came barreling past Pierce.

A bully was a bully. Pierce thought of his son and what he had to deal with in kindergarten. Without a lot of help and intervention, little Kenny would grow up to be like Dave. It was a sobering thought.

Thank heaven Cracroft would no longer be a threat to Diana. Just thinking about her made him excited for evening to come. There was nothing like going off duty knowing he would walk through the front door of his house to find her and Cory there waiting for him.

LESLIE TURNED INTO THE driveway and pressed the remote. Out of the corner of her eye she saw a note taped to the front door. The sight of it caused her body to break out in a cold sweat.

Though she'd wanted to drive straight to Pierce's office, she couldn't. Not when Cory was due home any second.

Once she'd parked inside the garage, she raced through the house to open the front door and remove the note.

"You can both go to hell!"

Leslie read the words and thought she was going to be sick right there. But she fought it because she could see Cory running toward the house carrying his backpack.

She stuffed it in her pocket. "Hi! How was school?"

"Recess was fun."

Of course. She took the backpack from him. He ran to the bathroom, then found her in the kitchen.

"Are you hungry?"

"No. Can I have a juice box?"

"One juice box coming up." She opened the fridge and handed it to him.

"Thanks, Diana."

Of his own volition, he'd just thanked her. They were making progress.

"You're welcome. What did you draw at school today?"

"A picture of the White House."

"Ooh. Can I see it?"

"Yes." He opened his backpack she'd set on the table. "That's the president and me and Daddy!"

"Do I see a dog in there, too?"

"Yes."

"Is it yours?"

"Yes."

"Your daddy's going to have to see this. It's a wonderful picture! You're a fine little artist, do you know that?"

"Kenny said it was stupid."

"Kids always say that when they're jealous. You just have to ignore them. Since it's so beautiful out, how would you like to walk to headquarters with me?"

His eyebrows lifted in surprise. "To see Daddy?"

"Yes. I think it would be kind of fun to surprise him, don't you?"

"Shall I take my picture?"

"Of course. He'll want to show it to Sally and Mindy. You know how daddies like to brag about their kids."

"Daddy says it's not nice to brag."

"He meant a person shouldn't brag about them-selves, but I know he brags about you all the time."

Cory blinked. "He does?"

"Yes. It's because he loves you."

"I know. I love him, too."

She smiled. "Shall we go? I'll lock the door behind us."

Being with Cory was pure delight. On their way she asked him if he'd learned any songs. He said no, but he could recite the Pledge of Allegiance.

When he'd finished saying it perfectly, the urge to hug him was so strong it was almost painful to have to refrain. "That was so impressive I'm going to rec-ord it before you go to bed tonight."

He giggled.

When they reached headquarters, she opened the door. Cory ran inside ahead of her. Like a homing pigeon he knew exactly where to go.

"Hi, Sally? Is my daddy here?"

The older woman smiled. "He sure is. Go on in."

Leslie stayed put to give father and son a chance to be alone. However, it wasn't long before Cory poked his head out the door. "Come on, Diana!"

It never failed that, when she was about to see Pierce, her heart raced like the proverbial freight train.

How different were the circumstances than the first time she'd laid eyes on the handsome, rather forbid-ding chief ranger of Grand Teton National Park.

As she stepped over the threshold of his inner sanc-tum, his eyes trapped hers. He knew she would never have disturbed him at work unless there was a vital reason.

"Your son's artwork is so outstanding, I told him you'd want everybody to see it."

His glance shifted to Cory. "That's the kind of news I like to hear. Before I look at it and start bragging, why don't you go get a jawbreaker out of the machine in front, champ?" Pierce pulled a quarter from his pocket and handed it to his son.

"Thanks!" Cory sent a secret smile to Diana before he dashed out the door. The shared moment thrilled her.

Once he'd disappeared, she pulled the wrinkled note from her pocket and handed it to Pierce. "I found this taped to the front door when I got home from Jackson a little while ago."

"You can both go to hell!"

Pierce ground his teeth before raising his eyes to Diana, whose frightened expression brought out his most protective instincts.

"If Dave did anything to you…"

"No." She shook her head. "I never saw him," she said in a tremulous voice.

Cracroft had crossed his last line. Pierce put the note in a file, then reached for the phone to call Security and have them round up Ed and escort him from the park immediately. As he hung up, his son ran back into his office.

"Let's see that masterpiece of yours."

Cory pulled it from his pocket. Pierce spread it out on the desk to give it a thorough examination. The stick figures were hilarious. "I agree with Diana. This drawing is extra special. Is that the president's dog or yours?"

He took the discolored jawbreaker out of his mouth. "Mine."

Pierce chuckled. "What's his name?"

"Max! He's from Planet X."

"Planet X…" Pierce noticed Diana smiling broadly. Her beauty robbed him of breath. "Well… I'm sure Sally and Mindy have never seen a dog from Planet X. Let's go show them." He got up from his chair.

"I'll be back," he said to her in his Arnold Schwarzenegger voice. She burst into laughter.

Cory giggled. "You're funny, Daddy."

His staff made a big fuss over Cory and his drawing. By the time they returned to his office where Diana was waiting, Pierce had made a decision that would get them away from the park for a few hours.

"This calls for a celebration. I heard they were showing the Disney version of Robin Hood at the drive-in movie in Jackson. What do you say we go?"

Cory let out an excited whoop and jerked around to look at Diana. "Do you want to see it with us?"

With that question Pierce's heart resumed beating.

"I'd love to. It's one of my nephew's favorites."

"Does anyone need to use the bathroom before we leave?"

"Nope."

Diana shook her head.

"Then let's get out of here."

When they reached the parking lot, Cory scrambled in the truck first. It was all Pierce could do not to pull Diana into his arms instead of helping her into the cab.

Her hair brushed against his cheek, sending a waft

of delicious peach scent past his nostrils. Such utter femininity aroused longings he needed to satisfy soon or go a little mad.

A half hour later, while they munched on hot dogs and potato chips waiting for the movie's intro to end, Pierce said, "The last time I was here with you, you were a little baby who cried so hard we had to take you to the clinic because you'd come down with roseola."

"What's that?" Cory asked.

"A high fever that gave you a rash."

"What was the movie?"

Pierce chuckled. "I don't remember. I was too worried about you."

"Josh once got roseola, too," Diana chimed in. "I thought my sister was going to have a heart attack."

"How come?"

"Because high temperatures can be dangerous."

Cory's head swerved to Pierce once more. "Were you scared?"

"Yes."

"I thought you never got scared."

Pierce ruffled his son's hair. "When you love someone as much as I love you, then you worry."

He turned to Diana. "Are you scared 'cos Josh is sick now?"

Diana shook her head. "Not scared, just concerned until I know his tummy's better."

"He threw up this morning, Daddy, so he had to stay home from kindergarten."

"That's no fun."

Once the actual show began, Cory became immersed in the story. Three-fourths of the way through the film his head fell against Pierce's shoulder. Two late nights in a row had taken their toll.

His gaze wandered to Diana. She appeared to be enjoying the movie, as if she weren't aware of him. It was time to find out...

"Diana?" he whispered. She turned to him, instantly alert. "I want you next to me. Help me move Cory against your door. Then he can rest his head against the window."

To his satisfaction she seemed eager to accommodate his request. Soon Cory was propped in the corner while her warm, supple body was planted firmly against Pierce's side, exactly the way he'd been craving.

Once his arm had gone around her shoulders he said, "Do you want some more popcorn?"

"No, thank you."

"Neither do I," he murmured, his gaze on her distinctive profile. "Right now I feel seventeen again, wondering if I dare make a move on the girl I've been dying to get alone since school started."

He heard her quiet gasp. "If you don't make it soon, I might expire right here," she admitted.

Pierce didn't have to do anything. She gravitated to him and gave him her mouth. It tasted of popcorn and salt and butter and peanut butter candy. It tasted of Diana, who was all warmth and beauty. It tasted of a woman who gave so completely, her deepening kiss filled him with ecstasy.

They made out through the rest of the movie, creating heat that built slowly and steadily. It wasn't until headlights flashed and motors started revving that Pierce realized the show was over.

It was agony to have to wrench his lips from hers. Her moan of protest was proof of her entrancement. "I know it's early in the year and all the other guys are lined up for their turn, but I don't want you seeing anyone else but me. Go steady with me, Diana."

She rested her forehead against his. He could feel her smile. "Are you willing to stop seeing all the other girls who fantasize about you?"

He undid his badge and pinned it on her sweater. "That's it. That's my trademark. I've never given it to anyone before."

"Pierce—"

Her cry disturbed Cory, who sat up and rubbed his eyes. "Hey—the show ended." He looked at the two of them and blinked. "How did I get over here?"

"I moved you so you'd be more comfortable, champ."

"Oh." His gaze traveled to Diana. "How come you've got Daddy's badge on?"

"I—I was pretending what it would be like to be a ranger." She removed it and handed it back to Pierce.

It was a good thing Diana was still able to function. He needed a few more minutes.

"You could be a ranger if you wanted to. Gilly King was one."

"What happened to her?"

"She had to go to work at another park," Cory stated.

"How come?" Diana imitated his son before looking at Pierce.

He averted his eyes to put his badge back on. Then he started the engine. "I don't remember."

"Yes you do, Daddy. You're the one who sent her away."

He put the truck in gear and pulled behind the last of the cars exiting the drive-in. "I didn't send her away. She asked for a transfer. One of the other rangers paid her too much attention."

Pierce felt Diana's involuntary shudder, before Cory said "Oh" and sat back to eat the rest of the popcorn.

One glance at her after they'd arrived home told him she knew Dave Cracroft had been the one responsible. Pierce had wanted to keep that knowledge from her, but it was too late now. The damage had been done. All because he'd lost his head in her arms.

After they pulled into the garage, Pierce opened the door for Cory to jump down. "Go in the house and get yourself ready for bed. I'll be there in a minute to tuck you in."

"Okay."

Diana came next. Unlike Cory, however, he caught her fully in his arms, needing to feel the length of her against him for a moment. "You haven't changed your mind, have you?"

"What do you mean?"

"This." Hungry to know rapture once more, he searched for her mouth, but she evaded his lips.

"We can't! Cory might see us."

He could feel her heart racing frantically against his chest. "Cory knows why he ended up on the other side of the cab. Now tell me what I need to hear."

She lifted dazed eyes to him. "You know I don't have a desire to be with anyone else, but we mustn't do this again."

Pierce felt as if he'd been shoved off the wall of the Teton's north face to plunge helplessly into the void. "Why in the hell not?"

"Because I'm Cory's temporary nanny."

"Temporary?" he demanded.

She broke free of his grasp, unwilling to look at him. "He could decide he doesn't like me."

"No."

"Nothing's written in stone—" she cried in anguish before rushing into the house.

Whatever was frightening her was making them both crazy. After raking a hand through his hair in puzzlement and frustration, he locked the truck, then went around to make sure the car was locked.

It wasn't.

His gaze flicked to the newspaper on the seat of the cab.

He reached for it before locking the door.

The *New York Chronicler.*

Pierce wasn't surprised she'd bought one of the major East Coast newspapers. Naturally she liked to keep in touch. But she already did that through e-mails and phone calls.

As he stood there deep in thought, he couldn't help but wonder if there was something in it she was looking for. Something specific that was tied to her fear.

Tired of playing guessing games he rushed after her, intent on getting answers. Tonight at the drive-in she'd given him a taste of paradise. But that would never be enough for him now. Pierce wouldn't be satisfied until they were both living it.

When he entered the house, she was cleaning up the living room. "You left this in the car."

"Oh—thank you!" She took the newspaper from him, but a pained expression had broken out on her face. "I'm sure I forgot to lock the car, too!

"When I was driving in from Jackson earlier today and saw the note from Dave on the front door, I was so afraid Cory would see it, I forgot everything else and dashed through the house to remove it."

Her explanation had given him the answer to one question at least. "I'm just thankful Dave didn't decide to hang around and harass you."

In front of his eyes, she lost color.

He reached for her, grasping her shoulders. "What did I say, Diana? You went pale on me again."

"I was thinking about that female ranger. What did Dave do to her?"

"Nothing physically harmful. It was more a case of his not leaving her alone."

"The poor thing," she whispered.

"It started happening after his wife divorced him. He has needed help for years. I've ordered him to start treatment at a hospital in Salt Lake for the next couple of months. He's been escorted out of the park under armed guard. Dave has been told that if he takes one step onto park property now, he'll be arrested."

"That's good," she whispered, but her pronounced pallor reminded him of the day he'd come home for lunch and had found her in a similar state. Only this was much worse.

"For the love of heaven, what's wrong? I know this has something to do with your ex-fiancé."

"You're right," she blurted with surprising honesty. "It does." He could see her throat working. "I should have told you about him when I called you from Salt Lake. No—" She shook her head. "I should never have called you period—"

"Daddy? I'm ready to say my prayers."

At the sound of Cory's voice, Pierce said, "Don't move from this spot. I'll be right back."

Five minutes later he'd kissed his son good-night and had returned to the living room to find her pacing.

"Cory's asleep. Now that we won't be disturbed, I want to hear the reason why you should never have called me."

She took a shuddering breath. "B-because you're going to despise me for having dragged you and Cory into something that has the potential to be life-threatening."

The conviction in her voice carried the ring of truth. A chill started to penetrate his flesh. In a pure revelation he realized he was finally going to learn her guilty secret. And God help him, he knew he wasn't going to like it.

He grimaced. "Go on."

"My ex-fiancé's name is Edward Strickland. The Dr. Jekyll part of him is a single, thirty-eight-year-old journalist for the *New York Chronicler,* a-and the Mr. Hyde part of him is a divorced, violent psychopath with a police record of spousal abuse.

"After I broke our engagement he stalked me for a month and virtually destroyed my life, so I couldn't take a step outside my sister's house, let alone go to work or even exist.

"Detective Santini, an expert assigned to my case, couldn't give me a good prognosis for the future. After discussing everything with Roger and Diana, I made the decision to disappear with a new identity.''

A nerve twitched in Pierce's cheek. ''Who are you?''

''I'm Leslie Hopkins, Diana's younger sister.''

Despise wasn't the word he would have used.

With Gilly King's fear of Dave still fresh in his mind, he could never despise anyone running away from a desperate situation. But Pierce had to admit he was disappointed she hadn't told him the truth up-front. It would have saved both of them a lot of unnecessary grief.

If he had known, he would have set up extra precautions for everyone's protection. But what he would or wouldn't have done was a moot point now....

''How much younger are you?''

''I turned twenty-eight in August.''

''Somehow I knew you couldn't be thirty,'' he muttered.

''The roots of my hair are champagne-blond, and I wore it long before Diana fixed me up to look like her.''

He now had an explanation for the fifty-dollar hair appointment.

''Roger's last name is Farrow. He's an attorney who warned me that lying to you was a federal offense, that I could go to prison. He advised me to find an anonymous office job.''

She kneaded her hands. ''It didn't surprise me my sister tried to discourage you from hiring me. But it hurt because neither of them could understand how much I wanted to help you with Cory.

''Life really changed for me after Daddy died. I

became insecure, and Mother's death made that insecurity worse.

"Not only was I a prime candidate for someone like Ed, whose sick possessiveness I didn't recognize at the outset, I'm afraid that when you told me about Cory losing his mother, I endowed him with a lot of my feelings.

"He's a very precious boy. I could tell from simply looking at his picture in your office. I thought that as long as I couldn't continue with my career, then taking care of a child like my own niece and nephew was the kind of work that made the most sense to me.

"I love the out-of-doors, and though I'd never been to Grand Teton National Park, it sounded like a beautiful, safe haven. Of course I wasn't thinking about anyone else's safety but my own.

"You and your son were in a lot of pain. I thought if I could ease Cory's fears, then you wouldn't have to give up your career and it would all be worth it."

Tears welled in her eyes. "It shows you how hysterical I had become, how unconscionably selfish. I ran away from a madman who still continues to harass my family, a crazy who will eventually trace me to the most beautiful place on earth where he could very well hurt you and Cory, or worse."

By now her face glistened with tears. "You have no idea how much I loathe myself for what I've done. I can't believe what I've done to you. There has to be something wrong with me to be so frightened, I actually lied to you.

"I guess I was so convinced you wouldn't hire me if you knew the truth, I didn't even consider doing the honorable thing. That's what's killing me now.

You're such an honorable man. You don't deserve this, not after all the pain you and Cory have been through since your wife died. I'm so sorry, Pierce. So sorry.''

Diana, Diana. Except that she wasn't Diana. She was Leslie....

''How did you meet Ed Strickland?''

''Through the newspaper. I'm a photojournalist for the *New York Chronicler*.''

Everything was making sense.

His eyes closed for a minute as he remembered thinking she must have learned a lot from her father to know her way around a camera. During their hike she'd been so meticulous in setting up her shots.

Her job with the *Chronicler* explained her interest in recording him on their drive to Yellowstone, the professional manner in which she'd asked questions.

''Are there pictures of one of your photo shoots in that edition you picked up in Jackson?''

She nodded. ''My boss told Diana the Sunday paper came out with the last of a series I've been working on, but I still haven't looked at it yet.''

Another piece of the puzzle had just fit into place, one he wanted to see for himself.

''I presume you live in New York.''

''Yes,'' she whispered. ''I have an apartment in downtown Manhattan. Diana and Roger are the ones who live in New Jersey.''

Pierce rubbed the front of his face with his hand, trying to absorb it all.

''Eight months ago Ed and I happened to be staying at the same hotel in Miami while we were covering different stories for the paper. He works for the

national news department and was doing some investigative reporting on the Haitian immigrants being
turned away from Florida waters.

"My boss is the science editor at the same paper.
Normally my work takes me around the globe, but on
this particular assignment I was sent to the Everglades
to get film on the endangered panther.

"Though I didn't realize it then, it was a case of
being in the wrong place at the wrong time with the
wrong person. We dated four months before getting
engaged, but during that time we weren't together all
that often.

"I'd been working on a layout dealing with the
world's disappearing rain forests, so we had to find
time in between my trips to Brazil, Malaysia, Australia and Madagascar."

Her life as a photographer was one big adventure.

"The three-week photo shoot to Madagascar was
my last one for the series before the wedding. Thank
heaven for Maureen Strickland, his ex-wife, who had
the courage to come forward before the invitations
went out and warn me he was mentally ill.

"Of course I didn't believe her. As soon as Ed got
back I told him what had happened, that this woman
had approached me in front of the newspaper building
with this fantastic story. To my shock he admitted
he'd been married to her, but it was a period of his
life that was over and he'd wanted to forget it."

Good grief. No wonder it had upset her to find out
Cracroft hadn't introduced himself as a divorced man.

"Roger found the police record on Ed. It verified
everything she'd told me and more. At that point I
realized I was engaged to someone I didn't even

know. I called off the wedding. That's when the real nightmare began.''

For the next few minutes Pierce's blood curdled as he listened to the details of things her ex-fiancé had done after breaking into her apartment, not once but many times, even though she'd changed her locks. It was a tale of terror.

''Since he hasn't been able to find me, he's been enraged. I know he's looking for me because his harassment of the family for information has been constant. He stalks everyone—Diana, Roger, Roger's parents, my friends, my colleagues.

''He leaves frantic messages on my answering machine day and night. I can't count the number of faxes and letters he has sent to Roger's work. He e-mails them at the house threatening suicide, preaching to me about forgiveness, quoting the Bible.

''Everything he says and does is so frightening. How he gets any work done for his boss is beyond my comprehension. The detective advised me not to tell anyone at the paper about him. It's his theory that if Ed's job were threatened in any way, he might become even more violent.''

Pierce could understand the detective's reasoning.

''My brother-in-law has been documenting everything so it can be used in court against him one day. Roger's a saint! A few days ago he hired a P.I., someone Detective Santini recommended, to keep tabs on Ed's apartment and trail him so we would know what he's up to. It's costing him a fortune just so we can stay advised of how close Ed is to picking up my trail.

''So far Ed believes I'm still hiding out in New

York. Nevertheless, he is an investigative reporter who knows how to track down a lead. There will come a day when he stumbles across a clue that brings him out to Utah.''

She hugged her arms to her waist. ''Halfway through that interview with you in your office, I realized you deserved to know the truth. That's why I bolted. But then—''

''But then I had you rounded up because I knew I'd scared you off without giving you a chance.''

Their eyes held. ''And instead of my coming clean, I held back because at that point I needed a savior. If I'd searched the world over, I couldn't have found anyone more perfect than you.''

Her confession put a whole new light on what had happened in the truck a little while ago. Right now she didn't know what she was feeling where he was concerned. Any man's arms would have been a comfort.

''The first night I stayed at your house I realized I couldn't go on with my lie. The only reason I didn't confess everything the next night was because I was convinced Cory would never be able to accept me. I honestly believed you'd be moving to Ashton by Sunday.''

Pierce had believed the same thing.

''Knowing Ed was still running around in circles back in New York, I figured what you didn't know couldn't hurt you yet. I fully intended to go back to Salt Lake on the weekend. I'd seen several jobs advertised for waitresses needed at a couple of mountain resorts. Neither of them would have involved children or a family who could be hurt.

"To my shock Cory turned everything around when he accepted me as his nanny. I knew then I had to tell you the truth, but I needed to find a time when Cory couldn't hear us talking and you weren't dealing with an emergency.

"Heaven knows I've done everything wrong!" she cried out in despair. More tears gushed down her cheeks. "I'm a horrible person and the world's worst judge of character. It was reckless of me to put your lives in danger. There's no excuse, no forgiveness for that.

"Please tell me what you'd like me to do and I'll do it. If you want, I'll leave tonight. I realize it means you'll have to uproot your lives and move to Ashton, but it's better than something happening to you and Cory because of my selfish actions.

"I've grown to love your son. If any harm were to come to him or you, I'd want to die."

Pierce took a deep breath. "A different kind of harm will come to Cory if you were suddenly to disappear out of his life now. The trust you've established with him is still fragile, yet growing stronger every day. I'm not willing to see that broken. The damage could be severe. Therefore nothing's going to change.

"Give me your cell phone. I want to call your brother-in-law tonight and have a talk with him."

"All right." She wiped her eyes. "It's in my bedroom. I'll go get it."

While she rushed off, he stood there reeling from her confession. Not because it had come as a surprise. It hadn't. He'd already suspected her ex-fiancé had put the fear in her.

What bothered him was the depth of his feelings for a woman he'd only known two weeks. A woman who needed him for the hiding place he could provide.

CHAPTER TWELVE

ROGER READ OVER A BRIEF for court in the morning,
then phoned Leslie's apartment to listen to the latest
voice messages before going up to bed.

Disturbed when he didn't hear any new ones from
Ed—which meant he could be anywhere looking for
her—Roger listened to the few calls left by her friends
who asked her to phone them back when she was
feeling up to it.

"Hi, Wonder Woman. It's Dean. How about that
layout in the *Chronicler?* Because of you, our department has achieved instant fame. That was a hell
of a series you shot.

"Sorry to hear you had to postpone your wedding
because of your sister's car accident. It really surprised me when your fiancé came to my office Friday
to tell me."

Roger's hand gripped the phone tighter. Dr. Dean
Eskelson was the head of the ecology and bioenvi-
ronmental department at the University of Tennessee
in Knoxville. Ed had gone hunting, all right....

What good was the P.I. if she didn't know about
this?

"I hate to admit I approve of the guy. He has to
be a good man to help you tend your sister's children
instead of honeymooning with you in the Serengeti.

Hopefully she'll get better soon and I'll be receiving a wedding invitation.

"Thanks for the personal photos of everyone you sent with him. The guys will love them. Give me a call one day when the situation has improved. We're due for one of our long talks. But for Ed Strickland... Well, you know what I'm trying to say."

Roger shook his head. Leslie had a lot of male admirers. Someone as sick and paranoid as Ed would have jumped to the conclusion she and Eskelson had been lovers in Madagascar when Leslie had been sent on that photo shoot for the newspaper.

There'd been three biologists from several universities exploring the Madagascar rain forest, all of whom had given their permission for her to take pictures for the paper.

Roger didn't doubt for a moment Ed was making the rounds of those professors now, hoping to catch her with one of them.

Though relieved he was off on a false lead, it filled Roger with fresh alarm that Rita Cardenas hadn't contacted him about this latest development.

"Honey?" he said when he'd gotten ready for bed and had climbed in next to his wife. "Did you happen to hear from the P.I. today?"

"Yes. She called early to tell us one of her assistants followed Ed to Tennessee on Friday. As far as I know, he's still there. She'll keep us informed."

So the P.I. was on top of things after all. His faith restored, he told Diana about the message Dr. Eskelson had left on Leslie's machine.

Her expression grew haunted. "We can't say anything to Leslie about this. I'm frightened, Roger."

She nestled against him. "He isn't going to quit until he finds her."

"He won't!" Determined about that, he pulled her closer and started kissing her. That was when the phone rang. "It's awfully late for anyone to be calling."

"Maybe it's Leslie!" she cried, lifting her head from his shoulder.

"Easy, honey. We have to listen before we pick up."

Roger recognized Rita's voice.

"The target is at the Knoxville airport waiting to board a flight to Denver, Colorado. My assistant found out one of the professors on the Madagascar trip, Alex Mayfield, left the day before to attend a biology seminar being held at the university in Boulder. Unless I hear from you in ten minutes with other instructions, I'll tell him to get on that plane with the target."

Roger reached for his cell phone, but Diana stopped him. "Don't call her."

"Honey—I'm not going to throw away good money while Ed's still running around in circles. You know this is costing us a fortune and Leslie's not in any danger at the moment."

"But at least we know where he is."

"I promise when he finds out Leslie isn't in Boulder, he'll be back in New York by tomorrow night."

He threw off the covers and sat up to call the P.I. back. When she picked up he said, "It's Roger Farrow. Just heard your message. I don't want Ed followed to Colorado. He'll return to New York before long."

"You can count on it. Is your wife on the line with you?"

"No," he answered, instantly alert.

"I had a look around his apartment today. It's not a pretty sight. He has turned his bedroom into a shrine. The place is wallpapered with pictures of his ex-wife and your sister-in-law, plus pages torn out of a Bible. Parts about forgiveness are circled in red pen. The missing underwear you mentioned some time ago is dangling from the ceiling.

"Parts of her smashed-up Nikon camera are in a box on top of his dresser. Among the items in his closet were a high-powered rifle, a handgun and ammo for both. I've already turned over the footage to the detective on her case."

After hearing what Rita had to say, he was glad he wasn't facing Diana right then. "Okay. Thanks for the information. Keep up the great work. I'll expect to hear from you after he's back in New York. Good night."

He'd barely clicked off when the phone rang again. Diana grabbed hold of his arm while they waited to hear who it was this time.

"This is Pierce Gallagher phoning from Moose, Wyoming. Forgive me for calling so late, but I have to speak to Roger right away. It's vital."

"Uh-oh." Diana moaned. "Leslie said she was going to tell him the truth tonight. I'm scared, Roger."

Roger wasn't too thrilled himself. It could be ugly. He got to his feet before answering. "Roger Farrow here, Mr. Gallagher. By now I have to assume you know Diana is really Leslie Hopkins, my wife's sister."

"Yes. When I hired her, I sensed something was wrong, but I was desperate to find a nanny for my son. She said enough right things to convince me to take a chance on her, anyway. Now that I know the whole truth, my major concern is to find out just how dangerous you believe Ed Strickland to be."

The chief ranger of Grand Teton National Park was a man of few words, very direct. Roger liked that. He also felt relief because he knew that deep down, the man had forgiven Leslie. Otherwise they wouldn't be having this conversation.

"I'll tell you everything I can. Give me a minute to go downstairs where I have all Ed's e-mails stored on the computer. After I've read them to you, you'll understand what we're up against."

It was half an hour later before they'd gone through everything and Roger had told him what the P.I. had found in Ed's apartment over the weekend.

After a telling silence Pierce Gallagher said, "Leslie's aware she's a very fortunate woman to have someone like you watching out for her, Roger."

"Leslie's a sweetheart. Right now, I'd say she's luckier than she knows to have an understanding employer like you. Needless to say, Diana and I love her. But all things considered, she must get another job someplace else so that you and your son won't be in harm's way."

"I'll take the necessary steps to protect us. What I'm hoping is that Strickland makes a mistake and gets himself arrested before he figures out where she's hiding. What's Detective Santini's number? I'd like to touch base with him."

"Excellent idea." Roger found it and gave it to him. "Mr. Gallagher?"

"Call me Pierce."

"Pierce—I know Leslie's heart. She took the loss of her parents harder than Diana did, I think. Though her deception was no small thing, she really did want to help Cory through his grief. I don't know if that's any consolation to you."

"It is." The huskiness in the other man's voice told Roger a lot. Pierce Gallagher was an exceptional man. "I'm sure we'll be talking again soon."

"No question about it. Good night, Pierce."

"HERE'S CAMERON'S BIRTHDAY present." Friday had come, the day Cory had been impatiently waiting for. "Have fun at the party!"

"I will. His parents are going to bring me home."

"Okay. I'll be waiting for you."

Before Leslie drove back to the house, she waited until Cory had joined the other kids playing on the lawn blowing soap bubbles.

Pierce had called earlier to inform her an emergency had cropped up and he wouldn't be home till late. Since Monday night there'd been so many calls on his time, they hadn't found another moment to talk when Cory wasn't around.

She half suspected Pierce stayed away on purpose. Things were different between them now that she'd told him the truth. If anything, she suffered worse guilt because he hadn't berated her or done anything that a less remarkable man would have done in retaliation.

After assuring her he'd taken the necessary steps

to ensure their safety, he'd gone about his business as if nothing had happened. Yet he'd put a professional distance between them she couldn't bridge. There would be no more intimate moments like that night at the drive-in. She'd ruined it.

He might have insisted she stay on in Moose for Cory's sake to keep his trust, but Pierce would never trust *her* again. Without it, she could never hope to mean anything more to him than just the person who took care of his son.

The thought of a whole Friday afternoon and evening alone seemed to exacerbate her pain. She decided now would be a good time to get started on her journal.

It would contain a workup of her essay for a brand-new photographic layout she was planning. A project that would never see the light of day, never be published, yet she was compelled to do it. This was a labor of love for her eyes only.

The title had come to her the night Pierce had returned home exhausted after finding the drowned grandfather wedged in the rocks. Heroes in Peril: Meet the Teton Rangers.

She sat at the kitchen table, then turned on her minirecorder to write down the answers Pierce had given her during their heavenly outing on Sunday.

Tell me about the road we're traveling right now.

"The Byway is an ancient Indian route. It passes through some of the continent's most wild and spectacular country, crossing the recreation lands of two national forests, Grand Teton National Park and the National Elk Refuge in Jackson Hole, and various private resorts. At the lower elevations you can see willow bottoms and sage-covered hills. But we'll climb dramatically into high alpine conifer forests.''

Could you describe the Teton Mountains for me?

''There are twelve Teton peaks reaching above 12,000 feet. The Grand Teton is 13,770 feet. Together they are high enough to support a dozen mountain glaciers. They're the youngest of the mountains in the Rocky Mountain system, yet the gentle slopes on the west side reveal some of North America's oldest rocks.

''Eons of glaciation caused by the rise of the Teton Range, as well as the erosion, have created conditions to allow numerous plant communities to thrive. You'll find sagebrush flats, ribbons of green riparian plants bordering rivers and streams, lodgepole pine and spruce forests, subalpine meadows and alpine stone fields. They support the habitat for a variety of animals, from the tiniest insects, birds and fish to small and large mammals. Humans have lived here for eleven thousand years.''

Leslie was so mesmerized by Pierce's deep, masculine voice and the precise way he stated his thoughts, she kept forgetting to write and had to rewind the tape over and over to get it all down.

What about the bears?

''When Daddy was young, he and his friend got chased by a jaw-chomping mother grizzly, huh, Daddy? He climbed up a tree and tried to help his friend, but the bear laddered the tree—''

''Diana doesn't want to hear about that, Cory.''

She pressed the Pause button. Pierce's friend had obviously died, or he would have said something about the story having a happy ending. The horror of what he must have lived through haunted her.

Not wanting to think about it, she released the button.

"When Lewis and Clark crossed the Rockies in 1804, about a hundred thousand grizzlies roamed the western half of the continental United States. Two hundred years later, they had lost ninety-nine percent of their original range to settlement. Now there are only about one thousand in the six populations of grizzlies living in the mountains of Wyoming, Montana, and Idaho. The Greater Yellowstone Ecosystem, which includes the Tetons, is home to one population. Only recently, however, have grizzlies been spotted within the boundaries of Teton Park."

It took several rewinds before she finished that segment. She was ready to start the next portion of the tape dealing with dry lightning when she heard the sound of the garage door opening.

Her heart raced out of rhythm. He'd come home much earlier than she'd expected! Excitement had her jumping up from the chair.

When he didn't come right in the house, she hurried over to the door and opened it. "Pierce?" she called out.

"Oh!" she cried when it was another man who approached first, carrying a large sack.

"Sorry to have startled you. I'm Nick Kincaid."

"Jessica's father!"

"Yes." He smiled. "And you're Leslie."

Pierce's friend was a very attractive ranger about his height and age.

"It's so nice to meet you. Please come in."

She looked past his shoulder to Pierce. He held a box in his arms. Little cries were coming from inside it.

Leslie squealed in delight. "You got Cory a dog!"

Their eyes met before he looked away. "Nick knows some people from Boise who breed basset hounds, so we drove there and picked up this little female."

"Is Maxine from Planet X, too?"

Pierce burst into laughter. It reminded her of the old Pierce for a moment. That thought was something to cherish.

She closed the door, then hurried over to look in the box. "Oh—isn't she adorable!" The little puppy licked her fingers. Leslie raised her head. "Cory's going to die of excitement when he walks in."

"That's the idea," Pierce said with a smile.

"I'm going to leave you two alone."

Leslie stood up. "Please don't go, Nick." Please don't go. I need you to ease the tension. "I made spaghetti for dinner. All I have to do is warm it up."

"I'd like to stay, but Jessica's waiting for me."

"Take the truck and go get her," Pierce suggested. "I'll drive you home later." Pierce handed him the keys. "We're going to need all the help we can get with a new baby in the house."

After Nick took off, Leslie sat on the floor and cuddled the newest addition to Pierce's family while he set up the doggy bed and bowls against the wall. No doubt he, too, wanted Nick around—but for a buffer. Another wound to her heart.

The phone rang. He answered it but didn't stay on long.

"That was Cory. He'll be home in a minute."

She looked up at him. "Do you have a camcorder?"

"Yes. Unfortunately, it's broken. I've been meaning to get it fixed."

"Here." She rose up and handed him the wiggly puppy. "I'll get my camera. We have to take pictures of him when he walks in and sees what you brought home."

She ran to the bedroom to grab it, and none too soon. On her way back through the house she saw the front door open. Cory made a beeline for the kitchen.

"Daddy? Leslie? Look at the prize I won!"

For the first few days he'd had trouble not calling her Diana. Pierce had been forced to sit him down and tell him that Leslie's old boyfriend had been trying to find her, so she'd been hiding from him and was using another name.

Dear Cory. He hadn't seemed the least bit upset about it. In fact, he'd been quite sympathetic and had told Leslie she didn't have to worry because his dad would protect all of them. "My dad's the chief ranger and can take care of anybody!" Leslie didn't doubt it for a second.

"Bring your prize over here," Pierce replied.

Cory hadn't seen Leslie yet. The dog was whimpering.

"Hey—what's that noise?"

She crept to the door of the kitchen.

Pierce stood in the middle of the room with his hands on his hips, a deadpan expression on his handsome face. "Why don't you look over in the corner?"

In the next few minutes she took shots from every camera angle possible. The pictures would tell it all. A boy and his dog. Talk about pure, unmitigated, total joy—

By the time Nick and Jessica walked into the kitchen, Leslie had put a fresh roll of film in the camera.

Cory ran over to them, holding his puppy against his chest. "This is my dog!" Tears of happiness rolled down his cheeks.

Leslie kept clicking away.

Jessica was just as taken with the puppy and made sounds like a little mother. "What are you going to name her?"

"Her?" Cory looked up at his father for verification.

Pierce nodded. "She's a girl. They make a better pet."

"What do *you* think I should call her, Daddy?"

Leslie melted at the smile he flashed his son. "It's your dog, Charlie Brown."

Cory blinked. "I'll call her Lucy. What do you think?" He looked at Leslie. The fact that he wanted her input excited her. Though the gulf between her and Pierce seemed greater than ever, she'd never felt so close to his son.

"I think it's a perfect name. She was always one of my favorite cartoon characters when I was young."

"Lucy it is!" Pierce declared.

"Can she have some spaghetti, Daddy?"

To Leslie, Pierce's laughter was the most beautiful sound in the world.

CHAPTER THIRTEEN

MONDAY AFTERNOON ROGER left the courthouse pleased to have won the case for his client. The jury had deliberated three days before rendering an innocent verdict. All he wanted to do now was go home and kick back while he watched the Knicks game.

"Honey? Where are you?" he called to his wife the second he entered the house.

"In the family room!" Amy came running to greet him. He caught her in his arms and gave her a kiss. Together they found Diana, who was folding clothes while Josh watched TV. She looked up when they came in.

"How did your court case go?"

"We won!"

"That's terrific, honey!"

"Hey, Daddy? Remember, there's no school tomorrow 'cos it's teachers' work day. Are we going sailing? You promised."

"I've been planning on it, sport, but only if it's good weather."

"It is! See?" He'd clicked to the weather channel. The forecast didn't sound too bad for early October.

"While you two finish watching, I'll put dinner on the table. Come on, Amy." Diana reached for their daughter and started for the door.

''And now for the top weather story of the evening. A ferocious thunderstorm that struck the Yellowstone-Teton area of the Rockies this afternoon caused significant damage to both parks.''

Roger saw his wife stop in her tracks and wheel around to listen.

''Power was knocked out, boats were scattered on Jackson Lake and the Grassy Lake Road was closed until further notice because about 175 trees toppled across it in its first three miles alone.

''One tree that fell on a Nissan Pathfinder on Highway 89 about a mile north of the Moran entrance seriously injured six-year-old Cameron Morgan of Moose, Wyoming, the son of one of the rangers who was riding with his mother.''

''Hey—he's *my* age!'' Josh blurted.

''Ironically, young Cameron had just been to the doctor for his six-month checkup.''

Not only did the mention of Moose capture their attention—the boy named Cameron sounded familiar to Roger. He could swear that was one of Cory's friends Leslie had talked about. Diana recognized his name, too. Her shocked gaze flew to his.

''Both had to be extricated from their vehicle.''

Josh turned his head. ''Daddy? What does that mean?''

''Someone had to help them get out of their car.''

''That's bad, huh?''

''Not necessarily.''

''The boy is in the hospital in stable condition. His mother was treated at the hospital and released. Total damage to the parks is not yet known.

''Other areas of the country are reporting torna—''

Roger walked over and shut it off. "Come on. Let's help your mom with dinner."

There was no reason to think Leslie was in any difficulty, but knowing Diana, she'd worry and fret until she'd heard from her sister.

As soon as dinner was over they checked their e-mail, but there was no message. When the kids had been put to bed and there was still no word, Roger was starting to feel a little antsy himself but would never admit it to his wife.

"Come on, honey. Let's turn in. You know as well as I do Leslie will contact us as soon as she can."

"That's what's got me nervous."

"Maybe she took Cory to the hospital so they could visit his friend. There could be a dozen explanations."

"You're right, but I can't stop thinking that tree might have fallen on her and Cory."

He was way ahead of his wife. With reporting as detailed as that, if it had been Leslie, any friends of theirs who heard the evening news would be phoning to talk about the coincidence of there being two Diana Farrows. That was all Ed would need to hear to put the missing piece of the puzzle in place.

Roger had been talking with Pierce Gallagher on a daily basis since their first conversation. They'd both agreed that for the time being, Leslie would go on being Diana except around Pierce's closest friends.

The chief ranger had taken measures to tighten security within the park. He'd asked Roger to e-mail him photos of Ed. Flyers had been made up and distributed to the other rangers, who were keeping a lookout for him. Roger had to admire the way he had everything under control. It was no wonder Leslie felt safe with him.

Heaven knew he and Diana slept better at night, except that tonight they were anxious to find out about Cory's little friend. Roger sighed. There was always something to weigh them down.

So far Ed hadn't returned to New York. That wasn't good news, especially when no one knew where he was right now.

"SET ME DOWN AT COULTER BAY."

"Will do, Pierce."

The pilot completed the circle of Jackson Lake before landing the chopper in the parking lot where one of the rangers had organized a search-and-rescue operation for any missing boaters. It was dark out now.

The governor emerged from the helicopter first. "Pierce? As soon as I get back, I'll give the order for you to receive the backup and equipment you need to clear all those trees from the Grassy Lake area."

"Thanks, Governor. I appreciate you getting here so fast."

"The park's one of my top priorities. I don't recall storm damage as severe as this in a long time. If you need anything else, call me."

"I'm hoping I won't have to, but until everyone has reported in, you might be hearing from me again before the night is out."

The two men shook hands before Pierce jumped out of the helicopter with the rotors still whirring. Rex was waiting for him.

"Good news, Pierce. All missing boaters are now

accounted for. The superintendent wants a status report as soon as you can give it to him."

Pierce waited to talk until the chopper was airborne and had veered north. "The governor's releasing emergency funds to clear the trees."

"With the department so underfunded, that's a big relief!"

"Amen. What have you heard from Gros Ventre and Signal Mountain?"

"So far so good."

"Anything new on Cameron and his mother?"

"I spoke to Gary a half hour ago. They taped her ribs to minimize the pain before releasing her. Cameron has a concussion, but he's going to be all right. If there are no complications, they'll release him to go home in the morning."

"Thank God." First Gary's cut hand, now this. The Morgan family had received more than their quota of bad luck.

Rex nodded. "The news made my day. There's more good news. Power should be restored to the park by midnight."

The tension started to leave Pierce's body. He took a quick survey of the activity surrounding them. "Considering the violence of the storm, it's a miracle there haven't been any fatalities reported."

"Everyone's saying the same thing."

"I'm on my way to headquarters to run operations from there for the rest of the night. En route I'll give the superintendent a call." He clapped Rex on the shoulder. "You're a good man to have around, especially in a crisis." With that, Pierce turned and headed for his truck.

Behind him he heard Rex say, "You know why, Pierce. Every day I'm learning from the pro."

Pierce waved to him. *I'm no pro yet,* he muttered to himself as he climbed into the cab and took off for Moose.

When word had first reached him about Cameron and his mother being pinned in the Pathfinder, it'd been a struggle to keep his reaction from the other rangers. With his emotions so raw, his mind could easily imagine the same accident having happened to Cory and Leslie.

To his everlasting relief, a couple of quick cell phone calls had assured him they were both home safe and sound with Lucy. At the time he talked to them, they weren't aware of the Morgans' accident. He'd decided to keep it to himself until he knew more about their condition.

Needing to hear their voices now, he phoned Leslie first. She picked up on the second ring.

"Pierce? I'm so glad you called—we just heard about Cameron and his mom. It has really upset Cory," she said in a hushed tone.

"I can imagine. Is he right there?"

"Yes."

"Let me talk to him."

He didn't have to wait long. "Daddy?"

"Hi, champ. Your buddy Cameron's going to be fine. He's got a big headache, but that's all. From what I understand, you'll be able to go over to his house and visit him tomorrow."

"Can I take Lucy?"

"Sure."

"He wants a dog just like her."

"I don't doubt it."

"How soon are you coming home?"

"Probably not until morning."

"Heck."

"You know what? It's time for bed, anyway. When you wake up in the morning, I'll be home."

"Okay."

"I love you."

"I love you, too."

"Put Leslie back on, will you?"

"Leslie?" his son called to her. "Daddy wants to talk to you again. Cameron's got a headache, but I can go over to his house tomorrow. He says I can take Lucy."

"That's wonderful news," she said to Cory before speaking into the mouthpiece again. "Hello, Pierce?"

"It *is* wonderful," he murmured. "But what's even more wonderful is that neither of you were out in that storm this afternoon."

"When we went on a little walk with Lucy so Cory could take some pictures of her, I noticed how black the sky was getting. It looked so ominous to me, I didn't dare let Cory go to school."

He had to clear his throat before he could talk. "You always know to do the right thing where he's concerned, Leslie. At the last minute the school buses were canceled, otherwise there would have been mayhem."

"I called Jessica to see if she was all right. She said she was fine, but I could tell the storm made her nervous so I invited her to come over. She had dinner with us and stayed until Nick came for her."

"I'm sure he was grateful you were there for his daughter. Thank you for being there for my son."

"You don't need to thank me. Jessica was a comfort to Cory after we heard from Logan's mother about the accident. I'm so glad they're all right." Her voice trembled.

"So am I. Strangely enough, although visitors to the park lost boats and gear, those two were the only people seriously injured today."

"Then that's a blessing."

"It is." He swallowed hard. "Much as I'd like to talk longer, I have to report in to the superintendent. Just so you know, I'll be at headquarters in a few minutes and will stay there to work tonight."

"We're glad you're going to be close by."

Her admission shouldn't have sent a thrill of excitement through his body, but it did. It was getting harder on him to live under the same roof with her without being close. Very close. But it wouldn't be fair—she was so vulnerable right now. He didn't want to pressure her into being intimate. Oh, but he wanted that intimacy so badly. When would she be ready? Maybe never.

"Me, too. Talk to you later."

Once they'd clicked off, he rang the superintendent and gave him a report. By the time Pierce reached headquarters, he was gratified to see that the skeleton staff had been there manning the post and had turned on the emergency generator.

Sally gave him the latest bulletins, pouring in from all areas of the park. He thanked her and the others, then told them to go on home.

A few minutes later he thought he was alone until he heard footsteps coming down the hall. "Sally?"

"Surprise, Daddy!"

Surprise was the operative word all right. When he lifted his head, his eyes beheld a marvelous sight. The two people he cared about most in the world had entered his office bearing gifts.

Leslie's smile seduced him on the spot. "You're always taking care of everybody else, so we thought we'd take care of you for a change."

"Yeah," Cory concurred.

They'd brought him a thermos of hot coffee, fried chicken, potato salad and his favorite chocolate cake.

When he'd eaten half of everything he said, "This is heaven."

Her eyes searched his face with gratifying intensity. "We knew you would be hungry."

"Guess what, Daddy? There's a whole bunch of leaves and branches in the yard. And guess what else? I found my old black Tonka plane that got lost in the tree last year."

Pierce grinned. "Where did it land?"

"In the driveway. Leslie saw it when we took Lucy out."

"Lucky you. That was your favorite." Though he gave Cory a hug, his gaze clung to Leslie's. "What would the Gallagher family do without her?"

She averted her eyes, but not before he saw color fill her cheeks. His heart raced. If Ed Strickland weren't in their lives, everything could be different.

The irony was that Pierce would never have met Leslie if it hadn't been for her psycho ex-fiancé. Hell.

"Chief?"

A voice caused him to look beyond her to the doorway. It was the two younger rangers who'd pulled Leslie over when she'd been driving Pierce's car. He'd been so far away in thought, he hadn't been aware they had company.

"Come in."

"Sorry to disturb you." They both tipped their hats to Leslie. "We've done a sweep of the main roads. The work crews are out clearing debris. By morning, traffic should be able to move as usual."

"Sounds good. Go on home and get some sleep. We're going to need all the help we can get in the next few days clearing the Grassy Lake Road area."

"Is it true what was said on the news? There are 175 trees down?"

"From the helicopter I counted close to two hundred."

"Oh, man—"

"Oh, man, is right. And there's fresh snow. It's a mess."

"See you later, then." One of them looked at Leslie expectantly. "Ms. Farrow? I hope you've forgiven us for pulling you over that day."

Leslie chuckled. "There's nothing to forgive. You thought I'd stolen Pierce's car. I must say your gentlemanly behavior was impressive."

"Thank you." The two young rangers grinned.

"I've chalked it up to one of my unforgettable adventures in the Tetons. When I leave, I'll have that memory to take with me."

"You're leaving?"

"No, Cory—" Leslie rushed to reassure him because he'd sounded so panicked just then. "I only meant some day."

"Oh."

Pierce's son wasn't the only one to have an adverse reaction to her words. His heart still hadn't resumed its normal rhythm.

He looked pointedly at the two rangers, who acted as if they were waiting for Leslie to ask them to stay. "Good night."

They promptly responded in kind and left.

To his chagrin their departure caused her to stand up. "I think Cory and I had better go home to Lucy so you can get some work done."

"She squealed like Piglet when we left, Daddy."

Both he and Leslie laughed. "I'm not surprised. She's still a baby, but growing fast." He got to his feet. "Come on. I'll walk you to the car."

She shook her head. "There's no need for that. We know you're busy and will see you in the morning."

Why did he sense there was something else going on inside Leslie?

"Cory? Call me when you get home so I know you're safe."

His son gave him another hug.

Pierce's gaze flicked to Leslie's. "Thank you for dinner. It saved my life."

"Anytime," she said before they disappeared from his office.

More than anything in the world he wanted her to mean that.

Four phone calls later he heard from Cory.

"Daddy?"

"Hi! Is everything okay?"

"Yes. Lucy's asleep in her bed."

"That's good."

"Daddy?" he whispered. "How come Leslie's going to go away some day?"

The air caught in Pierce's lungs. "Maybe she won't. Maybe she'll like it here so much, she won't want to leave."

"I hope she doesn't."

Pierce's heart leaped. "I don't want her to go, either."

"When Jessica started to cry, Leslie made her feel better."

"How come she cried?"

"'Cos Nick couldn't come home. She got scared of the storm."

"But you weren't scared, were you, champ?"

"No, 'cos Leslie was with me."

He gripped the phone tighter. A month ago he couldn't have imagined Cory saying that to him. "She's a pretty great person to have around when you need her."

"She played SWAT team with me. We looked for bad guys and called each other on our cell phones when we found one. She can talk funny like that lady in *Ghostbusters*."

"You mean the one who answers the telephone at the fire station?"

"Yes." He giggled.

For some reason that was one of Cory's favorite parts in the film. If anyone could do a strong Bronx accent like that, he assumed Leslie could. Did she have any idea how much she delighted Cory?

When Pierce had talked to Jim Archer earlier in the

day to coordinate the governor's flight schedule over both parks, his friend let it drop that Cory had only phoned Janice once since they'd moved. Now his wife was starting to feel bad.

Though Pierce assured Jim his son would never forget Janice, he was secretly thrilled Cory had grown so attached to Leslie already.

"Do you want to know a secret?"

"What?" Cory asked.

"When I hired Leslie, she promised to stay for a whole year."

"She did?"

"Yes. By next year Lucy will be all grown up and Leslie won't want to leave either of you."

"'Specially if Lucy has babies. Leslie says she loves babies."

A smile broke out on Pierce's face. "She does, huh?"

"Yup. She says she's always wanted three or four."

Three or four? Pierce was prepared to do his best to make that dream come true. *Maybe one day, Leslie.*

LESLIE HEARD THE GARAGE DOOR open. She glanced at her watch. It was five o'clock in the morning. Pierce had to be exhausted.

Excited he was home, even if she wouldn't be able to talk to him until much later, she lay in bed until he'd gone to his room, then she got up to turn on her laptop. Because of yesterday's events she hadn't tried to contact her sister. Now she had so much to tell her, she hardly knew where to start.

There were two e-mails waiting for her. She opened the one sent last night.

Leslie? It was all over the news about Cory's little friend and his mother being injured in that terrible storm. Please answer this as soon as you can. We need to know you're all right!

Guilt assailed Leslie. She had no idea the national news had given out names. Was it any wonder Diana sounded frantic?

She opened the second e-mail.

Call ASAP.

Without wasting a second, Leslie reached for her cell and phoned her sister.

"Thank heavens it's you, honey!"

"I'm sorry to have worried you, Diana. A lot has been going on here." In the next few minutes she brought her sister up to date on everything. "Now I have to know about Ed. What has the P.I. said he's been doing?"

Leslie was horrified when Diana told her he'd flown from Knoxville to Denver to hunt down Alex Mayfield.

"He's a madman, Diana." Tears streamed down her face. "What if he hurts Alex? You don't know how terrible it is to think that everyone I've ever known or associated with in the past is in danger!"

"I won't tell you I understand everything you're feeling, honey. All I can do is remind you he hasn't hurt anyone yet. The best news is, he still doesn't know where you are."

Leslie rocked back and forth on the bed. "But he's never going to stop looking. I can feel it. Do you remember when we were little and how scared we got watching the angel of death in *The Ten Commandments?*

"I used to get so terrified when I saw that eerie green mist come out of the sky and start filling the streets looking for the first born. It gave me nightmares for years.

"That's how Ed makes me feel. Like he's filling the streets looking for me. He just keeps coming as if he were an inexorable tide and there's no escape."

"Stop it, Leslie!" her sister chastised her.

"I can't stop it, and I can't expect you two to go on paying for my mistakes while I'm living here in a fool's paradise. Because of my poor judgment in getting involved with a monster like Ed, you and your family are being made to suffer.

"Roger makes a wonderful living, but he didn't get a law degree to finance the bills the P.I. is sending him because of my lunatic ex-fiancé. This wild-goose chase could go on for months and months. I couldn't live with myself if that were the case."

The silence on Diana's end lasted a long time. "You can't walk out on Pierce now. Cory needs you too much."

"I know," she whispered in agony. "But if Ed does eventually find out I'm here, he won't let anyone stand in his way trying to get to me. Not Pierce, not Cory. I've done an evil thing coming here and ruining their lives."

"Pierce Gallagher sounds like a big boy who can take care of himself and anyone else."

Leslie smiled through the tears. "That's what Cory says about his father. He has no fear that way."

"Then maybe you should take lessons from him."

THE DAY AFTER THE BIG STORM had done its worst, a cold front moved in. At a seven-thousand-foot elevation the rain had turned to snow, making working conditions miserable for the men driving the bulldozers and running the chain saws.

Trucks kept coming to haul away the trees. Between the ice and the mud and the debris, Pierce thought the area looked like it had been bombed.

Thankfully by Thursday noon, he declared the job finished and told everyone to go on home and get some rest. One by one the last of the trucks and heavy equipment moved out.

Nick stayed behind to help him put up some road signs that had been uprooted and blown into the snow by the gale-force winds.

"There's one more missing." Pierce raised the binoculars to his eyes and scanned the terrain. "I see the tip of it up on that ledge."

"I swear a tornado swept through here."

"I'm sure you're right. While you finish pounding that sign in good and deep, I'll get the other one."

Thoughts of going home to Leslie and Cory in the next few minutes charged his body with adrenaline. He climbed the side of the ravine without feeling any pain and heaved himself onto the icy ledge.

"You're never going to believe it, Nick!"

"What?" he shouted up at him.

"The post of this sign impaled the rock exactly like a stake through a vampire's heart."

"That I've got to see."

In a few minutes Nick had climbed his way up. When he saw it he said, "We'll have to get your resident photographer out here."

There were a lot of things Pierce wanted to do with his resident photographer.

They both pulled on the sign. "It's not budging," Pierce said.

"Nope. It's here to stay for posterity."

The word brought a certain conversation with Leslie and Cory to mind. Pierce started to tell his friend about it as they began moving off the ledge.

Suddenly his left arm felt strange. A cold sensation ran from his shoulder to his wrist. He lost his grip. With a cry he tumbled down the side of the ravine.

When he looked up, Nick's white face was staring down at him. "Dear God, Pierce—what happened?"

"I don't know. It's my left arm. I felt it go numb."

Nick moved around to Pierce's side where he could examine him. A strange cry came out of his throat. "You've been shot in the shoulder!"

"Shot?" Pierce couldn't comprehend it.

"That was no accident," Nick whispered. "Come on. We've got to get out of here."

Nick helped him to his feet and they ran for cover. Before reaching Nick's truck another shot whistled past Pierce's ear, missing it by a hair.

"Get in!" Nick pushed him inside as a third shot made a zinging sound overhead. He shut the door before running around to the driver's side. They took off at full speed, causing the truck to shimmy in the snow.

The movement of being shoved had created a searing pain in his shoulder, but he knew that shove had saved his life.

He was beginning to feel light-headed and nauseous. Nick was on the phone. It sounded like he was calling out the army and the marines.

"You heard me. It's the chief. Someone tried to kill him. He needs help *now,* and I want every inch of this terrain scoured for the sniper."

"It's only a flesh wound," Pierce whispered, but Nick ignored him. In a few minutes Pierce heard a helicopter in the distance.

"You'll be at the hospital in Jackson before you know it," Nick said in a shaken voice. "I knew some of the ranchers were angry because we've introduced the grizzlies back into the park, but I never dreamed they'd go so far as to try to pick you off. Dear God, Pierce…"

"If I didn't know Cracroft had kept his initial appointment with the doctor in Salt Lake, he'd be number one on my list."

"It doesn't mean he couldn't have doubled back here. If he's as crazy as I believe he is, he might have taken advantage of the storm to pack in without the rangers seeing him."

"You could be right. The guy hates my guts, but then so do those bikers from Los Angeles who tried to get past one of the rangers at the entrance last week. When I was summoned for help, the leader looked me in the eye and threatened to come back and raise hell."

Nick frowned. "I don't know what to think."

"Maybe those bullets were meant for you and the sniper was a bad shot, thank God," Pierce theorized.

"I suppose it's possible. I have my share of enemies, too."

Nick brought the truck to a stop near the spot where

the med-flight helicopter had landed. The paramedics came running with a stretcher.

"I'm worried about Leslie and Cory, Nick. I don't want them hearing this secondhand."

"I'll head to your house now to let Leslie know what happened. She'll want to bring Cory to the hospital to see you. Jessica and I will drive them."

"Nick?"

"I know what you're going to say. Whether either or both of us were targets, I'm concerned about our families, too. I'm going to call security to put Leslie and the kids under twenty-four-hour protection while this case is being investigated."

Pierce sighed with relief. "I owe you," he said as one of the paramedics opened the passenger door.

"We heard you took a bullet, chief," said one of the paramedics.

"I'm all right."

"Let us be the judge of that."

"I can walk to the helicopter."

"Maybe. But you're not going to."

"The hell I'm not!"

"Then at least lean on me."

Pierce eased his legs to the slushy ground and used his right hand to clutch the other man's shoulder. He moved through the snow to the chopper. Once he'd climbed inside, the men strapped him down. Pierce could hear two more helicopters coming.

"We're going to find out who did this," Nick assured him. "See you at the hospital in a little while. God bless." The door closed.

In another minute the rotors screamed and the helicopter lifted off. Pierce closed his eyes as the guys went to work on him.

"You're a lucky man, chief. Your wound is superficial, very little bleeding. They'll do an X ray, but I'm pretty sure once you're cleaned up, all you'll need is a dressing and antibiotics."

That was good enough for Pierce. The man had recently returned from the Gulf and had treated every rifle wound there was.

The more Pierce thought about it, the more he was convinced the sniper had purposely missed killing him.

He and Nick had been out in the open. They'd made slow-moving targets. Picking them off would have been easy, like shooting ducks in a barrel.

There was only one person Pierce could imagine who fit the profile of a person who would do such a thing. Cracroft.

He thought of the menacing glitter in Cracroft's eyes when he'd barreled past Pierce the morning he'd told him to turn in his badge. Perhaps it was a clue, an indication of a deranged mind that would enjoy toying with him first, then move in later on for the kill.

CHAPTER FOURTEEN

LESLIE WAS WHIPPING UP a batch of chocolate chip cookies when Pierce's house phone rang. She reached for the receiver to answer it. The caller ID indicated it was Logan's mom.

"Hello?"

"Leslie?"

"Yes?" The other woman didn't sound like herself. "Are you all right?"

"I was just going to ask you the same question."

Leslie's heart rate picked up speed. "Why do you ask?"

"Oh, dear, I assumed you would have been told by now."

"What?" she cried. "Is this about Cory? Was he hurt at school?"

"No, no. It's Pierce. My husband just phoned me to tell me a med-flight helicopter just flew him to the hospital in Jackson."

Dear God—

Her heart plunged to her stomach. She clutched the edge of the counter for support.

"What happened to him?"

"I don't know. My husband overheard one of the rangers talking about it and phoned to see if I'd heard anything. I just wanted to call and tell you I'm here for you if you need me to help with Cory.''

"Thank you so much. I'm going to leave for Jackson right now. I'll pick up Cory on the way. No matter what, his son needs to be there with him.''

"You're right. I'm so sorry to have been the one to upset you. Let me know if there's anything I can do.''

"I will.''

Leslie put the cookie dough in the fridge, then placed Lucy in her crated doggy area with food and water. After she grabbed her purse, she raced out to the garage. "Please, God—don't let it be serious, whatever it is—''

She backed out of the driveway and almost ran into Nick's truck. Her body shook so hard, she could hardly press the button so the window would go down.

He'd parked his truck in front of the house before approaching her side of the car. His grim countenance was all she needed to see to fear the worst.

She searched his face. "I just had a phone call from Logan's mom about Pierce.''

He frowned. "I was hoping to get here first.''

"How bad is he?'' she cried with her heart in her throat.

"He's going to be fine, Leslie, so stop agonizing.''

"Oh, thank you for telling me that! Thank you!'' She buried her face in her hands in an effort to get her emotions under control.

"Come on.'' He opened the door and helped her out. "I'll drive us to Jackson in your car. We'll pick up Jessica and Cory at school on the way to the hospital.''

Grateful for his support, she got in the passenger side with some assistance. In truth, she felt as weak as a kitten.

''I'm so glad you came.''

''I wouldn't be anywhere else. Pierce is my best friend.''

She knew how close the two men were. ''Tell me what happened to him.''

His head swerved toward hers. ''You don't know?''

''No—only that he'd been taken to the hospital in a helicopter. I guess I was thinking about what happened to Cameron's father, who went to the clinic with a cut hand. I was afraid Pierce might have cut his leg open with a chain saw or something.''

When Nick wasn't more forthcoming, she started to get nervous. ''Why aren't you saying anything?''

She heard his sharp intake of breath. ''He was shot in the shoulder.''

Leslie groaned. ''I don't understand. Did one of the rangers shoot him by accident? Were there wild animals around or something?''

''Or something,'' he muttered, but Leslie heard him.

''Are you telling me it *wasn't* an accident?''

In a few minutes he'd related the details to her. ''At first I thought it could be a random shot from a hunter's rifle. Though hunting's forbidden, it happens. But when a second and third shot were fired, barely missing us, I realized one or both of us was the hunted.''

She felt the blood drain from her face. "You don't have any idea who it was?"

"Off the top of our heads we came up with a few suspects, but it'll be up to the FBI to do a formal investigation."

It was Ed.

"Neither Cory nor Jessica can know about this," she whispered.

"I agree," Nick murmured. "When I phoned in, I asked the guys to keep the details hushed up."

"Thank heaven for your foresight. We'll tell the children his shoulder got cut while he was helping haul a tree away."

He pulled up to the curb in front of the school. "That's as good an explanation as any," he said before she started to get out. "Leslie? There's something else you should know."

She turned haunted eyes to him. "What is it?"

"I've asked that you and the kids be put under twenty-four-hour surveillance in case this is a revenge situation. Don't be surprised if you notice some undercover officers watching the house, following you when you leave."

"I'm glad to hear everyone will be protected. Thank you for telling me."

She felt his concerned gaze on her. "Are you all right? You look so pale. I swear to you Pierce climbed in that helicopter on his own two feet. They'll release him from the hospital in the morning."

"I believe you."

"His only concern was for you and Cory."

She bowed her head.

I know. My wretched cowardice and selfishness

have brought evil to the man and boy I love more than life itself.

I'm the one who deserves to die at Ed's hands, but before that happens I have to talk to Pierce.

"I'll be right back with Cory, then we can drive over to Jessica's school and get her."

"Do you want me to come in with you?" Nick asked. "I'm not sure you're steady enough to go alone."

She shook her head. "I'm fine. Really. I won't be long."

"DADDY?"

When Pierce heard Cory call to him, he breathed his first sigh of relief and opened his eyes. His son came running toward the hospital bed of his private room. A wan-looking Leslie trailed at a distance.

"Come over on this side so I can hug you, champ."

Cory did his bidding, then he stared at him through his glasses. "I heard you got cut by a sharp branch."

Pierce's gaze darted briefly to Leslie's. Her eyes communicated the implicit message that Cory had been spared the truth. Thank God.

"That's true. It caught my shoulder with a jagged end."

"Did you get all bloody?"

"Some."

"Does it hurt?"

"Not now."

"What's that needle in your hand?"

"They're giving me antibiotics so it won't get infected."

"Does it hurt?"

"No."

"Can you go home tonight?"

"I'd like to, but the doctor says I have to stay here until tomorrow so he can give me more antibiotics."

By now Leslie had seated herself in a chair at his other side. She must have seen his son's eyes fill because before Pierce could comfort him, she said, "Guess what, Cory? You can stay in here tonight with your daddy."

His little face lit up like a light bulb. "I can?"

"You bet. I'll ask the nurse to bring in a cot for you. You can sleep right by him and drink pop and juice."

"Hey—this is fun. Will you sleep in here, too?"

"Of course she will," Pierce answered for her. "Leslie's not going anyplace."

"Have you two forgotten Lucy?"

Pierce certainly had.

Cory let out a little gasp and put his hand to his mouth. "Do you think they let puppies in here?"

"No," Leslie declared. "Puppies need to stay home and be taken care of. But I won't leave for Moose until it's time for you to go to bed. How's that?"

"I wish you could bring Lucy to the hospital. If you put her in a box with a lid, nobody would know."

"Maybe not at first. But in the middle of the night she'll start squealing and scare all the patients."

Cory giggled. "You're funny, Leslie."

"It's true. Her squeal is very distinctive."

"Tell me about it," Pierce muttered, loving every moment of this conversation.

"Knock, knock."

He looked up to see Nick in the doorway with Jessica, who appeared a little worried about interrupting.

"How's the prettiest redhead this side of the Continental Divide?"

She grinned.

"Come on in, Jess, and join the party."

"Guess what? I get to stay all night with Daddy."

"How did you work that?" Jessica asked.

"Leslie said I could."

"You're lucky." She walked over to the side of the bed where Cory was perched. "Are you really okay, Pierce?"

"Couldn't be better."

She stared at him in disbelief. "You and Dad are just the same. You could be dying and you would never admit it."

"That's the way men are," Leslie interjected, rolling her eyes. "We're lucky we're women, Jessica. We can moan and groan and soak it for all we're worth, and the men feel sorry for us."

Jessica laughed before giving him a peck on the cheek.

Pierce never ceased to marvel over Leslie's ability to say the right thing to ease a difficult moment. Her timing was brilliant.

Nick put his hands on Cory's shoulders. "I don't know about you, but I haven't eaten since breakfast and I'm starving. How about you and Jessica having dinner with me in the hospital cafeteria, then we'll come back."

You're reading my mind, Nick.

"Do they have cheese pizza?"

"Let's go and find out."

"Come on, Leslie."

Though this was one time he needed to be alone with her, it thrilled Pierce his son had started including her in every aspect of his life. She had a unique quality about her he thought of as the Leslie Effect— natural infiltration more powerful than sorcery.

"Do you know what, Cory? Since I have to go back to Moose tonight, I'd better stay here and talk to the doctor when he comes on his rounds. He'll have instructions on how to take care of your daddy tomorrow after he comes home."

Cory blinked. "Will you have to stay in bed?"

"I don't think so, but I won't be able to work for a few days," Pierce replied.

"Do I have to go to school?"

"Why don't we wait until tomorrow to decide."

"Okay. See ya."

"Thanks," Pierce said, eyeing Nick.

"You're welcome. Come on, guys. I'm so hungry I could eat an elephant."

"No you couldn't," Cory said with a giggle as they left the room.

"I bet Dad would if it was all there was." Jessica's voice carried from the corridor.

Pierce laughed, but Leslie didn't join him.

Now that they were alone, her expression had darkened. He glimpsed pain in her eyes. Excruciating pain. Nick had to have told her the truth. She was blaming herself again.

"Leslie—" he said at the same moment she spoke his name.

"I *know* who shot you, Pierce." The throb of her voice reverberated in the hospital room.

He grimaced. "I do, too, and so does the FBI agent I discussed the case with a little while ago. There's an APB out on Cracroft as we speak."

"Dave? But he's in Salt Lake!"

"I don't think so. Come and sit down by me. You haven't even asked me how I am. Don't you want to hear the whole story?"

"Yes…o-of course I do," she stammered.

"It all started when Nick and I discovered this sign the storm had impaled into the rock. As soon as I'm better, we'll take Cory to see it and get a picture for posterity."

Pierce took his time telling her about his day, hoping to get her mind off the incident.

He thought he'd been making headway when she suddenly cried out, "It wasn't Dave who shot you— It was Ed!

"I know why he didn't kill you today, Pierce. He injured you to warn me that he's here, that he's in control, that I'm his possession and can never get away from him."

A sob escaped her throat. "What terrifies me is that he might be in the hospital right now, waiting to do something worse to you."

Tears gushed down her pale cheeks. "You've *got* to get more protection for you and Cory! You'll only need it as long as I'm here. If I leave the park tonight, he'll follow me because it's *me* he wants. Then the two of you will be safe. That's why I told Cory I couldn't spend the nigh—"

"Hi, Daddy!" His son came bouncing into the

room followed by Jessica and Nick. "They didn't have pizza, but the lady made me a peanut butter and jelly sandwich."

"That was nice of her." His gaze flicked to Nick. "How was the elephant steak?"

Jessica bubbled with laughter.

"They had something else on the menu tonight. I'm not sure what it was, but it filled me up."

"It was chicken-fried steak and I thought it was yummy."

"That's what it was?"

"Dad—" she chided her father, who wore a dead-pan expression.

"So how is our patient feeling?"

If only you knew.

"I have to admit I'm tired."

"So am I," Nick said. "If you're ready, Leslie, we'll go."

"There's been a change in plans," Pierce announced, ignoring Leslie's agonized expression. "Leslie has decided to sleep over after all."

"Goody," Cory blurted.

"There's only one problem."

"I'll take care of Lucy tonight!" Jessica cried out with an eagerness Pierce had been counting on. "Can I, Dad?"

Nick had picked up on Pierce's radar. "Of course."

"You're sure?"

"It's the least we can do for our chief."

"Thanks. The house key is the silver one on the chain with the car key."

His friend held them up. "Give me a call tomorrow, Pierce, and we'll come for you."

"Sounds good. I owe you."

His friend smiled. "You said that before."

Cory ran over to Jessica. "Tell Lucy I'll see her tomorrow."

"I will. Bye."

As soon as they left, the night nurse came in to hook up another bag of antibiotics and check his vital signs. "The doctor will be in shortly."

Pierce glanced at the clock. It was getting close to 9:00 p.m. "We're going to need two cots in here tonight. Can you arrange that?"

She looked around. "It'll be a squeeze, but if you can stand the togetherness, it's fine with me."

Togetherness was exactly what the doctor ordered. "We don't want to be disturbed."

"With two security guards outside your door, that's not going to happen."

"How come there are guards?" Cory asked.

"Because your father is a very important person. Even the governor called the desk a few minutes ago to find out how he was doing."

"Daddy's friends with the governor."

"That doesn't surprise me at all."

"Could we have a couple of cans of root beer and cola?"

"Sure thing."

After she left, Cory said, "Can I call Logan and Cameron and tell them I'm staying here tonight?"

The look of fear in Leslie's eyes needed no translation. The last thing Cory needed to hear was that Pierce had been shot.

"It's too late to phone, champ. You can talk to them tomorrow after we're home."

Another knock on the door sounded before a woman from housekeeping came in pushing a folded-up cot. Pierce watched Leslie rush to her assistance. Soon she had both cots extended end to end on his good side.

"You can lie by your daddy. First let's get your shoes and socks off. I'll put them on this table." In the process, the doctor came in. He smiled to see the setup.

"There's nothing like home sweet home."

"You got that right," Pierce quipped.

The doctor examined the wound. "It looks good."

"Can my daddy go home tomorrow?"

"I don't see why not."

Once he'd left, any residual anxiety had vanished from Cory's face. He climbed on top of the cot and sat cross-legged. Leslie had just removed her shoes when the nurse swept in with four cans of soda and some crackers.

"This looks cozy."

"We're very happy. Thank you for everything," Pierce told her.

Leslie handed everyone a pop. Finally they were settled and alone.

"Can we watch the weather channel, Daddy?"

Pierce pressed the remote. Good weather was forecast for the rest of the week, but there was a bad tornado in Louisiana. Cory's exclamation over a bathtub being the only thing left of a house prompted Pierce to tell him about the sign embedded in the rock where the rangers had been clearing away the trees.

"I want to see it!"

"We will when I'm better."

IT MUST HAVE BEEN THE middle of the night when a noise brought Leslie awake. She thought it was Cory until she saw Pierce coming out of the bathroom wheeling the stand holding his IV.

Leslie couldn't believe he was so calm and in control. You would never know by his seemingly relaxed, contented demeanor that he'd narrowly escaped death today. Or that he was pretending it was Dave Cracroft who'd shot at him when they both knew it could have been Ed.

Once again she suffered remorse over her actions—actions that had caused Pierce to end up in the hospital. Though her conscience had screamed at her not to get involved on that very first day, she hadn't listened.

She'd felt a force emanating from Pierce, a nobility of manhood that drew her like a magnet. Combined with her compassion for his motherless son, she could no more have walked away from them than she could have stopped breathing.

To her shock, instead of his going right back to bed, he moved in her direction and sat down on the side of the cot, forcing her to make room for him.

"Shh…" He put a finger to her lips to prevent her from talking. "I've been on the phone with Roger. He agrees with me that the chance of Ed being the one who took shots at me and Nick is very remote. It would make a lot more sense if Ed had broken into the house to kidnap you while you were there alone today."

"But—"

"But nothing. There's no reason to assume that just because he hasn't returned to New York, he knows where you are. I'm still firmly convinced Dave Cracroft is the culprit. Nick happens to agree with me and I'd trust his instincts over anyone else's conjectures."

Tears blurred her vision. "Oh, Pierce—if anything had happened to you today…" When she realized she was on the verge of blurting her love, she buried her face in the pillow.

His hand slid up her back to massage her heaving shoulders. "As long as you stay with me, nothing's going to happen to any of us."

She turned on her side to look at him out of tear-drenched eyes. "Maybe you're right about Dave. Even if you are, and it wasn't Ed who fired that rifle today, it's only a matter of time before that madman comes."

Pierce's jaw hardened. "Let him. He'll have to get past me first." He brushed her lips with his own before rising to his full, intimidating height. "Go to sleep, Leslie. You need it more than I do."

MIDMORNING ON SUNDAY, Pierce entered the conference room at headquarters, surprising the group of rangers, law enforcement officers and FBI assembled around the oval table. They took one look at him and broke into spontaneous applause.

He smiled. "It's good to see you, too."

Rex caught his eye across the expanse. "You weren't supposed to come to work until tomorrow at the earliest."

"I have things to do." The sling was a pain to wear, but it helped remind him not to make sudden movements. The doctor had cautioned him to keep his arm stationary until the wound had sufficiently healed.

Leslie had waited on him hand and foot, treating him with a nurse's strict professionalism. Cory had been home both days, so there'd been no opportunity for a long, frank talk with her about his feelings. But all that was about to change.

He turned to Dan Riker, the FBI agent. "What's the latest on Cracroft?"

"We know he hasn't kept any of his appointments at University Hospital since Monday. His motel room is under surveillance, but there's been no activity.

"The guys think he may be getting around on a motorcycle, so they're vetting every new and used dealership between Jackson and Salt Lake for information.

"One of the guys located his storage shed in Jackson and confiscated a rifle and shotgun from the facility. The forensics lab is checking to see if they were recently fired. A ballistics report on the bullets at the crime scene should tell us if there's a match."

Pierce rubbed his chin where he'd nicked himself shaving earlier. "You probably won't find one. Knowing Dave, he planned this out long before Thursday and has a secret cache of weapons and food in the backcountry where he can hold up indefinitely. I'm going with you to look for him."

"No way," Dan declared. "You're barely out of the hospital."

"You need me. Your men haven't grown up in these mountains. I have. Let's plan our strategy."

AFTER LESLIE HAD DRIVEN Cory over to Logan's house, she called Nick on his cell phone.

Please answer—

He picked up on the fourth ring. "Leslie?"

"Yes."

"I saw the caller ID. I'm still having trouble thinking of you as Leslie instead of Diana."

"It's a struggle for Cory, too."

"How's the patient today?"

"You know how he is, Nick." Her voice trembled. "I overheard him talking to you this morning, and I know that *you* know what he's planning." Her hand tightened on the phone. "You have to stop him!"

There was a ten-second silence on the other end before he said, "This has been coming on for a long time, Leslie. It's something Pierce has to do. It's the way he's made."

Leslie knew that.

"But he's still recovering from a gunshot wound. That makes him too vulnerable to do this."

After another period of quiet Nick followed with "He won't be alone. This is a manhunt for the experts. Pierce is the expert of them all."

"Nick—I can't stay here knowing he'll be out there. Let me ride with you. I promise not to get in the way. Just let me be there in the background."

"No, Leslie. The only reason Pierce can do this is because he knows you'll be home safe with Cory."

"Cory's at Logan's, where he's perfectly safe. But I can't stay here waiting in helpless agony. Let me help provide backup. I'm no stranger to mountains. You can show me how to load and fire a gun. For once in my life I'd like to be an asset instead of a liability.''

"Leslie…''

"I heard Pierce tell you he was going to leave at noon from work with the other men. I can be ready to go whenever you say. My only problem is, I don't have any gear.''

Again there was silence before he said, "I'll round up what you need and come by for you as soon as I can.''

Her eyes closed tightly. "Thank you.''

"You realize he may never speak to either one of us again.''

"I don't care. I have to be close to him. You don't understand.'' Her voice throbbed. "I don't think I could live without him now.''

"He's a lucky man to be loved by a woman like you.''

Her breath caught. "I was just going to say Pierce is blessed to have a friend who would lay down his life for him. That's you, Nick. I'm in awe of both of you.''

PIERCE KNEW EXACTLY WHERE Cracroft had set up camp.

Years before, when the two of them had been part of a search-and-rescue team looking for signs of a plane that had gone down, Pierce remembered Dave's comments about Berry Creek in the north end of the park.

"If a man wanted to hide from the world, this would be the place."

He knew Cracroft was waiting for him to come. That's what the shooting had been all about. To gain Pierce's attention and draw him to the remote spot— a place where two nine-hundred-pound male grizzlies could fight for supremacy of the territory.

That's how Dave saw the two of them. Survival of the fittest, because there was only room for one. But he'd made sure Pierce would come handicapped, because in his mind Pierce had handicapped *him* over the years.

October was a dangerous time of year, when the grizzlies who'd foraged into the park from the Yellowstone area headed to their dens in a crevice or a cave to sleep until spring. Their body temperatures didn't alter much, which meant they could be easily aroused by sound.

Dave would like that…driving the stakes higher to increase the risk that one of them wasn't going to make it out alive. It was a region even the most experienced mountaineers didn't like to navigate without a map or compass.

A two-day-old layer of snow couldn't hide the signs of recent grizzly activity. The group of thirty men had split up to cover the area where they figured Dave might hide. By the time Pierce had hiked seven miles in with a couple of the rangers, he'd seen fresh scat, paw prints, insect-mound diggings, dead hair and elk kill.

He'd trekked through burned-out forest and new forest, but it wasn't until he'd plunged down the steep ravine toward Berry Creek that he spotted human footprints. Gravity made his wound throb, but his elation in picking up Dave's trail counteracted any discomfort.

There were two hours of daylight left, enough time to put the handcuffs on him and send for a helicopter. He scanned the terrain before finding himself an outcropping of rocks that would give him protection. Using a hand signal, he warned the other two rangers to hold back. This was Pierce's fight.

Wedging himself between two slabs he shouted, "Cracroft? I'm here!"

Rifle shot struck rock directly above his head. The trajectory told him that he'd surprised the other man by coming in on the same side of the ravine.

"It's no use, Dave. There's a manhunt on for you."

"Go to hell, Gallagher!"

Cracroft couldn't be more than three hundred yards off.

"When they catch up to you, you'll be shot on sight. Let me take you in walking on your own two feet so you can get the help you need."

"I don't want your pity. I never wanted it," he ground out.

Pity?

Pierce rolled the word over on his tongue.

No… He wouldn't want another man's pity, either. It meant you weren't a man.

"So how do you want to do this, Dave?"

The answer came with a barrage of bullets. One whistled past Pierce's injured shoulder and ricocheted off the rocks. That meant Dave was gaining ground on him. That was good. It was exactly what Pierce wanted him to do.

He hunkered down and waited, listening for every sound.

Dave could track without making any noise. But he was fighting for his life now. In a minute Pierce would be able to hear labored breathing, because the human body responded with a mind of its own when it went into survival mode. It was something Dave wouldn't be able to hide.

Sure enough Pierce finally picked up a noise, but it wasn't human. The hair on his body stood up on end. He'd heard those same rasping huffs years before. They summoned the terrifying memory of his teenage friend being mauled to death.

Suddenly a great roar resounded in the ravine. More rifle shots rang out, followed by Dave's high-pitched cry of panic. Pierce climbed to the top of the boulder in time to witness Cracroft struggling to outrun what looked like a seven-hundred-pound grizzly.

The rifle fell from the other man's hands in an attempt to scale the nearest lodgepole pine, but he wasn't fast enough. Pierce raced down the ravine to close the gap between them.

"Help me, Gallagher!" His screams mingled with the bear's snarls.

On its hind legs now, the ravined grizzly pawed at Dave's left leg. Probably a hundred yards away from them, Pierce saw blood stream down the trunk as those four-inch claws ripped away leather and fabric to make strips of Dave's flesh. Pulling out his .416 Magnum loaded with four-hundred-grain bullets, Pierce took dead aim for the back of the bear's head and fired. Frenzied by the shock, it turned its great hulk of a body in Pierce's direction. It was still on its hind legs, smelling the air to get a sense of its surroundings.

The splendid creature who'd been minding his own business before being wrested from his den looked at Pierce the way one man acknowledges another before a fight to the death. It should have gone down already.

Before he took aim one more time, because that was all he was going to get, Pierce's last thought was what a tragic waste of both animal and human.

"I've got him!" Nick's unexpected voice sounded from the periphery. A final shot rang out. It toppled the bear. Pierce could see Dave dangling from the tree. The man had lost so much blood he'd gone into shock.

He turned to thank his friend for being his friend, but it was someone else who came running. Someone beautifully familiar. His heart pounded in his chest cavity as she came toward him.

"Pierce—"

When Leslie reached him, she clutched him around the chest in a hug as fierce as any bear's. "Pierce—" She cried his name over and over again, turning his agony into ecstasy. "Oh, darling—"

The gun fell to the ground as he crushed her in his arms. "Leslie—" he murmured before feverishly kissing her face, her eyes, her nose, her hair, her mouth.

"I love you," she whispered, kissing him long and hard until neither of them could breathe.

"Does this mean you're going to marry me? I've been in love with you from the beginning."

"So have I with you," she confessed, "but you know as well as I do Ed's a reality that's not going to go away. I can't do that to you.'' He felt her shudder resonate through his body. ''You've barely escaped death twice this week.''

He could hear two helicopters approaching. Before the world descended on them he wanted a commitment from her.

Kneading her arms, he said, ''You didn't answer my question, sweetheart.''

''Because I can't!'' She tried to pull away from him. He refused to let her go. A man would kill for the kind of love he saw coming from her eyes, but he also glimpsed raw pain in those haunted gold depths.

''It's my job to protect you, for better or worse.''

''With him alive it will always be for worse!'' her cry rang out.

''We'll deal with it.''

''You've forgotten Cory.''

He drew in a deep breath. ''What about my son?''

''I know he has learned to like me, but that's as far as it goes. On the way up, Nick was telling me about Jessica's fears. She has tolerated the few women he's had a relationship with, but there's all the difference in the world between like and love.''

Pierce tightened his hands on her shoulders. ''Let me tell you something, my love. If Nick had ever been able to give his heart to another woman, he wouldn't have let Jessica's feelings stand in the way. Unfortunately he's never met a woman to make him forget Samantha.

''Our situation's entirely different. All you have to do is remember how much Cory wanted you to stay at the hospital with us to know he'll embrace our marriage.''

"I don't think so," she said in a tremulous voice. "When you left for work this morning he acted like he'd lost his best friend. If, God forbid, anything happened to you, he wouldn't turn to me for comfort.''

He shifted his weight. "Nothing will happen to me, and the three of us are going to become a family.''

"No, Pierce—" She pulled out of his arms. "Wanting something doesn't necessarily make it so. Your little boy's psyche could be damaged beyond repair if we were to act too fast. A-and I could never be the wife I want to be to you knowing Ed is after me.

"For once in my life I'm going to do the right thing, the unselfish thing for everyone concerned, including *my* family. After I've helped you find a new nanny, I'm returning to New York.''

He saw black. "You call leaving me and Cory *unselfish?*''

"Hey, you two?" Nick spoke from a distance. "The chopper's waiting to fly us back to our trucks.''

"Answer me, Leslie!" he demanded, barely able to suppress his pain.

She averted her eyes. "We have to go.''

Without waiting for him, she hurried toward Nick. The agents in the other chopper had already loaded Dave and the other rangers inside and were taking off.

Shattered by her intransigence, Pierce picked up his gun and started after her. There had to be a way to reach her. He just had to figure out how....

After helping Leslie, Nick climbed inside. Pierce

followed with a private, heartfelt thank-you to his friend. After he shut the door, the pilot turned his head toward him. ''What do you want to do about the bear?''

''I'll contact Bill Shiffers. It's one of the radio-collared grizzlies his team is tracking. They'll be up tomorrow to take a look.''

''It's a damn shame.'' With those words the pilot turned on the motor.

''It's a tragedy,'' Pierce muttered, staring straight at Leslie.

CHAPTER FIFTEEN

THE TENSION INSIDE THE truck's cab was so unbearable, Leslie was grateful Pierce had official business to conduct on their way back to Moose. He made a dozen phone calls to the various men involved in the Cracroft manhunt. The conversations with the FBI agent and the governor were particularly revealing.

Word of the shooting earlier in the week had made the national news, attracting publicity to Pierce and the park. Unbeknownst to him, Leslie had filmed everything today including the moment when the grizzly had faced Pierce on its hind legs, ready to lunge.

That benchmark photograph, showing Pierce staring death in the face to save the man who'd shot him, would be the visible expression of her photographic essay titled Heroes in Peril: Meet the Teton Rangers.

Tonight when she couldn't sleep, she would finish writing it up. Tomorrow she would get the film developed and express-mail the photos and the disk to Roger's office. He could send a runner who would put the plain white envelope on her boss's desk at the *Chronicler.*

The photo essay would steal Lewis Fry's thunder, the journalist who'd been covering the news about the shooting for one of the cable channels. If she never accomplished another thing in her life, Leslie was grateful her profession would enable her to glorify Pierce and the rangers in a way no one else could do.

Night had fallen by the time he'd dropped her off at the house before driving to headquarters for a debriefing. While Pierce was still talking to Rex Hollister, Leslie opened the door of the truck and jumped out.

On the way in the front door, she phoned Logan's mom and asked her to bring Cory and Lucy home.

The other woman had already heard the news about Dave. "It was a horrible thing to happen, but I'm glad he's been stopped."

"So am I," Leslie murmured.

"Where's Pierce?"

"At headquarters by now."

"Is he all right?"

"Yes, but even if he weren't, we'd never know about it."

"My husband's the same way. He phoned me when the news got out about Dave and the grizzly. He's probably over there by now, too."

"How's Cory?"

"Do you know he has complained of a stomachache all afternoon?"

"You're kidding!"

"No. He didn't want dinner. I tried to get him to drink some ginger ale, but he didn't want that, either. It'll probably go away as soon as he walks in your house."

"I don't understand. It doesn't make sen— Oh, wait. Oh, no—" Leslie moaned. "I just remembered something. Neither of us had our cell phones turned on while we were hiking into Berry Creek."

"If he couldn't get you on the phone, that might be the reason. Then again maybe he has caught a bug."

"None of his friends are sick."

"The only thing that seemed to make him feel better was Lucy. She's entertained us all afternoon."

"Thank you for helping out today. You'll never know what it meant to me."

"I think I do. Pierce is a real heartbreaker."

Both Gallaghers were heartbreakers.

"We're leaving now. Be there in a second."

Leslie had barely hung up the jacket and taken off the boots Nick had loaned her when she heard Cory come in the front door.

"Leslie?"

"I'm in my bedroom!"

Tears filled her eyes the second she saw him in the doorway with Lucy at his heels. She loved him so much.

"How come you're here?" No boy should be wearing such a solemn expression. His question totally bewildered her. "Where else would I be?"

"In New York."

Her thoughts reeled. "Why would you think that?"

"'Cos."

"Oh, Cory—" she groaned. "You thought I'd gone away without telling you? Is that why you didn't feel good today?"

He nodded. His lower lip quivered.

"I would never do that to you."

"How come you didn't answer your phone?" he asked in a croaky voice.

She knew it!

"When I went to Jackson shopping with Nick, I forgot it was turned off."

"Daddy didn't answer his phone, either." A tear trickled down his cheek.

"Sometimes he can't if he has an emergency."

Cory stared at her. "Daddy said you promised to stay a whole year, but I don't ever want you to go away."

Her heart started to beat faster. "I won't if you don't want me to."

His face grew animated. "You won't?"

"No. I would miss you too much. I love you, Cory." There. She'd dared to say it at last.

"I love you, too."

They both reached for each other at the same time. Leslie didn't know a hug could last such a long, long time.

PIERCE STOOD IN THE DOORWAY watching and listening. The thing he'd been praying for had finally come to pass. He walked into her bedroom and pulled Cory onto the bed with him to give him a hug.

"Daddy!"

"The next time Leslie flies to New York to visit, we'll all go together."

"Can we go to New Jersey, too?"

When Leslie didn't say anything, Pierce found her hand and clasped it. "That's the first place we'll go so you can play with your cousins."

Cory blinked. "Cousins?"

"That's what Josh and Amy will be after Leslie marries me."

His statement sent a quiver through her body he

could feel. It also put the happiest smile on his son's face he'd ever seen. "Are you going to marry my daddy?"

"Do you want me to?"

"Yes. Don't you want to marry him?"

"More than anything in the world."

"You love him a lot, huh?"

"I love both of you, Cory."

Pierce squeezed her hand. "Then it's settled."

"Daddy? Can I call Logan and Cameron and tell them Leslie's going to be my new mommy?"

"Tomorrow morning you can phone anyone you want and announce that Leslie and I are engaged."

"But when's the wedding?"

"That's something we'll have to talk about later. Let's go out to the kitchen. I haven't had dinner yet and I'm starving."

"Me, too. Come on, Lucy."

Pierce held Leslie back when she started to follow Cory out of the room. He turned her to face him. She still had shadows in her eyes.

"I heard my son tell you he loved you, so you *have* to marry me now. After Linda died, I honestly didn't believe I could ever love another woman again, let alone with the kind of excitement and passion I felt as a younger man.

"Yet, here I am, holding and loving another woman whose beauty takes my breath away, who causes me to tremble when I even think of her. I don't have to wonder what kind of a mother she'll make, because she has already won my son's heart."

"Darling—"

He cupped her cheeks in his hands. "Let's not

worry about Ed Strickland. If or when he comes, he'll have to deal with me. What he has done to you is criminal, but if you let fear of him deprive us of a glorious future, that would be the greater crime.''

Her eyes fused with his. ''I know you're right. It's just that Cory's so young and vulnerable. I couldn't bear it if he were to come to any harm because Ed had tracked me down.''

Pierce shook his head. ''It's not going to happen. You saw his reaction today when he thought you'd gone back to New York. That's the only way he could ever be hurt.

''He can't wait to tell his friends you're going to be his new mother. You won him over with gentleness and infinite patience. What he feels for you goes soul-deep.

''I can relate,'' he whispered against her lips. ''When you came running to me in the ravine and I saw the look of love in your eyes, my being literally quaked.''

''Mine's quaking now—'' she cried, pressing her mouth urgently to his.

''I thought you were hungry, Daddy.''

With a moan of protest, he finally tore his lips from hers. ''I'm ravenous, Cory.'' But he was staring into her eyes as he said it.

''What does *ravenous* mean?''

A blushing Leslie turned in his arms so she faced Cory. ''It means he could eat an elephant.''

''That isn't quite what I had in mind,'' Pierce whispered, biting her earlobe. She laughed softly before escaping him.

''Do people really eat elephants?'' Cory asked as

the three of them headed for the other part of the house.

"Several of the guides on my trip to Malaysia ate stew made from the trunk of one."

"Ew. Did you eat it?"

"No. I had chicken, at least I think that's what it was."

Pierce never knew what was going to come out of her. He burst into laughter and gave her another squeeze once they'd reached the kitchen. The need to have constant physical contact with her had become an all-consuming need.

"D-do you want some chicken nuggets?" The betraying stammer told Pierce she craved his touch every bit as badly.

"No, thanks. Can I have a peanut butter and jelly sandwich?"

"That sounds good to me, too," Pierce murmured against her neck. "And a quart of milk. And after Cory goes back to bed, I'll have you for dessert."

DIANA THOUGHT SHE WAS dreaming that the phone was ringing, but when it seemed to go on forever, her eyelids fluttered open. She rose up on one elbow.

"Roger?" She shook his shoulder. "Your cell phone's ringing. It might be Leslie." He made a sound of protest. Who could blame him? It was only three-thirty in the morning. "Honey? Get the phone."

A grunting noise came out of him before he found it and said hello. Suddenly he sat up, wide-awake. "We'll be right down."

Alarmed, Diana scrambled out of her side of the bed and reached for her robe. "What's wrong?"

"That was Detective Santini. He's outside in the driveway and needs to talk to us ASAP."

She felt so sick, she swayed. "You don't think—"

"Don't jump to conclusions!" He so rarely snapped at her, she knew her husband was petrified, too. After he slipped on some sweats and a T-shirt, they hurried downstairs to let the detective inside.

"This is my partner, Detective Pandakis."

Roger invited them into the living room. Diana clung to his side as they sat down.

"Before I tell you the reason we're here, I need answers to a few questions." Detective Santini looked at Diana. "Is there someone who can vouch for your whereabouts at one o'clock your time yesterday afternoon?"

Diana blinked. She felt Roger's hand squeeze hers. "After I picked up Josh from kindergarten I was out doing errands with the children. We stopped at the Redman Nursery about that time to pick up a flat of geraniums. If you talk to the salesperson who waited on me, I'm sure he'd remember me."

"Do you have a sales slip? It'll show the time."

"I think it's still in the wastebasket under the kitchen sink."

"Mind if I take a look?" Detective Pandakis asked.

"No."

"What about you, Mr. Farrow?"

"I was at my office taking a deposition from a client. The time can be confirmed by my secretary as well as the recorded disk on the computer."

"What's your secretary's phone number?"

By the time the detective had talked with the other

woman and the other man had found the sales slip, Diana was dying inside.

"Thanks for your cooperation," Detective Santini said. "Now I can tell you that Edward Strickland was found dead in a Boulder, Colorado, hotel room yesterday."

Diana was incredulous. "Ed's dead?"

"That's right. He died of a gunshot wound to the head from a gun found near the body. It could have been self-inflicted, but there was no suicide note. Murder hasn't been ruled out."

Murder—

"The time of death was estimated at 11:00 a.m. Colorado time. A maid didn't discover the body until 7:00 p.m., at which time the hotel manager called the police.

"Once the information was fed into the police station in Manhattan, one of the guys recognized Strickland as the stalker on the case I was working on. He contacted me and that's why I came over here."

Diana stared at her husband. "I can't believe Ed's gone."

"Neither can I," Roger muttered, fully aware of what was going through the detective's mind. They all had a motive for killing Ed.

"Have you questioned Maureen Strickland?"

"We're looking for her now."

"What about Leslie? Does she know what's happened?"

"I'm sure she's being told and questioned as we speak."

"You can't seriously think Leslie had anything to do with his death!" Diana cried.

"Honey—" Roger put his arm around her. "Everyone's a suspect until they rule murder out."

"That's ridiculous!"

"Not to the police. If anyone had motive, she did. So did Maureen. But when the police are given proof Leslie was in Moose at the time he died, they'll cross her off the list. Honey? Did you check our e-mail before we went to bed?"

"Yes. There's nothing from anyone."

Roger turned to Detective Santini. "Maybe Ed left a message on Leslie's answering machine at the apartment."

The other man pulled out his cell phone once more. "Tell me how to retrieve her messages."

After Roger gave him instructions, the detective sat there listening for such a long time, Diana was jumping out of her skin.

"Here—listen to these," he finally said to Detective Pandakis.

Another long wait ensued before he handed the phone back to his partner with a nod.

Detective Santini's eyes flicked from Roger to Diana. "From the sound of it, Ed Strickland took his own life. The death of another human should never be a cause for celebration, but certainly in your sister's case, it ends the nightmare for all of you.

"I'll get in touch with the detective in Colorado. Combined with all your documentation, plus the video footage gathered by Rita Cardenas, it'll give him what he needs to wrap things up."

"*Roger!*" Diana shouted for joy the second the two men went out the front door. The happiness on her face as he turned to her was something he'd remember for the rest of his life.

"Mommy?" Josh called to her from the stairway landing. "What's happening?"

"We're celebrating because your aunt Leslie doesn't have to worry about Ed anymore." She sounded as euphoric as Roger felt.

"How come?" Josh wanted to know.

"Ed died tonight. No one knows why, but we do know one thing. He'll never be able to frighten anyone again."

"That's good. I want her to come home."

"I do, too. At least for a visit. I've got to call her, Roger."

"While you do that, I'll phone Mom and Dad and give them the good news. Come with me, sport. We'll tell them together." He grabbed Josh and disappeared upstairs.

IT WAS FOUR O'CLOCK IN THE morning when Leslie heard her cell phone ring. She jerked in Pierce's arms, but he held her fast. "I'll answer it."

She'd been half lying against him on the couch all night. Cory was asleep on the loveseat with Lucy, both of them covered with a blanket. After the harrowing experience in the mountains with Dave, the four of them needed to be together and just hold one another.

"It's Diana," he said after checking the caller ID.

This had to be news about Ed. Maybe the P.I. had tracked him to Salt Lake. What a painful irony just when Leslie couldn't wait to tell her sister she and Pierce were engaged.

"Leslie and Cory were here at eleven," she heard him say. "I was over at headquarters. Why?"

While Leslie was forced to wait for an explanation, a transformation suddenly came over Pierce. The lines of tension on his handsome face disappeared, yet his eyes studied her with a solemn expression. "Just a minute, Diana. I have to tell her—"

"Tell me what, darling?"

"Ed Strickland was found dead in a Boulder, Colorado, hotel room yesterday. The police believe it's a suicide, but there's still an investigation going on."

Leslie stared at Pierce while the news sank in. She could scarcely comprehend it. "Ed's really dead?"

He gave her a sober nod. "It happened about eleven yesterday morning."

Like someone in a trance, she slowly reached for the phone. "Diana?"

"Honey? I know you must be in shock right now, but it's true. Detective Santini just left the house. I hope God will forgive me for saying this, but I'm glad Ed's gone."

Tears trickled down Leslie's cheeks. "I am, too," she whispered. "Maybe now he'll find peace. He was just too sick. Oh, Diana—I can't believe it's over."

"Believe it, and embrace your new life with Pierce."

"I already have," her voice trembled. "We got engaged last night."

"Honey!"

Her sister's cry was filled with all the happiness and joy in the world. "We'll talk later. Right now you need Pierce, and he needs you." The line went dead.

Leslie clicked off, still in a state of shock.

"Sweetheart?" Pierce had barely murmured the endearment when his house phone rang. He let go of her with reluctance. "That'll be the police, I'm sure of it."

Those were prophetic words. After she'd followed him into the kitchen and he'd answered it, he whispered, "There's a detective outside the house. He wants to come in and ask us a few questions."

Leslie nodded.

After he hung up, he pulled her tightly against him. "So many emotions to deal with all at once. I know there's a part of you that's going to grieve for a while. Ed must have had a lot of good qualities, otherwise a woman as remarkable as you would never have fallen in love with him."

Leslie hadn't thought she could love Pierce more, but she was wrong....

CHAPTER SIXTEEN

"AND SO WE REMEMBER Edward Strickland as a beloved son and a fine journalist who has gone home to join his parents and find eternal peace. Let us pray."

The pastor of the church Ed had occasionally attended bowed his head to give the final benediction.

Cory held one of Leslie's hands. Pierce clasped the other and pressed it against his heart.

As she heard the words of the prayer, her mind traveled back to the farewell message Ed had left on her answering machine. He hadn't been able to handle being fired from the paper. He hadn't been able to handle a failed marriage and a failed engagement.

Before the funeral Leslie had met with Maureen. They'd talked about Ed's sad childhood, how he'd been orphaned and abandoned in Africa, which must have left an indelible mark on his psyche.

Though other missionary couples had tried to help raise him, his grief had caused him to turn to a more worldly life. But his soul was always at war. He believed a woman was supposed to stay at a man's side like his mother had done, yet he'd been attracted to women who wanted to have more active roles of their own. In the end, he broke.

The reign of terror was finally over. Ed's spirit had

left his body. Leslie could finally believe it. She felt herself let it all go.

In the next instant she looked into Pierce's eyes and saw the promise of a glorious future in them. His smile was too sweet. It filled her heart with joy.

A LATE NOVEMBER STORM had swept into the Tetons and hadn't let up yet. The wind moaned eerily around the eaves of the little cabin at Grayson's and pelted the windows with snow. It might be ten degrees in the white world outside, but Leslie was so on fire for her gorgeous new husband, she was oblivious to the elements.

The rapture of his lovemaking throughout the night had been a revelation. She would never be able to get enough of him. It was embarrassing how much she ached to know his possession again.

"Mrs. Gallagher?" came her bridegroom's low, vibrant voice in the early hours of the morning. "Are you awake?"

"Yes—" Leslie lay on her side with her back against the warmth of his hair-roughened chest. She'd never known such happiness in her life.

"Then why aren't you doing something about it?"

A wave of heat rose from the tips of her toes to the crown of her head. "Because I haven't left you alone since we got into bed."

"If you think I want to be left alone, then you don't know me at all. I need you, sweetheart."

The longing in his voice had her turning to him in a frenzy of want. With their bodies entangled, he started kissing her again until the heat of passion burned hotter and hotter, filling them both with the kind of ecstasy that left them breathless and trembling.

"I love you," he cried into her hair several hours later. "As traumatic as your past nightmare was, I can't be sorry it brought you into my world. When I think what I would have missed if you hadn't answered my ad."

"I've been thinking about that all night, darling." She found his mouth and kissed him with almost primitive savagery. It was shocking to realize she was capable of such violent sensual emotion where he was concerned.

"Deep down I was so excited when you sent a ranger to bring me back to headquarters," she admitted. "I felt an intense attraction to you the second you strode into your office. In or out of uniform, you're a spectacular man, Pierce Gallagher, and you're all mine."

His fingers twined in her hair. "All that day while I was working at Lizard Creek waiting for three o'clock to come, I nursed this secret dread that you were some desperate female out to snag herself a husband at any cost. But it was love at first sight for both of us. Somewhere inside of ourselves, we both knew it."

She slid on top of him, kissing every inch of his face and hair. "I *was* a very desperate female, convinced there was no man alive I could trust. But the second I looked into those fierce blue eyes of yours, I felt myself falling through space toward you."

He crushed her against him. "If they looked fierce it was because your intelligence and beauty terrified me. I hadn't expected someone like you to come into my life.

"My emotions rocketed from one end of the scale to the other. Would you turn out to be all the wonderful things your presence, your essence, seemed to promise?"

"I had the opposite problem." She kissed his compelling male mouth again, unable to help herself. "I didn't have to wonder anything about you. I knew in an instant Chief Ranger Gallagher was the man my heart had been looking for all my life.

"But would this rugged individualist, secure in his world, want me? At the end of the day, would this ultimate protector and loving father of an adorable boy named Cory be able to look past my faults?

"Would he be able to forgive me when it was truth time and I had to tell him I'd virtually lied about everything, beginning with my name?" Her voice quavered.

Pierce's eyes grew moist. "You know the answer to all those questions."

"I adore you, Pierce. I love you, I love you, I love you," she murmured against his mouth until they were driven to find fulfillment once more. Leslie lost all track of time and place. When one of their phones rang, Pierce groaned his displeasure.

"Let it ring, sweetheart. We only got married in the park chapel yesterday afternoon. We're on our honeymoon."

"Darling—you know it's Cory."

"But he's at our house with Lucy and your family having the time of his life."

"One day he'll have the time of his life away from

us, but right now he still needs reassurance we're here.''

''It's your fault he can always reach us.'' With low laughter rumbling out of him, he reached for the phone. Leslie nestled closer against him.

''Hi, champ. Yup. We're so happy we can't believe it.'' His eyes played over her face while they chatted for a minute. ''She's right here.''

Pierce handed her the phone, but he continued to kiss her neck and shoulders.

''H-hi, darling. Are you having a good time with Amy and Josh?''

''Yes. We've been outside building a snowman with Uncle Roger and Nick and Jessica. Lucy's scared of it and keeps barking.''

''Oh, the poor little thing.''

''How come you haven't come home yet? Aunt Diana and Josh's grandparents have fixed a big lunch and everyone's hungry!''

''We're on our way.''

''Okay. Hurry!''

''We will.''

''I love you.''

''I love you, too.''

Pierce took the phone out of her hand and hung up.

''I love you, too,'' he mimicked her.

Leslie looked down at the man she'd married. ''Have I told you there's no place I'd rather be than in my ranger's arms?''

He smiled. ''All night long. You're sure you're not going to miss your job at the paper?''

''Darling—I started out as a freelance photographer. The layout I did on you and the Teton Rangers is going to be published soon. There'll be more layouts and photo shoots on dozens of subjects I'll continue doing for the rest of my life. But this is the season when true love came into mine. Who knows if more children are waiting to belong to our family. I don't want to miss a second of it.''

"Neither do I." He kissed her long and passionately. "I want to stay in this bed with you forever."

"So do I, but our son won't let us, and there's always tonight when I'm alone with you again. And tomorrow night, and the next and the next for the rest of our lives."

"I'll remind you of that the first time you tell me you've got a headache."

She laughed before kissing the end of his nose. "I don't get headaches, you lucky man."

"I'm so lucky, it's scary." His voice sounded shaky.

"According to our son, chief rangers don't get scared."

"It's a lie."

"I'll never tell as long as you give me one more kiss to sustain me."

The phone rang again.

As they scrambled to get ready, happy laughter swelled beyond the confines of the little snow-swept cabin to the very tip of the Granddaddy Teton standing guard over them.

* * * * *

Watch for Nick's story
Coming in October 2004

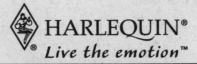

BOUND *for* TEMPTATION

A Frontiers of the Heart Novel

TESS LESUE

Praise for *Bound for Eden*

"Western aficionados will welcome a refreshing new voice in the sub-genre."
—RT Book Reviews

"I look forward to the next book by Tess LeSue."
—The Reading Cafe

"Lots of humor, engaging and completely lovable characters, *Bound for Eden* was just what I was looking for in a book escape."
—Tome Tender

"I adored Tess LeSue's *Bound for Eden*! Her voice is brilliant, funny and immediately draws you into the book. The hero is sexy and protective, the heroine is fierce and independent, and I couldn't stop turning pages."
—*New York Times* bestselling author Jessica Clare

"Tess LeSue has written a great Western romance with all the sass, fun and riveting action a reader could want. This novel is a rollicking ride with more twists and turns than a bronco with a burr under his saddle . . . You can't finish *Bound for Eden* without a smile on your face."
—*USA Today* bestselling author May McGoldrick

"I was blown away by the sparkling brilliance of [LeSue's] writing. She has a real gift for historical atmosphere, compelling characters, sexual tension and witty dialogue."
—Anna Campbell

"[Tess's] writing is lively and taut and generates emotion. Her characters spring to life and her stories move at a fast pace."
—Anne Gracie

"An accomplished mix of comedy and suspense, I found myself cheering with the heroine as she boldly navigates the journey to Oregon and, eventually, her freedom. I absolutely loved it."
—Victoria Purman

Titles by Tess LeSue

BOUND FOR EDEN
BOUND FOR SIN
BOUND FOR TEMPTATION

BOUND

for

TEMPTATION

Tess LeSue

JOVE
New York

A JOVE BOOK
Published by Berkley
An imprint of Penguin Random House LLC
1745 Broadway, New York, New York 10019

Copyright © 2018 by Tess LeSue
Excerpt from *Bound for Eden* copyright © 2018 by Tess LeSue
Penguin Random House supports copyright. Copyright fuels creativity, encourages
diverse voices, promotes free speech, and creates a vibrant culture. Thank you for buying
an authorized edition of this book and for complying with copyright laws by not
reproducing, scanning, or distributing any part of it in any form without permission.
You are supporting writers and allowing Penguin Random House to continue to
publish books for every reader.

A JOVE BOOK, BERKLEY, and the BERKLEY & B colophon
are registered trademarks of Penguin Random House LLC.

ISBN: 9780451492616

First Edition: December 2018

Printed in the United States of America
1   3   5   7   9   10   8   6   4   2

Cover design by Alana Colucci
Cowboy by Claudio Dogar-Marinesco; Horse by Iulia Khabibullina/Shutterstock; Wagon
by Terri Butler Photography/Shutterstock;
Grand Teton Mountains by aoldman/GettyImages

For Kirby,

my shining son.

ACKNOWLEDGMENTS

This book was written in the Australian summer of 2018, mostly at my kitchen table. I'd like to thank my family, who dragged me out in the sunlight when I needed it, who made me laugh (as they always do) and who unfailingly reminded me that I have feet of clay. This book is dedicated to my son, Kirby, who feels things as deeply as Tom does and who has the soul of a poet (or a mathematician . . . but then I guess theoretical mathematics is a kind of poetry, so maybe he's both). Thanks, Kirby, for being the calm in the middle of many storms; there are times when you are my rock. Thank you also to his sister, Isla, who is sassier than any heroine and will probably conquer the world one day and have you all in thrall. Trust me, you'll love it.

And Jonny. Just when I think you might drop to a four, you hold a torch during a blackout so I can complete my edits and you manage to remain a solid five. Maybe even a five and a half on a good day.

As always: thanks to my parents and my brother. And now Ash too. Good choice, bro.

Thank you to Dean and Dot, Sam and Anna and Sarah and Emma (Anna and Emma: I stole your names) and Nick. You guys are higher than fives. Much higher.

Thanks to Lynn, my disco queen. How in hell would I have survived these last few years without you? Who would dance with me? And who understands the madness of our biz like you do? No one. You're a ten.

Chelsea, my friend. Look at us! Who knew we'd not only find our feet but learn to fly! Go us. I am at the other end of a phone whenever you need me, and the other end of a bar even when you don't.

The magnificent women of SARA (Victoria, Bronwyn, Trish, Pam and Anne in particular!) and RWA. And Writers SA.

And of course thank you to Flinders University, where I get to teach some amazing humans and spend my life in the company of books. Shout out here to Amy Mead, who has become my collaborator and friend, and to Patrick Allington. I'm also going to throw Elizabeth Weeks in here because she made me a dress, and that dress makes me very happy.

Enormous thanks to Sol for checking my Spanish (any remaining errors are mine). Love to you and Dave and the little one.

Thanks to my agent, Clare.

And to the team at Berkley for being *amazing*. Maybe even better than amazing.

Thank you to Kristine Swartz. My lord, woman, you can edit. I am deeply grateful for your wisdom and skills and the way you tell me I have toilet paper on my shoe (metaphorically speaking). Thank you!

Last and most importantly, thank *you* for reading the book. I wrote it for you. I hope you enjoy it. I'm thankful you are reading it and hope we meet again.

✻ 1 ✻

Mokelumne Hill, California, 1850

SHE WAS RICH. Standing in her office over the whore-house saloon, Seline watched as the lawyer's fountain pen scratched at the ledger, forming a beautiful little billow of zeros. She had to pinch herself. In less than a year, the Heart of Gold had made her wealthier than she'd ever dreamed of being. And this wasn't even all of it. She still had two other businesses to cash in. Once she'd sold the other whorehouses in Angels Camp and Mariposa, she'd be almost as rich as Midas himself.

She watched as the prissy eastern lawyer transposed all of those lovely zeros onto the contract, her heart a tight little ball in her chest. Each zero he added was a further nail in the coffin of her current life. Good-bye, Seline. Good-bye, mining town. Good-bye, *men*. That money meant a nice little house in San Francisco, maybe even one with a view of the bay. It meant finishing her days when the sun was setting, rather than working through the night. No more hitting her pillow as dawn was breaking. It meant sitting on her lonesome drinking her first coffee of the day, in peace, without having to settle accounts and shoo out the last malingerers filling up her beds. It meant hammering out no more quarrels and mopping up no more tears and helping no more damn fool girls. Once she'd collected the last of her money, Seline planned to never see the inside of another whorehouse in her life.

"You're buying one hell of a business," she told Justine, who was equally transfixed by the ink flowing from the nib of the lawyer's fancy fountain pen.

"Don't I know it," Jussy said. She looked a little green at how much it was costing her. But she was no fool. She was getting the whorehouse at a cut price; if it weren't for Hec Boehm running Seline outta town, the place would have gone for more. But with a man like Hec snapping at her skirts, Seline was just happy to grab what she could get. Luckily, what she could get was eye-wateringly wonderful.

Mr. Teague put the gold dust in neatly folded brown squares of paper and lined up the rows of banknotes, using the beautiful little gold nuggets to weigh the stacks down.

"You'd best be depositing all of that in the bank, quick smart," Mr. Teague told her, peering up over his crooked spectacles. "Moke Hill is no place for a . . . ahem . . . lady . . . to be carrying around a fortune like that."

Seline ignored him. Even if she planned to stay in town—which she didn't—she didn't believe in banks. Especially not the one in Mokelumne Hill, which was run by Wilbur Stroud, a man who liked to be tied to a chair naked while Seline's girls dressed up like nuns and told him that he was a very naughty boy. Sometimes, when business was especially stressful at the bank, he'd even ask the nuns to take a strap to him.

No. Seline would look after her own money, thank you very much.

"Would you like me to read you the documents?" Teague asked.

Seline snatched them off him. Honestly. These men were all alike. They thought being a whore meant you were stupid. How did he think she could run her businesses without *reading*? She went through the contract first, and then the deeds to the building and the business. Justine peered over her shoulder. They each found a couple of errors, which Teague swiftly corrected and initialed, looking sour.

Seline's hands were sweaty as she took the corrected documents back from him and checked them one last time. There in the thicket of fancy legal words was her freedom. From Hec Boehm and Moke Hill, and best of all, from whoredom. And right at the bottom of the contract was a space for her to write her name. Her *real* name. The one she hadn't used for nigh on twelve years . . .

"You sign first," she told Justine, her voice a little unsteady. Hell. It was the thought of that name, she supposed. It was like seeing a ghost . . . a ghost that brought with it an ugly mudslide of memories. The weight on her. The pain. The smell of his rank corn liquor sweat. The feel of a hand clamped over her mouth and nose.

She exhaled. She hadn't been quick enough to get out of the way, that was all. Not then, and not now. Usually, she could jump aside before the memories hit. And there were more memories than she cared to count; the sludge of her past was a relentless tide, an avalanche of shame and fear, prone to sucking her down and drowning her alive.

But they were just memories, she told herself fiercely, as she watched Justine bend over the documents, pen in hand.

They were the *past*. And this, right here, right now, was the beginning of her *future*.

And her future was going to be a gold-plated, beautiful thing.

Justine finished her signature with a flourish and handed the pen to Seline. "All yours, boss."

"No, honey," Seline said, shaking off her ugly past and the whipped little creature she'd been, and adopting her fancy welcome-to-the-whorehouse drawl, "it's all *yours* now. *Boss*."

And as she signed the deed, her black signature an energetic slash on the page, she did so with her real name. With the name of the girl who had been left back in Tennessee all those years ago, scared and alone and with no other option than to let men buy her body by the hour.

Emma Jane Palmer.

She was free.

OR, ALMOST FREE. First she had to get out of town without Hec Boehm or any of his greasy henchmen seeing her.

"He's got those Koerners parked downstairs waiting for you, and that Dutch thug is watching the back door," Justine told her. The newly promoted madam was eager to get Emma out of her whorehouse as quickly as possible. She didn't fancy her expensive business the target of Hec's violence, not when she'd just paid her life savings for it.

"Don't fret, Teague's going to tell Hec I've sold up. He's headed to Hec's place now." Emma swept her fortune into the saddlebags she had waiting on the floor. The bags were deliciously heavy. She was glad the office had a connecting door to her room, so she didn't have to go out on the landing to get there, dragging her fortune with her. She knew Kipp Koerner would be watching the office door, probably without blinking. That man was like a tick on a dog when it came to doing Hec's business. His brother Carter, on the other hand, was just as liable to be liquored up and counting his coins to do the nasty with JoBeth or Mona. He favored the young-looking ones.

"'Don't fret,' she says," Justine parroted, following her into the bedroom. "It don't matter a lick if he knows you sold, so long as you're *here*."

Didn't Emma know it. She dropped the saddlebags and yanked her carpetbag out from under the bed. "Teague's also going to tell Mr. Boehm that I'll receive him tomorrow, at 9 p.m. sharp. To give him my decision." Justine didn't look reassured. "Teague will also pass on that my answer will of course be *yes*," Emma told her, as though that solved everything.

Jussy looked less convinced than ever. "And why would you sell this place, if you were planning on staying in Moke Hill?"

Emma fluttered her eyelashes. "To devote my full attentions to his pleasure." She snorted. "Or so Teague will tell him—along with how much it will cost him to have me. He did say he wanted me exclusively. And that sure as hell can't happen if I'm busy running this joint every night." It would also flatter his vanity, the thought of having her completely to himself. He'd already offered to set her up in a little place of her own, right on the main street across from the Heart of Gold. She'd be like his personal canary, hung right where everyone could see him strutting in and out of her gilded cage. He wanted one and all to know that he'd conquered the unconquerable whore. And he wanted to reinforce that she was, when all was said and done, still just a whore after all.

She'd made the price absolutely ridiculous. She didn't

think Hec would believe anything less, considering how much of a stink she'd kicked up over the whole business. Unconsciously, she touched her fingers to her neck. The bruises were just about gone now, but the memory of his hands around her throat was too fresh for comfort.

There was a sharp knock, and she and Justine both jumped. Hell. Was that him now? She'd been *sure* he'd wait until tomorrow. He was enjoying the theater of her defeat too much to cut it short. Little did the fat pig know that she wasn't defeated at all. She'd be halfway to Mariposa before he worked out that she wasn't here.

"Boss?" Virgil's voice was muffled through the closed door.

"Yes?" both Emma and Justine answered. Whoops. It was going to take a while to remember that she wasn't the boss anymore: Justine was. She gave Justine an apologetic look.

"You still want to open at the usual time?" Virge asked through the door.

"God, yes!" Despite her best intentions, Emma couldn't help responding. Nothing would tip Hec off faster than if the Heart of Gold was shuttered up past opening time. She needed him to think that she was still here. Still here and weeping into her pillow that the mighty Hec Boehm had bested her.

Emma hadn't turned a trick since she'd stopped her wagons in Moke Hill just under a year ago. She'd been well and truly done letting men paw at her. She'd spent too many years flat on her back for the profit of others; it was *her* turn to make the money. And she was a *good* madam. She paid her girls fair and helped them move on as fast as they could. Very few girls liked whoring; it was something a girl did when she was out of options. Seline made sure that they could do it safely and save their money to start over. She watched them light out after a couple of months, cashed up and free of the trade, and she couldn't wait to follow in their footsteps. But she was in it to make more than just a *handful* of cash; the Heart of Gold was her ticket to freedom *forever*. It took time to build that kind of nest egg; she'd been patient, and now her time had come, and she was glad to say that, since coming to Moke Hill, she'd bought her ticket out of here without letting a single man poke his stick into her. Her body was hers again, and hers alone, and she planned to keep it that way. No matter how much gold the mud-splattered miners offered her, she turned them down. Seline was bright as a peacock, strutting the bar downstairs, teasing and laughing and making sure they all had a good time—but that good time wasn't going to be with her. Her girls were as fancy as she could make them: scrubbed and scented and dressed to the nines. And the miners were happy enough when she turned them aside, so long as it was into the arms of one of her girls.

But not Hec Boehm. That man had taken one look at Seline and decided that *he* was going to be the man to knock her flat on her back and keep her there. He was the kind of man who had to play with other people's toys, Emma thought sourly; a selfish spoiled brat of a man. And he had all of Moke Hill in his sweaty fist.

"Will you be down soon?" Virgil asked through the door. "We're opening up, and we need you to play hostess."

"*I'll* be down," Justine told Virgil firmly. "It's my place now."

Emma took the unsubtle hint and left Justine to deal with Virgil. She turned her attention to packing. So long as the place opened as usual, she was happy. She dusted off her carpetbag. It was pitifully small, but she had to travel

light. It was such a shame to leave all her pretty dresses behind though, she thought with a sigh. Still, she couldn't
very well wear screaming pink satin now that she wasn't
running a whorehouse. She ran her fingers regretfully over
her favorite dress, which was heaped on the chair where
she'd left it the night before. No more frills and furbelows
for her . . . let alone her peacock feather headdress, which
sat in pride of place on her dresser. She felt a pang about
leaving it, but what use were peacock feathers now? She
was hardly going to wear them baking bread or tending her
kitchen garden, was she? She'd have to get herself some
nice, simple clothes. Something dowdy and respectable.
Gingham maybe. Hell. Not gingham. She'd rather be dead
than wear gingham. If Hec Boehm hadn't been such a hasty
old hog, she would have had time to prepare properly, she
thought grumpily, and there would have been no question
of resorting to gingham.

"I have to get ready," Justine said once Virge had gone,
"so you'd best stop telling me not to fret and start working
out how to deal with Hec Boehm and his boys."

"You worry too much." Emma sounded more confident
than she felt. "As usual. I've already got a plan."

Justine rolled her eyes. Emma's plans were notorious.
"What plan?"

Emma threw open the big wardrobe opposite her bed
and rifled through it. There was a screech of hangers on the
metal rod. The wardrobe was stuffed full. This was where
she kept the girls' best gear, as well as her own. She yanked
out gowns, tossing them on the bed. Oh, it hurt to leave
them behind. Maybe she could just take one . . .

"*What* plan?" Justine demanded.

"*This* one." Emma found what she was looking for and
brandished the coat hanger high in triumph. Well, as high

as she could. The damn thing weighed a ton. It was like holding up a sack of potatoes. "I'm going to be a nun!"

"You're not serious."

"Of course I'm serious! It's a *great* plan." She turned the heavy black habit around and gave it a quick once-over. It was an ugly thing, made of many layers of coarsely woven wool, and it was as heavy as sin. It was like a big old black tent. No one would make out her shape under it, and the wimple would hide her blazing red hair perfectly. If she wiped the paint off her face, she was sure no one would recognize her. She looked totally different without the rouge and the kohl. More like a hick straight off a farm than a fancy lady.

"It's the daftest thing you've suggested yet." Justine sat on the bed and put her face in her hands. "What did I do? Hec's going to torch this place, and *you're* dressing up like a nun. I've just bought a pile of ashes."

"Don't be like that." Emma wrestled with the habit, trying to get it off the hanger. There were so many pieces to it. How in hell did you put it on? No wonder Wilbur never got the girls naked. He wouldn't have been able to afford the time it took.

"Don't you think they'll find it odd to see a nun leaving a whorehouse?" Justine asked, exasperated. "Especially when they didn't see her *enter* it?"

Trust Justine to go throwing logic at her.

"It ain't my fault Hec got all het up and impatient," Emma told her. "I'm doing the best with what I've got." She tossed the loose pieces of the habit over her dressing chair, where the black cloth looked even coarser and uglier against her pink dress. She turned her attention to the biggest, most sack-like part of it, trying to work out which end was the head.

Her instincts told her the nun getup would work, and Emma had learned to trust her instincts. They'd kept her alive this far.

People were *nice* to nuns. Respectful. She wasn't likely to be accosted traveling to Mariposa in this outfit. It was the safest way to go—especially carrying a fortune in her saddle-bags.

"You've got to stop looking for problems," she told Justine as she wedged the habit under her arm and hunted through the bottom of the wardrobe for her old black boots, "and start thinking in terms of solutions."

"This ain't a solution! It's just plain crazy."

"Hush." Emma crawled backward out of the wardrobe, boots in hand. "What's crazy is nagging me when it ain't my fault. You want to go nagging someone, go nag old Hec. He's the reason for all this fuss and bother." She dropped the boots on the floor by the chair and turned her back to Justine. "Unbutton me, will you?" She heard Jussy sigh as she got to her feet. "You worry too much," Emma said kindly as Justine started on the little buttons running down the back of the purple taffeta gown. Emma played with the precious little scalloped frill on her sleeve. How was she going to leave this behind? She loved this dress. It had a double layer of fancy flouncing near the hem that had taken her forever to sew. And it looked so nice with those pea-cock feathers.

Justine ignored her and kept on with the buttons.

They were totally unprepared when the door burst open.

Justine shrieked and Emma leaped for the chair, half coming out of her purple dress in the process. Her gun was somewhere under the pink satin gown, where she'd left it the night before. Stupid. She should have kept it close.

She snatched up the Colt, turning it on the intruder.

"Goddamn it, Calla!" she swore when she saw who had burst in. "I mighta shot you!"

Calla was staring wide eyed at the pistol, which was still pointed at her chest. "Why in hell are you wanting to shoot me?"

"Didn't anyone ever tell you to knock?"

The Mexican girl pulled a face. "No one ever told me I'd be *shot* for not knocking."

"Well, I'm telling you now." Emma's hand was shaking as she lowered the pistol. "Now close that door. Can't you see I ain't entirely decent?"

"I've got a letter for you," Calla said as she closed the door. She was mighty calm for someone who'd almost been shot. But then, in Moke Hill almost getting shot happened on a weekly basis. "Virge said to bring it straight up. It's from Hec Boehm."

Justine snatched it out of her hand. "You can go now," she said shortly.

Emma snatched the note off Justine. "You can go too," she suggested.

"No." Justine and Calla spoke in unison, equally annoyed.

Emma kept hold of the pistol as she read the note. She was shaking something fierce now. She turned her back on the girls so they couldn't see. The letters swam before her eyes as she struggled to read Hec's crabbed handwriting.

"It's a love letter," she said, feeling weak with relief. Oh, thank God. The idiot had believed her when she said she would think about becoming his mistress. And he'd clearly believed Teague that she was looking to say yes.

"A love letter?" Justine sounded disbelieving. "From Hec Boehm?"

"Well, a love letter of sorts." It was more of a detailed

map of what he was going to do to her. That was about as loving as a man like Hec Boehm was likely to get. He seemed to think she'd enjoy his—what did he call it?—*manly persuasion*. She thrust the note at Justine and wriggled out of her purple taffeta dress. It rustled as it fell to the floor. Emma jumped over the skirts and snatched up the tented part of the nun's habit. She could feel the phantom press of Hec's hands around her throat. The sooner she was out of here, the better.

"Oh Lord." Justine sounded ill. "This is worse than I thought. He's a lot more than keen on you. He's *besotted*. What's he going to do when he finds you've gone? He'll kill *me*."

Emma had worried about that. But she had a plan. "I'll leave him a note."

"A note?"

Emma was glad Justine wasn't the one with the gun. She was looking a little murderous. "Listen before you judge," she cautioned. Why didn't people ever trust her? Hadn't she shown herself to be a sensible woman? Hadn't she brought a couple of wagonloads of whores two thousand miles from Missouri, across those horrid plains, without losing a single one to disease or disaster? Hadn't she built a thriving business? In fact, not one thriving business, but *three*? But people still treated her like she didn't know what she was doing.

"How do you put this thing on?" she asked, confounded by the habit. No matter which way she turned, she couldn't make heads or tails of it.

"Put the shift on first," Calla told her, stepping up to help. She'd been raised on a mission and threw herself into the role of Mother Superior with vigor when Wilbur came calling. As she helped Emma into the sack-like shift and then lowered the even heavier full body apron over the top, she didn't bother to ask why her boss was dressing up as a nun. The Heart of Gold was the kind of place where it was best not to ask too many questions.

"How's a note going to help?"

Unless you were Justine. Justine never *stopped* asking questions.

"It's not just about the note," Emma said, distracted by the contraption Calla was trying to cram onto her head. "It'll be the whole setup."

"You know, proper nuns would cut their hair off," Calla said, as she yanked the white coif down over Emma's ears.

"Good thing I ain't a proper nun." Although she *had* been wondering how to get the henna out of her hair. Henna didn't fade. Maybe cutting her hair wasn't such a bad idea. It could be part of her whole fresh start, and when her hair grew back, it would be her natural color. *Emma Jane Palmer's* natural color. She didn't quite remember what that color was anymore. Reddish. But probably darker now that she was a grown woman.

"*What* whole setup? You give me such a headache!" Justine was whipping herself into a frenzy. She'd have to learn some serenity if she wanted to survive running this place.

"You should try wearing this thing, if you want to talk headaches." Emma attempted to wedge her fingers between her forehead and the coif. It was pinching off the blood supply to her brain.

"*What whole setup?*" Justine was so angry her eyeballs were just about bulging out of her head.

Emma took pity on her and put her out of her misery. "I'll tell him we're playing a little game, honey. He likes his games. At least according to the girls. Most of the time I think he's more interested in playing than in poking."

"You can say that again," Calla agreed, hefting the stiff headdress over Emma's coif. "Sometimes he likes to play hide-and-seek. We leave clothes scattered about like clues, and he has to come find us. We're supposed to be naked when he does, but often we cheat. He quite likes having a reason to get all angry and give us a spanking."

"It never ceases to amaze me how many men like spanking," Emma mused.

"I don't mind a spanking myself," Calla admitted. "It's better than being poked. I don't mind anything that keeps them busy, to be honest, so long as they poke less."

"Are you suggesting that you're going to play *hide-and-seek* with Hec Boehm?" Justine sounded appalled.

"Of course not. I'm just going to *tell* him I'm playing hide-and-seek. I've already written the note—it's over there by the peacock feathers."

Justine all but dove for it. Emma saw her nose wrinkle as she read it.

"Did I lay it on too thick?" Emma asked.

"This is insane," Justine muttered.

Emma watched her closely. Her gut told her the plan would work. But maybe her gut was an idiot.

Justine looked up. Her dark eyes were frightened. But not *as* frightened as they had been. "You're going to send him on a wild-goose chase to Fiebre del Oro?"

"Clever, isn't it?" Emma couldn't keep the smugness out of her voice. It wasn't just clever; it was on the verge of genius. Everyone knew she'd funded Dottie to set up a whorehouse in the gold town up north. It made sense that she'd go there.

Her lusty little note to Hec should prove a successful bit of bait, anyway. He fancied himself a hunter, so she'd play the prey. She'd have the girls set up her room for Hec's arrival tomorrow. Candlelight, a hot bath, the good Spanish wine set out in the best glasses. Rose petals floating on the surface of the water, she thought in a fit of inspiration. Calla had done that once for the judge, and it had worked a treat. She'd have Gina and JoBeth lead him upstairs, where they would prepare him for her. He'd like that. They could undress him and bathe him, and maybe give his little soldier a tug if that's what he was up for. They could feed him the wine until he was all hot and pink from it. Towel him down. Then Gina could read him Seline's note—Gina was the only one of the two of them who could read, so it would have to be her—while JoBeth acted out all the things Seline promised to do to Hec when he finally found her. That note (and JoBeth's close attentions) should get Hec into the game. Then he could light out the next morning for Dottie's place at Fiebre del Oro, where Dottie would have another room ready for him, with her home brew instead of Spanish wine, and her German twins instead of Gina and JoBeth. Emma had sent Blossom's boy, Henry, on to Fiebre del Oro already, with a second note and instructions for Dottie. She'd paid generously for the German girls' time and included a nice extra chunk of cash for Dottie too. The twins could keep Hec happily entertained for the night, reading Seline's promises to him, while they used their plump white bodies on him. The note would send him on to Sutter's Mill next, to a whorehouse named the Silver Tongue. A whorehouse that didn't actually exist, but it would take Hec a while to realize it. By the time he'd worked out she'd tricked him and he had ridden all the way back to Moke Hill, she'd be safely through Angels Camp and Mariposa, where she'd sell off her shares in her other whorehouses. By the time old Hec reached Angels Camp, she'd be off to San Francisco, to buy herself that nice little house with a view of the bay. And by then she'd be a demure little nobody in gingham—hell, not gingham; surely muslin would be dowdy enough—and men like Hec Boehm wouldn't look twice at her. She'd be boring Miss Emma Palmer, with reddish hair and not-so-dowdy muslin gowns, tending her cabbage patch and growing freckled in the sun. Hec would be tearing up California looking for a woman who no longer existed.

It was genius.

"Clever!" Justine was shaking. "You think it's *clever?*"

Uh-oh. Justine was still mad.

"And what's he going to do to *me* when he gets back to Moke Hill?" Justine was looking peaky.

"That's the cleverest bit!" Emma beamed at her. "That's when you give him the *other* note!"

Justine's hand was starting to clench around the first note, and Emma had to pry it out of her hand. She didn't fancy rewriting it; she was on a tight schedule. Calla followed her as she moved, jabbing the black nun's veil into place with hairpins.

"He'll shoot me before I can give him any more damn notes!" Justine shouted.

"Hush. You don't want the Koerners to hear you, do you?"

"Tilt your head back," Calla instructed Emma.

"There's more to this contraption?" Hell, no wonder nuns were celibate.

Calla laughed and wrapped the wimple-bib around Emma's neck.

"What's the other note say?" Justine asked through clenched teeth.

"Just that he's not to shoot you because you're going to give him ten percent of the take from now on."

"I'm *what?!*"

"It's perfect! That man would walk over hot coals to pick up a dropped dime. He ain't going to hurt you if it hurts business, and as we all know, business at the Heart of Gold is *good*."

"That ten percent ain't yours to give away," Justine raged. "It's *mine*!"

"Fine, don't give it to him, then. But he might shoot you if'n you don't."

Justine cast about to see if there was a weapon handy. But the only one was in Emma's hot little hand.

"You selfish, two-faced . . ."

"Hush, Justine," Emma snapped. "Stop talking before you say things you'll regret. I've been good to you, and you *know* I've been good to you. It hurts me that you don't trust me."

"Trust you! After this!"

Emma frowned. It didn't matter how nice you were to people; they always wanted to believe the worst of you. "You honestly think I'd treat you bad? After all we've been through together?"

"You just did," Justine said bitterly.

"No, honey, I just saved you from getting shot by Hec Boehm." Emma moved to the dresser and opened the top drawer. Buried in her tangle of unmentionables was a sheaf of papers. "If you think I'd steal from one of my girls, you don't know me at all." She held the papers out to Justine, who looked at them suspiciously.

"What's that?"

"My shares in Dottie's place in Fiebre del Oro. I had Teague put them in your name. It's a forty percent share. It'll more than compensate for the ten percent you'll lose to Hec from this place. It'll also give you wiggle room if he demands more. You can give him up to forty percent of here, without putting yourself out of pocket. Dottie's place is the biggest whorehouse in that hellhole; it's making more than here already. No one but us three here and Dottie need to know you own it. And Calla won't tell, will you?"

"Nope." Calla's voice was muffled. She had her head stuck in the wardrobe. Scavenging through Emma's gowns, probably, now she knew her ex-boss was leaving town.

Justine wilted. She read the documents, looking peakier by the minute. This time her pinched look was caused by flat-out shame.

"I'm sorry, Seline. I shoulda known you'd treat me fair."

Yes, she should have. Emma was surprised to find herself on the brink of tears. It shouldn't hurt to be thought ill of. But it did.

"My name ain't Seline. It's Emma," was all she could manage to say in reply.

Justine nodded and rolled the papers up. "*Sister* Emma," she corrected shakily, taking in the getup.

Emma looked down at herself. "You gotta admit, it's a good plan."

Justine nodded again, and when she spoke, her voice was tight. "I gotta admit . . . it's better than I gave you credit for." She looked like she was going to cry for a moment, but pressed her lips hard together and pushed her emotions back down. That was something they were all good at. You didn't survive around here if you weren't. "You might need a belt," Justine observed.

"I got one!" Calla came crawling out of the wardrobe, waving a belt. In the other hand she was dragging a heavy mass of black wool.

"What the hell is that?" Emma asked.

"I'm coming with you," Calla said brightly, holding up another habit. "You need someone to show you how to act like a nun! And I want to go south. I got enough money saved to get myself back home."

"Of course," Justine muttered, "because getting *one* nun out of here unseen wasn't hard enough."

"Justine . . ." Emma warned.

"I know, boss," she sighed. "Focus on the solutions, not the problems."

❦ 2 ❧

Mariposa, California

Tom Slater was barely a day ahead of the bounty hunters. He'd ridden without sleep for more than two days through the blazing August heat, and he wasn't happy about it. He'd had to send his men on to Mexico without him, while he took this damn fool detour. And all because that crazy Indian wouldn't keep a low profile. No matter how many times he told the idiot to cut his hair and dress like a white man, Deathrider wouldn't do it.

"I did that once for your brother," he said in a bored voice, "and people still tried to kill me."

"You deserve to get shot," Tom told him, when he found him in Mariposa.

Deathrider was stretched out in the shade of a black oak, behind the Mariposa bunkhouse, which shared a yard with the fanciest-looking whorehouse Tom had ever seen. The place had so much white trim that it put him in mind of a wedding cake. Its fussy prettiness was in stark contrast to the unpainted timbers of the bunkhouse, which were barely hanging together. The pairing of whorehouse and bunk-house was probably profitable, no matter how incongruous the buildings looked beside each other; he doubted the men spent much time in the bunkhouse when there were whores so close by. And by the looks of them, these whores were *fancy*. A few of them were lolling in the shade on the back porch, whispering and shooting cheeky glances at Death-rider. Hell. They probably had every idea who was stretched out here under the black oak. The most wanted man in California, if not the whole west.

Deathrider looked completely at ease, dozing, his dog sleeping in a dusty heap beside him. Deathrider's old com-padre Micah Pearce was also nearby. He was a striking-looking man, with cheekbones like blades and quick dark eyes. Even dressed in a rumpled suit, with his hair crammed up under a hat, he didn't pass for white. Nor did he want to. Seated out here, on full display, he was as unmistakable as Deathrider. Which wouldn't serve them at all well when the hunters came to town.

To Tom's disgust, the book Micah was reading from was the very one that had caused all the fuss when he was in Frisco. "What the hell are you doing? He's got a price on his head because of that trash." Tom snatched the book out of Micah's hands and threw it at Deathrider. It missed him, slapping into the dirt next to the somnolent Indian's head. Dog startled and gave an irritated bark.

"They've got a bet running in Frisco," Tom warned his friend. "You've got to get out of the territory. People all through the goldfields are gambling on who will shoot you first; there's big money in it."

Deathrider opened one lazy eye. "You ride here all the way from Oregon to tell me that? You Slater boys have too much energy."

"I was just getting to the good part," Micah complained. "We were up to the part where the Plague of the West kidnaps the white boy. I think he plans to drink the kid's blood."

"They're on the hunt for you again," Tom warned his friend, "and they know you're here in Mariposa. You got less'n a day on them."

Deathrider didn't move. In fact, the blasted fool yawned.

"The prize is up to more'n a hundred dollars!" Tom could have throttled him. He didn't want to be here in the goldfields, wasting his precious time. He had work to do.

"Is that all?"

"Talk to him, will you?" Tom begged, looking to Micah. "You can usually yap some sense into him."

"Not sure I want to. For a hundred dollars I might kill him myself."

Deathrider snorted. "You couldn't kill a groundhog if you were standing on its tail."

"No one'd pay me a hundred dollars for a groundhog."

"It's *all* of them this time." Tom bent and collected the latest Archer dime novel out of the dirt. He rolled it up. "Cactus Joe, Pete Hamble, Irish George and English George, and Kennedy goddamn Voss."

That got Deathrider's attention. Kennedy Voss was a sadistic son of a bitch.

"And guess who's with them?"

"I can't imagine there's anyone left," Deathrider said dryly.

"A.A. Archer herself."

Deathrider uncoiled like a snake. "I beg your pardon?"

As much as Tom wanted to slap him with the dime novel, he was glad when Deathrider took it out of his hands. It meant the idiot was finally paying attention.

"She's writing a book about it. *The Great Hunt,* or some nonsense. She was writing down every word they said. There was a big to-do at LeFoy's Palladium."

"How do you know all this?" Deathrider's long fingers smoothed out the dime novel. It resisted his attentions, curling up again.

"Are you even listening to me? Everyone within miles of San Francisco knows. The place was a circus. They went from bar to bar, whipping up interest. And then there was an accounting at LeFoy's, where each bet was recorded in a book. Every man and his dog was betting against you. And that Archer woman was following along, writing it all down."

"I don't know why she bothers. She makes it all up anyway," Micah said.

"Who has the best odds?" Deathrider asked.

"Voss, by a mile."

"I should lay a bet," Micah mused.

Tom shot him a horrified look.

"Don't look so peaky. I know where my loyalties lie." Micah grinned. "And only a white man would be stupid enough to bet against White Wolf."

"You say they're a day away?" Deathrider was thumbing through the battered book.

"If that." Tom didn't like the smile hovering at his friend's mouth. Deathrider didn't usually smile. The sight of it was unnerving.

"I've always wanted to meet the author," he said quietly. "Maybe she can sign my copy."

Tom didn't know which was more frightening, the smile or the moment when it disappeared. "Even if the author is accompanied by a dozen hardened killers?" he asked, exasperated.

There was no response.

"Matt was right," he complained. Deathrider wasn't even listening to his arguments. "You're as hardheaded as a rhinoceros."

"I've never seen a rhinoceros," Micah said. "But I expect they're not much different from buffalo. Buffalo have powerful hard heads."

Tom ignored him. "You could come to Mexico with me, the both of you. I can always use more hands on the trail, and by the time we're back up this way, the whole mess will have blown over."

"You think we could find more of these dime novels?" Deathrider asked, as though Tom hadn't even spoken. He was absorbed by the crumpled copy of *The Plague of the West Rides Again*. He read it silently, licking his thumb occasionally to turn a page.

"You want to read *more* of that rubbish?" If he didn't know better, he would think Deathrider was drunk. But Deathrider had barely touched a drop since that trouble he'd gotten into with Matt in Kearney. It was too dangerous when a man might sneak up on you any minute and shoot you clean through.

"I bet some of those whores have a book or two." Micah scrambled to his feet. He didn't need much encouragement to visit the whorehouse across the yard.

Deathrider nodded like that was sage advice.

"You ain't serious." Maybe they were *both* drunk. Hadn't they heard him? Kennedy Voss was coming.

But they *were* serious. Seriously walking toward the wedding cake of a whorehouse, looking for more dime novels, even though a posse of men was headed here at breakneck speed, each looking to be the one to shoot Deathrider and take his head back to Frisco.

This was why Tom liked cows better than people. At least a cow made sense. Feed it, water it, keep it close to its herd, and it went where you wanted it to go. Not like people. People made no damn sense in the least.

"Have you read this?" Deathrider called over his shoulder, holding up the battered dime novel.

Of course he hadn't damn well read it.

"You might find it educational," Deathrider told him.

Tom didn't deign to answer that.

"Especially since you're in it." Deathrider was halfway across the yard before Tom registered what he'd said.

"What?"

Deathrider kept walking.

"What do you mean, 'since you're in it'?"

Deathrider tossed the book over his shoulder. Tom fumbled to catch it.

"Have a look at page seventy-five," Deathrider called back at him.

No. No, no, no. Please, no.

But there it was, in black and white, on page seventy-five: his own name. *Tom Slater.*

As a snake sheds its skin, so the Plague of the West sheds his names, slithering westward, now in Indian buckskins, now in denim and cotton; yesterday he went by the name Deathrider, today he dresses like a white man, with a white man's name. Today he is Tom Slater. One of the infamous Slater Brothers.

Oh no. No, no, no, no. This wasn't happening. What in hell was his name doing in there? And what was this rubbish about the *infamous Slater Brothers*? Infamous for what? His brothers did nothing more exciting than split wood and read their children to sleep at night. And as for *him*, the *real* Tom Slater, all he'd done for years was drive cattle up and down the country. He certainly hadn't been *slithering westward*, kidnapping and . . . ah hell, drinking blood.

"Nate!" he yelled after Deathrider. "What in hell is my name doing in here?"

Deathrider shrugged. "You'll have to ask the lady when she gets here."

"Maybe you're in one of the other books too," Micah suggested. "You might even be as famous as White Wolf."

"Might be worse than that," Deathrider said mildly, pushing open the back door to the whorehouse. "Stay," he instructed his dog. Dog obeyed, plonking himself down right in Tom's way.

"Worse?" Tom clambered over the dog. "What in hell does that mean?" He had a bad feeling about this.

That bad feeling only got stronger when they entered the whorehouse, plunging through the kitchen and into the main parlor. It wasn't just that the place was as frothy on the inside as it looked on the outside, or that it stank like a perfume bottle. No. Tom's dread came from the way the madam lit up when she saw them. And from the name that exploded from her.

"Tom!"

Tom had never seen the woman before in his life. He would have remembered. He racked his brains. No. No memory at all of a tall brunette, let alone one in yards of orange skirts with her breasts exploding out of her bodice.

What in hell was happening? The real Tom Slater watched in astonishment as the whore threw her arms around Deathrider and just about squeezed the life out of him.

Deathrider showed no surprise. Not even a flicker.

"Oh, Tom," the whore said, pulling back to look up at

him, "I thought you might have left. We're in powerful need of some help."

"Tom . . . ?" Tom couldn't keep the anger out of his voice. "*Tom.* I think we need to talk."

"YOU'D BETTER EXPLAIN yourself."

They were upstairs in the madam's office. It was a plain room, with a solid desk, neatly stacked with papers, with the quills and inkpots lined up like soldiers next to the ledgers; it was the desk of a very neat person. A very businesslike neat person. It looked nothing like the rest of the house.

Micah had opted to stay downstairs with the whores and a freshly uncorked bottle of brandy. He was a peaceable man, and this didn't look to be a peaceable conversation.

"How many names do you go by?" Tom snapped.

"More than I care to remember."

"Well, I want mine back."

"You can't blame me for this one," Deathrider told him calmly. "This is Matt's fault."

Of course it was. Tom wished his younger brother were here, so he could slap him upside the head. Trust Matt to make a bad situation worse. He listened as Deathrider outlined their adventures the year before, about getting shot in Kearney, about his infection and about Matt's crazy plan to fake Deathrider's death and pass him off as his brother instead. Tom had heard parts of the story before, but he'd certainly never heard the part where Deathrider had gone by the name *Tom Slater*. What kind of idiot was his brother? He'd known Deathrider was a hunted man, and he hadn't said a goddamn word about this mess to Tom. How could he not have even warned his brother that the men out to kill Deathrider would be looking for one *Tom Slater*? The full import of it hit Tom like a stampede. Holy hell. Those men riding out from Frisco might end up on *his* trail.

Tom had to work hard to keep his temper, and he wasn't a man usually prone to anger. Just wait till he got back to Utopia. Matt would learn what a horse whip was really for.

After a long silence, when it was clear Tom's temper wasn't going to slip its leash, Deathrider finally spoke again. "Let me see what Ella wants. Then we'll go through those books and find out what's been said about you. If I can fix it, I will."

"Fix it?" Tom was finding it hard to stay calm. "How on earth can you *fix it*? My name is in that goddamn book! It's not like you can erase every copy!"

Deathrider's eerily pale eyes were as cool as ever. "No. But she can always write another book."

Tom was startled into a bitter laugh. "Sure. Because she's prone to telling the truth."

"People can be persuaded." His tone was arctic, and that terrifying ghost of a smile was back on his lips. The door clicked behind him as he left.

Tom flung the book at the closed door. It hit with a sad little *smack* and didn't make him feel better in the slightest. He should never have come to Mariposa. He should have gone with Emilio and the boys. He should just go now. He glanced at the open window. There was still plenty of daylight. But the thought of the trail was almost too much to bear. He needed sleep. He'd managed a couple of naps in the saddle, but it wasn't enough to keep a man going.

He sank into the chair behind the desk. He wasn't sure he had it in him to ever get up again. All the fight seemed to have gone out of him. Why had he come here anyway? Deathrider could look after himself. Tom could have just sent one of his men; he didn't have to come in person. Despite the heat of the sun throbbing through waxed blinds at the window, the world suddenly seemed gray and cold and limp. He had what his father used to call the saddle sads. They were prone to hitting when you stopped moving. *It's nothing a decent feed and a good night's sleep won't improve,* he used to say. Luke and Matt said it now, usually to their wives in the midst of an argument. It often made the argument worse. *I'm not tired, you idiot,* Alex would shout (she was more of a shouter than Matt's wife, who tended to go terrifyingly silent when she was really mad), *stop telling me I'm tired.* Tom was glad to be out of the house, really. Home had changed. Once, it had just been the three of them: Luke, Matt and him. But now home was chaos. Happy chaos, but chaos just the same. It was full to the rafters since Matt and Georgiana had arrived with their pack of kids. They were building a place of their own, but it wouldn't be finished for a good long while. Tom had moved up to the attic to give them more space until then. It was odd how lonely it felt being in such a full house, listening to voices drift upstairs, tripping over boots and wooden toys. It seemed like the more people they crammed into the house, the lonelier he felt. When he'd left at the end of spring, he'd been ready for the quiet of the trail. On the trail, it made sense to feel lonely. And at least you were moving, heading somewhere—hopefully away from the mixed-up empty feeling that welled up inside you when you stopped.

A knock at the door startled him out of his broody thoughts, and a woman came in with a tray. She didn't look to be a whore. She was dressed in simple homespun, with an apron tied neatly around her waist.

"Don't get up," she scolded, when he made to stand. "Tom says you're half-dead from the trail."

Tom. His temper flared again. *He* was Tom.

"I've brought coffee and fresh biscuits. They're still warm from the pan, and trust me, you'll want to eat them while they're hot. It's Seline's recipe, and she's the best cook this side of the Rocky Mountains. She puts me to shame." She put the tray on the edge of the desk. "And Tom said to send you in some books." She turned and looked over her shoulder at the open door. "Come on, Winnie."

A shy little girl crept through the open door. She couldn't have been more than ten, and she was all but dwarfed by the stack of books she was carrying. Each and every one of them dime novels, Tom saw.

"Thank you," he said, even though the words felt stuck in his gullet. How many of those stupid books had his name in them?

The woman took the books off the girl and put them on the desk in front of Tom. "I'm Anna and this is Winnie."

"Nice to be meeting you. I'm . . . Tom." He'd be damned if he was letting Deathrider keep his name.

"Another Tom." She smiled at him. He forced himself to smile back. There was no *another* about it. *He* was Tom. He took up a book, to keep from saying something he might regret. It wasn't Anna's fault he was in a mood. Or that Deathrider and Matt were imbeciles, or that this wretched Archer woman was a bigger liar than Mephistopheles . . . It was just the way things were, he thought grimly.

"Don't bend the cover," Anna scolded Tom as she poured his coffee. "That one's my favorite."

He hadn't been aware of his hand clenching around the book. He unclenched and glanced at the cover. There was an etching of a wild mountain man and a swooning woman. Presumably, the woman was swooning because of the bear looming over them. The mountain man should have been paying more attention to the bear and less attention to the woman, in Tom's opinion.

"That's the story of Little Bill Lench and the Widow Dell," Anna sighed moonily.

"I assume they survive the bear," Tom said dryly, taking the coffee from her.

"Oh yes, indeed. Little Bill makes her a lovely bearskin coat out of it." Anna passed him a jug of cream. He shook his head. He liked his coffee black. And in quantity. The dainty china cup she'd given him held barely a thimbleful. He tossed it back and reached for the pot.

"I feel sorry for the bear," the little girl said in a half whisper. Tom glanced up. She was clinging close to the door, watching him with cautious eyes.

"The bear!" Anna snorted. She was busy sawing biscuits in half and slathering them with butter. She piled them on a plate and passed them to Tom. "That bear would have eaten them up, my girl, just like Mr. Tom here is going to eat up these biscuits."

"Would you like one?" Tom offered the plate to the girl.

Her eyes widened, and she shook her head vigorously. "I'm not to take things from strange men." She paused. "Or any men."

Anna smiled. "Good girl." She buttered another biscuit and handed it to the girl herself. "We're strict on that," she told Tom, "this being a house of ill repute and all. We don't want any nasties taking advantage of our girl, do we, Winnie?"

Winnie shook her head. She'd already crammed half the biscuit in her mouth.

He hated to think of the kind of men who'd take advantage of a girl as young as Winnie. "Is she your daughter?" he asked Anna.

"Oh bless, no. Though I'm touched you think I could turn out something as pretty as Winnie."

"I'm an orphan," Winnie told him gravely.

"Poor little mite," Anna clucked. "She was half-starved when she came begging at the kitchen door last winter. Ella let me take her on, on condition that she earn her keep."

"I clean out the fireplaces," the girl told Tom proudly.

"And you do a right good job of it too." Anna tugged at her braid.

The coffee was doing its task. Tom's saddle sads were retreating. He poured himself another cup and turned his attention to the biscuits. "They're good," he admitted, relaxing against the chair back in pure pleasure. He hadn't eaten a hot meal in days. The biscuits were buttery and just slightly crumbly; they melted in his mouth.

"Everything at *La Noche* is good," Anna said primly. "Pleasure is our business."

Tom kept his gaze on his plate. He didn't want her thinking he wanted any other pleasure than coffee and biscuits. He was too tired for whoring. He wasn't much for it at the best of times, to be honest, and he certainly wasn't in the mood this afternoon, no matter how fine and fancy those whores downstairs had looked.

"Come on, Winnie, let's leave Mr. Tom to his reading." Anna held her hand out to the little girl. "Mr. Slater said he'd be back directly," she told Tom.

A chunk of biscuit lodged in his throat when she called Deathrider "Mr. Slater."

"You should read the new one first," the little girl told him, her words coming in a nervous rush. "It's about a lady and a mail-order groom."

"Oh yes, that one's delightful," Anna agreed as she led the child from the room, "and it has our Mr. Slater in it too!"

Did it now? Tom picked through the stack of books until he found the one they meant. It was so cheaply printed that the newsprint had bled across the cover. His stomach dropped when he saw the title. *The Notorious Widow Smith and her Mail-Order Husband.*

Oh God. It was about Matt and Georgiana. He felt sick as he thumbed through it. It wasn't accurate, but it was close enough to the truth to be recognizable. At least the beginning was: it had Georgiana's advertisement and the flock of suitors who had answered it. But then the book introduced the Slater brothers: Matt and Tom. Matt was a hulking brute with all the intelligence of a stuffed moose (she got that right enough, Tom thought uncharitably), and then there was Matt's brother. Tom Slater. The Plague of the West. A shape-shifting Indian, who could turn himself into a wolf at will, and could also appear as a white man. At this point, the novel diverged considerably from fact. And not in a good way. Tom's skin crawled as he read about the exploits of the notorious widow and her brutish husband. And every time he saw his own name, he jerked, as though snakebit.

By the time Deathrider returned, Tom had finished the scurrilous rag and was in a filthy temper.

His friend paused in the doorway. "I'd hoped some food and rest might have improved your outlook."

"It did," Tom snapped. "Without it, I might have belted you. Do you have any idea what that woman has said about us?" He waved the book.

"Us?"

"*Me. All mixed up with you. Us.*"

Deathrider nodded. "I have some idea." He closed the door and leaned against it. "But we have other problems right now."

"We?"

"Well . . . *They* have problems."

"Why do you always talk in riddles?" The whole day had taken on a nightmarish cast. Tom knew it was partly because he hadn't slept, but how in hell could he sleep, knowing a posse was on its way, and Tom Slater was in their sights? Deathrider/Tom Slater or *him,* what did it matter? None of them had ever seen Deathrider in the flesh, so how were they to know which was which? One Tom Slater would be as good as another. "Who has time for riddles, goddamn it. Haven't you listened to a word I've said? There's a *hunt* on. For *us.*"

"You said you're headed for Mexico?" Deathrider asked.

"I *was*, before I got snarled up in this nightmare."

"You need to sleep, Slater," his friend told him. "You're wound tighter than a clock spring."

"Nate," Tom said tersely, rising from his seat, "you listen to me, and you listen to me good: they're less than a day behind me, and they're armed to the teeth. If we don't get out of here now, we're going to be hunting trophies."

"I believe you." Deathrider met his gaze. His icy eyes were steady and grave. Finally. He was listening. "We'll ride out before morning."

Tom let out his breath. He hadn't been aware he'd been holding it. "Good."

"I'll take care of everything," Deathrider promised, "provisions, extra mounts: everything. And while I do that, I need you to get some sleep." He cut Tom off when he made to protest. "You'll need to be fresh. The next few days are going to involve some hard riding."

"There's no time."

"There's the time it will take me to get things organized.

Use it. Ella said you can use her room. Get some shut-eye. You're no good to us without it."

"Us?" Reluctantly, Tom followed his friend through to the madam's bedroom.

"Yeah, us." Deathrider yanked the bedroom blinds down, blocking the late-afternoon sun. "Now shut up and sleep. We'll leave after moonset tonight, when it's dark."

He was getting his way, Tom realized. He'd done it. The stubborn Indian was actually going to be leaving town with him.

But if he was getting his way, why did he feel so uneasy? There was something in Deathrider's expression he didn't like. Something about the way he said the word *us*.

Who was *us?*

"Is HE AS good-looking as his brothers?" Emma couldn't resist asking, even though she knew she had better things to worry about. When she and Calla had finally straggled into Mariposa, hotter than pigs on spits in their thick woolen nun's habits and worn ragged from their dealings in Angels Camp, she'd been relieved to hear Deathrider was in town—but she hadn't been expecting him to be with a *Slater*. Her stomach had just about dropped out at the news. At first, she'd thought, stupidly, that it might be Luke.

Deathrider shot her a curious look. They were in the stables, where he was checking over the wagon she'd just bought. Calla was done riding a horse in this getup. She said it was just asking for trouble. Besides, the small cart they'd hitched to their packhorse wasn't coping with the weight of the luggage. It looked fit to rattle a wheel off.

Thank God for Deathrider. And thank God he was in a mood to help her. Ella had said he would. "It's *Tom*," Ella insisted. "He was always good to us."

He had been good to them. Along with Matt Slater, he'd

had their backs on that horrid trail out from Missouri. Emma couldn't count the number of times he'd got between her and a mean drunk who was looking to rough her up. He was a stand-up guy.

"You want to know if he's *good-looking*?" Deathrider said now, staring at her like she'd lost her mind.

"It's a simple enough question," she said defensively. "Generally speaking, those Slaters are a fine-looking bunch of men." He didn't need to know that it wasn't Matt she was thinking of. Matt Slater was a nice enough sort, big and strong and sexy in a bearish kind of way, but Luke Slater was still the finest man she'd ever seen. The finest and the kindest . . . the sweetest and the gentlest and the most incredible . . . oh, best not to follow those thoughts. Thoughts of Luke still hurt, even all these years later. She cringed at the memory of the last time she'd seen him, when she'd begged him to take her with him . . . and of the sweet but horrified way that he'd said no.

"He's tall. Dark." Deathrider shrugged.

Men. They had no idea. Emma sighed. "I'd ask Ella, but she thinks *you're* Tom Slater. There ain't no way to ask her how he compares to the other Slaters without giving the game up."

"It's probably best if I stay Tom Slater for now," Deathrider told her without looking up from the wagon. "Especially with the posse coming."

"As if Hec wasn't enough trouble," Emma sighed. Damn Hec and his low animal intelligence. That man sure did have an instinct. He hadn't gone one foot farther than Fiebre del Oro. Like an old hunting dog catching a whiff of its prey, he'd headed back to Moke Hill instead of carrying on to Sutter's Mill. Blossom's boy, Henry, had come tearing down to Angels Camp, all in a lather, full of stories about

Hec's rage and the hunting party he was getting up to come after her.

"I guess you could say I got a posse after me now too," she said to the Indian.

"Mine's bigger." Deathrider held his hand out for the hammer.

Emma passed it to him. "They all think that, honey," she told him dryly.

He gave her an amused look.

"I swear to God," she complained as she watched him work, "what man even thinks straight when he has buxom German twins sucking at him?"

"A man who doesn't like Germans?"

Emma snorted. "Hec *is* German. And in my experience, he likes any woman who's as white as curd."

"Sex ain't what drives some men."

She snorted again.

Deathrider stopped working. "You've got to consider, Seline, that for him it might not be about sex at all."

"Emma," she corrected.

"Emma." He fixed her with his eerie pale blue stare. "Whoring doesn't show you an accurate measure of a man."

"No," she agreed, "it sure don't."

"It shows you a certain kind of man, with certain kinds of drives. There are men who aren't driven by lust; some men like other things more. Like power."

She nodded. That seemed true enough. Even the ones who were driven by sex didn't seem driven by it in the same ways. Some hammered at you like they wanted to hurt you; others hated you for seeing them in need; some were so lonely they were like children in your arms. And then there were the lovers. The ones who were shy and tentative, who touched you like you might break; the ones who liked to pretend you were a lady and just about court you into bed. And then there was Luke . . .

Hell. She'd thought she'd exorcized that man. Now here he was again, popping into her head uninvited.

"Hec's not looking to screw you," Deathrider said bluntly. "At least not in the physical sense."

Emma shivered, even though she'd already known it. No. Hec Boehm wasn't looking to screw her. A screw would be simple. Hec wanted to *own* her. To dominate her. To destroy her.

"Men like that are the worst kind," Deathrider sighed. "You can't reason with them. At least lust is an itch you can scratch, even if it is mindless."

Emma took a shaky breath. She knew it. She'd had some experience of it before. Just not with someone as rich and dogged as Hec; not with someone with the capacity to hunt her the way Hec was going to hunt her.

"You can't go to San Francisco," Deathrider warned her. "He knows that's where you're headed next. It'd be like running straight into a corral."

It wasn't what she wanted to hear. "I ain't letting him stop me," she said hotly. She had a *plan*. And that plan included a house with a view of the bay, a kitchen and a vegetable garden.

"Don't die of stubbornness." Deathrider slapped the side of the now-fixed wagon. "Your girl Calla wants to go back to her hometown of Magdalena, and here's Tom headed to Mexico. Seems like fate to me. Go along with them down south, cozy up for the winter, and head to San Francisco next year, when Hec's out of wind."

Emma was many things, but dumb wasn't one of them. She knew it was stupid to go to Frisco when it was the first place Hec would look for her after Mariposa. But it burned her up to let him chase her away from her plans. She'd worked *hard*. She'd earned the right to her little house with its view of the bay.

But Deathrider was right. And it might burn her up, but she was smart enough to know sense when she heard it.

"He know you're dressed like that?" Deathrider asked, looking the ugly nun's habit up and down.

Emma shook her head. "Not as far as I know."

"Good. That'll help."

"He might find out when he gets here and talks to Ella though." Because Hec would scare the living daylights out of her to get information. Or hurt her. Damn him. Emma fretted over her old friend's safety.

"He won't need to talk to Ella."

"Why not?"

"Because it'll be clear where you went," Deathrider said. "I promise you he'll be through this town quicker than a jackrabbit through a burrow."

"What in hell are you planning?" Emma couldn't understand why the Indian looked so amused.

"We'll get your posse tangled up with my posse and lead them well away from you."

"I *knew* you were insecure about the size of your posse. You're just trying to make yours bigger."

He almost smiled at that.

"How on earth do you plan to get him chasing after *you* instead of me?" she asked, following him out of the stable. "He might want to keep his posse to himself." She winced as the hot August sun hit her full in the face. She'd sweated this nasty habit through so many times over it was permanently steamy. Just stepping back into the sunlight had her sweating again. Hadn't nuns ever heard of *cotton*?

"He won't be chasing after *me*," Deathrider assured her.

"Stop talking in riddles," she complained, hiking up the leaden black skirts and traipsing after him back to the whorehouse. "I'm too hot and tired for it."

Deathrider held the porch door open for her. "Hec's still going to be chasing after you. Seline, I mean. And we're going to let him. He's just not going to know that what he's really chasing is Micah in a dress."

"MICAH IN A *what*?" Micah was none too happy to hear Deathrider's plan either. They'd fetched him to help load gear onto the wagon. Calla and Emma had formed a chain, handing things up to the men, who tied everything down as firmly as they could.

"Seline and I are old friends," Deathrider told him. "We traveled out to California together, so it makes sense we might take up with each other again. We make an eye-catching couple: the outlaw and the whore. People will remember us."

"Emma, not Seline," Emma corrected him.

"No. *Seline*. Hec doesn't know Emma and never will. And we want people to see the whore, not you."

Emma felt the words like a wash of sunshine on a cold day. It was true, she realized. Hec Boehm would never know Emma. Would never know *her*.

"Hec knows a whore in a fancy dress." Deathrider looked at the mountain of luggage still to be handed up. "What's in all of these?"

"Clothes," Calla said cheerfully. "She couldn't leave them behind."

Emma knew it was ridiculous to haul a wagonful of gowns with her, but she hadn't been able to bring herself to part with them. She *loved* her gowns. At first, she'd planned to take just one or two, but then there was the trouble of choosing between them. It was like choosing a favorite child. Besides, she'd *earned* those gowns, and she'd be damned if she'd leave them.

"They're worth a lot of money," Emma defended herself when Deathrider looked incredulous. "Do you have any idea what a yard of silk costs?"

"And what do two nuns need with silk?"

She scowled at him. She wasn't planning on *staying* a nun.

"Can Micah here borrow one of your fancy dresses?" Deathrider asked, yanking open one of the trunks.

"Not that one!" Emma yelped when he pulled out her favorite pink.

"It's got to be something Hec and his cronies will recognize from a distance. Something flashy." Deathrider held up the gaudy gown.

Emma scowled. Goddamn it. "Fine. Take the pink."

Deathrider tossed the pink dress to Micah, who was looking increasingly appalled. "You want me to do *what*?" he kept saying. Deathrider ignored him.

"How do you make your hair that orange color?" Deathrider asked Emma.

Orange! It had taken her hours to get this color! "It's *red*."

"You really should put your coif back on," Calla scolded her. "You're too recognizable without it."

"It's too hot," Emma growled, her gaze fixed on her beautiful pink dress, which was scrunched up in Micah's sweaty paw.

"I don't look like no whore," Micah sounded surly as all hell.

Emma looked him up and down. "He really doesn't," she agreed.

"He'll pass from a distance. Especially if we make his hair that orange color."

"Over my dead body." Micah's hand went to his glossy black hair.

"Just put a hat on him," Emma said. "I've got a pink bonnet in that hatbox over there." She'd never liked the bonnet much. It didn't have nearly enough trim.

"Orange hair would be better."

"We could make a wig," Calla suggested. "She was thinking about cutting it all off anyway." She eyed Emma's hennaed hair. "I could sew a swatch of it to the bonnet, so it falls down his back. Then Micah could just take it off whenever he wanted."

"Damn it, Nate. I haven't agreed to any of this." Micah had the pink dress in one fist and the tail of his long shining hair in his other.

"But you will," Deathrider told his friend calmly. "And I would do the same for you."

"I'd never ask you to!"

"It makes sense for Seline and Deathrider to ride together," Deathrider repeated patiently. "And we might as well kill two birds with one stone. The whore and the outlaw. It will make a good book for Miss Archer." His ice-blue eyes glinted. "We'll dress Micah up like Seline. We'll make a spectacle of ourselves as we leave Mariposa tomorrow, so when the posses come through, the whole town will be talking about it. We'll leave a clear trail they can follow and lead them well away from you."

"You want *two* posses on our trail?" Micah was looking peaky.

"Are two worse than one?" Deathrider shrugged. "One man or a hundred men, what does it matter when the purpose is the same? One man can shoot you just as dead as ten."

"You're not making me feel any better."

Deathrider gave him a quick grin. "Don't worry, it won't be for long. Deathrider and the whore will come to a quick end."

"You're still not making me feel any better."

Deathrider's gaze grew sly as it slid over Emma's hennaed locks. "We're going to slip into the Apacheria, and our little whore is going to find herself scalped by the Apaches. We can leave the hair for them to find. Maybe bits of the dress too."

"Apaches!" Micah sounded horrified.

"My dress!" Emma sounded even more horrified.

Deathrider laughed. "Imagine it. Kennedy Voss, Hec Boehm and all those witless white men blundering into the Apacheria. They won't walk out alive."

"Yes, but what about *us*? Who says *we'll* be able to walk out alive?"

Deathrider didn't look concerned. "They'll find evidence of our deaths, and that will be the end of the hunt. And when the Apaches find them, that will be the end of *them*. Problems solved."

"When these Apaches kill Deathrider, will he stay dead? Or is he going to rise up like last time?" Micah asked sourly. "Because there'll only be another posse if you pop back up again. And while I swore to be your brother, I'm about done with posses."

"I'm the Ghost of the Trails," Deathrider said. "Ghosts can't die."

"Now he's believing his own press," Micah grumbled to the whores.

"Fine," Emma sighed, "if we're going to do this, let's hurry up and do it." As she handed her luggage into the wagon, she cursed Hec Boehm. Not only was she losing her house on the bay, she was losing her pink gown, and now her *hair*. What did it even matter if this Slater brother was good-looking, she thought grumpily, when all he'd see when he looked at her was a bald, sweaty nun.

"HOLY HELL."

"You can't say that anymore," Calla scolded her. "You're a nun, remember? You have to practice, so when people are around, you won't slip up."

Emma barely heard her. Her gaze was riveted to the man at the washbasin in the yard below. She leaned through the window to get a better look. Dear God. There was only one person it could be. From behind, with his shirt off, he was the spitting image of Luke Slater. He had shoulders like sandstone cliffs, with skin the color of caramel. The muscles in his back bunched as he washed. Thick dark hair, exactly the color of Luke's, curled damply at the cords of his neck. Drops of water ran down his spine, between the flexing muscles. He was hypnotic. And she wasn't the only one to notice what a fine figure he cut. She saw Ella's girls gathering in the yard to watch him at his bath. He was standing in the lee of the stable, washing himself from the tin laundry tub. The sun was setting, long hot bars of it falling dusty through the gaps in the buildings. Shadows stretched across the yard, and the air was heavy and lazy. It was so still, Emma could hear every splash of the water in the laundry tub.

She was at the open window of Ella's office, trying to dry her hair. Calla had demanded that she wash it, so Micah would at least have a clean wig. The problem was, they didn't have a lot of time, and her hair took forever to dry. Watching Tom Slater at his bath was a surefire way to dry her off though, she thought witlessly; she was hotter'n a Dutch oven right now.

"Your hair is so much brighter when it's clean," Calla

was saying as she fussed through the desk drawers, looking for scissors. "And it looked like a rat's nest. What would Micah have thought?"

Emma didn't think Micah would give a toss if the hair was clean or dirty. But Calla was right that cleaning it brought out the color. It was screamingly red. It would be visible from a mile away, which was exactly what Deathrider needed. So she'd suffered through the soaping and the pain of the comb yanking through her tangles. And then she'd taken her place at the window to dry off and had seen *him*.

"If you have to swear," Calla suggested, "say *Madre de Dios*."

"Madre de Dios," Emma repeated numbly, as the man who looked like Luke Slater tipped a cup of water over his head. The water shone gold in the sunset, and his back was chased with slick bronze. Droplets glittered. Oh my God, she'd forgotten how beautiful he was.

"Holy hell!" Calla had finally seen him too.

"You can't say that anymore." Emma couldn't resist needling her.

"Who is *that*?"

"That, I believe," she said, her voice thick with admiration, "is the real Tom Slater."

He put her so in mind of Luke that Emma had a sudden shock when the man turned to face them. This man was very clearly *not* Luke Slater. The resemblance was there, but . . . *How was it even possible?* . . . This man put Luke to shame. Where Luke had been thickly muscled, this man was leaner, more defined. The gold-lit water etched the rippling hard length of his body, outlining each and every muscle as it flexed. She'd had no idea that a man could even have so many muscles in him.

"*Madre de Dios.*" There was genuine reverence in Emma's voice as she drank in the sight of him. He pushed the wet hair back from his face. Oh. My. God. That *face*. Lean cheeked, hard jawed, it was all glorious golden planes and angles. Black stubble only served to outline its hard perfection.

"God have mercy," Calla breathed.

They watched breathlessly as he finished his ablutions and dried off, running a thin towel over his chest, pausing to rub the whorls of dark hair between his nipples. Emma had the urge to go down and help him.

She felt a stab of jealousy as she realized one of Ella's girls had the same urge. It was one of the young ones, a pretty little fresh-faced girl. She all but skipped across the yard with a bigger, more useful towel. Her voice drifted clearly up to the open window.

"Do you need a hand?" the young whore asked, a giggle in her voice.

"Lucky cow," Calla sighed.

They watched as Tom took the towel, although he refused the help.

"We're going with *him*?" Calla was almost pushing Emma out the way as she tried to keep Tom Slater in her line of sight. Emma shivered as she realized it was true: they were going to be out on the trail with this man. Alone. With this beautiful, burnished man, who looked like Luke Slater, only—*How was it possible?*—even better. Suddenly, going to Mexico didn't seem so bad . . .

At least until she remembered that she was going to be a *nun*. She scowled as she watched the pretty young whore below bat her eyelashes and giggle. No man was going to look twice at her in the stinky old black habit. Unless it was to ask her to pray for him.

"I ain't never seen a man that beautiful," Calla marveled. "Although 'beautiful' doesn't seem the right word. He's better than beautiful."

They both made disappointed noises as Tom Slater pulled his shirt on, covering up all those lovely muscles.

"I bet she doesn't even charge him," Calla said enviously. "I wouldn't if I were her."

"You would if you were working for me," Emma told her sharply, but mostly out of habit. Calla's words had struck her like a splash of cold water. It was a reminder of who she was.

Of course, it didn't matter if she was a nun when he met her. Because if she wasn't a nun, she was a *whore*. Even though years had passed, the memory of Luke's shock, of his horror, was suddenly as fresh as if she'd seen it yesterday. It had never occurred to him that their time together was anything more than a transaction. He had meant the world to her, but for him, she had been just another night's entertainment. If she hadn't been available, he would have slept with another. And he had. She was just a body to him. The rest had been her imagination.

So, who cared if she was a nun? If she wasn't wearing the habit, a man like Tom Slater wouldn't even *see* her. All he'd see would be the bright hair and the makeup, the fancy underwear and the naked legs. All he would want from a woman like her was a poke. And then he might toss her an extra coin after he was finished, if she was lucky. Better to be invisible in the sweaty black habit than to face that again.

She felt the old sour shame. She must have lost her mind, thinking a man like Luke Slater would see anything but a whore when he looked at her. She wouldn't make that mistake again.

"Did you find the scissors?" she asked abruptly. "We're

running out of time." She stole a glance at her reflection in the mirror on the opposite wall. What did a nun need with all that glorious hair? She pushed aside the pang of regret. She wanted to get rid of the henna anyway, she reminded herself. And the hair would grow back.

And when all of this was over, she would crawl out of the nun's habit, grow back her own hair and be someone entirely new. Someone who wasn't a nun and wasn't a whore.

It was as easy as a snake shedding its skin.

Wasn't it?

❧ 4 ❧

"**W**HAT DO YOU mean you're not coming?" This day could just go to hell. Tom pressed the heels of his hands into his gritty eyes. He hadn't managed to sleep. He'd lain on the whore's bed in the hot room, his mind chewing at problems. Eventually, he'd given up in disgust and gone and washed up. He'd laundered his filthy clothes and then himself. But not even the cold water refreshed him.

"We *talked* about this," he implored Deathrider. "You said you were coming to Mexico."

"No," the damn fool said, as he slid into his fringed buckskin shirt, "I don't believe I did."

"You said we were riding out tonight!"

"I did say that."

The madman was making himself *more* conspicuous, Tom realized, as he watched Deathrider lace his buckskin collar and reach for a black-tipped eagle feather to knot into his loose hair. Earlier, he'd been dressed more or less like a white man. Now he looked like he'd ridden straight off the plains.

"You're supposed to be in hiding," Tom snapped at him.

"I will be. Eventually." His fingers made deft work of the knot and the feather thrust jauntily from his shining hair. He pulled a couple of locks back and knotted them below the feather, keeping his hair from his face. It made his features seem more angular. Harder.

"And where are you going to hide, dressed like that?"

Deathrider ignored him and turned his attention to his saddlebags.

Tom had found him in the loft of the stable, out behind the whorehouse, where he'd taken advantage of the quiet to organize his baggage and prepare for the journey. Or so Tom had assumed.

"Nate!" Tom tried to keep his voice even. "Just talk straight. Tell me what's going on."

Deathrider paused over his saddlebags and sighed. "There are these nuns . . ." he said slowly.

Nuns! Now Tom had heard everything. He listened in disbelief as his friend told him an outlandish tale about two beleaguered nuns who needed to get to Mexico. It was utterly ridiculous and made no sense at all.

"Why in hell would a man like Hec Boehm be hunting a pair of *nuns*?" Tom had been running cattle up to the goldfields for a couple of years and knew enough about Hec Boehm to know that he wasn't a man prone to socializing with *nuns*.

"How should I know?" Deathrider had turned back to his bags. "They asked me to help them, so I'm helping them."

Tom's eyes narrowed suspiciously. "Since when are you a Good Samaritan?" Forget Hec Boehm and nuns, *Deathrider* and nuns made no sense.

Deathrider shrugged. "I'm not completely heartless. You try looking into a nun's big eyes and turning her aside."

Tom planned to do just that. He wasn't about to go dragging a pair of nuns halfway across the territory, especially not down through Apache country and into the heart of Mexico. He had his own problems, without adding *nuns* to them.

"It ain't safe for them to be with me," he protested hotly. "Not when people think I'm *you*. You're putting their lives in danger."

"Go by another name for a while and it won't be a problem."

"I *like* my name." Tom wanted to kick something. "Besides, people know me down south. Changing my name would do jackshit."

"They're safer with you than they are alone."

"Why don't *you* take them?" he demanded, feeling belligerent. Deathrider was more trouble than he was worth, he thought churlishly. He should have left him for the posse to find. "Why get me to do it?"

"Because, as you're so fond of pointing out, I have a posse on my tail."

"So do they. Seems like you're a good match."

"You got sour since I saw you last," Deathrider said mildly.

Tom turned away to hide the fact that Deathrider's words had hit their mark. He *had* grown sour. Sour and tired and restless to the bone. Nothing made him happy anymore. Not being at home, not being on the trail. And the reason for it was something he was so ashamed of, he could barely face it.

He was in love with his brother's wife.

It was a sad, messed-up kind of love. It was pointless and hopeless: Alex didn't care for him; she was madly in love with Luke. Like so many other women, he thought tiredly. Women melted over Luke. But Luke only melted over one woman, and that woman was Alex.

And how could he not? She was perfect. Beautiful, sassy, smart, kind, funny. She brightened every room she entered. It was hell to share a house with her and to watch her and Luke together. But leaving made Tom no happier. When he was away, he felt like he had a hole through the middle of him, like the funnel of a tornado, pulling all the sunshine out of the day with shocking force.

He'd thought it would get easier after Luke had married Alex. He'd thought his feelings would fall into line. But if anything, they got worse. Even after his nieces were born, even when it was clear that Luke and Alex were blissfully happy, every passing year made Tom's feelings more powerful and more painful.

"I came here to help *you*," Tom told Deathrider, pushing away thoughts of Alex, and pretending he hadn't heard the *sour* comment, "not some damn nuns."

"This *will* help me."

Tom had walked into that one. He scowled.

"It won't be so bad," Deathrider reassured him. "I've traveled with one of them before, and she's no trouble at all. She won't complain or slow you up. She's an old hand on the trail. And she's a great cook."

"You traveled with a nun?"

"I've traveled with lots of people." Deathrider buckled his saddlebags and fixed Tom with his eerie ice-blue stare. "They need to get to the mission at Santa María Magdalena de Buquivaba. It's barely a four-day ride from Arizpe. I wouldn't ask if it was going to upset your schedule, but it won't put you out to take them. You can catch up with your party, just like you planned to anyway, and get someone in Arizpe to take the nuns on to Magdalena. I swear on my mother's life they won't be any trouble." His pale eyes twinkled. "After all, how much trouble can they be? They're *nuns*."

It was like being on a runaway horse: there was no getting off safely. Tom shifted irritably. "Your mother ain't even alive," he grumbled.

"I swear on her grave, then."

Tom wasn't happy about it. But he agreed. Gracelessly. And then he went inside and bought himself a half bottle of whiskey and sat down in the corner to burn time until he could collect the nuns and leave. Luke always said that knowing Deathrider was like hunting for honey. You never knew if things would end up sweet, or if you'd get a face full of bees.

Today was all bees, Tom thought darkly. A whole goddamn swarm of them.

EVEN WITH THE windows open, the room was hot and stuffy. There wasn't a lick of breeze, and the air was oppressive. Emma wasn't one to be idle at the best of times, but being cooped up tonight was driving her crazy. The heat only made things worse. Although the one good thing about losing all her hair, she supposed, was that it made things marginally cooler. Look how Calla's hair was stuck to her forehead in clumps. At least Emma didn't have that problem.

Emma sighed and watched the fat moths batter at the glass around the lamp. She could hear the roar of the saloon below as it geared up for the night's trade, and there was the constant sound of traffic in the hallway and the click of doors opening and closing as the whores and their customers came and went.

"I'm so bored I'd even turn a trick," Emma complained.

There was nothing remotely interesting to look at out of the window now Tom Slater had put his shirt on and gone inside; it was too hot to eat, and she'd flicked through all the stupid books piled up by the chaise. According to the clock on Ella's desk, there were hours yet to go before they could sneak away.

Calla snorted, not looking up from the needle she was trying to thread. She'd almost finished sewing swatches of Emma's shorn hair onto the pink bonnet. "Don't tempt fate."

Emma pulled a face. Fine. There was no way in hell she would actually turn a trick. But she was *bored*. And edgy as all hell.

Deathrider was a very welcome distraction when he appeared late in the evening. He stopped dead at the sight of her. "You cut your hair off."

"You like it?" she asked dryly. "I like to think of it as swamp fever glamor." She ran a hand over the soft fuzz on her scalp and darted a glance at the mirror. She looked mighty strange with a bald head. Her face was all eyes and cheekbones. Still. At least her ears didn't stick out.

Deathrider swore.

"You don't like bald women?"

He seemed really displeased. That irked her. Especially since it was heart-droppingly horrible to be this shorn. She felt ugly as sin. But her hair, or lack thereof, was none of his damn business. "I think it suits me." She made a show of preening in the mirror. She looked like a plucked parrot, she thought as she postured.

"And look." Calla held up the finished bonnet. "Now Micah will pass for her." She paused. "From a distance."

Deathrider put his hands on his hips and stared at the bonnet, deep in thought. "I need Seline to put in one last appearance," he said.

Emma laughed. And then she realized that he was serious. "That whore has *gone*," Emma told him firmly.

"I know. And I wouldn't ask, except I need witnesses to tell Boehm that you were definitely here. Witnesses who aren't Ella and the girls. And Micah won't pass for you up close, so I can't ask him to do it."

That was an understatement. Micah was barely going to pass for her a mile off, let alone at close proximity.

"What are you thinking?" Emma asked, her eyes narrowing. "Exactly?"

"You and I put in an appearance downstairs and make sure we're seen by everyone in the room." He cleared his throat. "And then . . . come up here."

"Are you blushing?" Emma laughed. "You *are*. Look, Calla! The Plague of the West is blushing!"

Calla squinted. "How can you tell?"

"Look at his ears."

"Oh yes."

"Are you finished?" Deathrider sighed.

"When the alternative is being bored? Not a chance." She laughed again.

"I don't know why you're blushing about coming upstairs with her later when you're up here with her *now*," Calla joined in.

"I believe Mr. Death here wants us to pretend to come up here to do the nasty together." She fluttered her eyelashes. "Isn't that right? You want me to solicit you downstairs? I assume you want me to be rather obvious about it?"

Deathrider nodded. The flush had spread from his ears to his cheeks. It was completely incongruous with his forbidding demeanor.

"You're as bashful as a virgin, Mr. Death," Calla said

impishly. "Don't worry, she won't actually deflower you. Unless you want her to."

"Whores," Deathrider muttered under his breath. "Can you be serious for a moment?"

"So long as it's only a moment." Emma rubbed her hand over her smooth scalp. It was becoming a tic. She turned over Deathrider's idea. She could see the logic in it. It was worth imprinting the sight of Deathrider and the whore on people before the posses rode in. "I suppose you want a show? Something they'll remember?"

"I did." Deathrider's pale gaze followed her hand as it ran over her bare head. "But I didn't realize you'd cut your hair off already."

"She can wear this," Calla offered brightly, holding out the bonnet. "It will make it more believable when they see Micah in it tomorrow."

Deathrider and Emma looked dubiously at the hanks of orange hair hanging off the pink bonnet.

"If people see me here, tonight, with you, Hec isn't likely to question Ella, is he?" Emma asked. "He won't need to."

"It's less likely," Deathrider agreed.

"And the more they gossip about us tomorrow, the less likely it gets?"

Deathrider nodded.

Emma had been fretting about Ella's safety, and she could see the sense in his plan, so she resigned herself and snatched the bonnet off Calla. "All right, Mr. Death, prepare to be deflowered."

He looked pained.

She put the bonnet on.

"No one's going to believe that's real hair," he said.

"Leave that to me. You'll be amazed what a girl can do."

"You're not going to wear that, are you?" He gave the stiff white nun's underdress a distasteful look.

"No. No, I won't." She laughed. "Honey, get yourself downstairs and prepare to be solicited."

"Give it half an hour. By then the saloon should be full." He stopped short at the door and swore. "Hell. I forgot about Tom."

"Tom?" Her stomach did a slow somersault at the memory of Tom Slater pouring water over his long, muscular body.

"Tom Slater," he clarified.

She rolled her eyes. Like she didn't know who he'd meant.

"He's going to see you later tonight. As a *nun*."

"And?"

"So if he sees you down there now, he's hardly going to believe you're a nun."

"I see." Emma cocked her head. "Don't fret, honey. He won't be seeing me at all. He'll be seeing Seline."

"You're a striking woman. He's not blind. He'll remember you."

Emma gave him a bashfully coquettish look. "Why, Mr. Death, are you flirting with me?"

"Maybe I can buy him a whore," Deathrider said thoughtfully. "If he's upstairs he won't see you."

Emma felt a surprisingly sour spurt of jealousy. Which was ridiculous, as she'd never even met Tom Slater. He could sleep with any whore he wanted—what should she care?

"You won't need to buy him a whore. He won't recognize me," Emma told him imperiously.

"Your eyes alone are too memorable."

"Honey, if he's looking at my eyes, I ain't doing my job

right. Now stop yapping and let a girl get to work." She flapped her hand. "Go on. Get."

"It sounds like she has a plan," Calla told him. "You really don't want to get between Seline and a plan."

Emma, she almost corrected, *not Seline.* But she didn't. Because tonight she really would be Seline. One last time.

❧ 5 ❧

HE WASN'T DRUNK. Not exactly. He was just . . . *cozy*. Somehow, Tom had finished the half bottle of whiskey. He'd also eaten a helping of Anna's chili, a plate of corn bread and a hunk of chocolate cake, and turned down offers from half a dozen whores. The more whiskey he drank, the harder it got for him to turn them down, and the harder it was to tear his eyes away from all the exposed skin. The girls here were clean and fancy, and they looked more willing than most. As a rule, whores made Tom uncomfortable. Most of them were an unhappy bunch. They might smile, but there were shadows in their eyes, and they tended to flinch like whipped dogs if you moved too quick or spoke too loud. And he didn't like the feeling that a woman was only lying with him because he'd paid her. It made him feel dirty and sad and small.

La Noche filled up as the night wore on, and after a while, the whores were busy enough to forget he was there. He watched a miner chase a lovely blond up the stairs and felt a stab of envy. Other guys made it look so easy. They didn't seem to feel sad about the whole transaction. They looked like they were having fun. It made Tom feel like a failure. Why couldn't whores come easy to him?

Forget whores. Why couldn't *women* come easy to him? Hell. Why couldn't *people?* His brothers were about the only people he felt comfortable with. And Emilio. He'd traveled with Emilio for so long that they were practically brothers. Women, though . . . women were a whole other matter. They were completely alien to him. He didn't know what they were thinking. They didn't talk plain like men did. There were all these secret rules he didn't know or understand. They were tender and gentle and prone to taking offense if you weren't careful.

Alex had been the first woman he'd ever had feelings for. Pretty much from first sight. And while she could be tender and gentle, she was also tough and plainspoken. She wasn't like other women. She made him comfortable.

And look how that had turned out.

That gem of a thought had him contemplating another bottle of whiskey.

"Thought you weren't planning on pitching a drunk tonight?" Deathrider said, coming out of nowhere, as he was wont to do. He loomed over Tom, his full Indian dress drawing more than a few nervous looks from the clientele.

"I ain't drunk. I'm just relaxed." Tom scowled at him. "No thanks to you."

"You know what would relax you better than booze? One of Ella's girls."

Tom's eyes narrowed. "I thought you didn't hold with whoring? That's what you said back in Oregon. You don't think women should be bought—ain't that what you said?"

"*I'm* not planning on buying one. I just thought you might find it helpful."

"You know I'm not one for them either," Tom muttered,

his gaze snagging on an expanse of exposed thigh across the room.

"Just like Matt," Deathrider sighed, following his gaze. "I must have traveled five thousand miles with that man, and I never saw him visit a single woman. No wonder he was so ornery."

"They don't come natural to us. Neither one of us ever had much to do with women," Tom said defensively.

"Why not? Your brother Luke hoard them all?"

Tom snorted. "You're funnier than you look."

"Luke sure liked his women."

Liked. Past tense. Women had lost their luster for him after he'd met Alex. She had that kind of effect. Tom reached for the whiskey bottle, then remembered it was empty. "You cain't talk anyway," Tom said, thrusting aside the empty bottle. "You don't seem to have much to do with women. If we're peculiar, you're peculiar too."

"You didn't just get sour, did you, Slater? You got cantankerous. Sometimes I feel like I'm talking to your little brother."

Tom grunted. He didn't relish the comparison. His brother Matt was famously contrary, whereas Tom had always been the even-tempered one. The peacemaker.

"Had" being the word. He didn't know *what* he was these days, but even-tempered sure wasn't it. He was all knotted up and sourer than a green lemon.

"Maybe if you enjoyed a woman now and again, you'd regain your sweet nature," Deathrider suggested.

"I'm getting another drink." Tom pushed up from the table and headed for the bar. "You want a glass?"

"No." Deathrider surveyed the room. "And it's probably best if we don't keep company."

"*You* came up to *me*," Tom grumbled under his breath. He

got a single shot of whiskey and stood at the bar, watching Deathrider move through the saloon. The maniac was practically *parading*. Like he wanted every last fool in Mariposa to get a clean shot at the Plague of the West. Tom watched the crowd part for him. A couple of the gold miners were sizing him up. They were starting to whisper. Tom had no doubt what they were whispering. *Ain't that him? Rides with Death? There's money on his head. Mighty big money . . .*

He should be called Flirts with Death, Tom grumped, tossing back the whiskey. Ah hell. Now look. There was some shifty fellow over there, fiddling with his firearm. The fellow's eyes were trained on Deathrider, and he had a hungry glint about him. That was a man who was counting reward money in his head. And look at Deathrider swanning about like he was at a town dance. Tom should just let the fellow shoot the idiot.

"You want another one?" the bartender asked.

"Not right now," Tom sighed. He didn't know why he bothered, he thought, as he inched his way around the saloon, keeping a sharp eye on the shifty fellow with the twitchy finger. Deathrider was begging for trouble, so why not let him find it?

Deathrider had paused opposite the grand staircase, in full view of the whole room. Tom made his way behind him. He kept his hand on his own Colt, his gaze darting from the shifty-looking fellow to the crush of miners around them. Any one of them could draw his weapon in a heartbeat. Goddamn it. The hair rose on the back of his neck. The place had the feel of a tinderbox.

But then a screech broke the mood. There was the sound of a door slamming against a wall upstairs, and a thick southern accent shattered through the hot night air: "Goddamn it all to hell, where did that man go?"

Every head turned to the gallery, Tom's included. That was about when he lost the ability to think clearly.

Leaning over the rail above was a buck-naked whore. Well, buck-naked except for an enormous shocking pink bonnet and a pair of knee-high boots. Bonnet and boots somehow had the effect of making her look even *more* naked. And goddamn, did she look *good* naked.

Tom had never seen anything like her in his life. She had the longest, firmest legs he'd ever seen. They just about went on forever. And then there were those breasts . . . they were pouty and round and sat high and proud. It was hard to look anywhere else. But then she giggled and stepped away from the railing, and his gaze dropped to the rest of her. Which was . . . bare. Tom flushed. Every inch of her was smooth and exposed. The sight had him immediately hard. And just when you thought she couldn't be any sexier, she turned coquettishly on her heel, revealing a plump derriere. Her screamingly red hair slapped at those delicious cheeks. Every inch of her was white. And Lord, did her inches ripple and bounce as she walked. It made him ache to watch.

"Sorry, boys," she called down, as she sashayed her way to the head of the stairs. Every eye in the room was glued to the roll of her hips and the bounce of those magnificent breasts. "I didn't mean to interrupt your fun. I was just looking for my . . . Ah, there he is!" As she reached the head of the stairs, she rested one hand on the newel-post and posed. Tom's heart just about stopped as she arched her back so her breasts thrust higher. He heard a pout in her voice but couldn't bring himself to look up at her face to see her expression. He was transfixed. Her nipples were large and almost as shockingly pink as her hat. Were they *rouged*?

"What kind of man are you to leave me in the lurch like that, sugar? Is that how they do things in your tribe? They ought to call you Disappoints to Death," she called down the stairs.

Tom jerked. Was she talking to *Deathrider?*

She was. Tom tore his gaze away, with more difficulty than he cared to admit, to see Deathrider standing, dumbstruck. And was he . . . ? He *was.* The implacable Indian was blushing. He'd turned a deep brick red.

"'I'll just be gone a moment,' he said," the whore complained. "And then he left me there all on my lonesome."

"I'll keep you company!" one of the miners shouted. There was a round of cheers, and then all hell broke loose as they shouted their admiration. Men hurried to count their coins and wave bills as they offered to buy her services.

They parted like the Red Sea as the whore laughed and descended the stairs. Tom broke out in a sweat as she neared. Her lips were the same pink as her nipples. He didn't make it higher. As soon as he thought of her nipples, his gaze was lost to them. And they *were* rouged. As she got closer, he could see the sharpness of the pink. It turned him on like nothing had turned him on before. There was something about the stark contrast between the pink rouge and her white skin. Not to mention the fact that as he watched, her nipples were hardening.

Up close she was even sexier. He could see the shimmer of perspiration on her collarbones and in the valley of her cleavage. He wondered if she'd taste salty. His ears roared, his heartbeat thunderous. He couldn't stop himself from staring. Her stomach was firm and white, her navel a teasing indentation, leading down to . . .

"Y'all will have to excuse us," she said throatily as she sidled up to Deathrider, disappearing from Tom's view. He inched sideways, in time to see her hands slide up his friend's chest. Deathrider seemed frozen in place.

"I'm afraid I'm booked tonight," the whore purred, "and I mean *all night*." Those pink-pink lips pressed against Deathrider's. There was a collective moan as the miners watched. Tom felt a wave of envy as he saw Deathrider's hands slide down the whore's back, settling over the round curves of her behind.

"Lucky bastard," someone yelled.

The whore whispered something in Deathrider's ear and then squealed as he threw her over his shoulder and plunged up the stairs, taking them two at a time. The whore giggled and blew the room a kiss. The miners catcalled and howled when Deathrider slammed the door behind them.

The minute the door slammed, it was like a spell had broken. Tom shivered. Hell. He'd been too long without a woman. His hand shook as he swiped the perspiration away from his top lip. He couldn't get the sight of those rouged nipples out of his mind. And he was itchy and throbbing and horny as an old bull because of it.

So horny he would have hired a whore, if there had been one to be found. But the redhead had caused a fever in *La Noche*, and every girl was booked up in her wake. Deathrider had the luck of the devil himself, Tom thought enviously, as he consoled himself by buying another half bottle of whiskey. He had to do something to calm himself. After all, he was supposed to meet a pair of *nuns* in a couple of hours. He could hardly face a nun while he was sporting an erection, could he? His gaze drifted back up to the closed door. Every bit of him wished he could swap places with Deathrider tonight. He scowled as he filled his glass. Goddamn it. *He* couldn't be accosted by a long-legged redhead with enormous bouncing breasts, could he? No. *Nuns* were his lot in life.

✤ 6 ✤

"WHAT THE HELL was that?" Deathrider just about threw her off his shoulder.

Emma untied the bonnet and tossed it to him. "*That,* my friend, was what they call a show." She fluttered her eyelashes. "You said you wanted drama, didn't you?"

Deathrider was still the color of a prairie sunset.

Emma laughed. She put her hands on her hips and posed. "And, like I promised, our Mr. Slater sure didn't notice my *face.*" The thought of Tom Slater and his hungry eyes sent a little shiver through her. My, oh my, but that man was divine. She'd seen him the minute she'd reached the head of the stairs. He'd been in the shadows directly behind Deathrider, his long body tense, his eyes trained on her. Dear God, and she'd thought his brother was charismatic. Tom was like a wild animal: poised, watchful, hypnotic. Everything about him seemed intense and measured and sexy as all hell. The way his eyes had fixed on her like he could eat her alive . . .

"You could have been raped!" Deathrider growled. "What if those men had rushed you?"

Emma rolled her eyes. Men. Always trying to tell her her business. "Honey. I've been doing this since I grew breasts. If I know anything, it's how to work a room."

"That was reckless and stupid." He snatched her scratchy white underdress off the chair and threw it at her. "Get some clothes on!"

Emma was enjoying his discomfort. She'd never seen him at all discomposed before. All men were the same, really. Show them a pair of breasts and they go soft in the head. She took her time with the dress, wriggling into it as slowly as she could. He turned his back on her.

"I think what you mean by 'reckless and stupid' is 'that was *inspired*, Emma, well done.'" She smoothed the dress down. "I'm decent. You can turn back around."

"It worked then?" Calla asked, yawning as she emerged from the attached bedroom.

"I think we were memorable." Emma grinned. She plonked herself down in the chair and began unlacing the boots. She swapped them for her own pair, which were far more comfortable. "They should be talking about us for a while. And everyone should recognize the bonnet and the hair tomorrow."

"Mr. Death looks like he caught sunburn," Calla observed. She made a show of peering out the window, looking for the sun. "Or was he moonstruck?"

"Stop calling me Mr. Death," Deathrider growled. Neither of them bothered to tell him that he had pink paint smeared all over his lips from Emma's kiss.

"Sure thing, sugar," Emma said cheerily. "Calla, can you help me with this wretched thing? I never can remember how it goes on."

"Tom will be out round back of the stable waiting for

you in a couple of hours," Deathrider said tersely. His pale eyes watched as Calla swathed Emma in yards of black.

"You seem a little pent up," Emma teased. "Maybe you ought to find some company. I know Ella has always had a soft spot for you."

"I'm supposed to be busy, remember? With a certain redhead."

"Lucky Micah." Emma winked at him. Once she was all nunned up and had washed the paint off her face, she twirled in front of him. "What do you think? Will Mr. Slater recognize me?"

"*I* barely recognize you," he said, more than a little grudgingly.

"Admit it, I make a fetching nun." She looked utterly revolting. She pulled at the head-splittingly tight coif. She looked like a big black crow. A big black *sweaty* crow. "By the time I reach Mexico, I'm going to smell like a swine," she sighed.

"Next town we stop in, we should buy a bottle of perfume," Calla suggested. "We can douse ourselves in it every morning."

"Like fragrant pigs," Emma snorted. She glanced at the clock. "We've got two hours to kill. Anyone fancy a hand of cards?"

AN HOUR AND a half later, Emma was happily counting her winnings; Deathrider had retreated to the window, where he hulked like a brooding gargoyle, and Calla had dozed off on the lounge. But they all started to their feet when someone abruptly pounded on the office door.

Someone who clearly wasn't going anywhere. The three of them stayed silent, but the knocking only grew louder and more insistent. The saloon was in full swing below, the noise of it a steady roar. It got louder by the hour. They hadn't anticipated that Emma's appearance would kick off a festival atmosphere. The hallway was busier than the California Trail in high summer. Emma assumed whoever was knocking had an itch to scratch and was looking for an available whore.

"Go away!" Deathrider growled at the door. "We're busy!"

They didn't go away. "It's me!" a muffled female voice called through the door.

"Who the hell is 'me'?" Deathrider hissed at Emma.

She shrugged. "How should I know?"

"Get in the bedroom, both of you. The last thing we need is for someone to spy two nuns." As he spoke, he pulled his buckskin shirt over his head in one smooth movement. He mussed his hair with both hands.

"Wait," Emma said, realizing what he was up to. She yanked the eagle feather half loose from his hair, so it dangled askew. "Maybe unlace the opening of your pants too." The pink smear of paint across his mouth would help. He looked like a man who had been well and truly bedded. She suppressed a laugh as she skipped off to the bedroom. She and Calla kept the door slightly ajar, so they could peer through and watch the show.

"What do you want?" he snarled as he opened the door to the office. "Can't you see I'm busy?"

They heard a soft cry of despair, and then there was the sound of crying.

"Anna!" Emma saw who'd come knocking and left her hiding place.

"Goddamn it, woman!" Deathrider glared at her. "Don't you ever do what you're told?"

"Seline?" Anna gasped.

Deathrider yanked her through the door and slammed it behind her. "Do you even know what *discreet* means?" he railed at Emma.

Anna had a child in her arms, Emma saw. A gangly scrap of a girl who had her face buried in Anna's neck and was shaking like a leaf.

"Hush up," Emma told Deathrider. "Can't you see that you're scaring her?"

Anna burst into loud sobs.

"And her too, by the look of it." Emma glared at him.

"Oh, Seline, they were at her." Anna could barely talk for crying.

Emma led the woman to the lounge and helped her lower into it. It was no easy feat, with an armful of gangly child. The girl had a death grip on Anna.

"Calla, can you pour a nip out of the decanter over there?" Emma ordered. She made soothing sounds and patted Anna until Calla brought the glass of whiskey. "It's the good stuff. From Tennessee," she told Anna, lifting the glass to the woman's lips. "It'll smack those tears right out of you."

Deathrider was looming like a gargoyle again. Emma shooed him away. "You're just making everyone nervy," she scolded.

"No one's meant to see you," he complained.

"It's only Anna. We go way back." Emma could see how frightened Anna and the child were of him. And no wonder. He was big and powerful and half-naked, and glowering at them like he might scalp them. Not that he scalped people. But judging by all the silly dime novels piled up in here, they were likely to think so. At least the pink lips made him slightly less threatening, she thought philosophically.

"Now, Anna, ignore him. He's completely harmless."

He glowered even more at that. It wasn't helping.

Emma turned her back on him. She heard Calla giggle. "Why don't you tell me what happened and we'll see what we can do? All problems have solutions."

That was one of Emma's favorite sayings. The familiarity of it seemed to comfort Anna, who took a deep hitching breath.

"Well," she said, still dripping tears, "we've been more than usually busy tonight. With the men riled up and all . . ."

Despite herself, Emma took some pride in that. She wondered if Tom Slater was as riled as the rest of them. Judging by the heat in his gaze and the way he hadn't been able to look away from her body, he certainly had been.

"There just aren't enough girls to go around," Anna said anxiously.

Emma was less proud of the savage glee she felt at the thought that Tom Slater might not have been able to douse his fire. She didn't want him to find relief with another woman. Which was absurd. They hadn't even *met*.

"One of the rougher ones came hunting in the kitchen for women. You know. Looking for cooks or kitchen maids. Or anyone really."

Emma flinched. Oh Lord. Here she was full of vanity, when Anna was sobbing and something clearly horrid had happened. "Please tell me he didn't hurt the child," she said weakly. Memories roiled. The sour smell of whiskey mash. The hand over her mouth, almost suffocating her. The pain. The weight. The pressure. The screams trapped inside her own head.

"He tried." Anna pulled the child closer. "But I didn't let him," she said fiercely.

"Good," Emma said, just as fiercely.

"I might have hit him over the head with a skillet." Anna's tears started fresh. "I think I might have killed him!"

"Well done." Emma registered Anna and Calla's shock, but she wasn't sorry. Any man who touched a child deserved a skillet to the head.

"They'll hang me for sure!" Anna erupted into sobs. And now that set the child off too. "And then what will happen to Winnie?"

"Get yourself together," Emma said sharply. "This is a time for solutions, remember? You can cry later."

Anna pressed her lips together to still her wails and nodded.

"I assume you're Winnie?" Emma asked, bending over Anna's shoulder. Two big brown eyes blinked up at her, swimming with tears. "Hello, Winnie," Emma said gently. "I'm Emma."

Calla cleared her throat noisily.

"Sister Emma," Emma amended. "And this is Sister Calla. We're nuns."

"Blessed Sisters of Christ," Calla confirmed, nodding and sounding pious.

Emma caught herself before she could roll her eyes. Calla really took the nun thing far too seriously.

"When did you become a *nun*?" Anna asked. She seemed utterly bewildered as she looked back and forth between Emma and Calla.

"Not long ago." That was barely even a lie. Emma returned her attention to Winnie. "Do you know what a nun is, honey?"

Winnie nodded.

"Nuns are good people," Emma continued. "People you can trust." She thought she heard Deathrider stifle a laugh, but when she looked over, he was busy putting on his shirt. "Isn't that right, Anna?"

"I've known . . . Sister Emma . . . a long time, Winnie," Anna assured the girl. "I'd trust her with my life."

Winnie's tears slowed.

"Now, Winnie, I'm going to ask you to go with Sister Calla into the bedroom there."

Winnie shook her head and made a panicked noise.

Calla squatted beside the lounge so her face was level with Winnie's. "We'll leave the door open, so you can see Anna," she suggested.

"Sister Calla is a nun, remember?" Emma soothed. "She's a good person. Someone you can trust. She'll help you wash your face and straighten yourself up. And you'll be able to see Anna through the door and hear our voices. I'll ask our friend here to mind the door to the hallway so no one can get in to hurt you."

Deathrider arched a brow at that, but he moved to the office door and, just like she'd asked, stood watch. Emma liked him more than ever for it.

After a fair bit more coaxing, Winnie let herself be led to the room next door. She shot worried glances back at Anna with each step.

"Well," Emma sighed, as soon as the child was next door and they could hear the splash of water in the wash-basin, "there's only one solution as far as I can see. You and the girl will have to come with us."

"What?" Deathrider didn't sound pleased.

"Keep your voice down," she said. "You'll scare the poor little mite all over again. Now, Anna, do you by any chance know if Ella keeps a nun's habit on hand . . . ?"

❋ 7 ❋

"**H**E'S DRUNK!"

They were late to meet Tom Slater by more than half an hour. It couldn't be helped, as they'd needed the time to get Anna disguised. Deathrider had grudgingly gone to hide the body Anna had left in the kitchen. He still hadn't returned by the time they left. Emma assumed he was fine, as they hadn't heard a hue and cry go up. She hated to leave without thanking him, but time was against them. She left a scrawled note on the desk and reluctantly left him to his own adventure.

It was quite an ordeal sneaking out of the whorehouse and getting the wagon harnessed and ready.

"Where is he?" Calla asked anxiously, glancing around the dark stable.

"Deathrider said he'd be round back. Now hush." Emma handed Winnie up into the wagon. "The rest of us are going to walk until we meet our guide, honey," she told the skittish girl. "You stay up there where you're safe. Anna, cover the lantern. Calla, can you lead the horses?" Emma grabbed hold of the mules by the harness and yanked. She tried her best to keep everyone quiet as they maneuvered around behind the stable. Across the yard the whorehouse was still lit up like a sunrise and the sound of slurry singing hung in the airless heat. The last thing she wanted was to be spotted by the drunken miners.

There was no sign of Tom Slater behind the stable that she could see. Where the hell was he? It was a moonless night and plenty dark, so it was hard to tell if he was here or not.

And then they heard a soft snore.

"Anna," Emma whispered, "uncover the lantern." She tied the mules to a post and crept toward the sound of snoring.

"He's drunk!" Calla exclaimed, when they eventually found him.

"Why, that's Tom!" Anna said, as soon as the lantern light hit the planes of Tom Slater's beautiful face.

"Anna! You *know* him?" Emma couldn't keep the exasperation from her voice. "Honestly. You couldn't have thought to mention that *before* we went to all the trouble to disguise you?"

"I didn't know you meant *this* Tom."

"What in hell was the point in disguising you if he *knows* you!"

"She needs to be disguised from other people anyway," Calla said, trying to head off a scene. "If the man she whacked with the skillet is dead, they might well send the sheriff out for her."

Fine. But Emma was still irked. They could have been here half an hour ago if they hadn't spent so much time on Anna's disguise. Emma bent down to shine the lantern in Tom Slater's face. He was fast asleep. There was the unmistakable stink of whiskey about him.

Oh, Tom, she thought, what have you done to yourself?

For some reason she was disappointed in him. Why, she didn't know. After all, he could be a regular drunkard for all she knew. Maybe he was never sober. But she was disappointed just the same. She guessed she had expected more from a Slater.

"Maybe he won't realize that it's Anna, even if he has met her before?" Calla said hopefully. "It's a pretty good disguise."

Emma wrinkled her nose. "There's no way she can stay hidden on the trail for that long. Not if he's seeing her every day for that many weeks. I hadn't planned for her to stay veiled the whole time—she'll die in the heat. We'll just have to tell him what happened and pray he plays along," she said with a sigh. "Anyone with a heart would." She hoped.

Thank goodness they hadn't dressed Anna as a nun, considering he'd met her already. That might have had him doubting Emma and Calla too, for if one nun was a fake, why not all? She guessed it was a stroke of fortune they hadn't found a nun's habit in Ella's supplies, after all. Clearly, the men of Mariposa didn't fancy being told that they were very naughty boys. Emma and Calla had settled on dressing Anna up like a grand Spanish lady instead.

"But I don't look a lick like a Mexican," Anna had protested, as they'd buttoned her into the high-necked black gown. It glittered with jet beads and was fancier than anything Anna had worn even when she'd been whoring in her youth. Which wasn't hard, as she'd been a garden-variety backroom kind of whore, and not the kind that belonged in a fancy wedding cake whorehouse like *La Noche*. She'd hated whoring with every fiber of her being and was glad years ago to give it up and be a cook instead. It was Seline who'd first convinced Dolly to employ her in the kitchen all those years ago in Missouri. Seline who'd patiently taught her how to cook, suffering through countless charred dinners and incinerated loaves of bread, defending her fiercely to Dolly, even when she couldn't produce an edible meal. *You'd best get her up to scratch,* the madam had told Seline, *or it's* your *pay I'll start docking.*

Everyone starts somewhere, Seline would insist. *Give her time.* Seline had never given up on her. Because of Seline, Anna could get herself a job wherever she went—and one that didn't require her to be flat on her back. And when she'd come west, Seline had fixed her up quick smart with a job here in Mariposa. Anna only let herself be crammed into this ridiculous glittering dress because she trusted Seline. *Sister Emma,* she corrected herself. She trusted Sister Emma. If Emma wanted her to play at being a grand foreign lady, she supposed she'd do it.

"You aren't going to be Mexican," Calla had told Anna, fussing with the mantilla. "You're Spanish. A grand Spanish lady who was widowed on the journey to the New World and is now joining her sister at the convent in Magdalena."

"But I don't look Spanish."

"Now you do." Calla yanked the black lace mantilla over Anna's face. "You are Doña Anna del Castillo." She'd stepped away with a flourish.

"But I don't speak Spanish!"

"Then don't speak," Emma suggested.

None of that was going to be a problem now, Emma thought. Not if Tom and Anna had already met. No fancy dress and black lace veil would convince him Anna-the-cook was Anna-the-grand-lady if she'd served him biscuits only a few hours before. Anna could just be her regular self on the trail and save the Spanish routine for when they passed through towns. Which was a good thing, or she would have had to stay mute for most of the journey.

"He's *drunk*," Calla repeated as Tom Slater gave a rolling snore. "What kind of man gets drunk before meeting a pair of nuns?"

"The kind who meets them out back of a whorehouse," Emma said tartly. She squatted in front of the drunkard and patted him on the cheek. "Wakey-wakey," she said as she kept patting him. He stirred irritably and blinked, pushing her hand away.

He frowned as he struggled to focus. Once he had, he jerked and scrambled to his feet. "Oh Christ," he said. "The nuns!"

"We'd appreciate it if you didn't blaspheme," Calla said primly.

"But we'll forgive you this time." Emma rose to her feet. My, he was a tall one. She was tall herself and did appreciate a tall man. "I'm Sister Emma," she said, offering her hand for him to shake. Tentatively, he took it. His hand was big and rough. He was looking a bit bewildered, poor love. He was still too far in his cups to be quite caught up to events. "Never mind about introductions now," she told him kindly. "We can bother about that kind of thing once the sun's up and you can see who's who. Now, where's your horse?"

"My horse?"

Emma heard Calla groan. Pointedly, she ignored her. "You must have a horse. I've not heard of a cowboy without a horse before, and Deathrider did say you were a cowboy."

"I have a horse." He lurched off into the darkness.

"We're all going to die," Calla said grimly.

"Now what kind of attitude is that?" Emma clucked.

"I've never known a cowboy who didn't tie one on now and again. Give him a chance."

They heard a thud off in the darkness.

Emma winced. "You all right, honey?"

There was a grunt.

Emma didn't like the looks on Calla's and Anna's faces. And she couldn't quite explain why she felt the need to defend Tom Slater. Perhaps because she'd seen him earlier tonight, looking lean and mean and capable as all hell. Or maybe it was because he'd looked rather adorable as he'd woken up. Or perhaps it was merely a hangover from her feelings for his brother. What did it matter? Emma wasn't one to dwell. She pushed the thoughts aside and did what she always did: kept on moving.

"Don't fret," she reassured the women. "I'm an old hand at traveling. Worst comes to worst, I'm sure I can get us to Magdalena just fine."

Neither of them looked reassured.

Fortunately, Tom Slater chose that moment to return. He was mounted on a sturdy paint, leading a packhorse behind him. Even drunk, he was easy in the saddle. He looked like he lived on a horse. Which he probably did.

"Are you ready?" he asked. His voice was gravelly and low.

"I was born ready, sugar." Emma shooed the women. "Calla, you drive the wagon. I'm going to ride." She'd had wagons enough on the trail out from Missouri and didn't plan to spend much time rattling around on that hellish contraption. Not that riding horseback in the black habit was much more pleasant. Saddles weren't designed for nuns. Or rather, nuns weren't designed for saddles. She had to hike the habit up and bunch it around her like a woolen blanket; needless to say, it wasn't the weather for woolen blankets. She'd worn a pair of buckskin breeches under the habit, which made things hotter but at least saved her from chafing against the saddle. Her sweet little mare skittered as she tried to settle herself. Emma gave her a reassuring scratch.

"Everyone ready?" she asked, once Calla had tied her horse to the back of the wagon and she and Anna had clambered up beside Winnie.

"Ready, boss."

"Wonderful. Mr. Slater? Would you like to lead?" Emma turned a bright smile his way. Not that he could see it in the darkness.

"Don't call me that," he growled.

Well. So far he lacked Luke's charm. He was more like Matt. Kind of surly. She pursed her lips. Shame. "What shall I call you?"

"Just Tom." He wheeled and flicked his reins, leading them away from the stable and the whorehouse and the rough old town of Mariposa, and into the darkness and the wild.

"JUST TOM" DIDN'T speak for the rest of the night, or well into the next morning. If he hadn't carried a lantern, they would have lost him in the darkness. He rode too far ahead to speak to and didn't show the slightest interest in them. Emma wondered if he'd fallen asleep in the saddle.

"Friendly sort, isn't he?" Calla said dryly.

"He seemed nice enough this afternoon," Anna protested. "He was sweet to Winnie."

Was he now? That made Emma feel better. Maybe it was just the drink that made him surly. "I'm sure we don't make such a great first impression ourselves," she said, striving for cheerfulness.

"His first impression was fine," Calla giggled, prompting thoughts of him pouring water over his hard, naked body. "It's his second that could do with some improvement."

Third, Emma corrected silently. Her second impression of Tom Slater was just as good as the first. She remembered him standing behind Deathrider in the saloon, his gaze smoldering as it devoured her naked body.

"Still," Calla continued, "any man who looks that good deserves a second chance."

"Amen, Sister." Emma laughed and settled in for a long night in the saddle. And it was a very long night. Time lost all meaning in the solid darkness; it was eerie riding when you could hardly see. Emma's mare, Bessie, picked her way carefully alongside the wagon. They followed a rough trail, the sound of the wagon rattling loudly in the open sprawl of the countryside. Once, they heard the terrifying scream of a bobcat in the distance. The mules got skittish, and Bessie danced under Emma nervously.

"That ole cat isn't interested in us," Emma soothed, trying to keep herself calm as much as the mare. Lord, but she was tired. She and Calla had done some hard miles these last few days. She didn't know how Calla was feeling, but she for one was as sore as a kicked kitten. She'd kill for a bed right now. A proper one; not the kind of catch-as-catch-can bed you found in bunkhouses and outposts, but the kind with a fat mattress and feather pillows. The kind like she'd had back in her room in Moke Hill.

Still, beggars couldn't be choosers. At least she was well away from Hec Boehm. Hopefully. She couldn't help but glance behind her. Thinking of him felt like summoning the devil. Her plan had seemed like such a great one back in Moke Hill. But now, out here on the dark trail, headed to

Mexico of all places, she wondered if she'd taken leave of her senses. She had no doubt word of Hec's wild-goose chase would have made the rounds of the goldfields by now. Miners were terrible gossips. He'd be completely humiliated, the butt of every joke from Sutter Creek to San Francisco. How gleeful they'd be that the mighty Hec Boehm had gone sniffing after a whore like a dog after a bitch in heat, while the whore in question had been laughing at him the entire time, playing with him like he was a mouse. Every saloon he entered would erupt with mockery when he showed his face. Which had seemed like a *wonderful* idea at the time . . .

Justine had been right. She hadn't thought this through. As they rode through the darkest heart of the night, she felt the cold horror of what she'd done wrap around her. Dear God, she'd made him a laughingstock. And of all the men she'd ever met, Hec Boehm was the most humorless, the one who could least abide ridicule. His pride was bigger than his fat head.

Despite the heat, she sank into the thick black habit, chilled to the bone. What if she could *never* come out of hiding? What if she had to be a nun for the rest of her life? As the night wore on, her mood grew bleaker. What if she had to stay in Mexico? If she had to keep her head shaved? If she had to grow old without ever wearing a pretty dress again? She got so lost in the tangle of her gloomy thoughts that she didn't notice the darkness was ebbing until Tom Slater came to a sudden stop. The night had faded to an ashy predawn, and the horizon was a blend of smudgy charcoal; the chaparral was emerging from the darkness as blurs of slightly lighter gray.

"We'll rest here for a few hours," Tom Slater told them

roughly. He threw his bedroll on the ground and was flat out and snoring before Calla had even brought the wagon to a standstill.

"I guess he was tired," Emma said mildly. He hadn't so much as watered his poor horses. Even though she was gritty-eyed with exhaustion, she took care of it for him, since she had to water her own animals anyway.

Calla watched disapprovingly. "I'm glad we're not paying him for his services," she sniffed. "Even free, he's overpriced."

"Let's give him a chance to sober up," Emma suggested, "before we go making judgments."

"We've been riding for hours," Calla muttered as she helped Emma pitch their tent. "If he's not sober yet, he might well never be."

Emma ignored her muttering. Tom Slater had been pretty sodden when they'd found him behind the stable. A few hours was hardly likely to sober him up. Emma guessed he'd only stopped riding because the early teeth of a hangover had sunk into him. That man was going to wake up with one pretty mean headache. Especially when the sun came up and hit him full in the face. Taking pity on him, she tethered his horse on the sunrise side of him, to block the sun, and gently rested his hat over his face.

"Aren't you going to sleep?" Calla asked, when Emma rummaged in the wagon for her sourdough starter.

"As soon as I've fed my yeast," she said, yawning. She'd brought her starter halfway across the country and wasn't about to starve it to death now. She scraped out half into a bowl and made short work of whipping up a dough for when they woke. It wouldn't have much time to rise, but the weather was so hot it should puff up enough to make a decent loaf. Once the dough was wrapped and rising, she hastily stirred flour and water into the starter and put the fat cork back in the neck of the clay pot. She made sure it was safely tucked away in the wagon and then crawled into the tent, which was far too crowded. They hadn't provisioned for Anna and Winnie; they'd have to do something about that in the next town, she thought as she wrestled her way out of the heavy black habit and fought to get the coif off her head. Feeling much cooler, she wriggled into place on the bedding, pushing Winnie's foot out of her face. Another tent certainly wouldn't go astray either.

"I was wondering," she said thoughtfully, as she struggled to get comfortable, "if it would be worth seeing how well Anna's disguise works . . ."

"What are you talking about?" Calla's voice was muffled. "You know he's already seen her."

"Exactly. He's the perfect person to try the disguise on. If *he* doesn't recognize her and he's already met her . . ."

"*You* were the one who said it wouldn't work."

"No one's going to take me for a lady!" Anna groaned.

"Don't be so negative." Emma gave Anna's leg a pat. At least she thought it was Anna's leg. It might have been Calla's. "You make a wonderful señora. And it can't hurt to try, can it?"

"If he stays this sauced, he's not likely to recognize his own horse, let alone Anna," Calla muttered.

Emma giggled. "He's pretty far gone, isn't he?"

"How can you laugh at a time like this?"

Emma rolled her eyes. "How can you not?"

❧ 8 ❧

"I GUESS I GOT some apologizing to do." It had taken Tom most of the day to work up to an apology. It had been mortifying to have the nuns emerge from the tent this morning to find him losing his stomach in the sagebrush. He hadn't been able to look them in the eye afterward. He had felt the disapproval coming off them in waves, particularly the little one.

He was disgusted with himself. Not that he wasn't as prone to a night out drinking as the next man, particularly at the end of a long cattle drive after weeks on the dusty, hot trail. But this hadn't been social or relaxing or fun. This had been a pure drowning of sorrows; the kind of drinking session Tom abhorred. He hated to see men drowning their problems in their cups. You saw too many men, both on the trail and in the goldfields, who couldn't handle their booze. They got liquored up on a nightly basis, blowing every cent they earned. As far as Tom could see, it caused more problems than it drowned.

And holy hell, had he been *drunk*. He hadn't been sauced like that in years. He had vague memories of riding queasily through the night, the sagebrush rising up like beasts in the darkness. He didn't remember stopping, but they clearly had, because when he had cracked his eyelids this morning to the searing morning light, he'd seen a canvas tent neatly pitched and the animals pegged and watered. He felt horrible when he woke, but it was nothing compared to how he felt when he sat up. It didn't take more than a moment for him to realize he was going to upend his stomach. He tripped over the tangle of his bedroll as he stumbled into the chaparral for what privacy he could find. To his mortification, it was the sound of his vomiting that woke the nuns.

"Mr. Slater? Are you all right?"

He'd groaned and screwed his eyes shut. Please don't come over, he prayed. But of course one of them did. What else could he expect from nuns? Sick men were their stock-in-trade.

"I'm fine," he'd grunted, staying crouched behind the bush. But of course he wasn't fine. He'd spent a good half an hour emptying his stomach, each retch making him feel lower than a bug. He was painfully aware that they could hear him.

To their credit, they did their best to save his pride. The one who'd come to check on him left a water flask within easy reach, as well as a pail of water and a washcloth for him to wipe up with when he was done. Then she retreated, and before long he heard soft voices, the crackling of a fire, and then he could smell coffee. Once the sickness had subsided, he crouched in the dust with the damp washcloth on the back of his neck, trying to breathe. After a while, the smell of coffee didn't turn his stomach anymore, and actually started smelling pretty good.

He was still sweating hard and feeling poisonous when

he emerged shamefaced from the bushes. He kept his gaze fixed firmly on his toes.

"We'd best ride out," he said. His tongue was thick in his dry mouth. "We're still too close to Mariposa for comfort." He paused. "Probably." He was humiliated to realize he had no idea how far from Mariposa they actually were, or if they were even on the right path. He cleared his throat. "I just need to scout ahead quickly," he told them. "If you can have everything packed up and be ready to go by the time I get back, that would be good."

"Don't you want something to eat before you go? Or some coffee?"

His stomach lurched. Oh God, no. Not again. He couldn't vomit in front of them *again*. He turned on his heel and gave saddling his paint his full attention.

"Do you think he'll be back?" he heard one of them sigh as he rode off. He just about died of shame. What kind of man did they take him for? His mother would be turning over in her grave.

Tom didn't know what had gotten into him. Things had seemed so simple on the road from Frisco to Mariposa. Find Deathrider and warn him, and then take him on down to Mexico. He hadn't bargained on posses and nuns and Deathrider stealing his name. But, if he was honest with himself, that wasn't what had caused the drinking. He hadn't been thinking about any of that as he knocked back the whiskey. He hadn't been thinking about much of anything at all; he'd just been trying to stop that tornado inside of him, the one that just kept on sucking at him, stripping him of life and turning him into storm wreckage. It didn't make no sense to be feeling as wild and empty as he did. Nothing had happened to bring it on; it was just there. It grew every day, a sense that nothing mattered, and that he was all alone and lost.

Quite literally lost today, he realized. He had no idea where they were.

He was also disturbed to see that it was mighty late in the day. Getting on close to midday by the look, and scorching hot already. He'd wasted too much time. Hell, he hoped he hadn't ridden them right into Deathrider's path. What if those posses were close by? What kind of idiot was he, getting fall-down drunk when there were men out hunting him? And not just him, but the women he was supposed to be protecting. *Nuns.* What kind of man led *nuns* into danger? He ignored his somersaulting stomach and the waves of nausea and gave the surrounds his close attention. He didn't recognize anything. Wherever they were was nowhere he'd ever been before.

He galloped back to the campsite. If he didn't know where they were, he better get them moving, or they were at risk of Hec Boehm or Kennedy Voss or some other son of a bitch blundering into them. His best bet was to point them south and hope they'd hit a landmark soon. With any luck, they'd ride into one of the big ranches or he'd find a marker of some kind, or at the very least a fence they could follow.

"We'd best get moving," he said when he got back.

They were efficient; he had to give them that. The tent was packed and the fire was damped and they were already harnessing the mules. There were four of them in total: two nuns, a señora in a black veil, and a child, who was sheltering from the sun under the canvas of the wagon. The nuns were younger than he expected. Much younger. And prettier, he thought uncomfortably. The tall one might even be called beautiful. Striking, anyways. She put him in mind of a cougar, all slow, graceful movements and tawny eyes. She had a smattering of freckles on her fresh-scrubbed cheeks, and her sharp-cornered mouth seemed to be quirked in a permanent look of amusement. He wondered what led a woman that pretty to be a nun.

"Curious, are you?" she asked, cocking her head. Her question was blunt as a sledgehammer.

He flushed. Had he been staring? He had been, he knew he had been. Which wasn't like him. What in hell was going on with him? The whore last night, the nun today . . . His brothers would have a field day if they could see him. Matt always said Tom took more interest in cows than in women. *Maybe if we could find a girl who was happy to sit in the middle of the herd and wait for him to rope her . . . ?* Luke wasn't convinced: *Even if he roped one, he wouldn't know what to do with her.* These days, Alex was likely to chip in too: *If you want a lady, you have to talk to them, Tom.* Then Matt would start in again: *Talk to them? Hell, he has to* look *at them first.* Well, he'd certainly been looking lately. His mind filled with the image of the naked whore: her long legs and rouged nipples and all that glorious bare skin.

He realized the second nun, the little one, was glowering at him. He forced his mind away from the whore.

"Well, Mr. Slater, I would imagine you *are* curious," the tall one continued, in a southern accent so thick it was like syrup, "as we haven't been properly introduced yet. Are you planning on dragging us across country without asking our names?"

His flush became a full-blown blush. He couldn't really remember last night. Was she saying he hadn't even introduced himself? "We've been in a rush," he said defensively.

He was painfully aware of his poor manners. And on top of his disgraceful behavior last night and his gross display this morning . . .

"It won't take a minute. I'm Sister Emma." She held out her hand for him to shake. She had a firm grip. Her skin was warm and smooth.

He had a powerful sense of déjà vu. "*Have* we done this before?"

"Last night." She grinned. There was something impish in her expression that didn't match the nunnish garb. Her eyes sparkled; they put Tom in mind of a gemstone brooch his mother had worn when he was a child. Tiger's eye, it was called. It had rippled with layers of brown and gold and all the shades in between. But the nun's eyes had something extra too: twinkles of hazy green, like summer light through oak leaves. The colors swirled and shifted. They were teasing eyes, and they gave Tom the queerest feeling.

"But you didn't meet everyone last night," the nun was saying. "Just me."

He'd held her hand a touch too long, he realized, dropping it like it was a hot coal.

"This here is Sister Calla." Sister Emma barreled on with the introductions.

The little nun gave him a sharp nod. She didn't seem to like him in the least. Tom couldn't say he blamed her.

"And I think you know Winnie."

The child was peering nervously from the wagon. It was the girl from the whorehouse, he realized. The one who'd brought him the stack of dime novels. He tipped his hat at her, and she ducked back down out of sight. He had to admit he was glad to see the little 'un get away from *La Noche*, and who safer to send a child with than a couple of nuns?

"And this . . ." Sister Emma cleared her throat as she introduced the veiled woman in black. "This is . . . Doña Anna del Castillo. She's headed for the mission at Santa María Magdalena de Buquivaba too."

"Bienvenida, señora," Tom said politely, tipping his hat again.

The señora gave a squeak and nodded her head in response. Then she made a dash for the wagon. Tom cringed. He wasn't making a good impression.

"You speak Spanish?" the little one, Sister Calla, asked him, her almond-shaped eyes lighting up. She was dark eyed and caramel skinned and had a soft Mexican accent.

"Crecí en México," he told her, feeling her thaw with every word he spoke. "My mother was Mexican. I was born there."

"Where in Mexico are you from? How long have you been away? I haven't been home for so many years! I can't wait to get back." The little nun erupted in a stream of Spanish. Her eyes were shining as the words flowed from her. She'd definitely thawed.

Tom could see that the taller nun—Sister Emma, the one with the startling golden-green eyes—couldn't understand a word.

"He's from Mexico!" Sister Calla told her companion.

"I guessed." Sister Emma's lips were quirking again as she watched the little nun take Tom's arm in delight. Tom wished Sister Emma wouldn't smile like that. It did strange things to his already weak stomach.

"We have to go," he said lamely.

"We'll talk tonight," Sister Calla said, squeezing his arm. "You can tell me where you're from."

"Arizpe. I'm from Arizpe." He edged out of her grasp.

"Arizpe! But that's so close to Magdalena." Sister Calla

was just about exploding with joy. "*I'm* from Magdalena. Just think, we might have met before."

"I mean originally. Now I'm from Oregon." At least that's where he spent his winters.

"Do you know Arturo Robles? Or Don Leon? Or Miguel Ángel Leon?"

"I do," he replied in Spanish. She lit up like the sun breaking free of clouds. "I do business with Don Leon and his son," Tom explained.

"You two will have a lot to talk about tonight," Sister Emma said.

He nodded, keeping his gaze away from her. He wasn't going to make the mistake of looking at her again. He'd done enough staring for one day.

"We've got some traveling to do until then," he grunted. "We should get going."

"Wait. I have something for you." Sister Emma had stepped in his path as he made to leave. "Here." She handed him a small wooden pail.

He frowned at it.

"It won't bite you."

Close up, her eyes were a marvel. Like summer grasses: a perfect blend of gold and wheat, speckled with green. He would have kept staring if she hadn't turned away to mount her mare. Despite the weight of her robes, she swung athletically into the saddle. The black habit rode up, showing an incredibly long, shapely leg, clad in tight buckskin. She saw him watching and flicked the hem of her habit down, to cover herself.

Goddamn it. He was ogling a *nun*. Surely, he couldn't get much lower. He turned his attention to the pail.

"It's lunch," she told him. "It'll be cold, but it's better than nothing."

It was much better than nothing. It was *good*. Once they were riding, he dug into it. She'd packed him some big wedges of fresh bread, and damn if it wasn't the best bread he'd ever eaten. Now that the nausea was subsiding, he was powerfully hungry. Under the bread, she'd also packed some thick-cut slices of ham and an apple. He was still hungry when he'd finished, so he fished some jerky out of his saddlebag. Shame he'd missed the coffee, he thought. The food had brightened his mood considerably, but coffee would have rounded things off nicely. Before he headed out to scout farther afield, he returned the sister's pail and thanked her.

"If I'da known you were that hungry, I would have packed more," she said. She was smiling again. She sure seemed to be a sunny sort, for a nun. Especially for a nun who was being hunted by a man like Hec Boehm. But Tom guessed religious types must have a certain level of fortitude.

"If you'da packed more, I would have eaten it," he told her. "Especially the bread."

She looked mighty pleased with herself. God, she was pretty.

God*damn* it. What was *wrong* with him?

"Are you armed?" he asked abruptly.

"What?" That knocked the sun out of her.

"Do you have a weapon?" he asked. "I need to scout ahead. I might have to go a fair way, and I don't want to leave you unarmed. I know you got some mean sorts on your tail."

She flinched and he almost groaned. He forgot he was dealing with a woman. He probably could have done that with more finesse.

"Just in case," he said hurriedly.

"I have this." She pulled a Colt from the folds of her habit. Judging by her grip on the stock, she was used to handling it.

"You can fire it?"

"Honey, I can hit a possum at fifty paces."

He was startled into a laugh. It was the incongruity of her thick accent and cocky expression with the sober black habit. "Not sure how many possums you'll run into in broad daylight," he said.

"Aw now, Hec Boehm ain't much more than a big old fat possum."

She had kind eyes, he thought stupidly, as he realized she was trying to put him at ease.

"Don't worry, honey," she said, "we'll be fine while you go off scouting. I'll make sure we follow your tracks. And I'll keep the pistol handy."

There was something about her voice, he thought as he rode off through the chaparral. She didn't sound the way he'd imagined a nun would sound. Her voice was woodsy and slow and full of fun. But then he'd always been a sucker for a southern accent. The whore last night had had one, and so did Alex. They warmed him up like a shot of straight bourbon. Sister Emma's was stronger than Alex's, somehow both twangier but also more of a drawl. There were no edges to her words; they ran together like a flow of molasses on a hot day. When she said his name, she made it last for several slow heartbeats.

The booze had muddled him. The booze and the August heat and the sheer bizarreness of the past day. He pulled his hat down lower to block the sun and relaxed into what was going to be a long afternoon of riding. One day he'd find a woman who would steal his heart away from Alex, he reassured himself. Maybe someone with one of those sexy ac-

cents. Maybe he should take himself off to the South. He
wondered if there were more women like Alex back there
in Mississippi. Or maybe he should ask Sister Emma where
she was from—he sure did like the way she sounded.

By the time the day was easing, he'd twigged where they
were. He steered them slightly westward, so they'd hit the
town of Second Carrot in another day or so. He needed provisions if they were going to get down to Mexico. And it
was probably a good idea to put their ears to the ground and
see if there was any word about those posses. He hoped
Deathrider and Micah had cleared Mariposa safely. Someone in Second Carrot would probably have word about the
bet in Frisco and whether the bounty hunters were all in a
bunch or whether they'd spread out. The news would be too
juicy not to have spread.

The nuns looked relieved to hear they were reasonably
close to a town. He had the feeling they didn't completely
trust him, which made him cringe in shame. He set store by
his reputation as a solid man, and it pained him to have
made such a poor impression.

"I guess I got some apologizing to do," he said eventually, once they'd pitched camp and his chores were done. It
had taken him all day to work up to it. The women paused
what they were doing and looked up at him, surprised. Sister Emma was kneading a slab of dough, while Sister Calla
and Doña Anna were preparing the evening meal. Winnie
was standing close by the veiled señora; she'd been quiet
and jumpy all evening. The sky was a streaky bay of purples and oranges behind them, and shadows were creeping
out from the chaparral and sage. Even though the sun had
set, the heat was still rising from the baked earth. It was
shaping up to be another airlessly hot night.

"I'm not much of a drinker." He continued his apology

shamefaced. He was glad the light was fading so he didn't have to see their expressions clearly. "I ain't been in a state like that in years. There's no excuse for it, but I've been traveling hard and I hadn't slept or eaten and the booze hit me; I should have known better than to drink, considering I had a responsibility to you. I just want to assure you that it won't happen again."

There was a long silence that tested Tom's nerves. Then Sister Emma started laughing.

"Good Lord, man, you'd think you'd killed someone!" She went back to kneading her bread, still laughing. "You ain't the first man to fall into the bottle, and you won't be the last."

Tom frowned and turned to Sister Calla and the señora. It was impossible to see Doña Anna's expression through her veil, but he imagined her body language was less amused than Sister Emma's. Sister Calla merely shrugged and went back to work.

"It wasn't right," he insisted, still frowning. "You were my responsibility and I let you down."

"Oh hush." Sister Emma shaped her dough into a large ball. "We seem to be doing just fine. We made it out of Mariposa, we're on the right track, we've got a nice supper cooking, and"—she announced with a flourish, dropping her dough into a Dutch oven—"there'll be fresh bread for breakfast!"

"I made you worry," he insisted.

"A little worry never killed anyone." She wiped her floury hands and gave him a sideways look. "And there's worse in the world than a man who pitched an inconvenient drunk."

"I'm trying to apologize."

"I'm trying to tell you that you don't need to."

"I *want* to," he snapped.

She rose to her feet so they were eye to eye. "Fine. Apology accepted. We forgive you." Her expression grew impish again. "After all, we're nuns. It's what we do."

Apologizing should have made him feel better, but instead he felt vaguely ridiculous. Maybe it was just women, he thought as the night wore on. He'd never spent much time with womenfolk, and here he was in the middle of nowhere with nothing but females. It made sense that he felt on the back foot. Nothing about women was the same as men. Usually, his men would be sprawled around the fire with a couple of bottles of mescal; they'd be talking and joking and telling off-color tales. Food would be rice and beans. There'd be no tents unless it was raining; the men would sling their bedrolls around the fire, and there'd be tobacco and laughs until their weary bodies led them to sleep.

There was no rice and beans tonight and certainly no off-color jokes. Instead, there was a potpie and quiet. Tom had no idea how they'd managed to magic up a pie so tasty in such a short time, let alone on a campfire. The pastry just about melted when it broke apart. They served it in actual china bowls—no pewter to be seen—and even handed him a napkin.

"Would you like more, Mr. Slater?" Sister Emma was filling his bowl even as she asked the question.

He had three helpings and mopped up the gravy with the piecrust. He didn't miss Emilio's cooking, that was for sure. Although he did miss the ease of being with his men. He felt like an oaf around these ladies. It didn't help that they were so quiet. He cleared his throat a couple of times and almost spoke, but when their eyes turned to him, he froze up. He didn't have anything to say to them. He was glad when they retired for the night into their tent. Only then could he relax. He banked the fire and unfurled his bedroll. His mind was overstuffed with the events of the past few days. If he hadn't stopped by San Francisco, none of this would have happened, he thought wistfully. He'd just be going about his normal life.

Damn Deathrider.

His gaze drifted to the tent, which was glowing like a firefly in the darkness. He could see shadows moving within. He'd always thought nuns were dour old women. *Disappointed* old women. But these two were young and fresh and happy enough. They seemed to take everything in stride. Doña Anna was far more nunnish than they were. She barely spoke and put him in mind of a bat, with her flowing black veil. Tom wondered if she was off to take her vows at the mission. Some widows did, didn't they? And why else would she be traveling with nuns?

He hadn't been raised with much religion himself. They'd had a Bible, which Luke had read from on Sundays . . . when he remembered . . . when he was around and he remembered, anyway. More often than not he wasn't around, and Matt and Tom tended to leave the Bible on the shelf when he was gone. When more people moved to the valley, they'd taken to going to the informal Sunday services, just to be neighborly. Then Alex had come to town, and her brother was a minister, so after that there were proper services. There was even a little whitewashed chapel in town, and Alex was strict about the whole family attending every week.

Alex. She'd changed everything. He remembered the day she'd arrived, upending everything as surely as an earthquake. He remembered seeing her on the porch that first time, and competing with Matt for her attention. He'd never seen a woman so pretty in his entire life, or one with such spunk. She'd turned their house upside down, and when everything settled and his idiot brother had finally come to his senses and married her, nothing had been the same again. The house was full of people and noise; there was always coffee on the stove and muddy boots strewn by the door; the dining table was crowded with people and laden with food. And presiding over all of it was Alex, glowing and happy. And at the other end of the table, puffed up with pride like a peacock, was Tom's brother Luke. Luke, who half the time had no idea how lucky he was.

As he idly watched the stars winking above, Tom wondered for the millionth time if things would have been different if he'd met Alex before Luke had. The familiar daydreams curled to life, simple daydreams of going courting. Of liking a girl and having her like you back.

"Damnation, it's hotter'n Satan's armpit in there!" Without warning, Sister Emma exploded from the tent, fighting with the heavy folds of her habit as she went.

Tom's daydreams blew away like smoke, and he propped himself up, watching as the nun tripped over her skirts and struggled to pull the edges of her coif away from her face. Gone was the composed and quiet woman of earlier in the evening. All of her grace had disappeared, and she was a hot, flustered mess.

"How in all the seven hells do you *sleep* out here?" she complained. "The earth is like a damn hot plate!"

She sure had a salty mouth for a nun.

"It's probably cooler outside the tent," he said mildly.

"You know where it's cooler? San Francisco! By the *sea*." She reached into the tent and yanked out a blanket, which she dumped on the other side of the fire.

He stayed quiet as she settled herself down. Not that she settled at all. She tossed and turned and wrestled with her habit, muttering the entire time. A couple of times he thought he heard a particularly filthy epithet.

The sound of her was oddly soothing. It was more like being with Emilio and the boys.

"Is there any sea nearby where you live, Mr. Slater?" she asked. He could hear her kicking at her heavy skirts.

"Not close by, no."

"That's a shame."

"Not really. I've never had much to do with the sea."

"I've never even seen it," she sighed, "but I always wanted to."

"You won't see it in Magdalena. It's a fair piece inland."

"You don't say." She sounded disgusted. She was silent for about half a minute. "What's it like?"

"Magdalena? 'Bout what you'd expect. There's a mission. Cows."

"No. Not Magdalena. The *sea*."

"Oh." How on earth did you describe the ocean? "It's like a big lake, I guess. You ever seen a lake?" He sensed that didn't please her. "You seen the great prairies?" he asked.

She laughed. "Are you serious? I came west overland—I've seen more prairie than a girl ever needs to."

"The ocean is like that, but with water instead of grass."

There was silence. He guessed she was trying to imagine it.

"When the wind blows, everything ripples. Instead of seed heads flicking, imagine waves chasing across the surface, all white tipped. It's like a breathing thing. And it changes color. Sometimes it's so bright blue and green it don't seem real, and at other times it's a real iron gray. The sun glints off it like someone's thrown silver dollars all across it."

After another long silence, he heard a soft laugh in the darkness. "Mercy, Mr. Slater, I wasn't expecting you to be a poet."

"I ain't. I'm just telling it like it is."

There was a soft sigh, so soft he barely heard it. And then the silence held, and they were both left to their thoughts in the darkness.

❧ 9 ❧

"*THIS* IS A town?" Emma's heart plummeted as she looked around. Second Carrot was barely a trading post, let alone a town. There were only two buildings, for heaven's sake! And they both looked like they might fall down at any moment. "You sure you don't want to keep going until we find First Carrot?"

He smiled at that. There was clearly a sense of humor in him. He'd be all serious, and then when she made a wisecrack, out came that toe-curlingly gorgeous smile. Which was something, as he was the angriest man she'd ever met. The man carried a veritable *anvil* of anger around with him. And he was the worst kind of angry too; he was the kind who didn't even *know* he was angry. It wasn't the flashy kind of anger, not the kind that made a man yell or hit; it was the inward kind, the kind that made a body barren and empty eyed. Emma wondered what made him that way. His brothers sure hadn't been like that. Luke was just about the most happy-go-lucky man she'd ever met, and Matt was just . . . Matt. He acted tough, but inside he was all tender heart. This Slater was something else entirely. He was a volcano . . . The man himself was molten and buried deep.

But you had to give it to him: he was a *beautiful* volcano. After a couple of days on the trail, he was rumpled and bearded and sultry as all get-out. The rasp of black stubble made his cheekbones and jaw stronger and his lips more pronounced. And then there were his eyes . . . Those eyes were nothing like his brother's. Where Luke's were dark, his were green, a faded minty green made even more startling by his jet-black eyelashes. Every time she caught sight of them, all the breath was knocked from her lungs. They were so clear. Like the waters of a shallow creek. Only *green*.

"There ain't no First Carrot, Sister," he said, flicking his reins around the hitching post. It was a very askew hitching post that looked like it had been hammered together by a child. A blind one. "This is all the Carrot you're going to get."

They'd settled into a fairly comfortable companionship, she and Tom Slater. Enough that she had relaxed her guard on acting nunnish. Not that she'd done a good job of it in the first place. Calla, on the other hand, got more devout by the minute; any day now she might actually grow a halo. Emma wasn't one for halos herself. Even if she'd had one—which she most certainly did not—she doubted she could manage to keep it polished. No. It was better to keep your feet solidly on the ground than to go wishing after wings.

"Well, heck. They don't look like they'd stock much of anything here. They ain't likely to have another tent, are they?" Emma slid from her horse as the wagon rattled up to join them on Main Street. She knew it was Main Street because there was a sign. Although it wasn't spelled right. They liked their signs around here. There'd been another one half a mile back: "Wellkom toe Second Carrot!"

"I need another tent," Emma insisted. "Ours is a furnace with all the bodies crammed in there; I can't sleep in that .hotbox."

"You *haven't* been sleeping in there," Calla said tightly as she joined Emma and Tom by the store. "You've been sleeping outside."

Emma rolled her eyes. Calla didn't like the idea of Emma spending the night unchaperoned with Tom Slater. *We're supposed to be nuns,* she'd hissed at Emma more times than Emma could count. *Have some modesty!* Like there was anything immodest about sleeping on the opposite side of the campfire to a man. Besides, she wasn't a nun; she was a goddamn whore! They all were. The time for worrying about her modesty was long past. You could put a whore in a habit, but it didn't wash her clean.

"And I'm going to *keep* sleeping outside if there's no tent to be had here," she announced belligerently. "You ought to try it. It's a hell of a lot cooler. Well, not a hell of a lot. But some." If she could ditch the habit, the heat would be more bearable. This thing was heavy and scratchy and suffocating, and she was cooking alive in it. When they finally got safely to Magdalena, she was going to burn the wretched thing.

She stomped up the stairs after Tom and followed him into the building, which had a hand-painted sign reading "Storr."

"There ain't no one here." Emma took in the empty room.

"But the door wasn't locked," Winnie said, cautiously inching over the threshold. She'd started coming out of her shell the last day or so.

"Guess because there's nothing to steal." Emma ran a finger over the table and wrinkled her nose when it came away thick with dust. "Maybe it's abandoned."

"It ain't abandoned. Stu's probably just out hunting." Tom dropped his saddlebags inside the door.

"He should do less hunting and more cleaning." Emma peered into the recesses of the store. She suspected the shape in the dim corner might be a dead rat. Or maybe a possum. She hoped it was a possum, because it was enormous, and she didn't fancy running into any giant rats. "How many people live here?" she asked.

Tom shrugged. "It changes, depending. It's one of those places people pass through. There's always basic supplies—like beans—and some fresh game." He cleared his throat. "And they do a pretty fair trade in liquor," he added.

Emma grinned. Mercy, he was cute when he got embarrassed, and he was still plenty embarrassed about his drinking. That spoke to the quality of the man, she thought. And he'd been a very well-behaved drunk. She sure could tell him some stories about the ways men behaved when they were liquored up . . . Well . . . she could if she weren't pretending to be a stuffy old nun.

"Liquor is the devil's drink," Calla intoned.

Emma almost lost her composure at that. Calla looked away quickly. Emma was relieved to see the girl's lips twitch. Oh, thank heavens; it was nice to know the old Calla was still in there. Especially since Calla made the best beer in Moke Hill and it would be a tragedy if she quit brewing forever.

But she did like the fetching way Mr. Slater blushed at Calla's words. High color suited him. Hell, anything suited him.

"Might be best if we pass through quickly then, Sister," he said awkwardly, tapping his dusty hat against his leg. "This place can get a bit rowdy in the evenings."

Emma looked around in sheer disbelief. There weren't

no one to get rowdy that she could see. "I think it will be fine," she assured him. It was late afternoon, and she didn't fancy rushing, even though it didn't look like there was much to keep them there. And Second Carrot was better than no carrot at all.

"You sure?" Tom ran an anxious hand through his hair.

"Honey, if we weren't shocked by the goldfields, we won't be shocked here."

"Who said we weren't shocked?" Calla complained quietly after Tom had gone to see to the animals and set up a campsite. "Your heart ain't in this nun business."

"Bite your tongue, little Calida. We both know my heart is exactly where it's supposed to be." She slung an arm around Calla's shoulders and gave her a squeeze. "I think I'm doing an excellent job. Considering."

Calla rolled her eyes.

"I've kept my clothes on," Emma teased, "and I haven't propositioned anyone. Yet."

"There ain't been anyone to proposition."

"Oh ho ho, there ain't, huh?" Emma nodded at the doorway as Tom Slater ambled past, leading the mules. "That there looks like prime propositioning material." She sighed admiringly.

Calla snorted. They both knew Emma hadn't slept with a man in nigh on a year and that she was mighty happy to keep it that way.

Still, a girl could enjoy the view, Emma thought, watching that lovely long man at work. It was such a shame when he moseyed out of sight.

There was a sneeze, and then Anna's voice came from the back of the Storr. "There's some fabric back here," she called. "There might be some canvas you can make into a tent."

"You're useful for a fancy lady, ain't you?" Emma said as she found Anna in the darkened rear storeroom where goods were stacked haphazardly. There were bags of coffee beans next to piles of firewood next to coils of hemp rope next to cook pots, everything teetering in a chaotic maze.

Anna sneezed again. She held out her veil and sneezed a few more times in quick succession.

"Watch out for rodents," Emma said as she inched cautiously into the chaos. She peered at the rolls of cloth. "None of that looks like canvas." Something caught her eye. She perked up and dragged it out of the stack. It came with a plume of dust that set both of them off sneezing.

"Look, Calla, cotton!" she exclaimed gleefully, emerging from the storeroom.

"*Sister* Calla," Calla reminded her darkly. And that's when Emma saw they weren't alone.

Four men hulked in the doorway. They were terrible rough sorts. The sort who gave you pause, even when you met them in full daylight, with witnesses. They seemed nonplussed to have company, particularly female company. All four were armed to the teeth. They'd been hunting, Emma assumed. Hopefully not people. Winnie was just about hiding under Calla's skirts in fear. Calla wasn't much bigger than the girl but was standing her ground; on the outside she looked serene, but Emma knew her well enough to see the tension in her. She'd known enough men like these to be wary.

"Well, howdy," Emma said brightly. She'd learned that brazenness worked best in these situations. Show no fear. Claim control of the interaction before they did. Set the rules. "I assume one of you is the proprietor of this fine establishment? How much for the cotton?"

Thank God she was dressed as a nun. "Wasn't it a good

idea?" she whispered to Calla later, once they'd bought supplies. "*No one* takes advantage of a nun! He didn't even haggle with me."

It turned out the men were more scared of them than they were of the men. The sight of nuns had knocked them sideways. They watched Emma with startled, almost frightened eyes as she chattered at them. By the time Tom came in from sorting the animals, she'd taken care of the introductions and was happily buying provisions. They watched her like she was a wild animal who might turn on them at any minute. Men. Show them a whore and they fell over themselves to get at her; show them a nun and they about wet their pants with fear. Even when it was the exact same woman.

She and Calla bundled up their haul and left Tom to soothe the poor dears.

"What do you need with all that cotton?" Calla asked, bewildered by the armful of fabric Emma was so excited about. "You can't make a tent out of cotton."

"Forget the tent. You could give me some praise now and admit it was a good idea for us to dress as nuns. Look how they leave us alone! We'd be in some trouble without these getups."

"It was a *great* idea. You're very clever. Now what's with the cotton?"

"You're being smart with me, but I *am* very clever. I'm going to make us new habits."

"You're what?"

Emma grinned. "I'm going to make us *cotton* habits. So we don't sweat ourselves out of existence."

"But it ain't black!"

"It's almost black."

"It's navy!"

"Navy's close enough to black. I'd rather be navy and survive the summer than stay in black and be cooked."

Calla closed her eyes and seemed to mouth a silent Hail Mary. "You can't," she said once she'd finished her prayer.

"I can and I shall." Emma brushed her hands clean of dust. "I can't see that God cares what color our habits are. In fact, He's probably outraged at the whole endeavor and has already washed His hands of us. Changing our lie from black to navy ain't going to send us to hell any faster."

"But no one will believe it if we're navy! We won't look like nuns."

"Rubbish. Most people are right gullible, Calla. Didn't I teach you anything?" It was true. Call a sheep a cow, and most people would go right along with you, so long as you did it confident enough. Look at them inside, treating Anna like she was a grand lady. The original four men had been joined by another half dozen heavily armed ruffians, and each and every one of them was just about bowing to the fancy señora. Luckily, none of them spoke Spanish. It probably wouldn't even matter if they did; Tom spoke Spanish at Anna the first day or so, and she just remained resolutely silent and eventually he gave up. Probably figured her for the nervous sort. Or maybe he thought she was mute. But it certainly didn't have him questioning who she was.

"They want to know if we'd care to eat with them," Tom told them quietly, joining them in their corner of the Storr.

"Guess it would be rude not to," Emma said cheerfully. "Unless you think it ain't safe?"

"I reckon it's safe enough. They're acting respectful and all."

They were indeed. Painfully so. They apologized for each curse, darting alarmed looks at the women. "Sorry, Sister," they mumbled constantly.

"What's for supper?" Emma asked them, striving for a kind of schoolmarmish chipper tone.

"Possum."

Of course it was possum. It had to be, didn't it? She only hoped it was fresh.

"You like possum?" Stu the Storr owner asked, seeming anxious to please.

"I grew up on possum," Emma told him brightly. That at least was true enough. She'd eaten more possum than she cared to admit. Her daddy trapped them, and her ma turned them into stew, pie, sausages and anything else she could manage. Emma kept her smile fixed in place, even though the memory of greasy possum meat turned her stomach. "Can we add to the table?" she suggested, not quite able to keep the desperation from her voice. "I reckon we can rustle up a couple of dishes too. And I can make some corn bread."

"I'll help." Tom followed her outside. "Thank you," he groaned once they were clear of the Storr. "I *hate* possum." He squinted at the patchy woods. "Reckon I can get a rabbit or something?"

"Depends. How good a shot are you?"

He gave her a disgruntled look and she laughed. Men and their pride.

"I guess by the size of you, you'll do just fine. You must eat something to get that big." She fluttered her eyelashes dramatically.

He laughed. "You're sassy for a nun, ain't you?"

It was a knack, she thought with a grin, getting him to laugh. When he laughed, he relaxed. His eyes were bottle green in the late-afternoon sun, and his dimples flickered as he met her gaze.

"*All* nuns are sassy," she assured him loftily. "You

clearly ain't known many or you'd recognize that for a fact."

"I ain't known *any* before you. Least not that I remember."

Was it her imagination or was there a flash of admiration in his eyes? Whether it was her imagination or not, it caused a very real quickening of her heartbeat.

"Well, I'm standard for a nun. You can take my word for it." She had a sudden urge to go hunting with him. Corn bread didn't take no time at all; she could make it when she got back. "You know what else is standard for a nun?" she said.

He shook his head, looking simultaneously manly and also like a shy little boy.

"Marksmanship," she announced.

"Marksmanship?" Up went his thick black eyebrows.

"Marksmanship is standard for a nun. All nuns are excellent shots." She placed the heel of her hand on her holster, which was slung from the leather belt around her hips.

"They are?" There went those dimples again.

"It's one of the tests they give you before they hand you your crucifix."

"Is it? And what do they get you to shoot at?"

"Arks." It was the first thing she thought of, and the sheer ridiculousness of it almost had her giggling.

He laughed. "And why would they want you shooting arks?"

"I think the real question is why *wouldn't* they want you shooting at arks?" She glanced at the low sun. "We should get moving before we lose the light."

"Wouldn't want to miss those arks," he said dryly.

"Bet you a dollar I shoot something before you do." She set off out of the town. It took her roughly ten strides to be at the town limits.

"I didn't know nuns were allowed to gamble."

"And why not?"

"For a start, it don't seem fair. Since you have God on your side and all." He led her into the sparsely wooded area ahead.

"I'll make it fairer." She turned her face to the sky. "God? It's Sister Emma. Remember me? That's right, the one with the ark-shooting record. Sorry to trouble You, but would You mind stepping aside for this one? Just to even the odds?" She offered Tom her hand to shake. "Happy now? A dollar for first catch?"

Oh, his dimples gave her such a light-headed feeling. He was sexy enough when he was a volcano, but this smiling version of him was devastating.

Emma gave him an angelic look and drew her Colt. She wanted to win the bet.

❧ 10 ❧

"**Y**OU'D THINK A place called Second Carrot would at least stock a carrot," Emma said as she sucked the last of the meat off a quail drumstick. Quail might not be the most filling game, but it tasted a damn sight better than possum. Shame there were no carrots, as they would have gone perfectly with quail, and God knew they could all do with some fresh vegetables. But even though it was late summer, the men of Second Carrot had no fresh greens or squash or summer fruit; there wasn't so much as a vegetable garden or a field to be seen. They seemed to subsist entirely on meat and fried dough. Emma couldn't bear the thought of it, so she'd gone and foraged in the woods and had found some fennel, goosefoot and sorrel growing wild. She would have loved to have a cucumber or a carrot or two to toss through the leaves. It was utterly criminal that they didn't have a kitchen garden, considering how fertile the land was around here.

"It's plain misleading to call a town Second Carrot when there are no carrots," she said, licking her fingers.

The men shared a confused look. "Why would there be carrots?"

She paused. "I assume there must have been carrots here once? At least two of them anyway."

She saw Tom Slater just about choke on his corn bread.

What was so funny? Why was he laughing? An idea itched at the back of her mind. Dear God, surely not . . .

"Why exactly did you settle here?" she asked the men suspiciously.

"For the gold," Stu told her, mopping the grease off his chin with his sleeve.

Oh, for the love of . . . Second *Karat*. Emma groaned. God save her from illiterate miners. It didn't even make sense. *Two* karats: did gold even come in weights that small?

"I didn't think there was gold this far south," Calla said.

There wasn't, Emma thought, exasperated. Look at the place. If there'd been so much as a sniff of gold, it would be clogged with miners.

"In the streams there is," Stu said. "It washes down from the goldfields."

"It does?" Emma didn't believe him. "Rich pickings, is it?"

"Look." He dug in his pocket and brought out a vial. It seemed to be filled with water. "See the gold?" He held it up to the lamplight. Tiny flecks sparkled in the water.

Emma bit her tongue. He looked so proud of his glittery water, and who was she to shatter a man's illusions? She doubted he'd ever seen proper gold dust, let alone a nugget. She was sitting on a fortune in gold herself. Quite literally. She had it stitched into the waistband and pockets of her breeches, where it would stay until she used it to buy herself a house by the bay. Some of the nuggets were as big as her knuckles and dug into her something fierce.

"It's very pretty," she said, trying to sound admiring. She was aware of Tom Slater in the corner of her vision, hiding a smile as he sawed off another hunk of corn bread. She sure did love the way that man ate. It was a shame they didn't have any butter; a nice slathering of salted butter was just what corn bread needed.

After the food was finished and everything had been washed up, the men milled around awkwardly. Emma had a fair idea of what their problem was. They were itching to break out the moonshine but weren't keen to do it with the nuns present. Stu offered them private use of his room for the night, but Emma politely declined. She didn't fancy sleeping in the dust, worrying about rats the size of possums; she also didn't fancy being within hearing of their late-night drinking session. Especially considering the sneaky little looks a couple of the men were already giving Anna and Winnie. Particularly Winnie. It would never cease to amaze her how many men wanted to poke at a child. It was something that turned her stomach; she'd never countenanced it in any place she'd worked, and certainly not in the ones she'd owned. She took note of which men snuck looks at little Winnie and resolved to sleep with her Colt close by.

Tom had similar thoughts, clearly, because while they were busy cooking, he'd snuck off and pitched their camp a fair piece from town, over an embankment and hidden in a thicket of cottonwoods next to a creek. The tent was screened by thick brush, and he'd backed the wagon behind a stand of trees, with the animals pegged farther on, where they could feed on the dry summer grasses. When he led the women through the scrappy woods to the camp, Emma gave him a curious look. He'd gone to an awful lot of trouble to make sure they were well hidden. It was an informal kind of fort, with the banks and trees and creek acting as natural barriers. They had to descend a fairly sharp slope to reach the campsite. Clearly, he'd made it as difficult as possible for someone to creep up on them. She doubted a drunk could navigate it without waking everyone in the camp, especially in the dark. It was difficult enough to get down the slope now, sober and with the lingering summer twilight still offering enough light to see by.

"How on earth did you get the wagon down here?" she asked, astonished, as she held on to a tree trunk to keep from sliding down the hill.

"With difficulty," he said with a quick grin. He held out his hand to help her down the last of the slope. His fingers closed around hers. His skin was warm and, oh my . . . Sparks shot through her. Cascades of sparkles, like pinpoints of fire in her blood.

Oh *dear*. She hadn't felt sparks like that in years. Sparks like that led you smack bang into trouble. Those sparks got you all dazzled, and by the time you got clear again, some man had gone and chipped away at your heart. Men like Rory Baker, who'd run off with her when she was fourteen. She'd been desperate to get away from Duck Creek, and just the slightest glimmer of sparks from Rory had sent her off and away. She'd taken nothing with her but her late mother's starter dough and the clothes on her back; she'd held on to the starter all these years, but lost Rory within a couple of weeks. He'd abandoned her in Paducah, Kentucky, leaving her high and dry. He hadn't paid the bill for their lodging, and she hadn't had a cent to her name, so the landlord had taken payment roughly, and against Emma's will.

She pushed that memory away quickly. There was no point dwelling on it. You couldn't change the past.

She certainly wouldn't change the good bits, like the sparks when she'd met Mr. Aaron Nash, who was from the east and talked fancy. Oh, hadn't he swept her right off her feet . . . and right onto her back. He'd been full of pretty dreams, promising to marry her and take her to New York. By then she was working in a whorehouse in St. Louis; she'd colored her hair and was going by the name Seline. She still remembered Mr. Nash's pretty stories about New York: about snow falling on gaslit streets; about riding in horse-drawn carriages; about theaters and restaurants, dancing girls and lecture halls; about the sunlight glancing off the harbor on hot summer days and sailboats racing to keep the wind. Those stories were the only thing Mr. Nash had left her with when he'd run off. Well, those and a baby in her belly.

There were half a dozen other spark-causers who had turned her head when she was still young enough to hope for better. Each and every one of them talked sweet, enjoyed her body and then left her with nothing but a sore heart. Rory, Mr. Nash, Gerd Schultz, Ennio Salvi, Luke Slater . . . Although if she was honest, Luke had been the only one who'd never promised her the moon: he'd only ever been a nicer-than-normal paying customer; anything more had all been in her imagination. She'd led *herself* astray that time. And what woman didn't, when it came to Luke Slater?

And that had been the *last* time. She'd been done with men after Luke. They were customers and that was all. Anything more hurt too bad. None of them wanted a woman; they just wanted a body. They certainly didn't want the person who came with the body. The minute she started hampering their fun, they were off like a shot. And she couldn't take another chip in her heart. It wasn't even the men who made the worst chips; it was the babies they left her with. The babies who also left her, one by one, some before they'd finished growing, others during childbirth and, worst of all, the ones who lived a day or a week or a month and then succumbed to coughs or fevers or simply died in the night. A heart took a beating from losing babies. It might even get a little twisted, a little crippled. So she'd started taking Dolly's contraceptive concoction and decided to banish the sparks from her life. They weren't worth the pain.

Only now here they were again . . . fountains of them swirling through her every time Tom Slater smiled.

Still. What harm could a few sparks do in *this* situation? Tom Slater thought she was a nun. If you thought about it, it was actually the perfect time to enjoy some sparks. There was no risk. She could tease and flirt, admire those dimples and those shoulders . . . and those eyes . . . and those hard, muscular thighs in those tight dark pants . . . Well, now, there was no harm in it, was there? she thought as her gaze lingered on his legs. She was a *nun*. The very nature of her nunhood meant everything would stop at a little innocent flirting. There wouldn't—*couldn't*—be any touching, any kissing, any taking things further than darting glances and some teasing. And he sure was fun to tease.

She watched as he helped Anna down the slope. Her heart gave a girlish little skip at his chivalry. She bit her lip. She'd never had much chance to be a regular girl, she thought with a stab of longing. She hadn't had the chance to sweetly flirt like real girls did, like *good* girls did. No one had cast cow eyes at her in church or walked her home or asked her daddy if he could come visiting. No one had brought her fresh-picked flowers or written her love notes. No. There hadn't been youthful courtship for her. Instead, from the age of thirteen, she'd had a sweaty hand shoved over her mouth and a searing pain between her legs.

Don't think about it.

She *wouldn't* think about it. Because once you started, you couldn't stop. And she wouldn't let him ruin one more thing in her life. Especially this. Because she was a *nun*, goddamn it, and nuns were *safe*. And why the hell shouldn't she enjoy a spark or two while she was safe?

"I was thinking we should skip the campfire tonight," Tom suggested softly, so only she could hear. He was squinting back up at the embankment. "We've already eaten, and we certainly don't need it for warmth."

She frowned, all thoughts of sparks and flirting flying from her. "You're really that worried about the men?"

"Just a couple of them. I didn't like the way . . ."

"They were looking at Winnie? Me neither."

"Winnie?" His eyebrows shot up. "I didn't like the way they were looking at *you*. You and Calla both."

"What?" she squeaked. "But we're *nuns*."

"You thought they were looking at Winnie?" It was getting difficult to see his expression in the gathering purple darkness, but she thought there was a look of pure horror on his face. "What the hell is wrong with people?" he muttered.

Emma thought she should probably say something nunlike there, something about sin or the devil. Jesus had probably said something on the topic of what the hell was wrong with people. If she'd been a proper nun, she might have known what it was.

"Some people are just sons of bitches." She doubted Jesus had said that. But he should have.

"I'll stand guard tonight," Tom reassured her. "I doubt they'll do anything; they were probably just looking. But you never know. Stu's moonshine could stir them up. Especially as there ain't no women in Second Carrot, and I'd bet none of those men have seen a real one in a good long while." He sighed. "I'm afraid it can be rough out here for women, Sister."

"It's rough everywhere for women, Mr. Slater," she said tartly. "And you can't keep guard all night. You'll need to sleep eventually. We can take turns keeping watch."

"No," he said shortly. "It's my job to get you safely to Mexico. *I'll* stand watch."

"Yeah, well, it's *me* they're looking to violate."

He flinched. By now, he was merely an indigo silhouette in the gathering darkness, but she saw how his silhouette jerked at her words.

"I'm a good shot—you saw me earlier." She tried to lighten the mood. "I got the silver dollar to prove it."

He was silent.

"Tom?"

"I'm thinking," he said shortly. "Fine. You can stand watch. But we'll do it together. We can keep each other awake. Can you talk to Sister Calla and Doña Anna? They'll need to be absolutely quiet tonight. And we can't use lanterns."

His seriousness gave her a chill. Hell. She didn't fancy fighting off a bunch of drunken fools. "Maybe we're worrying for nothing?"

"Maybe. But I'd rather worry for nothing than be caught unawares."

So would she, she thought with a shiver as she made for the tent to warn the others. Calla clearly already had an inkling, as she'd grabbed the shotgun from the wagon and had it loaded and resting on her lap.

"Guess none of us are planning on sleeping tonight," Emma said mildly.

EMMA WAS WOUND tighter than a clock spring for a good couple of hours. Every snapping twig and rustling leaf made her finger tighten on the trigger. And there were noises aplenty as darkness drew in and the nocturnal wildlife foraged by the creek. It was enough to make a girl a nervous wreck. Calla and Anna had Winnie sandwiched between them in the tent, the shotgun in easy reach. They'd all slipped off to sleep pretty quick, despite the tension. Tom had planted himself in front of the tent and was facing the embankment. He leaned against a tree trunk, his revolver resting on his thigh. Emma joined him, perched anxiously on a rock. Distantly, they could hear voices from the direction of Second Carrot; the sound carried clearly through the hot summer air. Even though she couldn't make out words, the voices sounded fractious.

"Men always sound like they're arguing when they're drunk," Emma whispered.

"That's because they often are." There was a smile in Tom's voice.

"Why is that, do you think?" She was twitchy as all get-out.

"It's the same with all animals," he said softly, adjusting his position to get more comfortable. He didn't seem twitchy at all. "You should see what happens when you get a couple of bull steers together. Especially when there's females about."

Emma rolled her eyes. "You reckon they'd stop if they knew the lady cows thought they were stupid for doing it?"

"No, I don't reckon they would. Cattle are notoriously immune to judgment."

Now it was her turn to laugh. He was surprisingly funny. You wouldn't expect it when you met him. And in her experience, men that good-looking seldom had wit.

Laughing broke her tension. She left the rock and joined him, sitting against the tree next to his. She made sure to position herself so she could still see his bulk in the dimness. Somehow the sight of him kept her calm.

A sickle moon was rising, casting ashy light through the still cottonwood leaves and lining everything with silver. Frogs were singing by the creek.

"I reckon it might rain," Tom said.

Emma looked dubiously at the patches of clear sky visible through the canopy above. The stars glittered, unobstructed by the slightest trace of cloud.

"Frogs get louder when it's about to rain," he told her. Emma laughed again. She thought that was about the biggest load of rubbish she'd ever heard. There'd been plenty of bullfrogs back in Duck Creek, and they'd set to croaking up a storm every evening, come rain or shine. They'd never seemed daunted by a clear sky, and neither did these California frogs.

"You wait," he said. He tilted his head back to look up at the sky. A shaft of silver moonlight fell through the canopy, catching the side of his face. Emma's gaze traced his silvered jaw and the planes of his high cheekbones. On the surface, he was so calm, she thought. He was a solid presence, quiet, reassuring. But she could see the tightness of the muscles in his jaw, and the two frown lines between his eyebrows. He wasn't what he seemed, this man. Not one bit. What was he thinking when he was all quiet like this? What caused those shadows that chased across his face? What made him so deathly serious, when clearly, there was a sense of humor in there somewhere? He was a man who needed to laugh more, she decided. He had no call being so grave when he was young and strong and so damn good-looking. Life was his for the taking. So why was he out here in the wilderness with a couple of nuns, instead of off taking it?

As she watched him, his head snapped around. Frightened, she followed his gaze. She couldn't see anything. His eyes narrowed and the gun rose. His gaze flicked to her, and he lifted a finger to his lips, warning her to be silent.

She froze. What on earth had he heard? What had he *seen?*

She couldn't see anything.

As they sat frozen, she realized she couldn't hear voices drifting over from Second Carrot anymore. It was suspiciously quiet. But it wasn't that late; there was no way they would have packed in the drinking yet . . .

Then the frogs gave pause.

Goddamn it. She cocked her own weapon and followed his gaze to the embankment. As they sat there frozen, a breeze skittered through their campsite, breaking the perfect stillness. The frogs started up again, and she realized she'd been holding her breath. She exhaled shakily, trying to stay as silent as possible.

Then she heard the voices. They were faint but heading their way. Tom gestured for her to come to him. She crept over, and he pulled her behind the tree with him. She saw him check over his shoulder at the tent. It should be well enough hidden. Emma hoped that the horses didn't start whickering.

"Maybe they left?" The man's voice came from the other side of the embankment. It was one of those brutes from Second Carrot. Emma's blood ran hot and cold. Memories of past assaults were rising like a tide, and it took everything she had to force them down, to not let the fear take her.

She jumped when Tom's hand settled on the small of her back. He must have sensed her panic, because he gave her a couple of soothing rubs.

"Wouldn't you?" A second voice joined the first. "There's a fortune riding on his head. And he ain't stupid, or he wouldn't have lasted this long."

Emma frowned. *He?*

Tom's hand went deathly still on her back.

"He didn't look like no Indian."

Oh no. *No.*

"He's passing for a white man now. That's what they said in Frisco. And you heard Stu: that was definitely Tom Slater."

Emma heard Tom's breath catch. This time it was her turn to lay a soothing hand on him. Startled, he met her gaze. They were only inches apart. She gave a small shake of her head. *Stay silent,* she begged with her eyes. *Please.*

The wind picked up, gusting, rustling the leaves overhead. It was a moody sound.

"His eyes were pretty pale, weren't they?" the second man said, not sounding entirely convinced.

His friend ignored him. "I woulda run off too if I was him." The two men kept walking. "He wouldn't stand a chance against all of us."

"You sure he wouldn't have camped? He might be up a ways still. He couldn't be dragging all those women through the dark. Especially *those* women—they looked the tender sort."

Tender! She was outraged. She'd show them tender. Those fatheads wouldn't have survived a single *day* of her life. Or Calla's. Or Anna's.

"If they were going to pitch camp, they would have done it back near town." There was a long pause. "Maybe he's gone and turned himself into a wolf . . . They say he can do that."

A wolf? These two were too dumb to live. And who the hell could confuse Tom with Deathrider? Tom Slater was the least outlaw-looking man Emma had ever seen. He had fine and upstanding written all over him.

"Maybe so. But what about the women? He cain't be turning them into no wolves." Only he said *woofs* instead of "wolves." Emma bet he was the idiot who wrote all the signs.

"Yeah, I guess." There was a pause. "You reckon he's kidnapped those nuns? And that little white girl?"

Emma gasped. "Hush," Tom whispered in her ear. He'd pulled her tight against him so she could barely move.

"Of course he's kidnapped them. You saw how jumpy they were."

"Goddamn."

Kidnapped! They weren't kidnapped. And they'd been jumpy because they were alone in the middle of nowhere with men who hadn't bathed in months and served up possum for dinner, not because they were here with Tom Slater!

Emma flinched when they heard a piercing whistle sound from back toward Second Carrot.

"Looks like they've found them!" The pair couldn't contain their excitement. They were heading to town in a flash, eager not to miss the lynching.

"Hell," Tom growled once they were gone.

"We should go now, while they're distracted." Emma made for the tent, but Tom yanked her back.

"Wait." He kept his voice low. "I'm worried it's a trap."

"How much money is on Deathrider's head?" Emma asked.

"Too much." The anger was coming off him like heat from a stove. In the distance, they could hear dogs barking. Tom swore. "If they get the dogs out for us, we're out of luck."

Emma's heart was thundering. "I don't believe in luck," she said. The wind had picked up and was blowing her heavy woolen veil. She had to hold it back with her hands.

"I guess you don't have to believe in luck, being a nun. You've got God on your side."

She pulled a face. She wasn't sure God had *ever* been on her side, but if He ever had been, He certainly wasn't now—not when she was impersonating one of His women.

Still. She was alive and whole, wasn't she? She had a brain in her head to plan her way out of this mess, didn't she? So maybe He wasn't too displeased with her. "I wish your frogs were right and it *was* about to rain," she said to Tom. "Rain would sure put a stop to the dogs sniffing us out." But at the mention of rain an idea struck her. "Rain!"

"Where?" He looked up. There was no rain.

"No, I mean"—she shook her head—"I have a plan. Can you harness the wagon?" She made for the tent, but he grabbed her arm.

"Tell me," he said tightly.

"The creek. It'll hide our scent from the dogs. We won't leave tracks." She didn't need to say more. He melted away into the darkness to deal with the wagon. She hurried to the tent and woke the others. "Forget about packing up the tent," she ordered. "We'll get another one. Quick. Move! Don't ask questions. Be as quiet as possible."

Tom harnessed the wagon in record time. Emma briefly

explained the situation to the others. She pushed Calla and
Anna toward the wagon and handed Winnie up onto the
seat. "The creek," Emma told them. Her heart was thundering. It felt like it could just about burst in her chest. "Take
the wagon into the creek. Follow it downstream. Go as fast
and as quiet as you can." If the dogs managed to track them
this far (which they would), they'd soon lose the trail when
it disappeared into the water. Emma's main concern was
that the wagon was slow and their pursuers would be on
horseback; it would take them no time at all to catch up to
the wagon. "Go, Calla. Don't wait for us! And if they catch
you, shoot to kill!" They both knew what happened to
women who got caught. She gave her friend's arm a
squeeze, and then she slapped the lead mule's flank. "Good
luck!"

Once the wagon was off into the creek, making more
noise than Emma cared for, she helped Tom throw the saddlebags over the pack animals.

"It's a good plan," Tom said approvingly as he cinched
the last buckle. There was the low rumble of thunder. "Now
we want that rain. That'll stop them from making it even
this far, which will give us more time."

Yes. Please let it rain. Emma mounted her mare. *Dear
God, I know I ain't been good. I may have broken more
commandments than You ever thought of, but I ain't knowingly done harm, and I've always looked out for those less
fortunate than myself. If You could see to it in Your heart
to be clement right now and let it rain, I promise I'll do better. I don't know how, but I will.*

Thunder cracked above and she jumped. She might have
been too presumptuous. But then, as they surged into the
creek after the wagon, the first fat drops of rain began to
fall. Startled, she looked skyward. Heavy drops spattered

her face. Maybe there was something to this nun thing after all.

"I guess you were right about those bullfrogs," she told Tom, but he didn't hear her over the sound of the wind and the rain.

❧ 11 ❧

I T WAS A terrifying night. They kept in the creek until it
was too swollen to be safe. Emma's habit was sodden
and heavy, and the veil pulled at her neck until her muscles
were screaming. They couldn't hear any trace of dogs or
men over the bluster of the wind, and she was in constant
fear that they were right behind her. She wasn't able to see
two feet ahead, and she had to trust to her horse's surefoot-
edness on the slippery creek bed.

When they finally left the creek, Calla, Anna and Winnie had to get out of the wagon and help push it up the
banks. By the time they'd got it over the lip of the embankment, they were exhausted. But Tom hurried them on. "We
want to be well away before dawn."

It didn't feel like dawn would ever come. Without Tom,
she might have just sat down in the mud, but he drove them
on, sounding as calm as if he were relaxing by the campfire. His calmness was mighty soothing. After a time, the
rain slowed and then stopped. It wasn't just hot now, but
humid. Emma rode engulfed in the pungent stink of wet
wool and her own body odor.

"We have to make a choice soon," Tom told her quietly, dropping back to ride beside her. The wretched night was finally fading, she realized, because she could make out his shape in the darkness. "I can take us through ranchero territory, or we can push farther east, into the Apacheria."

"That's where Deathrider went," Emma protested. "If we go that way, we might end up with the Second Carrot men *and* Hec *and* Deathrider's bounty hunters after us. Not to mention the Apaches." The thought of Hec was enough to make her sit down and cry. Or shoot things.

"With any luck, Hec and the others have run into the Apaches themselves by now."

"Which is something *we* don't want to do," she said, panicked. She'd heard enough about the Apaches to know that she didn't want to run into them.

"We have to risk them to get to Magdalena anyway—it's right in the path of their plunder trails."

"Their *what?* No, don't answer that. I don't want to know." She swallowed. "I suppose there's a good reason you're even considering it as an option, rather than simply taking us through the rancheros' lands?"

"The rancheros know me," he said, sounding wearier by the minute. "I take their cattle up to the goldfields and sell them on. I can't go by a fake name here; they know very well that *I'm* Tom Slater. Anyone looking for 'Tom Slater' is going to know that I was here. Then we'll have a dozen bounty hunters on our trail."

"But why would your friends give you away? Why wouldn't they protect you?"

"They ain't my friends. We just do business. I don't doubt that some of them will shoot me themselves if they can collect the bounty." He rubbed tiredly at his bristling beard. "Word sure spreads quick, don't it? That place is no bigger than a fleabite."

"But they must *know* you ain't the Plague of the West!"

"I ain't betting my life or yours on it."

Madre de Dios. Apaches or rancheros? If that wasn't a poisoned chalice, she didn't know what was.

"There's a third choice," he said slowly. "It seems mad for you to suffer because of me. No one knows *you* here, so there's no reason for you to risk your lives in the Apacheria. I can leave you here and you can push on through the rancheros' lands on your own. The rancheros are Catholic; I'm sure they'll give you safe passage."

"No," she said, horrified at the thought of leaving him. They were hunting him, for heaven's sake! What kind of person would she be if she abandoned him to the mob?

"As far as I can see, those are our only three choices."

"No," she said. "There are always more choices." She cut him off when he made to speak. "No! Let me think."

"There's no other way," he said tiredly.

But there was. He just wasn't going to like it.

"THERE'S NO WAY in hell."

Emma didn't appreciate his tone. This was an *excellent* plan.

"No one is going to believe I'm a woman," he growled.

"Not an attractive woman," she agreed, "but then no one expects you to launch a thousand ships. And the veil will hide your face."

"They'll know it's me."

"I doubt it. You didn't know it was Anna."

"I'd met her *once*. They've met me dozens of times."

Emma's plan had required her to come clean about Anna. She hated to ruin Anna's disguise, but she needed to steal it for Tom. There was no choice. They didn't have any another suitable clothes for him; Calla's habit was far too small, or she might have dressed him up as a nun, and she couldn't give him *her* habit, because Hec was still after her and she needed to stay hidden. Also, she still needed *him* to believe they were nuns; she couldn't have him doubting *her.* And she didn't have time to sew a whole new habit out of the navy cotton. So he couldn't be a nun. And as for the gowns stored in her trunk, they were low-cut and fancy beyond belief—there was no way he'd pull that off. Besides, even if she had been able to sew a habit, or if he had fit into one of her gaudy gowns, there was still the problem of his *face*. No one was going to look at that chiseled face with its aquiline nose, strong jaw and *beard,* and believe he was a woman. Even if he shaved off the stubble. Some boys could have done it, but not this one. Posing him as a veiled señora was the best option. And it would work—she knew it would. If she let out the seams and the hem a little, the dress should fit him. And the lacy veil would cover him from head to waist.

"No one will ever suspect it's you! Why on earth would they? It's a perfect disguise!" she insisted.

He had a face on him like a mule. "I'm not doing it, so you can get the idea right out of your head."

"Anna, can you go and change? Throw the widow's weeds out to us once you're done, will you?" Emma went blithely on as though he wasn't being contrary.

"Oh, thank heavens, these beads keep snagging on everything." Anna had pulled the veil off as soon as Emma had revealed her identity, and she was eager to shuck the fancy dress off too.

Tom had been shocked to find out that it had been Anna under the veil all along. "But . . . why?"

When Emma told him why, he lowered his head and pinched his nose between his fingers. She wondered if he was prone to nosebleeds.

"Are you telling me that she's wanted by the law?"

"We're not sure," Emma said primly. "But we assume at the very least his friends might have formed a lynch mob."

He took a deep breath. "So we may have *four* posses out for us, if the man she hit with a frying pan has friends?"

"It seems so." She'd given him what she hoped was a charming smile.

"Are there any more you want to tell me about? Lynch mobs? Marshals? Any armies on the march for us?"

"Not yet, but give me time."

There was a ghost of a smile at that. But it hadn't lasted long. Now he was back to being difficult again. She could deal with it. She was just going to jolly him along until he gave in.

"Sister Emma?" The black dress glittered in the sun as Anna thrust it from the wagon. Emma snatched it off her and held it out to him.

Tom shook his head vehemently. "There is no way *in hell.*"

But there was. Not a pleasant way, but a way nonetheless. And this time the way included one hell of a lot of guilt. "You'd rather leave us here, in the middle of nowhere, at the mercy of men like those bastards in Second Carrot, than keep protecting us?"

"I said I'd stay with you," he growled.

"Stay with us? And put us in danger because everyone thinks you're the Plague of the West? Because of you we just got chased out of town! If you stay with us, we're going to end up shot through a dozen times over."

"So I'll leave you then! Which do you want?" A vein was pulsing in his temple.

"Neither! I want you to wear the damn dress and escort us safely to Mexico. It's only your stupid pride that's keeping us in danger!"

"My stupid . . . you name me *one man* who'd do this!"

She bit her tongue. He didn't need to know that they'd dressed Micah up like a whore.

"Exactly!" He sounded far too smug.

But he had no idea who he was dealing with. She had no scruples.

"Winnie!" Emma marched over to the wagon, where Winnie sat watching their discussion with wide eyes. Emma held out her arms. "Come here, honey."

"What are you doing?" Tom sounded horrified. Good.

Emma scooped Winnie into her arms and carried her toward Tom. The girl was far too old to be carried, but the effect was what mattered. Winnie's long legs slapped against hers as she walked.

Catching the scent of what she was up to, Tom's eyes narrowed menacingly. "Don't you dare," he warned.

Winnie burrowed her face into Emma's neck, keeping a wary eye on Tom.

"Don't do it." He stood his ground as she approached, looking blacker by the moment.

"What do you think will happen to her if you abandon us here?" Emma was merciless.

"I'm not abandoning her!"

"What do you think will happen to her if we're captured by the men hunting *you*?"

"This is low," he growled, "real, real low." He turned his back on her, and she heard him muttering under his breath.

Winnie frowned and looked up at Emma. Emma winked at her. "There, there, honey. I'm sure Tom doesn't really want to sacrifice you to the wild men."

He snapped around, glaring at her. Ah, now the volcano was starting to steam. Had she gone too far?

Or not far enough?

"I'm sure she'll understand when she's older that you couldn't compromise your manhood and wear a dress," Emma needled him. "Not even to save our virtues . . . and our lives."

"Give me that." He snatched the black dress off her. Then he jabbed a finger at her. "That was *low*. And you're a *nun*."

Emma tried not to grin as he stomped off with the dress. "That, honey, is a *real man*," she told Winnie, dropping a kiss on her head.

Winnie pulled a face. "I'm hungry."

"Me too. What's say we make some biscuits? We'll make extra for Mr. Slater. He's earned them."

❖ 12 ❖

THE FIRST PLACE they came to was *Gran Rancho de Gato*. It was a massive ranch of more than fifty thousand acres. Tom steered them toward it because *de Gato* was infinitely preferable to *El Lugar Rico*, which bordered it. Don Graciano Machado, the ranchero of *El Lugar Rico*, was infamous for his ruthlessness, and Tom wasn't risking a run-in with him. Machado wasn't scared of man or God. The *Lugar Rico* land had been seized from the Church during the secularization of the 1830s, and Machado lived in the old mission, where he sat like a desert king, reaping the profits from the land. Out here, he was a law unto himself, one not pleased by the encroaching *americanos*, who had been chipping away at his rights since the end of the Mexican-American War. More than a few Americans went missing on his land, never to be heard from again. No, Tom thought, eyeing the eastern horizon warily, best to keep well away. Especially in light of the way his luck was running.

Because, as if the posses and the death threats and the nuns and the heat weren't bad enough, the devil winds had started up too, kicking up dust and making the blazing day even hotter. His ridiculous getup was torture. The winds set the dress against him; the skirt blew up and smacked him in the face, no matter how many times he forced it down, and the black lace veil kept trying to strangle him. That stubborn nun wouldn't let him take it off, even though they were in the middle of nowhere and who the hell was going to see his face all the way out here? He could barely *see* through the goddamn thing. And he needed to see. Not just to keep watch for the posses and lynch mobs and bounty hunters, but also because he was anxious about wildfires. It was perfect conditions for them, and they were deadly. It was hard to watch for distant smoke when the veil made the whole world black and lacy. He put up with it for a while, but when the devil winds got so strong they were whistling in his ears, he tore the veil off. The nun set up complaining, but he ignored her. He'd rather be dead of a bullet than dead of a fire. And he was no good as a guide if he couldn't damn well *see*.

"I'll put it back on if we see people coming," he'd snapped.

So it was a relief when they rode onto *de Gato* land. Tom had been increasingly itchy at the thought of meeting Machado's vaqueros as they traversed the borderlands. His gaze moved restlessly over the sagebrush and chaparral, scanning for movement. Usually, you'd see a rider coming by the dust rising in their wake, but the winds meant dust was already flying.

"*De Gato* belongs to Don Joaquín José Rey," Tom told Emma as they rode on. "He should be hospitable enough. We won't reach the hacienda for a day or two, but we'll probably run into some of his vaqueros before then." He sighed as he realized her eyes had a suspicious shine. "If you keep laughing, I'm taking this goddamn dress off."

"I just forgot how pretty you look without your veil. And I'd thank you not to blaspheme," the wretched woman said, even as a giggle escaped her. "And I'm not laughing. It's just the dust getting to me."

Why the hell had he given in and worn this wretched thing? He pulled at the neckline of the suffocating dress. It dug into him in the most irritating places. His armpits were rubbed raw. He felt like a damn fool. He *was* a damn fool.

"When we stop somewhere, I'll see if I can make some adjustments," she said as she watched him wrestle with it.

"The hell you will," he snapped. "I ain't planning on staying in this thing for long, so there's no point in making it comfortable." They didn't have a mirror, so he couldn't see how ridiculous he looked, but he could imagine. He didn't know how women wore these things in this kind of heat. He was sweating like a pig. They'd even stuck gloves on him; he'd sweated them through, and it was a deeply unpleasant feeling. They were nothing at all like the work gloves he wore when he was with the herd. And anyways, work sweat was clean sweat. This was something else again, like being locked in a box in the full sun. He felt suffocated and helpless. "I don't see why I have to wear gloves when there's no one even about," he grumbled.

"You're the one who said we might run into vaqueros," she told him with a maddening show of patience. "And your knuckles are too hairy to pass for a woman's. You might have time to put the veil back on if we stumble into people, but you certainly ain't got time to put on the veil *and* the gloves. One or the other. You choose."

"You ain't very kind for a nun," he said sullenly.

"I'm the exact right amount of kind for a nun," she disagreed. "But you ain't in need of kindness; you're in need of a damn good bucking up. It's only a *dress*. Imagine how *I* feel, in this heavy old thing."

Startled, he took in her black habit. "It looks hot," he grunted.

She nodded, looking far too peppy, in his opinion. The woman could keep on shining even on the most miserable of days. Tom didn't know how she did it.

"How can you be so cheerful when it's so goddamn hot?" he demanded. He sounded like a sulky boy, which irritated him even more.

For the first time, he noticed how her fingers worried at her coif. She was sun flushed and damp with perspiration and was clearly trying to find a way to get some air against her hot head. He could feel the sweat running down his own bare neck. Imagine how oppressive her funny hat must be. He yanked irritably at the cloth pinching his armpits, uncomfortable with both the dress and his thoughts. He was of a mind to get his knife and just slash the underarms of the dress, so he could move. It might let some of the goddamn sweat out too. He reached for his canteen. He couldn't drink enough to make up for the moisture he was losing.

"You have to stop blaspheming," she warned him. "I'm getting mighty sick of telling you off for it."

"So don't tell me off."

"If I don't tell *you* off, Calla tells *me* off."

"Does she now?" He darted a glance back at the wagon. Sister Calla was rattling along on the bench, looking peaky from the heat.

Sister Emma followed his gaze and sighed. "I should swap with her for a spell. She's good to drive all the time; it's a god-awful way to spend the day."

"Don't blaspheme," he needled.

"God doesn't mind when *I* do it. I'm a *nun*." She turned and trotted back to the wagon to free Sister Calla.

Tom felt a pang as he watched her go. He liked riding with her. She was quick-witted and sassy and made the hours pass; without her, there was just the heat and the winds and this foul dress strangling him.

Once Sister Emma had spelled her, Sister Calla rode out to join him, chattering in Spanish about Magdalena and all the people they had in common. But it just wasn't the same.

"TAKE IT OFF."

"What?" That night in camp, Tom frowned up at Sister Emma, who was clicking her fingers at him.

"Take the dress off, and I'll see if I can fix it so it doesn't suffocate you."

"No." He wasn't about to undress in front of her. He just wanted to be left alone. He turned back to his whittling. He was only whittling in the first place so he didn't stare at her, and now here she was, disturbing him. And "disturbing" was the word for it. He'd found his gaze wandering all evening, following her every move. She was a tall woman. Regal. Like a queen. She moved through the camp, straight-backed and graceful, her heavy black skirts flowing around her. Unlike a queen, though, she worked. Hard. She never asked anyone to do a task she wouldn't do herself, and as a result, Calla and Anna respected her and did everything she asked, without complaint. She had the camp in impeccable order every night, with fresh food cooking and coffee percolating, and everyone's comfort cared for. And she did it with a smile. She laughed and teased and turned the weary day's end into a pleasure. In his whole life, he'd never seen a face as animated as hers, he thought as he watched her. Her mouth was sharp cornered and mobile, and her eyebrows seemed to express every passing feeling. He could have watched her all day and never grown tired of it. Now and then she caught him looking, and one eyebrow would go up. He'd snatch his gaze away, but before long, it roamed right back.

They'd camped by a stand of junipers, out of the worst of the winds, and Sister Emma had set Winnie to gathering a pile of the deadwood for the fire. Tom went along to help her, to get away from the nun for a bit. If he didn't stop staring, she was liable to think him softheaded. Besides, the kid needed help. She was a little scrap of a thing, and it panged him to see her struggling with an armful of wood. The least he could do was help her. Winnie was jumpy around him, so he made sure to maintain his distance and to keep them in sight of the nuns at all times. He didn't talk. He figured a jumpy child was a bit like an unbroken horse: at first you just wanted it to be comfortable with you being nearby. The longer he was around, the more likely it was she'd relax a little. Until then, he was happy enough to gather wood in silence. Juniper was good wood for whittling, and he had sifted through it as he went, looking for some decent hunks to work on. He needed something to distract him so he wouldn't stare at Emma. But even as he thought about staring, his gaze had drifted, finding Emma at her bread.

She had the same routine every night, like clockwork: as soon as she'd helped Calla and Anna pitch camp, she fed her starter, kneaded her bread and set bowls of dough out to prove. Sometimes she sang to herself while she worked. He didn't think she realized she was doing it. She had a pretty voice, sweeter than you'd expect from a woman with a tongue as sharp as hers. It drifted through the campsite and made the closing darkness seem almost homey. The songs she sang were as unexpected as the sweetness of her voice. There were no hymns or churchy things; in fact, some of the tunes were downright lewd.

When she had started on the lewd ones was about when he had resolved to spend the night with his eyes fixed on his whittling.

"Don't be so difficult," she scolded him now as she clicked her fingers for him to hand over the dress. He kept his eyes on his knife and ignored her, hoping she'd go away. Of course she didn't. She was the stubbornest woman he'd ever met.

"I don't need you to fix it," he muttered, shaving the wood with increasing agitation.

"Think of it this way: it means you don't have to wear it for a while."

He stopped whittling and squinted up at her. Actually, that seemed like a pretty fine argument. "What if someone comes?" he asked suspiciously. "You've been carping at me all day about being seen."

"Carping? I don't carp."

"Bitching, then." Hell, she was pretty when she got her ire up. "You were all het up about me being seen."

"Well, if someone comes and you get seen, then I guess you might get shot."

"I'll risk it." As much as he didn't fancy undressing in front of her, he fancied the hot dress even less.

"Wait!" She was laughing as he tried to pull the dress up and over his head. "You'll never get it off like that. You're ruining it!"

Beads had snapped as he yanked, falling to the ground with clattering sounds.

"Now I have to sew the beads back on too," she com-

plained, but there was no sting to her words. If she had to
sew beads, that meant more time he wouldn't have to wear
the damn dress. He contemplated snapping some more off.

"You have to undo all the buttons before you take it off,
you dunce," she scolded him. "Ain't you never undressed a
woman?" She grabbed him by the shoulders and turned
him. The feel of her hands sent shock waves through him.
He winced. Goddamn it. *No.* She was a nun. There weren't
going to be any shock waves. There just *weren't.* Not if he
had anything to say about it.

You don't notice women, remember? he told himself
fiercely. *You're famous for it.* Except that he clearly noticed
this one. More than noticed. Was fixated. Like a damn fool
rabbit frozen in front of a bobcat.

He felt the brush of her fingers though the cloth as she
freed the buttons down his back. The dress parted, and he
felt the kiss of air against his bare skin. He was immediately aware of every naked inch of his back, and he imagined he could feel her gaze as she looked him over.

"How racy of you, Mr. Slater," she teased, "not to wear
any undergarments."

He blushed. Which was ridiculous. She meant he wasn't
wearing *lady* undergarments. The thought of flimsy lady
underthings brought images to his mind that had him stiffening. And once the images started, they came like a flood,
including memories of that gorgeous whore with the rouged
nipples. Hell, no. Not now.

He scowled. Of *course* he was wearing undergarments.
He was still wearing his trousers under the dress, for Pete's
sake. But her words made him feel buck-naked, and he was
even more painfully aware of her now.

"All done. You can take it off now," she laughed, patting

him between the shoulder blades. He just about jumped out of his skin.

He got away from her as fast as he could, tossing the dress at her and heading for the other side of the campfire.

"You forgot your whittling," she called after him.

He didn't need it. He kept walking, heading for his saddlebags in search of a shirt. He couldn't be sitting opposite her half-naked.

"You ain't being very friendly," she said later, after supper was over and everything had been washed up and packed away. Anna had taken Winnie off to the wagon, which the women bedded beneath now that the tent was gone. With Winne and Anna abed, the sisters had settled down on either side of the lantern with their sewing. Sister Emma was still adjusting the hideous black gown of strangulation for him, while Sister Calla was sewing a length of navy cloth into a makeshift nun's habit for Anna. It had been Sister Emma's idea to disguise Anna as a nun, now that Tom had usurped her Spanish lady costume. That woman sure had a liking for dressing people up as things they weren't. The thought gave him pause.

"You still mad about wearing the dress? That why you've plonked yourself all the way over there?" she asked, as she sucked on the end of a strand of cotton before she threaded it through her needle. "I'd have thought you'd be used to the dress by now."

"It's an inhuman contraption."

She gave him an arch look. "And yet women wear them every day."

"I'd give anything to be wearing your dress instead of this," Sister Calla sighed, pulling at her coif. Since his conversation with Emma, Tom had noticed how often they both fussed with their funny hats. The pair of them jammed their fingers between the tight headdresses and their faces every minute or two. They must be uncomfortable as all hell.

"Why don't you take those things off?" he suggested. "They look powerful hot, and there ain't no one here but me and the ponies to see."

They exchanged a tense look. He guessed there was probably a rule about it, taking your funny nun hat off in front of a man. He wondered what they looked like without them. What *she* looked like. He didn't even know what color her hair was, he realized. Her eyebrows were brownish, so her hair probably was too. But was it curly or straight? Light brown or dark brown? He found he couldn't even imagine what she'd look like without the nun hat. In fact, he couldn't quite imagine what she'd look like in anything but nun clothes. His gaze wandered again, taking in the voluminous billow of Sister Emma's heavy black habit. It ballooned around her where she sat. He wondered what kind of shape she had under there.

"What if someone were to come along?" Sister Calla said anxiously. "These ain't quick to put back on."

"Then I guess you'd get shot right along with me." He poured himself a cup of coffee from the pot that Sister Emma kept warm by the fire.

"Probably best if we don't," Sister Emma said regretfully, turning back to her sewing.

Sister Calla nodded in agreement, looking despondent.

"Shame," Tom said, running a hand through his hair. "It feels mighty nice. Much cooler."

Emma threw a reel of cotton at him.

He caught it and grinned.

"It will be so nice to get to a town," Sister Calla sighed. "I would love a cool bath."

So would he, he thought as the devil winds picked up again, sending dust swirling. The gusts soughed through the junipers, making eerie sounds. *Ghosts are walking tonight,* Luke used to tease on windy nights like these when they were kids. It had always sent a shiver through Tom, the very thought of it. *Maybe it's Mamá,* Tom had thought after her death, even though he was old enough to know better by then. But he still thought it, even when he was the size of a man and responsible for his little brother, Matt. His father didn't believe in ghosts, and neither did Luke. It was just a joke. But when the devil winds blew, singing at the doors and windows, part of him wondered if she was out there, trying to come back, trying to talk to them, to come in from the wind. Because they'd left her to the winds, hadn't they? Buried in the hard ground next to the adobe hut on the edge of the desert, where their father had been foolish enough to claim land. Land where no rain fell and no crops grew, and where *Mamá* would stay forever, alone, blown by the devil winds.

"That's it for me," Sister Calla said abruptly, after a particularly wicked blast. She startled Tom back to the present as she gathered up her sewing and said her good nights. "It's just about done anyway; I'll finish it tomorrow. I'm going under the wagon. It's too nasty out here." She waited for Emma to join her, but the good sister showed no sign of budging. "Please tell me you're not planning to sleep out here?" she said disapprovingly. "There's no hot tent, so you got no call not to come sleep with us." She'd dropped her voice, but Tom could still hear her clearly. He didn't think he was supposed to be able to.

Emma didn't say anything.

"Sister?" Calla sounded more disapproving by the minute.

"You told me not to tell you, so I'm not telling you."

Calla made a *humphing* noise and headed for the wagon. Emma kept on sewing. Tom took up his whittling again, painfully aware that they were alone. He couldn't see his whittling very well now that the fire was dying down for the night, but he kept whittling anyway. It calmed his nerves.

"Ain't it a fine night?" she asked. She'd stopped sewing and was staring across the fire, straight at him.

"It's dark," he grunted. Just keep whittling, he told himself firmly.

"Of course it's dark, you idiot, it's nighttime. If it weren't dark, you wouldn't be able to see all the stars." She tilted her head back to admire the sky, which glittered with a vast swirl of stars. He followed her gaze. Curls of dust blew in patterns across the mica-glitter of the galaxy.

"There are a lot of them." It seemed a thing to say.

But apparently it wasn't the right thing to say, because she made a great show of rolling her eyes at him. "Where did all your poetry go?" she complained. "You were quite happy to wax lyrical about the sea."

"I did no such thing." He was irked by that. "I just told you the truth of things. *You* asked. I wouldn't have said anything about the sea if you hadn't asked."

She shot him a look. "And now I'm asking you to tell me the truth of things about the stars. What do those stars put you in mind of?"

He squinted up at them. "Honestly? It looks like someone's scattered a bunch of chicken feed up there." She got the giggles at that, which offended him. "*You asked*," he said, miffed.

"Chicken feed?"

"Well, it does," he grumbled.

"Maybe it does," she admitted, still laughing, "but there's no romance in it."

"Depends how much you like chickens."

"Hopefully not that much." She popped a pin in her mouth as she adjusted the armpit of the dress, and he thought he might be spared, but the pin came out soon enough. "You romance the girls back home with talk of chicken scratch stars when you go courting?" she teased.

"I ain't never been courting." He pulled a face. Why had he told her that? She didn't need to know about him and his history with girls. Or his lack of history with girls.

"I don't believe you, Mr. Slater. A handsome man like you." She darted a sideways glance at him, and his stomach did a slow somersault. "I'm sure the girls are all over you back home."

She thought he was handsome? Tom's knife slipped and nicked his finger. He sucked the bead of blood off his skin. "I've got two brothers better looking than me," he admitted. "The girls barely notice I exist."

She gave him a dubious look.

He was glad it was dark, because he was turning red. He wished they could go back to talking about the stars. He cast around for another topic of conversation. "Have you got brothers?" he asked, a trifle desperately.

"I do," she said, giving him a cheeky smile, "but none of them are better looking than me."

He bet. She was pretty good-looking. Especially when she smiled. She had one of those smiles that lit up her whole face; she was pretty without it, but when she smiled, she was breathtaking. And she smiled a lot. "Are they older or younger?" Look at your whittling, he told himself sternly. Or the stars. Look anywhere but at her, or you'll forget to blink, and she'll know you're staring, and she's a *nun* . . .

"Younger. There are three of them," she told him. *She* seemed perfectly relaxed. He doubted she knew the effect she had on him—after all, she was a nun, and nuns were about as innocent as they came. Even if they did have sly tawny eyes.

"And where are they?" He cleared his throat. "Are they out here in California too, or back in . . . ?" He was fishing. He knew he was doing it, but he couldn't help himself. He wanted to know where that accent came from, the one that sent shivers through him.

She laughed, but it was laughter with an edge. "No, they ain't out here. All of them are back in Duck Creek with our daddy. I ain't seen any of them since I was fourteen."

There was something in her manner that stopped him asking more about her family. There was a shadow there, and he didn't know her well enough to chase after it. "Where's Duck Creek?" he asked instead.

"Tennessee."

Tennessee, huh? Maybe one day he'd go and see if there were any other tawny-eyed, sexy-voiced women in Tennessee . . . ones who weren't nuns.

She didn't elaborate further on her birthplace, and he didn't push her. This tawny-eyed, sexy-voiced Tennessean clearly had a history, and not a very pleasant one, judging by her expression, which was cast into stark relief by the lantern. All her sunshine had faded, replaced by clouds. He wondered if the cause of the clouds was also the reason she'd become a nun. Had there been a man back in Tennessee, someone who'd broken her heart? Someone who'd come between her and her family? Although she said she hadn't seen them since she was fourteen, which was a bit young for a man to be the cause.

"How about you, Mr. Slater?" She shook off her clouds as she tried to smile at him again.

"How about me what?"

"You're from Mexico originally?"

He nodded. "We left when I was eight."

"That's when you moved to Oregon?"

"No. We went to El Paso first. Then when I was thirteen, we moved to California." He went back to whittling. He didn't like to think of that time. "A few years later we went to Oregon."

"I hear Oregon is beautiful," she said gently.

"It is. But no more beautiful than other places. It's just different." His knife flicked, sending shavings curling to the ground. "Utopia, where we live, is in the woods at the foothills of the mountains. It's thick with all the kinds of trees you can imagine. In fall, it's like the whole place has caught fire with color; the woods go amber and yellow and red so bright the color might as well be painted on. But it's no more beautiful than out here; it's only beautiful in a different way. The sight of the sun rising, glimmering through the sage, turning the dusty air golden . . . the mountains snowcapped in the distance . . . Mexico has its charm too: the long blue skies over the terra-cotta-tiled villages . . ." He stared into the coals, imagining the villages. And one village in particular. Arizpe. His old home.

But not anymore.

"Ah, there's my poet."

Her voice startled him. He'd been lost in the picture he'd conjured for himself. He met her gaze across the fire. There was wistfulness in her shadowed eyes, reflecting back the wave of feeling inside of him. It was unsettling.

"I wish I could see the world the way you do," she sighed.

"No, you don't."

"I do. I look around here and I see dust and toil, but when you describe it . . . it sounds magical."

"It's not magical," he sighed, putting down his whittling for the night. "It just is."

"Tom," she said softly as he stretched out on his bedroll.

He turned his head. She was holding out the black dress. "I finished it. It's all yours."

He didn't want it. But he took it. And then he lay back and looked up at the stars, which didn't look like scattered chicken feed at all. They looked like constellations of freckles, just like the ones scattered across the nose of a certain nun from Tennessee. But he could hardly tell her that, could he?

❖ 13 ❖

Two days later, they stumbled into trouble, or rather *more* trouble, in the form of English George and Irish George. When they first saw the cloud of dust, they thought they had run into Don Rey's vaqueros.

"Tell them we're fine," Tom told the nuns, quickly tossing the black veil over his head. "We don't need help. We just need to be granted safe passage through the ranch on our way to Magdalena. But make sure you stress that we don't need an escort—we're perfectly fine on our own. I won't talk unless I have to."

"Or you could pretend to be mute, and let me handle this. Like we discussed." As usual, Sister Emma wasn't prone to following instructions.

"I said I'd try." How hard he'd try might depend on how things turned out, he thought as he watched the dust cloud approach. But she didn't need to know that.

"If you do speak, you'd better put on a high voice, or we're done for," Sister Emma muttered. "You don't sound like a woman at all."

They watched the dust cloud anxiously. Tom kept his

hand on his pistol, which was well hidden under the veil. And he was glad that he did, because the dust cloud soon resolved into two men leading a line of packhorses. He could see that they weren't vaqueros after all. Tom swore under his breath. Bounty hunters, he guessed. Or *pistoleros*. They had the look. Flashy. Mean. Full of rat cunning.

One was decked out in a dusty suit, complete with bowler hat. He had an enormous walrus mustache and a pair of small round spectacles. The suit was a couple of sizes too small, and he looked rather like an overstuffed sausage, but he carried himself proud in the saddle. He rode like an experienced horseman, despite his roly-poly appearance and fancy clothes, and behind the spectacles, his gaze was as sharp as a knife. This was a man who cultivated a deceptively benign look, Tom thought, his nerves increasing. What he was looking at was a wolf in sheep's clothing.

Why couldn't anything be simple? Didn't they have enough to contend with, without adding wolves to the mix?

The wolf's companion was rangy and beak nosed, with spiky ginger eyebrows and a more overtly mean look. There was no suit for him; he was wrapped in a serape and wore a brown hat so battered it no longer had a shape. He was chewing tobacco, and as they slowed their horses to a walk, he spat a stream of brown juice, which hit the earth with a splatter.

"Ladies!" the fellow in the suit exclaimed. His round face was sunburned, and he was slick with sweat. He pulled a kerchief from his pocket and mopped at his face, smiling at the "ladies." His eyes didn't match his smile, Tom noted. They glinted as they passed over the group, taking in the horseflesh and the wagon, lingering on the saddlebags. Tom's fingers tightened on his pistol. He had a bad feeling about this.

"Nuns," the tobacco chewer in the shapeless hat grunted.

He squinted at them and crammed the hunk of tobacco between his lower lip and his teeth. Somehow it made him look even meaner.

"What a delightful surprise!" the fat one exclaimed, still mopping at himself. "To find *ladies* in the middle of nowhere like this!"

"Nuns," the tobacco chewer grunted again.

"Not all nuns," the fat one scolded, his gaze lingering on Tom's veiled figure. He had an English accent. It wasn't a fancy one, Tom observed, even though he was giving himself airs. "We have a señora and a lovely little one too." His gaze slipped over Winnie quickly, before returning to Tom. He smiled. Tom thought he was trying to be charming. He had about as much charm as a warthog.

"I think the delight is all ours," Sister Emma told him, sounding earnest and grateful and like a green girl straight off the farm. She was beaming at them, all wide-eyed and fresh, naïve as all get-out: the perfect picture of a harmless young nun. You'd never know she was a crack shot with her Colt. Tom felt a blossoming admiration for her. The last thing you wanted to do with men like these was make them wary of you. A wary *pistolero* was on a hair trigger.

"We're lost, you see," she continued. "You couldn't point us in the direction of Don Rey's hacienda, could you? We're his guests."

Tom jerked. Wait. What? What was the damn fool woman doing? The last thing they wanted to do was to end up at the hacienda. They were supposed to be hiding from people, not running headlong into them. The plan was to tell people they were *fine,* goddamn it. To move along with the minimum of fuss. To get across Rey's land as quickly as they damn well could. He cleared his throat, in warning, but she ignored him.

"We've got ourselves turned around," she was chattering, "and I hate to think of Don Rey being inconvenienced. He's been so kind to accommodate us on our journey to our new mission. Although," she said with a merry laugh, "I suppose he'll send some men to find us now we haven't arrived on time."

She was warning them off, he realized, his rage fizzling. And her instincts seemed to be good. The fat man and his friend went shifty at her words, glancing over their shoulders. Tom would bet they hadn't known they were on Rey's land, or that they were so close to the main house. The Englishman scanned the land around them for signs of approaching vaqueros. He didn't seem keen to find any. When he didn't see anything, he tilted his head, thinking for a moment. Then he smiled. "My good lady, we can do more than point you in the right direction. We can escort you!"

Hell. They didn't *want* a goddamn escort. And with these two as guides, they were likely to find themselves "escorted" somewhere and robbed blind. Or maybe worse. Tom wondered if he should just shoot them now. But he could hardly commit cold-blooded murder in front of *nuns*, could he? Although Anna was a fake nun, the other two weren't. He didn't think nuns would hold with murder, even if it was in self-defense. And then there was the child to think of.

"Oh no, we couldn't possibly inconvenience you," Sister Emma said hastily. "We wouldn't dream of taking you away from your business. Just point us in the right direction; I'm sure we'll find Don Rey and his men in no time."

"Nonsense, it's the least we can do."

No. The least they could do was just move right along and mind their own damn business.

"After all, my dear," the fat one continued expansively, "nothing is more important than helping those in need."

Tom saw Sister Emma's nose wrinkle imperceptibly at the man's heavy-handed attempt at Christian generosity. She shot Tom a quick look. She'd got them in a bind now. She could hardly claim they weren't in need when she'd just asked them for help, could she?

"It's a simple enough matter," their new friend insisted. "The hacienda should be this way." He gestured westward.

Tom had the luxury of rolling his eyes behind the veil. The hacienda wasn't that way at all. Which was for the best too, as he didn't particularly want to end up there. Playing the señora for a traveler or two was a very different matter from playing the señora to Don Rey, in his own home. Imagine it. Having to be the man's guest, dressed like this. And while Don Rey might be preferable to Don Machado, that didn't make him a pussycat. Playing the lady for a ranchero wasn't a situation he planned to get himself in. But neither did he want to go riding off at the mercy of a couple of greedy-eyed *pistoleros*. Hell. How were they going to wriggle out of this?

Sister Emma had the look of a bronco realizing it was corralled. But she wasn't a woman to be easily penned. She had a few good kicks in her. "Oh no," she said, keeping her eyes wide and guileless, "it's definitely not that way." She pointed southward. "I think it's over there."

There was another splatter as the *pistolero* in the battered brown hat spat tobacco juice. He squinted at them, and Tom prepared to fight. Brown Hat knew something was up. They had good instincts, men like these. If they didn't, they'd be dead by now.

"Thought you said you was lost?" Brown Hat drawled.

Tom watched as Sister Emma deflected him, spinning prettily told falsehoods, looking for all the world like she'd just stepped out of church. He wondered if she'd have to do penance for so many lies. Unfortunately, despite all her hard work, the *pistoleros* weren't swayed, and Tom and the nuns found themselves under "escort."

"I'm George," the fat one introduced himself cheerfully, as they all but herded the women southwest. Sister Emma was looking anxious. Her knuckles were white as she gripped the pommel of her saddle. He couldn't reassure her because of his goddamn veil.

"Nice to meet you, George. And who's your friend?" Emma asked, giving his quieter partner a wary look.

"He's also George."

Tom's stomach sank all the way to his toes. George. And George. Hell. The English accent . . . He knew these two. Well, he knew *of* them. And none of it was good. Judging by the shock on Emma's face, she'd heard of them too.

"Not . . . English George and Irish George, by any chance?" she asked weakly. Perhaps it was Tom's imagination, but he thought her voice shook.

Sister Calla gave a squeak when she heard the names. Sister Emma seemed hopeful that he would reply in the negative. But of course he didn't. That wouldn't have matched their luck on this trip.

"You've heard of us?" The fat fool puffed up at the thought of it. He looked uncannily like a bird as he turned a bright eye on the nuns. But Tom was more concerned with the other George, who had dropped back to ride behind them. Damn it. He wanted to keep them both in his line of sight.

"Oh my." Anna drained of color. She pulled Winnie closer and kept tight hold of her.

"Don't let our troublesome reputations deceive you," fat George continued, puffing up even further—if such a thing was possible. "We are, at heart, gentlemen."

Tom doubted it.

"That's a relief, English George." Sister Emma made the right noises, but Tom could see that she was dubious too. Good. This wasn't a man to relax around, or to trust.

The fat man gave a jovial laugh, even though his eyes were anything but jovial. "Don't let the accent fool you, dear sister. I'm *Irish* George. English George's over there."

Tom and Emma both swiveled in the saddle and craned their necks to see English George at the back of their wagon, taking inventory of their belongings.

"So you're Irish?" Emma was frowning as she watched English George coveting her goods.

"God no." The fat man cleared his throat as Sister Calla fixed him with a black look. "Forgive my blasphemy, sister."

Calla pursed her lips, oozing disapproval.

"I'm a Berkshire man." Irish George turned his attention back to Emma. He clearly preferred her open curiosity to Calla's brooding disapproval. "I'm from Reading." He took in her blank face. "In England."

"But . . . shouldn't *you* be called English George, then?"

Irish George laughed, clearly relishing the attention. "When George and I took up together, people were already calling him English George. So to save confusion, I went by Irish George."

"Even though you're not Irish?"

Tom slowed his paint until the horse had dropped back to the wagon, so he could ride next to Anna and Winnie. Calla gave him a startled look but nodded when he gestured at Anna and the girl. Both were white with fear, whereas Sister Emma seemed to be coping just fine. In fact, the more Irish George kept talking, the more pep she seemed to have. Tom wasn't too worried about her or Calla.

He rode stolidly by Anna's side, and he could see her

grow calmer, although she still had a death grip on the child. Winnie radiated fear, and Tom wished he could reassure her, but there was no way without giving the game up. He hoped his presence would help settle her a little.

He listened to Sister Emma conversing with Irish George, who clearly liked a natter. Tom was more concerned about English George, truth be told. From his vantage point next to the wagon, Tom could keep an eye on the man as he rode around them, taking a thorough inventory of their possessions. English George's rifle was resting loosely across his saddle, but Tom could see he was ready to fire at a moment's notice. Tom's mind was racing as he tried to find a way out of this bind. No solutions were forthcoming, bar outright murder. And there was no way he could shoot both of them without the women getting caught in the middle. He'd just have to bide his time for now . . .

"English George didn't sound very English to me." Sister Emma was keeping Irish George distracted and amenable at least. She was clearly worried about what English George was up to as much as Tom was, as she kept turning to look back at the wagon.

"Oh, he's not. I think his folks were Dutch."

"So why ain't he called Dutch George?" Sister Emma was sounding increasingly exasperated.

"Because he's from London."

"I thought you said he wasn't English?"

Irish George laughed. "London, Ohio."

"For the love of . . . Why on earth wouldn't they call him Ohio George, then?"

"It's supposed to be funny."

"Well, it ain't." Her nerves were clearly fraying, as she sounded more than a touch irritated. "It's just plain wrongheaded." Tom hoped she could keep her composure.

"How old's the girl?"

Tom had seen English George creeping up on the other side of the wagon, but Anna was startled into a soft scream.

"Hey," Irish George called back to them, "I promised these ladies we'd be gentlemen, E.G. I hope you're not making me out to be a liar."

"He just gave me a shock, that's all," Anna said shakily.

"It's a sin to startle nuns," Irish George told his partner. Then he laughed. "And if it ain't, it should be."

English George didn't respond. His gaze was riveted on Winnie. He was like a snake staring at its prey. Winnie shrunk back against Anna, and Tom's finger tightened on the trigger of his pistol.

"How old?" English George repeated in his toneless voice.

"She's just turned ten." A thread of anger was shot through the fear in Anna's voice.

"Why, we've been mighty rude, haven't we?" Sister Emma swept in, turning her horse and trotting back to join them. "We haven't introduced ourselves! And when you've been so kind to us." She all but inserted her horse between English George and the wagon. Tom didn't know how she did it, but she had an ability to control a conversation. She kept her voice bright and breezy, but he could see the way her tawny eyes narrowed. Under the naïve charm she was oozing, she was secretly seething.

"I'm Sister Emma," she said brightly, "and this is Sister Calla and Sister Anna. We're heading for our new mission at Santa María Magdalena de Buquivaba. The little one here is Winnie; she's joining our . . . nunhouse."

"Convent," Sister Calla interrupted. "We take orphans who have felt the call of God."

English George spat tobacco juice. It hit the wheel of the wagon. Winnie's nose wrinkled.

"What about her?" he grunted, jerking his head at Tom.

"Doña . . . Elvira?" Sister Emma turned to look at Tom too.

Elvira? For the love of . . .

"Doña Elvira is a widow." She was talking fast now. "She was ravaged by the pox that killed her husband."

The woman was a consummate liar. Tom bet her knees were rubbed raw from all the atoning she had to do at the end of her hard day's lying.

"As you can imagine, a pox-scarred woman of advancing age has no hope of another marriage." She had quite a story for Doña Elvira. "And her husband—God rest his soul—left her in penury. So she's going into seclusion at the . . . convent . . . in Magdalena."

"I'm sorry to hear of your loss, señora," Irish George said gallantly, even as his gaze slid over Tom's black form. Counting the jet beads, probably.

"How scarred is she?" English George asked.

Tom couldn't wait to hear.

"Dreadfully, I'm afraid." Emma lowered her voice, ostensibly so Doña Elvira wouldn't get her tender feelings hurt. "Scarred enough that I've seen grown men lose their lunch at the sight of her."

Tom doubted there was enough penance in the world for all the lies she was telling. She actually seemed to *enjoy* it. Her green-gold eyes sparkled as she got into her story.

"Shame," English George grunted, also giving Tom a once-over.

"Still," Irish George chipped in, "there are so few women out here, she might find a husband. And she has a nice enough form. If she leaves the veil on, a man might not mind."

Tom could have decked the bastard.

"Perhaps," Sister Emma agreed, her sharp-cornered mouth twitching, "but I think the man in question might get a rude shock if the veil should ever slip."

The man in question would get a rude shock even if the veil stayed on, Tom thought sourly.

"The girl's wasted in a convent." English George kicked his horse and rode ahead.

Tom almost swore. What did *that* mean? Nothing good.

"Now, George, remember ladies have sensibilities," Irish George called after him.

Yes, George, Tom thought as he watched the man fish a spyglass out of his saddlebag and scan the horizon, *ladies have sensibilities. Make one move toward that kid, and you'll find out how keen those sensibilities are.*

From the corner of his eye, Tom saw Emma whispering to Calla. Calla nodded and inched closer to Irish George. "You're very kind to escort us," Sister Calla gushed, all trace of her earlier disapproval gone. She led him ahead, just out of earshot of the wagon, peppering him with questions about himself. Irish George went along happily enough. He seemed the sort who was content so long as he had an audience.

"What are we going to do?" Sister Emma asked, once they were out of earshot.

"Get rid of them," Tom said tersely.

"Yes, but *how*?"

"There's only one how that I can think of," he admitted, "and I suspect you ain't going to like it."

❧ 14 ❧

THIS WAS THE worst thing about being a nun. Worse even than wearing the hellish black habit. You had to be *good*.

She might get away with a little cursing and a little blasphemy, but she certainly wasn't getting away with murder. Or even assault. Emma scowled at English George's back. Normally, she'd have no qualms about dealing with men like the Georges quickly, violently if necessary. But now she was a *nun*. And what kind of nun would leave two men tied up out here? If it weren't for Tom Slater, she'd be able to do as she liked. There wouldn't be anyone expecting *goodness* of her.

She turned her glower on Tom. Damn him. She couldn't make his face out through the veil, but she just knew he was expecting her to protest. So she had to protest. Because what kind of nun would agree to a plan like his? No kind of nun, that's what. And he was looking at her, just waiting for her to come out with some kind of nonsense about forgiveness and mercy.

Men. Why did they always back you into a corner? And where was it written that women had to be the voice of reason? She didn't *want* to be the voice of reason. She wanted to pull her Colt on the Georges for the way they'd strong-armed everyone. They'd had the nerve to corral the whole party, ignoring every last protest. No one wanted their damn escort! And *then* they had the gall to size Winnie and Tom up like they were pieces of meat. They were the worst kind of trail scum. And could she shoot them? *No.* Instead, here she was begging for their lives. It was enough to make a girl scream.

"You can't kill them," she said gracelessly, through grit-ted teeth.

"We'll just tie them up and leave them here." Tom was barely audible over the wind. His veil swirled around him.

I'll get the rope, she thought. If there's one thing whor-ing had taught her, it was how to tie a man up. But she couldn't very well tell him that. So she braced herself and did the *right thing*. The Christian thing. Goddamn it.

"We can't." Ugh. It was hard to say the words. Wasn't it possible that somewhere there were nuns who *could* tie a man up and leave him to his fate in the wilderness? Espe-cially if he posed a mortal threat to them? Nuns who under-stood that some situations warranted hard measures? Nuns who had a bit of flexibility over what the *right thing* might be? Warrior nuns? They must have those? She'd heard of warrior priests—they had those in the crusades. Back in Moke Hill, Justine had a book about them. It was a roman-tic book that all the girls begged her to read aloud from when business was slow. They particularly liked the swoony bits. But aside from the lord and lady and mooning and swooning, there were knights in it . . . ones who were also priests. Or something. They'd gone rampaging through the Holy Lands. Which apparently was fine, because God wanted it.

So God *could* be flexible about these things. And surely, if He could see what was going on here, *now*, God would want her to tie these men up. Emma had enough experience to know thieves when she saw them. Rapists too. And why on earth would God want her and the girls to get robbed and raped? If she didn't do *something*, raping and robbing was in the cards. She was sure of it.

"They'll die if we leave them tied up out here," she told Tom, not sounding entirely regretful about it. "The likelihood of anyone finding them before they die of thirst is pretty slim." But maybe someone would . . . And God wouldn't mind a little self-defense; she was certain of it. Maybe they could find a way to make sure someone found them . . .

But how? And if it didn't work and they died . . . She didn't think God would countenance murder. There was a whole commandment about that one. One of the important ones that people actually remembered.

Tom grunted. She got the impression that he didn't seem too happy about the idea of murder either.

"You ever killed anyone before?" she asked, curious.

"Not that I know of," he admitted.

Right. Murder wasn't really in the cards, then. But there *must* be a way of dealing with the Georges . . . She racked her brains. Everything she thought of led to the very real risk of the Georges dying out here in the middle of nowhere. Or to them tracking Emma down and exacting revenge . . . Neither was ideal. There *must* be a way. And she'd better find it before they stumbled into the ranchero's vaqueros and landed in . . . Oh.

"Now don't get mad . . ." she warned, as excitement zapped through her, "but I think I have a plan."

He groaned.

"Don't be like that. It's a good plan."

"As good as the one where you asked the Georges for directions?"

She scowled.

"Or as good as the one where you dressed me up like a woman?"

"I'm *good* at plans," she said hotly.

"According to who?"

"According to the fact that because of that dress you're alive right now and not shot through by the Georges. They look the bounty hunting type." Ha. She had him there. He went all sullen and quiet. Generously, she decided not to rub it in, and instead went back to telling him about her plan. "I've given it a lot of thought, and I've decided God is on board with the tying up business." She thought she heard a stifled moan but pressed on. "But I don't reckon He'd be too happy if we killed them."

"I bet."

He wasn't convinced yet, she could tell. But he would be. She had excellent powers of persuasion. "But if we make sure they don't *die*, that's fine. I think." She chewed on her lip. "Even though they haven't actually committed a crime . . . or done anything to us yet . . . except be pushy. And give me a bad feeling." She sighed. "It probably *is* a sin to tie them up before they've actually done anything . . ."

"Think of it like moving a spider out of your bed before it actually bites you," he suggested dryly.

She liked that. Yes. They were just a couple of spiders that needed moving along. By force. Because spiders didn't go about moving on their own. And they certainly didn't respond to sweet talk.

"There's one thing I'm confused about," he said.

"What?"

"Why did you say, 'don't get mad'? Tying them up was my idea in the first place. You're just agreeing with me."

"Oh." She forced a bright smile. "Because we won't be leaving them to die. We're going to take them with us."

"What?"

"Hush! Look, now you've gone and upset Irish George."

It was true. The fat spider had turned and was frowning back at them.

"Not only did you speak, when you're supposed to be mute, but you were loud," Emma scolded Tom. "And you sounded like a man. How am I going to explain that?"

"I can help," Anna suggested. She and Winnie had been still as mice, listening to every word. "Oh, Mr. George!" she called, in a deep voice. It didn't really sound like Tom's voice, but it would probably do. People were inclined to believe their eyes, and Irish George's eyes told him he was looking at three women and a girl.

Irish George stopped and waited for the wagon to catch up.

"We need to stop for a moment. Winnie's just told me she needs to go . . . well, *you know.* I *told* her to go last time we stopped, but do you think she listened?" Anna did her earnest best to give her voice a mannish timbre.

"Of course," Irish George said. He was more interested in talking to Calla than listening to Anna. Emma wasn't surprised. Calla was a very pretty girl, even if she was a nun, and pretty girls were hard to come by on the frontier. Maybe there was some way she could *use* his attraction to Calla . . .

"What's going on?" English George was back, spyglass still in hand. He was scowling. It looked to be his fixed expression, judging by the deep ravines of his frown lines.

"The little one needs to relieve herself." Irish George

flapped a hand at the sagebrush, where Anna was leading Winnie to privacy.

English George didn't look pleased. But they were supposed to be playing at escorts, rather than kidnappers, so he kept silent. Emma wondered how long it would take before his patience wore thin and he stopped the pretense.

"Would anyone fancy coffee while we've stopped? Lunch?" Emma suggested cheerily. "I have some leftovers from last night I can reheat."

"We don't have time," English George said.

"Now, now," Irish George tutted, giving him a look. "We ain't in a rush, are we? We said we'd get the ladies to their friend, and we will. But there's still plenty of light in the day. And we haven't had a proper meal since Frisco." He dismounted. "We've been living on hardtack and tea."

English George didn't look happy, but he didn't protest. He did, however, stay on his horse.

"What are you doing, offering them food?" Tom hissed at her as they quickly gathered wood for the cook fire.

"I thought we'd best get it over with as soon as possible," she whispered. "Might as well do it while they're eating. They'll have their hands and mouths full—it's the perfect time to stick a gun to their heads."

"Lady, you're crazy," Tom snapped. "What in hell are you thinking, taking them with us?"

"Trust me," she snapped back, "it makes *perfect* sense. I know what I'm doing. Wait until they're eating. I'll take Fat George, you take English George."

"And where in hell are you planning on taking them? All the way to Mexico?"

She ignored him and took her armful of wood back to the wagon.

"Excuse me, Mr. English George," she said as she brazened her way through a haphazard plan, "would you mind lighting the fire for us?" She squinted up at English George, who was still mounted and restlessly scanning the horizon. He sure was a mean-looking son of a bitch. The kind who'd beat a whore, she decided. She knew his type. "I have a wonderful rabbit pie," she told him, "and fresh bread from this morning. No butter, but you can't have everything."

"You don't want to miss Sister Emma's cooking," Calla told the Georges. Emma shot her a grateful look. While Calla didn't know what Emma was up to, she knew she was up to something. And trusted her.

Which is more than she could say for Tom Slater, Emma thought, as she saw him hanging back, his arms full of wood.

"Let me take that for you," Irish George intervened, taking the wood from Tom's arms. "A little lady like you shouldn't be carrying a load like that." This, despite the fact that Tom towered over him. "Come and sit over here, by me," Irish George invited, "while George over there builds the fire."

Emma froze. She had no idea what Tom was going to do. *Please don't do anything rash.* She breathed a sigh of relief when he followed Irish George to a fallen juniper log and sat beside him. She'd have to talk to him about manners later, though. He sat with his legs spread. It was giving Irish George the wrong idea.

"Come on, George," Irish George coaxed his friend. "We're waiting on you before we can have our supper." Irish George's plump pink tongue swiped at his lips as his eyes dropped to the skirt draped between Tom's splayed knees. Emma tried to catch Tom's attention, to gesture at him to act like a lady and sit with his ankles crossed, but the damn man wouldn't look at her.

Exuding surly discontent, English George dismounted and started on the fire. His companion, meanwhile, just about fell over himself trying to impress Doña Elvira. He'd either forgotten about her pox scars, or he'd decided that he didn't care. A woman's spread legs often had that effect on a man, Emma thought dryly. Doña Elvira was also the only non-nun here, and while Irish George might have been struck by Calla's pretty face, she *was* still a nun. Whereas Doña Elvira was a widow. And while she was ostensibly not an attractive one, Emma knew men. She figured George had done the odds and calculated Doña Elvira was a better bet. Ugly women weren't so choosy. Or so men liked to tell themselves. Although, to be fair, Tom made a decent-looking woman: he had an elegant build, and the well-padded dress did wonders for the impression of a willowy female body. Emma felt the urge to giggle. She wished she could see Tom's face as Irish George flirted with him.

"You're a shy one, aren't you?" Irish George was cooing.

"Oh, did I forget to mention that Doña Elvira is mute?" Emma said breezily on her way past to fetch the pie. "I'm afraid the pox took her tongue." She didn't know if that was entirely possible, but it sounded good. By the time she came back, pie in hand, she saw that Irish George had started getting handsy. He'd better watch out, she thought, feeling the urge to giggle again. Tom might well belt him one.

"What are you gentlemen doing all the way out here if you're not visiting Don Rey?" Emma asked lightly as she set to warming the leftovers.

"We're looking for someone," English George said shortly. Now that he had the fire going, he was watching his friend and the señora with narrowed eyes. Maybe he was jealous. That almost set Emma to giggling again. There was a touch of hysteria to it, but it was better than being afraid.

"Oh?" she said. "Who?" Although she had a sinking feeling that she already knew.

"An Indian," Irish George said with relish, trying to impress Doña Elvira. "A Plains Indian, not one from round here. He's wanted all through the west. You woulda heard of him . . ."

Oh dear. Here they went again . . .

"You woulda heard one of his names, anyway: Rides with Death, White Wolf, the Angel of Death, the Plague of the West . . ."

"Oh heavens!" Emma exclaimed, forcing a note of horror into her voice.

Calla took her cue from Emma. "He's not around *here*, is he?"

"He's passing for a white," English George spat. Like that was the worst possible thing the Plague of the West could do. "You might have even met him, without knowing it."

"No!" Emma gasped, feigning outrage. She had a hard time not rolling her eyes. She'd met him all right, and she liked him a damn sight better than she liked these two.

"He's going by the name Tom Slater," Irish George said. And then he swore. Loudly.

The curse startled Emma. She whipped around in time to see Tom's pistol settle threateningly in front of Irish George's nose. Goddamn him! She wasn't *ready*. And now look, before she could even reach for her Colt, English George had drawn his own pistol and pointed it directly at Tom's head. That wretched man had better have drawn his weapon because of Irish George's wandering hands and *not* because he had a bee in his bonnet about Deathrider using

his name! She could forgive punishing wandering hands—
she knew about that kind of rage firsthand—but she had a
nasty feeling it was the name that had done it. He was
mighty sensitive about it. But what did this kind of rash behavior accomplish? Nothing, that's what! Well, nothing except a pistol to the head.

"Doña Elvira doesn't like to be manhandled," Emma
said quickly. "She's got a hair trigger when it comes to being pawed."

Irish George gingerly removed his hand from Tom's
knee.

Emma had a momentary hope that she'd be able to sal-
vage the situation. But then Don Rey's vaqueros rode into
camp, and everything went well and truly to hell.

❧ 15 ❧

"IT'S NOT *MY* fault you got shot!" Emma felt like wringing his neck. He was the *worst* patient she'd ever had. "And it's not even a proper wound," she told him imperiously. "It's barely a graze."

"I'm missing half my hip," he growled. His green eyes were fierce in his white face.

"Don't be so dramatic."

They were cooped up together in a guest room at Don Rey's hacienda, where Emma had volunteered to nurse "poor Doña Elvira," who'd sustained a nasty injury during the scuffle with the Georges. When the vaqueros had ridden into camp, everything had devolved into total chaos. There had been a lot of shouting in Spanish, which Emma didn't understand in the slightest, and it had turned out neither of the Georges did either, which only seemed to make the vaqueros shout even more. Then, as if all the shouting wasn't enough, English George had gone and shot off his weapon. Everything went right to hell from there. Emma had screamed at Calla to get Anna and Winnie safe, before drawing her Colt and joining the fray. But she didn't know who on earth she should shoot. The camp was a cloud of dust, with horses wheeling and guns blazing, and her ears were ringing fit to split her head. And then suddenly it was calm. Without her even having to fire a shot, the Georges were defeated, trussed up and slung over their horses. It had all happened so fast she barely had time to blink. *Huh*, Emma thought as she watched the Georges struggle against their bonds, *it looks like God can be flexible after all*. It seemed He'd sent cowboys to do her dirty work for her; cowboys who were outraged by the idea of nuns being accosted.

Once the Georges had been subdued, the vaqueros flocked to the women, full of concern. "They saw the *pistoleros* threatening us with their weapons," Calla translated. "They're calling them godless *americanos*."

"Tell them they *are* godless, but only one of them is a proper *americano*," Emma said. "They can blame England for the other one." Now that it was all over, she could see that the vaqueros were mostly young, sweet-faced boys; they seemed as shaken by the whole situation as Emma was. They were reverently polite toward Calla as they chattered at her, doffing their hats and almost bowing.

"They're good Catholic boys; they're horrified that anyone would dare to attack a nun," Calla said.

"Tell them we are too." Emma straightened her habit.

"They drew on *us*," Irish George protested hotly from where he hung upside down over his horse.

Emma hid her Colt in the folds of her skirt. "Tell them these men manhandled us," she told Calla.

"Oh, I did," Calla said cheerfully.

"*We're* the victims here!" Irish George was yelling. All the blood had rushed to his head, turning his face a meaty pink. He looked like a cooked ham. "That bitch drew a gun on me! If you want to be trussing people up, you filthy Mexicans, you should truss up the señora!" That was all he managed to yell before they gagged him, but that's when Emma realized that Tom was missing. *Madre de Dios!* What if he'd been shot? What if they'd discovered that he was a man? What if they knew that he was *Tom Slater* and had trussed *him* to his horse?

"Where *is* the señora?" she'd asked, panicked.

The vaqueros hadn't seen any señoras. Emma clenched her teeth to bite back her curses. Where was he? She couldn't see any trace of the impossible man. Maybe he'd run off? But his horses were here. And he wasn't the kind of man to run off. She'd bet her life on it.

Oh no, no, no. She spied a black boot sticking out the back of the wagon. Please don't let him be hurt. Emma's heart sank as she ran.

He was slumped between the flour sacks in the back of the wagon. The veil had slid off him, showing his bent head, his dark hair damp and ruffled. His stubbled jaw was clenched in pain. Time seemed to slow down as she took in the dusty stretch of his long body. The gown was tattered at his hip. And there was blood. Lots of it. Splashes of blood were all over the flour sacks and in rusty patches on the earth at Emma's feet. Tom's gloved hands were slick with it as he pressed them to the wound. He opened his eyes, and they blazed in his white face, green as river ice glinting in the sun.

As though from a great distance, she heard the vaqueros coming, and she had the presence of mind—just—to throw the veil over Tom's head.

"The bastard shot me," he said. His voice sounded papery. Emma didn't like the sound of it.

"Don't talk," Emma told him. Her mind raced as she

yanked the flour sacks out and climbed into the wagon beside him. She managed to make him more comfortable by pushing the goods out of the way to make space for him. Gingerly, she nudged his hand off the wound.

"Leave it," he protested.

She ignored him. The whole side of his left hip was sodden with blood. She needed to stop the bleeding. She opened the nearest trunk and grabbed at the first thing her hand landed on. It was her powder blue "sweetheart" dress, the one she used for men who liked to pretend they were courting rather than whoring. She didn't have time to rip it; instead, she wadded it up and used it whole to stanch his bleeding. She pressed down hard on his hip, and he swore at her.

"Shut up," she said kindly, "or they'll hear you."

She needed to see to him . . . but she couldn't have anyone else *see* him. And how was she going to hike the dress up and deal with the wound without everyone seeing that the señora wasn't a señora at all?

"Doña Elvira has been wounded!" Emma told the vaqueros, who were piling up at the back of the wagon, their sweet faces full of concern. Calla and Anna were huge eyed, certain that Tom was about to be discovered. But the vaqueros didn't ask questions, and they were too shy and gentlemanly to so much as touch the señora. They were more than happy to leave the nursing to Sister Emma. Especially once she told them where the wound was. Emma patted her hip, close to her groin, and the vaqueros turned beet red and averted their eyes. That had done the trick nicely.

"They said they'll take us to the hacienda," Calla translated as the vaqueros packed up the camp for them and mounted their horses. Calla jumped onto the wagon seat and gathered the reins.

Anna deposited Winnie next to Calla and then helped Emma lace the canvas closed over the ends of the wagon, to give Emma privacy to tend Tom's wound. Before she finished the last knot, tying Emma in with her patient, Anna paused. "Do you know what you're doing?"

"Not really," Emma admitted.

"Make sure the wound is clean," Anna said. "Wash it if you can. But the main thing at this point is to stop the bleeding. I really should be in there to help you."

"Best not," Emma said. "He's unhappy enough that *I'm* here."

Unhappy was an understatement at best.

"Get," he snapped at her, when she crawled back to him over the rattling bucking trunks. With the canvas laced closed, the wagon was dim and baking hot. The stifling heat sapped Tom's strength, and he slapped her hands away with increasing weakness when she tried to help. *"Get."*

He'd ripped his veil off again. His hair was wet through with sweat, and he was white and clammy. But he was conscious, and his green eyes were clear, even if the lines around them were deep with pain.

"I'm telling you to *get*," he told her fiercely.

"Fine." Oh, she could have slapped him. Why did men have to be such idiots? "If you want to bleed to death, bleed to death. It's no skin off my nose."

"I'll look after it myself," he said, stubborn as a bull. He winced as he pulled himself into a sitting position. The violent shaking of the wagon was clearly causing him pain.

"*Fine.* Look after it yourself." She rolled her eyes. *Men.* She'd give him ten minutes before he was begging for her help. She busied herself getting water from the water barrel; she filled the pitcher and dug out a washcloth.

"Keep your back turned," he insisted.

"For the love of . . . You're bleeding to death, and you're worried about your *modesty*?"

"Turn. Your. Back."

She left the water next to him and wriggled around until she was facing the canvas hoop of the wagon. She could hear the rustle of the gown as he lifted the skirts to take a look at his hip, and then she heard him curse. It was a vigorous curse, so he clearly wasn't dying. That was something.

"How bad is it? Is it bad?" There was no answer. "Anna said to stop the bleeding before you do anything else," she said helpfully.

"I know what to do."

"I understand that you're in pain, but you really could be nicer, especially since I saved your life."

"You what?" The words were bitten off through clenched teeth. There was a world of pain in them.

Emma winced in sympathy. She hoped the bullet hadn't lodged in him somewhere. How in hell would she get it out? "If I hadn't whacked that dressing on your wound like that, you might have bled out," she said, talking to keep herself occupied as much as anything. So long as he was talking back, he wasn't passing out. Or dying. "You should be thanking me, instead of being all growly like a bear."

He grunted. It wasn't an apology, but at least he'd stopped cursing and carrying on.

"Has it stopped bleeding?" she asked. He'd lost an awful lot of blood. She wasn't sure how much more he could stand to lose.

He grunted again. She didn't know what that meant, so she snuck a peek at him. He was bent double, poking at his hip. His gown was hiked up around his armpits, and the sweetheart dress was wadded up in a ball on his lap. It was red-black with wet blood. The smell of it was thick and metallic in the close wagon.

"Is there a bullet that needs digging out?" she prodded.

"Doesn't look it."

Thank goodness. She exhaled. She hadn't even realized she'd been holding her breath. Her hands were shaking too, she saw now. "It went straight through?"

"Looks like it just grazed me," he admitted grudgingly.

A graze. She laughed. Out of sheer relief, but he took offense. He also caught her looking.

"It took a fair hunk of flesh with it." He glared at her.

"I saw the blood," she soothed. "I know it did."

That clearly wasn't the right thing to say either. He gave her a filthy look and turned back to his wound.

"Is it still bleeding?"

He didn't answer.

Honestly. "If it's still bleeding, you need to stanch it. Do you need fresh cloth?"

"Stop fussing."

"I'm not fussing, I'm *helping*."

"I don't need *help*. I just need you to be quiet for five minutes."

She managed two. Maybe less. "You know I'm a nun. You can let me help you. My whole life is devoted to helping people." It might be a lie, but it sounded so good she just about believed it. She started feeling quite righteous. "Helping people is what I *do*." It was kind of true, when you thought about it. She'd helped whole *towns full* of men in her time . . .

"Well, you ain't very good at it."

"I beg your pardon?" She gave up all pretense of keeping her back turned. "I happen to be *wonderful* at it."

"You're the reason I'm shot. That ain't particularly helpful."

That was just utter nonsense. *He* was the one who hadn't been able to keep his pistol in its holster. She would have told him so too, and in no uncertain words, if Calla hadn't chosen that moment to tell them they were approaching the hacienda.

"The what?" Tom frowned at her. "*What* did she say? Where are we going?"

She pursed her lips. Hell. Surely, he'd heard Calla translate the vaqueros? Come to think of it, he didn't even *need* the translation—he spoke Spanish. He must have heard? Oh God. She didn't fancy his reaction to this . . .

She cleared her throat. "We're going to Don Rey's hacienda," she said brightly. Sometimes saying bad things in a cheerful voice worked. You could turn people right around into thinking that a bad thing was a good thing. Although, judging by his face, perhaps not this time . . . Oh well. If cheerfulness didn't work, going on the offensive might. "Don't go pulling that face at me," she said, changing her tone. "You knew where we were going. You heard the vaqueros. You were right here when it was organized."

"I was a little preoccupied," he growled. "Goddamn it, woman, we're trying to *avoid* Don Rey, not be his house-guests. The man *knows* me. He's going to see right through this stupid disguise." He'd gone an alarming chalky color.

Hell. He hadn't stanched the bleeding at all. She ignored him as he railed at her about Don Rey and the hacienda. Let him get it out of his system. So long as he didn't set his blood pumping out faster and bleed himself to death. She found some more cloth to use as a makeshift bandage and shoved his hands out of the way.

"What are you doing?"

"What I should have done before, instead of letting you botch things; I'm *helping* you." She pressed the cloth to the wound. "Hold that down hard," she ordered him.

"I wasn't botching anything," he protested. But he held it down. As best he could; he was going a bit limp.

"Don't you pass out on me," she warned as she found an old petticoat. She dug out the sewing basket and found the scissors. "Make sure you're pressing hard."

"How are you going to make sure he doesn't recognize me?" he asked. His voice had that papery sound again.

"Stop talking," she said as she took the scissors to the petticoat. "Save your energy and let me worry about hiding you."

"Let me guess," he sighed, sounding weaker by the minute, "you have a plan."

"It's an *excellent* plan," she agreed, manhandling him as she wrapped the makeshift petticoat bandages around his hips, binding the cloth tight to the wound. The bleeding did seem to be slowing.

"God help me," he sighed, leaning back against the trunk as she tied off the bandage.

"He did," she said. "He sent you *me.*"

Tom Slater groaned and closed his eyes.

"Don't pass out until I get your veil back on," she told him.

But of course he did. The man was as contrary as they came.

She managed to get him presentable enough as they approached the gates of the hacienda. She'd pulled his gown back down over his blood-sodden wool trousers and pinned the veil into place. Her makeshift bandage worked a treat, and as far as she could see, the bleeding had slowed to a trickle. She made him as comfortable as she could and then climbed over the luggage to talk to Calla and Anna.

"Oh my, that's nice," she said when Anna unknotted the canvas and pulled it open so Emma could lean through. The rush of fresh air cleared Emma's head immediately. She leaned over the back of the wagon bench, resting on her elbows between Calla and Anna. She gave Winnie a wink, and the girl almost smiled. The poor kid was buckled as tight as a miser's saddlebags. Scenes like today's shooting weren't helping to unbuckle her any. "Oh *my*," Emma said again, when she caught sight of the hacienda over the mules' heads, "that's *nice*."

The Spanish-style gateway was topped with a bell, which a servant boy rang vigorously to announce the visitors. The gateway framed the hacienda, which was about the most magnificent thing Emma had ever seen. Against a backdrop of mountains chased gold by the end-of-day sun, the hacienda was blue and cool. It was a three-story building of archways and tiled stairs, with curlicue iron balconies and shadowed windows. The stucco was painted cobalt blue with snow-white trim and glowed in the shadows of the lush garden. It was magical, like stumbling on a fairy garden. There were palms and bright flowers, peacocks and parrots; there were fountains splashing and children running through the front courtyard. Fat orange hens pecked at the earth, and lazy dogs slept on the warm tiles.

"This is just about the nearest thing I've seen to Heaven," Emma said, amazed.

"Me too," Calla agreed.

"Who knew this was out here in the middle of nowhere?"

"Do you think we'll be able to bathe?" Anna asked. "Those fountains look tempting."

"God, I hope so," Emma laughed. "We're all overripe."

"Don't blaspheme," Calla reminded her. "Especially here—they're all Catholic."

"I can see that." Emma's gaze lingered on the cross on top of the domed roof at the side of the courtyard.

They followed the vaqueros into the beauty of the hacienda's front courtyard, the wagon rattling on the wide cobbled drive. The temperature dropped as they passed into the garden. Droplets from the fountain cooled the air. It was divine.

"I guess that's Don Rey," Emma said, as a man stepped out onto the front steps. He was impeccably dressed. Aristocratic. More than a little intimidating. But Emma had a good feeling about him; anyone who built an oasis as beautiful as this *had* to be a good person.

Tom groaned in the depths of the wagon behind her. He clearly didn't share her enthusiasm for the place.

"What are we doing about *him*?" Calla asked. She looked worried.

Emma patted her on the back. "Don't worry. Leave it to me."

She ignored the fact that Calla didn't seem soothed. Tom moaned again, and she told him to shush.

"Anna, can you and Winnie look after Doña Elvira while I speak to our hosts?" she said loudly, so the vaqueros could hear her. Then she dropped her voice to a whisper. "Make sure his veil stays on and he's completely covered."

Anna nodded.

"Calla," she whispered, leaning close to her friend, "can you come with me and make sure I sound like a proper nun?"

Calla sighed. "Why don't you let me do the talking? The

more you try to sound like a nun, the less you do. Besides, they may not even speak English."

"Just make sure you tell them that Doña Elvira is recovering from the pox as well as the gunshot . . . well, it's more of a graze than a gunshot . . . and tell them she's man-shy and modest . . . Actually, tell them she doesn't like people . . . except for me . . ."

Calla rolled her eyes. "I'll make sure you and the good señora have privacy, but I'm not spinning stupid tales."

"They're not stupid. And they've worked so far." Emma didn't like relinquishing control, but she had to admit that Calla did a marvelous job of things. She didn't understand a word of what her friend said, but Don Rey and his wife certainly seemed to. They had the most sympathetic expressions Emma had ever seen. Doña Maria actually seemed to blink back tears, and Don Rey took it as a personal affront that daughters of Christ had been assaulted on his land.

"He says he will see to their punishment personally," Calla translated.

"Oh. Well, do remind him about God liking mercy. Right?"

Calla gave her a pinched look and then translated. A moment later, she translated Don Rey's reply: "He says, 'The Bible also speaks of an eye for an eye.'"

"Oh well. Yes. I guess it does." Emma frowned. "But there's a whole bit after that, when Jesus came along."

Calla leaned in close. "Just stop talking now," she said, very quietly. "They may speak some English."

Emma bit her tongue, even though she had more to say on the subject of mercy. Also, she was feeling dreadfully guilty about the Georges. While she knew in her gut that they were horrid men, they hadn't actually *done* anything . . . yet. She hoped that Don Rey wasn't going to do anything too drastic to them. Uneasily, she watched him follow the vaqueros as they led the Georges away.

"Doña Maria says it is their honor to host sisters of charity," Calla told Emma as the mistress of the hacienda descended the stairs to organize transferring Doña Elvira to a makeshift stretcher. Emma rushed to help, so she could hold Tom's veil in place.

"I'm the only one she trusts," she gabbled as she stuck close to the stretcher.

"I told her the señora is sensitive about her disfigurement," Calla said after she'd finished translating Emma's chatter, "and that the señora has taken a vow of silence after her husband's death. I've suggested the señora be left exclusively to your care."

So she had told some "stupid tales" after all. Emma felt smug. Now Calla might give her some credit and understand how a stupid tale was entirely necessary now and again. Emma thought she'd done a *great* job keeping everyone safe so far. Well. Except for the whole Tom getting shot thing.

"Pobrecita," Doña Maria cooed, smiling at Emma and patting Tom's arm as she escorted the makeshift stretcher into the house. The mistress of the hacienda was as cool and lovely as her house. Emma prayed Tom didn't startle her by moaning. He didn't sound the slightest bit womanly.

If she'd thought the hacienda was beautiful on the outside, she was stunned by the interior. Built around a central courtyard, the house was high ceilinged and lusciously cool, full of archways and filtered light. Mosaics swirled on the floors, and chandeliers glittered overhead. Everywhere she looked, there were things growing: tall ferns in brass urns; pink, red and white geraniums in terra-cotta pots spilling down stairways and nestled in arches; great swathes of white and purple bougainvillea draped like bunting around the central courtyard. The air was perfumed with mock orange flowers and water and hot terra-cotta tiles.

There were servants everywhere Emma looked: sweeping and gardening, dusting and scrubbing. All of them were young. And they all looked to be Indian. Passing them as they wound through the hacienda, Emma had her first moment of unease. Doña Maria led them through the main entry hall and up a stairway to the second floor. She and Calla chatted in Spanish while Anna and Winnie followed along nervously behind. Tom stirred on the stretcher. Emma reached down and took his hand, and his fingers curled around hers.

"Hush," she said, bending down. "The señora is taking us to a room where I can see to you in private."

He squeezed her hand. Rather too hard in Emma's opinion. He just about ground her bones together.

Doña Maria opened a door and gestured the stretcher through.

"She says you and the señora shall stay here," Calla said in a hushed voice, as she and Emma stood awed, taking in the luxury of the room. "We'll be just next door . . . I hope our room looks like this . . ."

The room was huge and just as beautiful as the rest of the house. The floors were polished wood, splashed here and there with finely woven Mexican rugs; tapestries hung from the walls, softening the austerity of the white adobe; and there was a gigantic wooden bed, hung with a white muslin canopy, to keep out the mosquitos. A small sitting area had been arranged facing the double doors, which Doña Maria opened, to allow fresh air in. The sound of the fountain below drifted up, bringing with it the perfume of water. Oh my, Emma thought, this place was nicer than even the *fanciest* whorehouse.

And the *views*. The windows opposite the bed framed a majestic view of the mountains. They were lusciously purple as dusk drew in. You'd *never* get out of bed with a view like that.

"Doña Maria says she will have a pallet delivered for you to sleep on."

Oh. A pallet. Emma gave the enormous, pillowy bed a longing look. She saw the sense in it, of course, as her roommate was gravely injured, but she had to swallow her disappointment as the men lowered Tom onto the bed. She would have liked the big bed for herself, with the canopy and the view.

She noticed Tom left a smear of blood on the luxurious white comforter. "He'll get blood all over the bedding," Emma said, worried.

"She says not to fret. The servants will bring fresh bedding once you have seen to the wound."

Poor servants, Emma thought, pulling a face. Tom Slater was about to make an awful mess in here.

"The servants will be up directly with water and bandages and your bedding. She wants to know if there's anything else you need."

Emma shook her head. She was eager to get everyone out so she could check on Tom. She thanked Doña Maria profusely as she left. Emma could see that Calla was already getting impatient translating back and forth, so she cheekily threw in a few more "thank-yous" than necessary, just to tease her. Calla didn't seem to appreciate the humor of it.

Once they were gone, Emma locked the door behind

them, then hurried to close the balcony doors and draw the curtains, so no one would see a man emerge from under the señora's gown. She turned to the bed with a grin, waiting for Tom to express his gratitude. But *did* he express his gratitude? No. Instead, all he did was bitch at her. Within ten minutes of being alone with him, she wished she'd left him to Doña Maria after all. "Poor Doña Elvira" wasn't a *pobrecita* at all, whatever the hell that was, Emma thought crankily. She was just an ungrateful, bullheaded cowpuncher.

"It's not *my* fault you got shot!" Emma felt like wringing his neck. He was the *worst* patient she'd ever had. "And it's not even a proper wound," she told him imperiously. "It's barely a graze."

"I'm missing half my hip," he growled. His green eyes were fierce in his white face.

"Don't be so dramatic."

"How would you know if I'm being dramatic?" Tom snapped at her after she'd maligned his bullet graze. "You ain't seen it properly!"

"Only because you won't let me." She drew a calming breath. It didn't help. *She'd* been through a difficult day too. He should damn well remember that. "I can't help you if you won't let me *look at it*."

He glared at her.

"It's nothing I haven't seen before," she said primly.

He didn't look like he believed her. The idiot had *no idea*. She'd seen more naked men than she cared to count. Probably more gunshots too.

"I'll look after myself," he said stubbornly.

"Fine. You do that. But don't come crying to me when you pass out and hit your head."

"Turn your back."

"Again?" With a show of poor grace, she ostentatiously turned her back on him.

"You locked the door?" He sounded surlier than ever.

"You *saw* me do it."

He grunted. She heard the sound of him struggling to get the dress off.

"You want me to undo the buttons for you?" She kept her tone polite. Because she was a *nice* person.

"No."

Give her strength. "You won't get it off if you don't undo the buttons."

There was the sound of cloth tearing.

"Tom Slater!" Emma whipped around in horror as she took in the mess he'd made of the gown. "How dare you! What are you going to wear now?"

"Who told you to turn around?"

"Oh, for Pete's sake!" He'd gone a nasty shade of clay white. His hip was bloody, and he was tangled in a mess of torn fabric. "That's quite enough." She stalked over to the bed, which was as huge and impressive as everything else in the room. She had to climb up to even reach him. "Keep still!" She made short work of the buttons down his back, giving him a sharp smack when he tried to fight her. Then she yanked the ruined dress over his head, unmindful of his wound. He gave a pained howl.

"Hush up," she said, throwing the dress on the chair. "If you keep that racket up, everyone from here to Mexico will know you're a man." She tried to roll up her sleeves, but they were big loose things and kept flopping down again. "If you must scream, at least make it high-pitched."

He was covered with a sheen of perspiration and was

obviously running out of the energy to fight her. Good. Perhaps now he'd listen to sense.

"You," she said, jabbing her finger at him, "are going to do *everything* I tell you to do, do you hear? *I'm in charge.*"

There was a knock at the door. Hell. He was half-naked. No one was mistaking that wide, hairy chest for a woman's.

"Get under the comforter," she ordered. She yanked it out from under him. "Pull it over your head."

He could barely move, so she helped him.

"Stay still," she hissed. "And don't you dare say a word." She pulled the white mosquito curtains closed around the bed. They were sheer, but they were better than nothing. She made sure she couldn't see anything of him but a lump under the comforter before she opened the door. This lying business was hard on the nerves. Her heart was galloping like a herd of runaway horses.

She opened the door to a flood of servants. She stepped back to let them pass, astonished. How many people did it take to make up a bed? None of them spoke English. At least none of them responded to her when she spoke to them, so she assumed they didn't speak English. They trooped in, carrying bedding, a tin tub, buckets of warm water, towels and bandages.

Emma rushed to put herself between the servants and Tom's bed, so they wouldn't see him. She kept chattering in English, hoping they'd be distracted enough by her not to pay any attention to the lump in the bed. Most of the servants ignored her completely, keeping their eyes fixed on their tasks, but one girl gave her a nervous smile and nodded occasionally. Perhaps she understood a word or two. Emma wished she spoke Spanish. The Reys were of Spanish settler stock, so the household probably didn't know any

English. Calla had told her the rancheros were snobby about their origins and didn't like to be confused with the Mexicans. "Even their Spanish is snobby," Calla had sniffed. Emma didn't know about that, but they were sure rich, judging by all these servants. Money did have a way of making people give themselves airs.

Within no time at all, the servant girl had set up a pallet on the floor for Emma. It looked more comfortable than Emma's bed back in Moke Hill. They'd used feather quilts and white linen, and it appeared just like a fluffy white cloud. Emma was looking forward to crawling into it. She hadn't slept in a bed for the longest time.

By the time the servants left, they'd also unfolded a dressing screen around a brass tub full of steaming water. The servant girl paused by the door after her companions had trooped out. She said something in halting Spanish.

"*Gracias*," Emma hazarded.

"Do you have any idea what you're thanking her for?" Tom rasped after she'd locked the door behind the servants.

"Of course I do," Emma said imperiously. "I'm thanking her for my bed. And that bath, which I intend to make use of, so you'd better let me fix you up before that water goes cold!"

"You can't make use of it," he said, sounding appalled.

"And why not?"

"Because *I'm* here."

She quite enjoyed how panicked he sounded. He was almost lively. "The tub is screened."

"By that? You can just about see through it."

It was true. The panels of the dressing screen were made of cream-colored calico. The shadow of the tub was clearly visible through them.

"So close your eyes," she suggested with a shrug.

"It ain't decent," he protested.

"I'll tell you what," she said as she parted the canopy and pulled the comforter off him, "I won't mind when you're not decent, if you don't mind when I'm not." She reached for the waistband of his trousers.

"What the hell do you think you're doing?"

"Having a look at your hip."

He just about fell off the bed in his attempts to get away from her. His efforts had him bleeding again, and he covered the lovely white bed with blood. He also went from chalk white to bluish gray in a matter of seconds.

"Look at what you've done," she scolded. "You've made a mess and hurt yourself into the bargain. Now stop being such a child and let me take care of you."

His lips were blue. That couldn't be a good sign.

"Tom," she said, holding him down and looking him directly in the eye. "I'm a *nun*. I've seen naked men in my time. I've cared for them, I've bathed them . . ." She'd done a lot of other things to them too, but that was a story for another day. "Trust me. I won't be scandalized. I won't be shocked. I won't faint dead away. I will treat you gently and with respect."

He was frozen under her hands.

"I know this is embarrassing," she commiserated. "But a little embarrassment never killed anyone."

He closed his eyes.

"All right?"

He nodded imperceptibly.

About bloody time. Before he could change his mind, she flicked open the buttons and pulled his trousers off. And then Tom Slater was buck-naked and entirely at her mercy.

❖ 16 ❖

IT TOOK EVERY ounce of willpower Tom had not to get an erection. And it was no small task. He was sprawled on his back, naked as the day he was born, while the good sister scrubbed the grit out of his wound. She'd been kind enough to throw a towel across his nether regions, but it was the thinnest scrap of toweling Tom had ever seen, and since the wound was on his hip, she was only a hairbreadth from touching him every time she moved. His modesty was hanging by a thread. He stared at the white bed canopy, perspiring from the effort it took not to get visibly aroused. Somehow, even despite the pain of his wound, he found the whole situation disturbingly erotic. The September heat; the slow slide of the wet cloth over his skin; the strangely sexual juxtaposition of the stinging pain in his hip and the uncurling pleasure in the rest of his body; the smell of her; their silence; all of it combined to make him light-headed with lust. He'd never fantasized about nuns in his life—but he had a feeling they'd be featuring in his dreams from now on.

She wasn't businesslike about things, which was a big part of the problem. She moved slow and soft, and everything about her was earthy and sexy and hypnotic. Her fingers brushed against his hip and thigh as she cleaned his wound with the warm water. While one hand ran the washcloth over Tom's torn flesh, the other rested on his leg, the fingers curled around his calf. It was maddeningly distracting.

"I'm amazed you've got any blood left in you," she said as she wrung the washcloth out. The water in the basin was red. "I'm just going to change the water, and then I'll sponge you down."

Any blood that *was* left in him was rapidly heading south. He should absolutely take this opportunity to tell her to stop. She was too innocent to know better. She was a nun; she couldn't know the effect she was having on him. How could a chaste virgin have any idea of what it did to a man to be helpless and naked and *sponged?* She couldn't possibly know that his head was hot and steamy with delicious images, that he was aware of every last inch of himself, that he had to clench his fists to keep from touching her.

Get up. Cover yourself. Get out of this goddamn situation right now. But he couldn't bring himself to move. He felt drugged.

It was probably the blood loss.

Or maybe it was exhaustion.

Or, worst of all, maybe it was *her.* No woman had ever had this narcotic effect on him before. And she wasn't even *trying.*

That didn't bear thinking about.

"I've got blood all over me," she observed, as she came back with a basin of clean water. "I'll have to soak my habit after I bathe."

Christ. Don't think about her out of the habit. Don't think about her bathing. He closed his eyes so he wouldn't

stare at her; wouldn't imagine what she looked like without
the headdress, without the thick, shapeless black sack of a
habit; wouldn't imagine her body, white as milk from never
seeing the sun, soft, curving, slick with water from the
bath . . .

Hell. Closing his eyes just made the images *more* vivid.

"Try and relax," she said, and he heard the gentle splashing of water as she wet the sponge.

Relax. As if that was even a possibility. His teeth were
clenched, fit to crack.

He almost moaned when she started in on him again.
She couldn't wash him briskly, could she? With swift, practical strokes? No, she had to take her time, had to try to *relax*
him with long, lazy, warm circles. It was excruciating.

She started at his feet and worked up, and she was *thorough*. Every toe received detailed attention, and then she
worked her way up his legs, the cloth rubbing long arcs over
his tense muscles, the pressure firm enough to make him
wince, but after the pressure came incredible waves of pleasure; spirals of desire spread from her touch. He felt like
he was sinking through the bed. Time lost all meaning. He
was nothing but singing nerve endings and tingling skin.

When she reached his chest, he just about came off
the bed. His nipples were painfully sensitive; when the
sponge passed over them, he lost the battle with his willful
cock. It swelled hard against his stomach. It was taking all
his good sense as well as his blood supply. What he
wouldn't have given for her to slide that sponge down, over
his quivering, clenched stomach until she found the hard,
throbbing length of him.

He was going to hell. Who had thoughts like these about
nuns? He couldn't keep himself in check. Mumbling a panicked excuse, he rolled over onto his stomach.

"Watch your hip," she said, sounding worried.

To hell with his hip; it was his cock he was worried about. Specifically, that she would see it. The scrap of toweling wasn't doing anything to provide cover, and the damn thing was standing at attention like a flagpole. At least if he was facedown she couldn't see the effect she had on him. He pressed his face hard into the bed. *Tell her to stop. That's enough now.* But his idiot tongue wouldn't work. And then the sponge started up again, over the plains of his back and down his spine. It was warm and slick and firm: exquisitely torturous. And then, just when he thought it couldn't get *more* torturous, it did.

"You're mighty dirty," she said. And goddamn if her voice hadn't thickened . . . if there wasn't a huskiness to it . . . a tremor . . . a pulse of desire in it.

No. You're imagining it.

But *was* he? He certainly wasn't imagining the charged silence. It was like the air during a lightning storm. The hairs on the back of his neck stood on end with anticipation. He also didn't think he was imagining the slight hesitation in the swipe of the sponge. Or the faint sigh she gave . . .

He didn't know if he could take much more.

Luckily, he didn't have to find out, because a knock at the door saved him. Saved *them.* Because he didn't think he had imagined that sigh.

He felt an intense blend of relief and disappointment when she flung the comforter over him and went to answer the door. He was still aroused. Painfully so. He tried to get himself under control as he listened to her usher in more servants, who brought food and fresh water.

Sister Emma kept saying, *"Gracias,"* in an atrocious accent. "You're going to have to teach me to say a few things," she sighed after she'd closed the door on the servants.

He stayed silent. He didn't think it was a good idea for him to teach her *anything*. He thought the only thing he should be doing was staying well away from her. He pretended to be asleep. Not least because he couldn't be talking to a nun while he was rigid as a randy mustang.

He thought this was about as uncomfortable as he could get. But that was before she tried to bandage his hip. He stayed stubbornly on his stomach, keeping up the pretense of sleep. He threw a soft snore in for good measure. When she tried to roll him onto his side, he gripped the edge of the mattress and held firm. He felt her freeze. Maybe she had an inkling of why he was staying planted facedown at that point, because she retreated. He breathed a sigh of relief when she drew the comforter back over him and left him in peace.

At least he thought she was leaving him in peace . . . until a while later when she started shucking her clothes.

"I guess you're more tired than you are hungry," she'd sighed when she'd first retreated from him. He heard her sit down. Then nothing. The silence stretched out.

He opened his eyes a crack. She'd sat herself on the couch, next to the food. She'd poked through the covered clay pots, sniffing at the contents. Then she plucked a purple grape and sank back into the couch. She looked exhausted. But that didn't stop her from torturing him with the grape. How in hell did she make eating a grape look so sexy, so sinful? She didn't just eat the damn thing, she *played* with it. Her sharp-cornered lips sucked on it. *Slowly.* She stared into the middle distance, lost in thought, as her mouth drove him wild. He *hurt* from it.

When she was finished the grape, she bent double and unlaced her shoes. She moved with grace, unthreading each lace at a glacial pace. It gave him time to watch her.

She eased her boots off and flexed her feet. God, she was pretty. Natural. Unaffected.

"Well, Mr. Slater," she sighed, "if you're having a sleep, I'm going to take advantage of that bath." She stood abruptly and hiked her skirts up. He had to bite his tongue to stop from swearing. She was undressing *here*? In full view? Luckily for both of them, she had her riding breeches on under her skirts, so when she yanked her habit up, she didn't show him anything he hadn't already seen when she was mounting her horse. But then the woman went to take the breeches off too. As she worked the buttons, he screwed his eyes shut. His cock was like a ridgepole. She was getting *naked*. Right now. Right there. The woman wasn't just innocent; she was *dangerously* naïve. His eyes burned behind his eyelids. It took every ounce of self-control he had not to peek. He heard her humming as she shed her clothes. He didn't know how much longer his willpower would hold.

SHE KNEW HE wasn't asleep. He wasn't even making a good show of it. His breathing was irregular, his body was stiff as a board (in more ways than one), and he kept cracking an eyelid to spy on her. Emma tried not to laugh as she relaxed back in the tub. Now that she was safely behind the dressing screen, she could grin. That was one pent-up man. He radiated sheer, unadulterated need.

She was more flattered than she cared to admit. Especially since the woman he knew was smothered in heavy black wool and a silly hat, wasn't wearing a lick of paint and must smell to high heaven. Maybe he had a thing for smelly women.

She hadn't been expecting him to enjoy a wound cleaning that much. *She'd* been rather tingly at the sight of all that lovely bare male body, but it had come as a shock to realize he was tingling too. Not least because he was in pain. But also because he thought she was a *nun*.

But her nunhood certainly hadn't stopped him from standing at attention. She felt rather smug as she lathered up with the soap. The water was only tepid, but it was a hot evening, so Emma didn't care. It was bliss to scrub the dirt away. Her hands slid over the fuzz on her scalp. It was nice to know that even dirty and smelly and nunny, she could still make a man's body sing. Imagine how irresistible she'd be when she was *clean*.

She wasn't a fool. She knew nothing was going to happen between her and Tom Slater (for too many reasons to count), but it was soothing to know that it *could* happen if she wanted it to. She sang softly as she soaped herself. He was one beautiful man. He had the most divine body, golden skinned and muscular . . . Oh, those muscles . . . His arms, his chest, his stomach; every inch of him was hard and defined, and there was a delicious trail of hair disappearing under the towel she'd draped over his hips. She had to admit she'd stolen a peak before she'd covered him up and was unsurprised to find that he was just as well proportioned below the waist as he was above.

She hadn't felt sparks like these in years. If ever.

Sparks had never been simple for Emma, and even less simple when she'd been Seline. Desire was a complicated thing for a whore. And sex was more complicated still. Sex was a job. It was *work*. It wasn't romance and seduction and toe-curling lust. At least not for the whore. Most men took their pleasure quick, and they took it without a single thought for her side of the experience. They were paying *not* to think about her pleasure. There was no question of desire when a man took you like that. Sex was a chore and a labor. Using your hands or your mouth, or just letting them thrust away at you—it was a drudge of a job. And it chipped away at something inside of you. It dulled you. But now and then you sparked for a man. Sometimes for money, and sometimes not; sometimes a man took it slow and was courteous and seemed to care for your comfort through the experience, and a single spark might fizz. Now and then, you met a man like Luke Slater who wanted you to have as much fun as he did, and there would be a Catherine wheel of sparkles. But they were as rare as hen's teeth, and when they came along, you grabbed hold of them and enjoyed them for all that they were worth.

But *desire* for its own sake . . . that was a funny thing. Desire happened by accident, as a side effect. When you used your body for work, there was a blockage in your head that kept it dammed. But even with her history and her job, she'd always felt that there was the capacity for grace in lovemaking. Not in the kind of sex she had for money, but in real lovemaking. When a man wanted you and you wanted him and it was tender and gentle and you stayed pressed body to body long after the climax, holding each other through the night; when they shared themselves with you, dropping their guard and telling you intimacies; when you looked into their eyes and you saw right into their heart. Those were the keenest moments in her life, the ones that gave her hope.

Because life could be down-in-the-gutter bitter and dirty, and it was easy to despair. But now and then you saw a flash of something in people that lifted you up, that made you realize that above the gutter was the whole spread of sky with all of its blazing stars. So long as you had the strength to look up. And then people could show you what real grace was. Like that old prospector, McGinty, who had fallen like a stone for Nora Paul. Nora had been a whore for her whole grown-up life, and she wasn't young. She was missing teeth and had sad eyes; she had wrestled with a liking for the bottle and lost her son to whooping cough. She was a woman with a worn face and a sore heart. But McGinty had spent one night with her and lost his wits with love. When he looked at her, he didn't see a battered whore; he saw *Nora*. A girl who'd been born and raised in West Virginia, who liked tapioca pudding and mulberries eaten fresh from the tree, who cried when she heard a hymn well sung and who couldn't walk past a dog without giving it a pat. And damned if McGinty hadn't married Nora Paul and set her up in a white clapboard house by the stream where he panned for gold; damned if they didn't have a pack of dogs and didn't attend church on Sundays, where they sang together lustily, sharing a hymnbook; and damned if he didn't think he was the luckiest man on the face of the earth to get to sit next to Nora Paul and call her his wife. Oh yes, there was grace in lovemaking; some divine spark set off a blaze that turned lovemaking to love, and brought a body back to life.

Her thoughts had lost their way. Love had nothing to do with her and Tom Slater, or with his arousal under her sponge. Some men just had a hair trigger, that was all. She wondered if he was watching her shadow on the dressing screen. *There* was a thought with some sparks to it. She tingled as she rose from the tub, aware that the lantern would cast her shadow into relief against the dressing screen. She ran her hands down her body, and she could swear she heard his breath catch. She smiled. She might just be a retired whore, but she was a *top-notch* retired whore.

She hummed as she toweled herself dry. Once she was

dry, she had to face her stinking black habit. She wrinkled her nose. The underdress was just as bad. She tossed them both in the tub, submerging them in the soapy water. Then she tossed her undergarments in too. She couldn't wash her breeches, because her life savings were sewn into them. She'd just have to hope that a night of airing out would improve their fragrance. She couldn't be bothered scrubbing anything; she'd leave the gowns to soak for a bit. Now, what the hell was she going to wear while everything was wet?

She probably should have thought of that before she'd shoved everything in the tub. Oh well. Every problem had a solution. There was an Indian blanket neatly folded on a chair nearby. She could wrap up in that. She could turn anything into a dress, she thought smugly as she wound the blanket into a kind of Grecian wrap. There was a shaving mirror hanging from the dressing screen, and Emma contorted herself to see if she was decently covered. Now she had to do something about her hair—or lack of hair. Although . . . maybe it was best if he saw her like this, bareheaded as a bald eagle. She wasn't too worried that he'd recognize her as the redheaded whore from *La Noche,* now that she didn't have the nun hat on; she thought that would have happened by now if it was going to happen. And it might be best to damp him down by showing him her baldness; it seemed cruel to keep him all het up when nothing could happen between them. And nothing would cool him off faster than her peach-fuzz head. It was a stark reminder of her nunhood—if the hideous black habit hadn't been enough. She also thought she looked genuinely awful, and that would help to damp him down too.

She felt bizarrely shy as she stepped out from behind the screen. He was still pretending to be asleep. She ran her hand over her scalp. Her vanity was already starting to ache. She *liked* the admiration in his eyes. She wasn't looking forward to it fading when he caught sight of her.

She shook off the damn fool feeling. *Stop it.* Pining over some pretty man she could never have wasn't going to do anyone any good.

Why couldn't you have him? He's right there. He clearly wouldn't mind . . .

No. She wasn't doing that again. These were dangerous thoughts; they glittered like fool's gold, but like fool's gold, they weren't worth keeping. She'd promised herself she wouldn't lead herself to heartbreak again, and she always kept her promises.

"The food's getting cold," she said, straightening her shoulders and gathering her pride. Who cared if the admiration in his eyes fizzled and died once he saw her bald head? That was what she *wanted*. Wasn't it?

He didn't respond, still clinging to the pretense of sleep. She shrugged and crossed the room to the couch. It was no skin off her nose if he wanted to eat cold beans.

She knew he was watching her as she curled up on the couch, tucking the Indian blanket tightly around her. "It was a shame not to eat it fresh," she sighed, as she made herself a plate, "but I'd rather be clean when I eat, than all mucky and hot like I was. I don't know how you bore the stench of me." When she lifted the lids on the clay pots, delicious aromas filled the room. Spicy beans, onions and tomato, roasted peppers. She heard his stomach rumble.

"Want me to bring you a plate?" she asked dryly. There was no response. Fine. Let him wait. She took a tortilla and attacked the peppers and beans. The food was good. She sighed happily. She loved food. Everything about it. Good food filled her with a sense of total well-being, even when times were hard.

Her ma had been a good cook. Emma's earliest memories were of the smell of fresh bread baking and the taste of salted butter melted into fat, yeasty hunks of it. Her mama made so many kinds of bread: sourdough, soda bread, corn bread, French bread, rye, potato bread, pumpkin loaf. Every lunch hour there was a meal to make your mouth water: grits and okra, catfish and peppery greens, and all kinds of beans in all kinds of ways, all of it accompanied by steaming-hot bread. Everyone went back to work in the afternoon happy, even when the farm was floundering. Emma's ma could even make possum palatable, which was no mean feat. She'd known how to make a feast out of lean cracklings, and Emma's youngest, happiest girlhood had been spent at her mother's side, kneading and chopping, stirring and scrubbing. Food and happiness were closely linked. When Ma got sick, the feasts had stopped, and any happiness Emma had felt melted away. It didn't come back.

Sad thoughts didn't belong with good food, so Emma pushed them away and concentrated on the oily goodness of the peppers. She wished she had some corn bread too, to mop up the juices. The tortillas were good, but they were nothing on her corn bread. The thought of corn bread reminded her of her starter, which was still with their luggage and needed feeding. She'd have to ask the servant girl to bring it up, or maybe she could go to it. She wouldn't mind a walk in the fresh air, but she couldn't leave Tom alone, in case someone came in. She glanced over at him. He wasn't quite quick enough to close his eyes before she caught him.

She grinned. "There's no point in pretending, honey. I can hear your stomach complaining from here. And I don't blame it; this is mighty good food. I'll bring you a plate." Humming, she piled high a plate for him and poured him a glass of spring water from the jug. Night had fallen while she bathed, and the lanterns cast long shadows. She stood next to the bed patiently, watching the shadows dance on the planes of his face. He was still on his stomach, cheek pressed to the mattress, eyes stubbornly closed.

She wondered if he was still aroused. She shouldn't have entertained the thought, because it caused a fountain of sparks, and she was trying not to encourage sparks. The problem was he was *gorgeous*. Just looking at him sent her into spark territory. He put every man she'd ever met to shame. Look at those cheekbones. Those lips. Those thick black eyelashes. He was magnificent. And even more so because he didn't seem to know it. Unlike his brother Luke, Tom seemed to be utterly clueless about how beautiful he was. While Luke used his looks to charm, Tom just went through the world like he was a regular old cowhand; there was no flirting, no sideways looks, no meltingly knowing smiles. He was just plain old Tom, and whether he was with men or women, his behavior was the same.

Only . . . she hadn't really seen him with a proper woman, had she? In their time together, he'd only been around nuns and veiled señoras and children. There'd been no one at all to flirt with. He wasn't likely to act more than a simple cowhand with nuns and children. How could she know what he was like with *women*, when she'd yet to see him with a woman he could charm? *Except for Seline.* She felt her stomach clench as she remembered that hot look he'd given her back in Mariposa, when she'd posed stark-naked on the staircase. He hadn't been plain old cowhand Tom then, had he? He'd been a smoldering dark presence behind Deathrider, all leashed animal desire and burning eyes. She envied the women who'd felt the full force of *that* Tom Slater. Her gaze ran over the shape of his body beneath the thin comforter. Lucky, lucky women.

If he *was* still aroused, he wasn't likely to roll over while she was standing here. Because he was a *nice* man, and he thought she was a nun. Even if she hadn't been a nun, he probably wouldn't have rolled over. He didn't seem the sort to foist himself on women, even when the woman in question had forced him into a cheeky sponge bath.

"I'll just leave your plate here," she said, not quite able to keep the note of regret out of her voice. She set the plate on the bed in front of him, close enough that the smell would tantalize him. "There's a glass of water on the floor next to the bed too," she added, placing the glass on the floor. "Eat up before the food's stone-cold, and before the servants come back for the dirty dishes."

She retreated, heading behind the screen to wash her clothes. Through the calico, she could see his silhouette as he stirred. She had to smile at his completely unbelievable show of stretching and yawning and pretending to wake.

"How's your hip, honey?" she called.

He muttered something. Lord, he was adorable. She wrestled with the soaking wet habit. He was like a boy in a man's body. Awkward, shy, but also powerful—there was all that volcanic energy seething under the calm.

"I thought you already had a bath," he said. His voice was tight.

"I did. Now I'm giving my stinky clothes a bath." She could hear his spoon scraping the plate as he shoveled food in. He sure sounded hungry. "There's still food in the pots, if you want seconds," she told him.

He grunted.

"Yell out when you want it. Don't go getting up and tearing at your wound."

He grunted again. But before she'd even wrung out her wet clothes, he was asking sheepishly for seconds.

Coming out from behind the screen felt even harder this time, now that she knew he was definitely looking at her. She found herself blushing—and she hadn't blushed since she was a green girl. She cringed when his gaze lingered on her head. She brushed her hand over her scalp. Goddamn it. She hated this feeling. This was the reason she'd sworn off men. They made you feel so goddamn vulnerable.

Hellfire. What did she care what he thought? She *didn't*. Let him look all he wanted. She forced herself to keep her hand at her side, away from the peach fuzz on her scalp. She lifted her chin and went to collect his plate. He was staring. So let him stare.

"You have to cut it all off when you take your vows," she lied, feeling the need to answer his unasked question. It barely even felt like lying. She hated herself for the note of defensiveness in her voice. It made her feel weak. "Vanity has no place for a nun." She didn't know for certain that was true, but it probably was. Look at what they wore. And Calla had said so, and she knew more about nuns than was reasonable. Especially for a whore.

"It don't look too bad," he said. He was clearly trying to be polite, but it just made her feel grumpy.

"It don't matter how it looks," she snapped, snatching the plate out of his hand. "That's the whole point."

He stayed silent as she marched to the food and tipped the clay pots out onto his plate. She thrust the food at him and stalked back to her washing. For some reason, her eyes were hot and itchy. Like she was about to cry. But that was stupid. Why in hell would she cry just because some idiot man saw her with a shaved head? She *wouldn't*. And that was that.

❧ 17 ❧

THE NEXT FEW days were a sweet oasis. Somehow, Emma managed to keep Tom hidden from view as the servants changed the sheets and emptied the bathwater, delivered food and laundered their clothes. Once or twice she hid him in Calla and Anna's room, especially the first day, before Emma had managed to hastily mend the black dress he'd ripped to shreds. There were a few close moments, but overall, they'd kept him secret remarkably well.

Emma fetched her sewing and her starter from the wagon, and the five of them enjoyed a well-earned rest after the shenanigans on the trail. She kept her starter happy, sending batches of dough down to the kitchens (because she had to use the starter anyway and it was sinful to waste such nice yeast), and sewed up a new underdress for her horrid habit (so she'd have a spare, which would allow her to wash more frequently). She and Anna cut down and altered a couple of the simpler muslin gowns in Emma's trunks for Winnie, who was wide-eyed with pleasure at inheriting such finery. They slept late, in their divinely soft beds, and filled up on wonderful fresh food.

Gran Rancho de Gato was a sublime place to rest. The hot days were blunted by the cool of the fountains and the gardens, and when the balcony doors and the windows were thrown open, the smell of water and flowers perfumed the air. Through the windows, they watched the changing sun on the mountains: blue and silver in the early mornings, golden in the bright of day, brassy in the waning and lushly purple as night drew in. Emma had never seen such beauty in her entire life. It gave a girl ideas.

"One day, I'm going to have a house just like this," she sighed. She and Calla were sprawled on the couches, enjoying the morning sun, while Anna had taken Winnie to play in the gardens. The girl had blossomed now that they'd taken a few days to rest. She was well fed and well slept, and had come out of her shell. She particularly enjoyed Doña Maria's doting and the presence of other children. Emma could hear the sound of squeals and splashing water and smiled. She stretched out her fingers, which ached from sewing. Now that they'd finished Winnie's dresses, Doña Maria had given her an old black gown to alter, to replace Tom's ruined señora's outfit. Emma had tried her best to fix the black dress, but it had been too badly damaged to repair effectively. It looked a fright. Fortunately, Doña Maria had a trunk of old clothes that had belonged to her mother, who had been a tall woman by the looks of it. Which was good, because "Doña Elvira" was tall herself. The black dress Doña Maria delivered was terribly out of fashion but beggars couldn't be choosers. It might even work in their favor, as it would make Tom even less attractive to men like Irish George, with his wandering hands. Emma had been working on the dress all morning, much to Tom's displeasure. He got more cantankerous each time she made him have a fitting.

"Oh yes," she sighed again, pausing her sewing to watch

the bougainvillea bob in the breeze and the sunshine slant across the courtyard, "one day I shall have a house *just* like this. Only by the sea."

"A house like this?" Tom said, in his usual grumpy way. The man was like a bear with a sore head. He refused to stay in bed and play the invalid, and was prone to pacing, which set Emma's nerves on edge. "A house like this, for nuns?"

Ugh. There was the nun thing again. It always tripped her up. "Why not?" she said, even though Calla was giving her warning looks. "Why can't nuns have a bit of prettiness in their lives?"

"I thought you swore a vow of poverty?"

She really could stab him with a needle sometimes. He was such a sourpuss. "Dreams don't cost anything," she said primly. "I can *dream* I have a house like this."

"Me too," Calla said. Oh, that was a relief. For a while there, Emma had thought she was going to join in with the sourness. Emma had enough sourness from Tom; she didn't need it from both of them. Calla might have soured if Emma had insisted that nuns *could* have houses like this, but when Emma kept it to dreams, she relaxed. Poor nuns. You'd think a vow of chastity was enough. Poverty seemed to be gilding the lily, in Emma's humble opinion. If *she* ran a nunhouse, she'd only make them choose one: chastity *or* poverty. The chaste ones could live in luxury like this, and the poor ones could find comfort in love. That seemed like a fair trade.

But it was ideas like those that showed why she'd never really be a nun, she supposed.

"I'd have a house like this but with the balcony facing the mountains," Calla said happily, falling into the dream like she was sinking into a warm bath. She smiled as she stared out the window at the view. "You could sit out there as the sun was setting. I'd have a couch like this on the balcony too, so I could put my feet up at the end of the day."

"I'd have my bath out there," Emma topped her. "A nice, hot, steaming bath as the stars came out overhead. You could watch the moon rise over the mountains."

They'd played this game on the trail out from Missouri, and then again on slow nights in the Heart of Gold. *If I could,* it was called. Over the months, Emma's *coulds* had solidified into a single dream: *If I could* I would have a house by the bay, where I could watch the water from my windows. *If I could* I would have a big sunny kitchen, with pots of herbs on the windowsills and bread in the oven. *If I could* I would have a garden with a vegetable patch, fruit trees and chickens, and a bit of lawn to lie on and watch the clouds. *If I could* I'd have a place to call my own, where I could be safe and I could be warm, and no one would come pawing at me in the night. *If I could* I would be free to say *no* and to close the door. And lock it.

"If I could I'd sleep in until morning was just about done," Calla said longingly, "and someone would bring me breakfast in bed."

Yes. "If I could I'd have pancakes and syrup every morning and never get fat."

"If I could," Calla sang, "I'd have *champagne* with my pancakes."

"Followed by a bath scented with French perfume."

"By my French maid!"

Oh yes!

"*If I could* I'd get the hell out of here," Tom snapped.

No. Emma glared at him. "You're ruining the game."

"Game? I don't see any game. What I see is us sitting around while the posses get ever closer. We need to leave. *Now.*"

He was right. Emma hated him for it, but he was. They should have left already; "Doña Elvira" was well enough to travel, and there was nothing else keeping them here—it was just that Don Rey's hospitality was so seductive. It was so nice to sleep on a pillowy mattress, between soft sheets, even if it was on the floor; it was so nice to have a warm bath drawn and hot food delivered; it was so nice not to have to wash pots or suffer sunburn, or to get a sore rear from bouncing along on a horse all day.

"You need to tell them that we're leaving," he insisted.

"I will." Stone-faced, she went back to her sewing. She didn't want to leave yet. Surely, one more day wouldn't hurt . . .

"When will you tell them?"

"At dinner tonight."

The mention of dinner made him even grumpier. They'd all been invited to a formal dinner downstairs in the courtyard. To say that Tom was unhappy about it was an understatement. The last thing he wanted was to be appearing veiled and acting the woman in front of the Reys.

"You have a death wish," he snapped. "I'm not going."

"Fine. We'll say you're sick." She went blithely on with her sewing. "But it seems to me that a gentleman like Don Rey won't be happy to let us leave tomorrow if you're sick. He's a good Catholic. He's not about to let a gunshot nun-to-be go wandering into the wilderness, where she might die."

He swore under his breath and resumed his pacing.

"It's much better if he thinks you're fit and well."

Which he *was*. Rudely so. Tom thrummed with suppressed energy. He clearly wasn't a man designed to recline in luxury. He couldn't sit still for half a minute. Even at night he thrashed about, wrestling the sheets like they were his mortal enemy. She guessed he was so used to sleeping rough that comfort was anathema to him.

Either that or he was having naughty dreams.

She grinned at her sewing. It had been patently clear that seeing her bald head hadn't dampened his interest at all. The man watched her every move, and his eyes got that smoldering look she'd seen back in Mariposa. Only this time, he was looking at *her* and not Seline. Emma knew that shouldn't have pleased her so mightily, but it did. He gave *her* naughty dreams (such languid, loose, lovely dreams), so she thought it was only fair if he suffered too. Because, *Madre de Dios,* it was torture sleeping near him. It seemed ridiculous, because she slept near him on the trail. But it was worse in here. There was something about the privacy of it; once the curtains were drawn and the doors were locked, their room became a plush little cocoon. The hush of it, the sensual slide of the sheets against Emma's skin, that charge that was always in the air when the two of them were alone together, the sound of his uneven breath, the warm masculine smell of him . . . Who knew that sleeping on a pallet on the floor *next* to a man could be so erotic? There was no touching, no talking, no kissing, no looking . . . but Emma spent every night loose limbed and lazy with desire. More than once she had an urge to join him in that big plush bed, an urge that was so strong she almost gave in to it. *Tom.* How many times had she almost purred his name? Had almost invited him to join her on the floor . . .

Yes, perhaps he was right. Perhaps the sooner they left, the better. It would put him in a sweeter temper, for a start.

"You know, I'm shocked you'd want to live in a place like this," he said, giving her a spiky look, "being waited on hand and foot."

She rolled her eyes. There he went grumbling again.

"By slaves."

She stabbed herself with the needle. *"What?"*

"I would have thought slavery went against your grain. You being a nun and all."

And that's when Emma learned the truth about the armies of servants who had made her life so blissful these past few days.

"They're indentured," Tom explained. He seemed astonished that she hadn't known.

"They're *what?*" Emma was frozen.

That was when she learned the truth about *Gran Rancho de Gato*. She felt like she'd had the rug pulled out from under her. It was like learning that up was down. She'd been busy in Moke Hill these past few months and hadn't kept up with territorial politics. Oh, she'd heard men talk in her saloon about California's impending statehood in the fall, and the usual rubbish about the Mexicans, but somehow she'd missed the news that California was up and enslaving Indians now.

"Men like Rey have always had Indians working for them," Tom told her. "Most not entirely by choice, but as of a few months ago, it's law."

"What do you mean it's law?"

"Just what I said: it's the law. Indian children are fair game for indenture; they got no rights. Any famer or miner or whoever can press an Indian kid into labor, so long as that farmer or miner is white. White-white or Hispanic-white don't matter, so long as you're not black or Indian. You must have seen them in Moke Hill? There's Indians all through the goldfields, working people's claims for them, keeping their camps."

She felt sick. "Warming their beds?"

He flushed. "Yeah," he admitted, "I guess that's a true thing."

Slaves. She looked at her pillowy bed and fancy room with new eyes. Oh God. All those young servants. *Slaves.*

"Did you know about this?" she asked Calla.

"Not about the law," Calla admitted guiltily, "but I knew those kids didn't look too happy to be here."

Shame bit Emma hard. Why hadn't *she* noticed? How could she have made those kids fetch and carry for her the way she had? How could she be sitting here all comfortable on a couch in the sunshine while they labored for her against their will?

The sound of the gate bell ringing cut through Emma's swirling black thoughts. "What's that?"

"Someone's coming." Tom threw his veil over his head and headed for the courtyard balcony. Their room didn't face the front courtyard, so they couldn't see who was riding into *de Gato* from where they were. Emma and Calla followed him as he stalked the galleried balcony that wrapped around the inner courtyard, until he reached the front of the house. Emma couldn't help but notice the servants setting up the dinner table in the courtyard below. So many of them. She hated to think how many there were in houses like these all across California. How many heart-broken parents grieved their loss?

Ahead, there was a narrow passageway to a small front balcony, which overlooked the front courtyard and gate. The three of them stood, gripping the curlicue iron railing. Doña Maria emerged onto the small balcony beside theirs, the one that led to the Reys' private rooms.

"Buenos días," the mistress of the house said, smiling. Emma looked at her differently now too. It must have taken some servant hours to do her elaborate coiffure this morning.

"Ask her who's coming," Tom whispered to Calla. Emma could barely hear him over the clanging of the bell.

"You ask her, Emma," Calla complained quietly. "I'm sick of talking to her, and she wants to practice her English."

"I don't care who the hell asks her," Tom hissed, "just do it."

Emma trod on his foot. He shouldn't be talking at all; he couldn't sound like a woman if he tried, and he didn't seem to have any interest in actually trying.

"*Excusez-moi*, Doña Maria," she started, trying not to show her newfound distaste for the woman.

"That's French," Tom hissed.

Emma pressed down harder on his foot. "You're expecting visitors?"

"Visitors?" Doña Maria pursed her lips and seemed to struggle for a moment. Then she grimaced and looked at Calla.

"*Los visitantes*," Calla supplied.

"Ah." Doña Maria nodded, smiling. "*Sí.* Our . . . visitors. Our visitors the . . . our . . . *Los vecinos* . . ." Doña Maria gave Calla an apologetic look.

"It's their neighbors," Calla said, sighing.

Tom swore under his breath. Since weight alone wasn't working, Emma stomped on his foot. She heard him grunt.

"How lovely," Emma said politely, ignoring him. "Do they visit often?"

They watched as a group rode through the gates. They were mounted on glossy, expensive horseflesh. At the head of the group was an older man with the aplomb of a pirate. He tossed his reins to a servant boy and swung from the saddle, his teeth flashing white in his swarthy face as he greeted his host. Don Rey had descended to greet him; in this man's presence, the aristocratic Don Rey seemed diminished somehow.

"Machado," Tom groaned softly.

Since stomping clearly wasn't working either, Emma

pinched him. Annoyed, he grabbed her hand and kept hold of it.

"Doña Maria says Don Machado is their closest neighbor," Calla translated. "He is the . . ." She paused, at a loss. She looked to Tom for help. "It kind of means leader? Lawkeeper? Peacemaker?"

"Despot," Tom suggested. He was speaking too quietly for Doña Maria to hear him, but he shouldn't have been speaking at all. Emma glared at him.

"He's come to collect the Georges," Calla translated.

"What?" Emma snapped around at that.

"She says Don Rey is handing them over to Don Machado. He will punish them."

Emma had a bad feeling. "Punish them how?"

"He'll hang them," Tom said quietly. "That's what he does."

Emma gripped the railing. Hang them? But they hadn't done anything. Not really. Oh, she was certainly going to hell for this.

"Don Machado will dine tonight with us," Doña Maria said in broken English. She looked to Calla to see if she'd said it correctly and beamed when Calla nodded.

Below, the Dons had turned to wave to Doña Maria. She waved gaily back. Don Machado's gaze lingered on the trio on the balcony next to her, taking in the black garb and veils. He said something quietly to Don Rey, and they laughed. The hair stood up on the back of Emma's neck. Oh yes, she had a *very* bad feeling about this.

❧ 18 ❧

DINNER SHOULD HAVE been lovely. They ate late, after a sultry darkness had fallen, at a long, festive table running down the central courtyard. The flaming torches sent shadows leaping in the archways and chased the bougainvillea blossoms with brassy light. A guitarist played and sang softly next to the fountain, the music blending with the splash of the water. There was Spanish wine, and the air was heady with the smell of roasting meats.

It should have been a wonderful night, Emma thought, feeling surly as she peered over the railing of the gallery and down at the table below. She had been looking forward to it. "Had" being the operative word. She could hardly enjoy it now, could she? Firstly, because all of those lovely smells were coming from a kitchen worked by stolen children, and secondly, because of the damn Georges. They were going to be hanged, and it was her fault. What was she going to do? She couldn't see them *hanged,* not when they hadn't done anything wrong.

Well, based on their reputation, they probably *had* done something wrong, somewhere, to someone. But that wasn't enough of a thing to hang them on. You couldn't kill a man because he *looked* dangerous and had *probably* committed a crime at some point. At least she couldn't. And her conscience was paining her about it.

It kept paining her as she trudged downstairs with the others to meet their hosts.

"Hey," Tom hissed, grabbing her firmly by the arm when she tried to hang back, "you ain't going anywhere. You stay right next to me, you hear?"

"You're supposed to be mute," she reminded him primly. But she had to admit she was glad to find they were seated together. Calla and Anna had been put way down at the other end, near the mistress of the house; so she could practice her English, Emma supposed. Calla didn't look too pleased about it. Emma was just glad she wasn't with her. Not that sitting with Tom and making sure he didn't give away his disguise was a picnic. The man was hopeless at acting like a woman. He strode about like he was still wearing his spurs.

"How the hell am I supposed to eat in this thing?" he muttered from under the veil as they took their seats along the table. They were squarely in the middle, away from their host at one end, and their hostess and Machado at the other.

"What do you mean how are you supposed to eat? Use your cutlery and chew with your mouth closed."

Tom made a disgusted noise.

Emma tried to smile at the servant who pulled her seat out for her. How old was he? Fourteen? Thirteen? Younger? It didn't bear thinking about. *"Gracias,"* she said three or four times. He nodded but didn't meet her eye or smile at her.

"Your accent is atrocious," Tom complained. He hadn't waited to be seated. He'd yanked his own chair out and sat in it like a cowhand sitting on a tree stump.

"Stop talking," she hissed at him. "And keep your knees together. You're a lady, remember?"

She managed to keep a polite expression through their hissed exchange. She was well practiced in looking polite when she felt anything but. The chairs around her filled up with Machado's companions and Don Rey's sons, and she put her back into staying polite. She'd taken a severe dislike to the Dons and their ilk now. None of the men seated around her spoke English, which she supposed made her night easier. Once it was clear to all involved that they couldn't converse, the men talked among themselves in Spanish, Tom played mute, and Emma was left to the food. And the food was *good*. Someone around here sure knew how to barbecue. Emma piled her plate high with roast pork and grilled steak and helped herself to corn on the cob and bread and stuffed peppers. She saw the men give her surprised looks. Undaunted, she put a whack of butter on her corn and reached for the greens.

"Food's about the only pleasure a nun's got," she told them brightly.

She heard Tom make a stifled noise under his veil.

"Well, it is," she told him. "And why ain't you eating?" Ignoring his obvious disapproval, she loaded his plate too. "You just slip the food under the damn veil," she scolded him quietly. "Women do it every day. There ain't no reason you cain't do it too."

He trod on her foot under the table. She yanked her foot away and gave him a sharp kick. She heard his pained intake of breath.

"Don't you go spoiling my dinner," she hissed. "I've had a rotten day. Hell, a rotten *year*. The least you can do is let me enjoy some of this food."

As she spoke, the servant girl who always came with

their breakfast—the one who had tried to talk to her that first day they arrived—reached over her shoulder to pour her some wine. Emma flinched. She felt an inch high. Who was she was to be talking about having a rotten year? What did she know about rotten years? Nothing, compared to this girl.

She took a big gulp of wine. Tom's foot found hers again and gave her a warning tap. She glared at him and purposefully drained the whole glass. Machado's men were watching her agog.

"It's good wine," she told them. There wasn't a commandment saying nuns couldn't drink wine, so they could damn well stare all they wanted. She had nothing to feel guilty about. The servant girl topped her up, and she raised her glass in salute.

"You've had enough," Tom whispered, leaning close.

"I've had one."

"Which is enough."

"I can't hear you. You're mute." She ignored him and concentrated on the food. Even plagued by ill thoughts, food was a comfort. Wine too. Especially wine this good.

It was a shame to waste such a gorgeous night, she thought wistfully as she gazed down the table. The weather was balmy, the candles flickered and danced, the food was wonderful, and the wine was divine. If only there were no slaves, no Georges, no posses and no damn heavy, hot nun's habit. She glanced at Tom, who was cutting his food into pieces but not eating much of it. If only this place was empty except for the two of them. If only he was out of that stupid black dress and into those tight pants of his. If only she was in one of her fancy dresses, with one of her even fancier corsets pushing her assets up all plump and on show. He wouldn't be stomping on her foot *then*. Oh no.

Her thoughts were all over the place. How on earth had she gone from worrying about the Georges being hanged to showing Tom Slater her assets?

The stress of it all was addling her wits. Or maybe it was the wine.

Try as she might, and she tried hard as she ate, she couldn't think of a solution to the problem of the Georges. The night wore on, the men grew loose with drink, the musician had to sing louder to be heard and the platters were cleared away.

"It's a shame you can't talk, señora," she sighed, resting her chin on her hand and giving Tom a rueful look.

He leaned close. "I want to go."

"I bet. But we can't go yet."

"Why not?" It was amazing he managed to get the words out from between such gritted teeth.

"Because," she said, as though speaking to a dunce, "we ain't had dessert yet."

He slumped back in his chair. She could feel the disbelief radiating off him.

"Don't judge me," she snapped. "You got no idea what it's like giving up all earthly pleasures but food. You think it's easy forgoing the sins of the flesh?" She cleared her throat. "Not that I've necessarily had them, mind you. But I can imagine what I'm missing." She'd had too much to drink. Clearly. "A little pastry does much to soothe the soul," she told him haughtily. For her sake, she hoped dessert came soon. She needed to stop talking.

"You have to admit," she said, when the plates were put before them, "it was worth the wait."

"Nothing is worth this," he muttered. He'd grown tenser by the minute. He was also spreading his legs again. She rapped him on the knee to remind him.

"*This* is." Emma lifted the edge of his veil and shoved a spoonful of custard cream in his mouth. She heard him sputter. No one around them noticed or cared. They were all yapping away in Spanish.

"This might be the best custard cream I've ever had," she said breezily, spooning some into her own mouth. "And these fritters are worth dying for."

"*Buñuelos*," Tom said in a murmur so soft she barely caught it.

"I can't hear you."

"I know," he grumbled. "I'm mute."

"No. I mean I didn't catch what you said."

"*Buñuelos*. They're called *buñuelos*. *Buñuelos de viento.*"

Emma was too busy eating them to reply, but she filed the name away. She'd find the recipe somehow. "Ain't you going to eat yours?" she asked, astonished that Tom hadn't so much as touched his.

He shook his head.

Cheerfully, she swapped her empty plate for his full one and set to work. She was halfway through her second helping when she heard the hue and cry go up. The bell over the courtyard gate was ringing furiously. Distantly, they could hear shouting from the front courtyard. A servant came dashing in, and the dinner erupted into chaos.

"What's happening?" she demanded, not able to understand a word anyone was saying.

"Hell," Tom swore, seizing her by the elbow and hauling her to her feet. "It's English George and Irish George."

"What about them?"

"They've escaped."

❧ 19 ❧

TOM HAD TO grit his teeth to keep from yelling. He wanted *out*. Out of this hacienda, out of this goddamn black dress and out of this mess with these mad nuns. Most of all, he wanted out of these mixed-up feelings he got every time he looked at Sister Emma. Even when she was lying straight to his face, she made his heart twist and his stomach fall and his skin itch. Who knew a woman could do this to a man? He'd never felt this way, not in his life, not once. Not even for Alex, he realized with a shock. And he loved Alex.

Didn't he?

Thinking about Alex made him feel like yelling even more. He didn't *like* feeling like this.

He hauled Sister Emma up the stairs, ignoring her questions. He'd told her all she needed to know. The Georges were out. And Tom was plenty worried. Those two *pistoleros* were mean as slaughterhouse rats and liable to come calling for revenge.

"You're *sure* that's what they said?" Sister Emma demanded, wriggling out of his grasp as they reached their room.

"Get packing," he said shortly. "We're done here."

"It's the middle of the night!"

"That never stopped you before." He started throwing things into bags.

"You're *sure* they said the Georges escaped?" She was like a dog with a bone. She just wasn't going to let up.

"I'm sure."

"Oh, thank God!"

"Thank God?" Tom had a sinking feeling. He straightened and lifted his veil, fixing her with a steely look. "Did you have anything to do with this?"

"No." But the wretched woman was smiling.

She'd lied to him too many times for him to trust her now. There was an etched tin cross on the wall. He snatched it from its hook and held it out. She looked at it, confused.

"Swear on it," he said.

"What?"

"Swear on that cross that you had nothing to do with their escape."

She narrowed her eyes. "Don't you trust me, Mr. Slater?"

"No."

She crossed her arms. "I don't think I've ever given you reason to mistrust me."

He looked at her in disbelief. "You told me Anna was a mute señora," he reminded her.

"Well." She rolled her eyes. "*That* isn't anything to hold against me."

"You've been lying to Don Rey about me."

"I only did that to protect you."

"If you're telling the truth, you'll have no trouble holding that cross and swearing on it, will you?"

"Why would I lie?"

"I have no idea," he growled. "Why in hell would you?"

"Fine," she snapped, "give me that." She snatched the cross off him. "I swear I had nothing to do with it," she intoned.

"At all."

She pressed her lips together. He *knew* it. She was lying. Or at least dodging the full truth.

"What have you done?"

"Nothing!"

"What have you *done*?"

"Nothing!" She looked down at the crucifix. "It's just . . . I might be glad they escaped."

"You what?"

"I'm a little bit glad," she admitted. "I didn't hold with them getting the rope when they hadn't done anything. That's all."

They were interrupted by Anna, who came tapping at the doors to the balcony. "Sorry, I didn't mean to interrupt . . ." Her gaze dropped to the crucifix. "I'll just collect Winnie and leave you to it, shall I?"

"Winnie?" Tom frowned at her. "She's not here."

"She must be—she's not in our room."

"She isn't?"

He and Emma exchanged a look. Winnie had been left tucked up tight in bed when they all went down to dinner.

"Are you sure she's not in there?" Emma headed for the adjoining room.

Tom made to follow, but Anna stopped him. "Your veil," she protested. "There are people everywhere."

Sighing, he pulled the black veil back over his face. By the time he got to Calla and Anna's room, Emma and Calla had yanked all the bedding off the beds and were looking through the wardrobe. He could hear Emma cursing. "She's not here," she said, emerging from the wardrobe.

"I told you that," Anna said. She was beginning to wring her hands. "You don't think anything has happened to her, do you? I should never have left her. What was I thinking? I got all turned upside down by the thought of a fancy dinner, and I assumed she could watch us from the balcony if she got worried, or if she felt lonely."

"Don't move," Tom told both of them. He wondered if he could track the girl. He wasn't used to tracking people indoors. "Where would you go, if you were a little girl?" he asked.

"I'd want to see the party," Emma said immediately. She walked to the railing overlooking the central courtyard. He collected a lamp and followed. Below, the servants were clearing away the tables and chairs.

"I'd want to see all the fancy people and the food and listen to the music," Calla added.

Sister Emma slid along the railing, moving slowly around the gallery. "I'd want to see it from every angle."

He followed her. While Emma stared down into the courtyard, Tom held the lamp up, checking the doorways around the gallery.

"There," he said, as he spied a flash of color. It was a blanket. The kind a small girl might wrap around her as she went wandering a gallery at nighttime.

"We need the girl, not the blanket," Sister Emma told him, continuing her prowl along the balcony. Tom picked up the blanket and tried not to feel irked.

"Down this end she would have been able to see you properly, Anna." Sister Emma stopped at the far end of the gallery. The four of them paused and stared down at the courtyard below.

"Maybe she fell asleep somewhere up here," Tom mused, scanning the doorways. But a horrifying fear was taking shape. There was a stairway by the exterior balcony, the same balcony they'd stood on as they'd watched Machado arrive. Tom moved out onto it; the garden was still, the torches guttering. The gate was standing ajar, left open by the Dons after they'd ridden out in pursuit.

The sight of the gate gave him a bad feeling. A very bad feeling.

"We need to find her," Sister Emma said, and judging by the barely suppressed panic in her voice, she was having the same bad feeling he was.

"I'm *trying* to find her," he snapped. But hell. They'd have to comb every inch of the place . . . and what if she wasn't there . . . what if . . .

"I don't see how *standing here* is finding her," Sister Emma railed at him.

"Enough," Anna ordered. She'd clearly had enough of both of them. It was time for action, not carping. Impatiently, Anna took control of the search. "You hush for good now," Anna hissed at Tom. "You're mute, remember?"

Mute be damned.

"You hush too," Anna snapped at Emma when she went to talk. "You can snip at each other once we've found Winnie. Until then, you can shut your yaps and get looking."

Shamefaced, the three of them followed Anna down the stairs and into the front courtyard.

"We'll split up," Anna said firmly. "Calla and I'll search the church and garden; you two take the courtyards."

"You sure you want to leave them together?" Calla asked.

"You want either of them?" Anna said sharply, stalking off. Calla clearly didn't as she went trotting after her.

"They took her, didn't they?" Sister Emma said bluntly, as soon as Anna was out of earshot.

"We don't know that yet." Tom did his duty and searched the courtyard.

"We're wasting time! If they took her, we need to go after them!"

"She might still be here," he snapped. "There's no point tearing off into the dark on a wild-goose chase if she's curled up in a corner somewhere asleep."

"You must be kidding! That kid is too timid to be out of Anna's sight for half a minute—you really think she came down here in the dark all by herself!"

"She ain't in the church," Anna said desperately, as she returned to find them still barking at each other.

"We haven't checked the stables or the rest of the house, or the servants' quarters for that matter," Tom said, trying to sound soothing. He gave Emma a warning look. There was no point in upsetting Anna more than she was already, not before they knew what was what.

"She's probably back in the house," Sister Emma agreed with him stiffly, and he was grateful for it, no matter how grudging it was. "Maybe she's in the kitchens, or curled up on one of those comfy chairs in the big room. Maybe she's even gone back to your room and found us gone."

Tom highly doubted it, but it was good to see Anna strengthen at the thought. Calla looked far less convinced. She and Emma exchanged a charged look.

"Why don't you all go and look in the house?" Tom suggested. "I'll check the stable and servants' quarters."

"I'm coming with you," Sister Emma said belligerently.

"Oh good," he said sourly.

Fortunately for both of them, she stopped carping at him as they searched the gardens on their way to the stable.

There were precious few people left about; they could hear voices drifting from the servants' quarters, but the stables were quiet. Quiet and in disarray from Rey and Machado's hastily put together lynch mob; lanterns still burned on the hooks, illuminating the gaping stall doors.

They heard a noise from the far stall.

"Winnie!"

Tom tried to grab hold of her, but the fool woman was dashing for the stall before he could stop her. He swore.

"Emma!" he yelled, his voice cracking in fear. "You got no idea who's in there!" He managed to reach her as she skidded to a halt in front of the stall. He pulled her behind him.

"It ain't Winnie," he told her furiously, "and you should know better. What if it had been the Georges?"

"It ain't," she said, shoving him out of the way.

It sure wasn't. It was three Indian kids, poised in the middle of harnessing a horse.

"Hey," Sister Emma said. "I know her! It's that servant girl! What's she doing?"

"Stealing horses by the look of it," Tom said, observing the three of them, frozen in the act of saddling a couple of Don Rey's horses. "He'll hang you if you take those," he said to the kids. Then repeated it in Spanish. "Horse theft is a hanging offense."

"You can have one of my animals," Emma said hastily while he was still translating himself. "There's no need to steal."

He sighed. Did she honestly think all three of them could ride out of here on a single animal? Hell. The three of them looked powerfully young as they stood there in the stall. The boys were big, and they were strong, but they were clearly still just boys.

"You can have one of my packhorses too," he said grudgingly. They were going to be in a world of trouble as it was, without adding horse theft to the list.

They looked at him in astonishment and more than a little fear. He swore as he realized why. He'd forgotten he was supposed to be a woman.

Sister Emma glared at him. And then she started up with her lies again. "Doña Elvira got her voice back—isn't it a miracle? It's a bit low and rough, as the pox clearly damaged her throat but the Lord works in mysterious ways, doesn't He?"

Tom spoke over her, in Spanish, which he knew she didn't understand. "Have you seen the girl we were traveling with? This high." He gestured with his hand. "Dark hair, big eyes, answers to the name Winnie. I know *you've* seen her before," he said to the girl. "Have you seen her tonight? She's missing."

The girl shook her head, but one of the boys behind her said something quietly. They had a quick, animated discussion with their backs to Tom and Sister Emma.

"What are they saying?" Sister Emma demanded.

"I don't know. I don't know the language. It's not Spanish."

She glared at him. "You know they're probably talking about how you're actually a man. You just couldn't keep your mouth shut, could you?"

"Señor?" The girl interrupted them. "We saw the girl. Tonight she was wearing a white nightdress. A fancy one. And she had her hair in braids. Yes?"

Tom nodded yes. Sister Emma was looking back and forth between them. Tom knew she wouldn't be able to hold her tongue for much longer.

"She went with her father," the girl told him.

"We go now," the bigger of two Indian boys said firmly in Spanish. "If you can't give us horse, we take these."

"Wait." Tom blocked their way. He ripped his veil off. Who the hell were they going to tell anyway? The minute they set foot off the property, they'd be fugitives. "No one's going anywhere until we know where the girl is."

The Indian boy took a step back. He looked Tom up and down.

"Don't think about it too much," Sister Emma advised him cheerfully. "Some men just like to dress in women's clothes."

Tom ignored her. "What do you mean she went with her father? She doesn't have a father."

"What are you saying?" Sister Emma demanded. "And why do you need your veil off to say it? Do they know where Winnie is?"

There was more conversation between the three, in a language Tom didn't know.

"That didn't look good. Why is she rolling her eyes?" Sister Emma was just about frothing at the mouth now. "What's she *saying*? You're being deliberately cruel. Stop punishing me."

"Would you hush for five minutes and let me get to the bottom of this? I'm not punishing you, goddamn it."

"Don't blaspheme."

He didn't dignify that with a response. "You're saying a man took Winnie?" he prodded the Indian kids.

"He said he was her father," the girl repeated, shooting her companions a dirty look.

"*Who* said he was her father?"

There was another exchange between the boys.

"The fat man," the girl clarified. "The one everyone is hunting."

Irish George. Tom's fists clenched. If that grabby-handed two-bit *pistolero* was here now, he'd smack him in his fat face.

"He's not her father," Tom said tightly, trying to keep a rein on his temper.

"What's going on?" Sister Emma slapped him on the arm. "Tell me. That look on your face is worrying me."

"The Georges have her."

"Goddamn it!"

"Hush," he snapped. "Do you want half the household to come running?"

"Yes! We need to go after them!"

"Honey," he said, barely managing to keep his voice even, "if you scream bloody murder and half the house comes running, what do you think they're going to do to *them?*" He jerked his head at the Indian kids. "It's pretty clear they're lighting out of here."

Emma blanched.

"He's not her father?" The girl looked appalled. She turned and railed at the two boys, particularly at the one who hadn't spoken yet.

"Does your friend speak Spanish?" Tom had to raise his voice to be heard over her scolding.

"No," the bigger boy said. "He's new to the ranch." The boy sized him up. "Were you serious about giving us horses?"

"On one condition. You help us track those bastards."

The boy laughed. "Not for all the horses in this stable. We're going home."

"Goddamn it all to hell!" Sister Emma stomped her boot. "If'n you don't start translating, I'm going to pitch a fit! And I'll be so loud the goddamn king of Mexico will come running."

"Mexico doesn't have a king."

"She's a nun?" The boy seemed dubious.

"Apparently. But then I'm apparently a woman."

"They headed south," the girl said. "If you give us horses, we'll help you."

The first boy wasn't pleased.

"If you don't start telling me what's going on, Slater, I'm going to shoot you." Sister Emma wasn't joking. The crazy woman was reaching for her gun.

"Calm down, woman, they're going to help us."

"We didn't say that," the boy objected, still in Spanish.

"Yes," the girl disagreed, in halting English this time, "we did. We'll help you, sister. We'll find the girl."

"Guess I won't need this, then." Sister Emma took her hand off her gun.

Don't be too sure. Tom regarded their motley group. How on earth they were going to get the girl away from the Georges without anyone getting hurt was beyond him. And then there'd be the matter of Don Rey and Don Machado . . .

"I'll go get Anna and Calla." The nun went off half-cocked as usual. "We'll need to take our wagon. I doubt we'll be coming back here. While I'm gone, you work out how we're going to get out of here without everyone seeing us."

Tom pinched the bridge of his nose. Why did everything always have to become a circus with this woman?

❧ 20 ❧

"**THEY'RE HEADED FOR** *Hueco del Diablo*." Black Horse was grim when he delivered the news. He was the older of the boys and had proven to be worth his weight in gold. He was Serrano, *Taaqtam* in his language, and this was Serrano land; Black Horse knew it well enough to be a fine guide. More importantly, he knew it well enough to keep them out of the Dons' way. The other two were as foreign as Tom was here; the girl, Two Moon, was Cahuilla from farther south, and Spear Fisher, the one who spoke no white languages, was Miwok and a long way from home.

They were three days out from *de Gato*, rattling along after the Georges' trail. There was no sign of pursuers yet, but Tom kept watch over his shoulder, knowing they would appear eventually. He wasn't lucky enough to have shaken them completely.

"*Hueco del Diablo*? How do you know?" Tension made him short. But hell. *Hueco del Diablo*. Of all the goddamn places.

"What else is this way?" Black Horse said matter-of-factly.

Nothing. That's what. Tom winced to think of Winnie being led into that hellhole. The poor kid. He only hoped they could reach her before she was put on the slave market.

"What is it?" Sister Emma called as she trotted up.

"Good luck telling her this one," Black Horse said under his breath, giving Tom a pitying look as he rode ahead.

Tom winced. He didn't relish telling Sister Emma that Winnie was headed for the most infamous black market in all the territories.

"You found something?" she asked hopefully. She pulled her mare up. Her face was pinched, and she had circles under her eyes the color of bruises. Guilt was gnawing away at her something fierce, and it made her hot-tempered and difficult.

"No." He tried to be patient, he really did. He wanted to be the kind of man who was patient. He'd always thought of himself as the solid sort. But the truth was, the thought of that little girl out here with those two animals unmanned him. He veered between white-hot rage and sucking black despair. It made him as hot-tempered and difficult as Sister Emma was. The upshot of which was that they were often at each other's throats.

"We haven't found anything," he told her. "But we think we know where they're going." He nudged his horse into a trot. He'd rather they were still moving while they had this conversation.

"Where?" she demanded, following. "Goddamn it, Slater, would you stop being so high-handed and *talk to me?*"

Fine. She wanted him to talk, he'd damn well talk. But she wasn't going to like it. "There's a place called *Hueco del Diablo*." He couldn't look at her as he told her. The expression on her face would be his undoing. He only hoped she'd get mad rather than cry. He could handle anger, but tears would be the end of him. He'd be liable to goddamn well cry too, the state he was in. They hadn't slept, they were living on hardtack, they were sunburned and high strung and played out: it wasn't a good place to be, considering the mess they were about to head into.

"The Devil's Hollow," he translated for her.

"That don't sound good."

"It's not." He bit the bullet. "It's a slave market, Sister."

He expected her to erupt; he expected shouting and cursing and threats of violence. But what he got was silence.

"It ain't anything legal," he continued. "It's informal and unlawful and dangerous as all get-out. It's run in a cut in the rock that ain't big enough to be a canyon but is plenty big enough to hide them from view. They mostly trade in Indian kids, selling them to the Dons for labor."

"You ain't serious." The tone in her voice was one he hadn't heard before.

He looked over. Hell. She looked like she might just faint right off the horse. He reached over and took her reins and put a steadying hand on her back. "Drink some water," he said. "Come on, honey. You look like that habit is cooking you alive."

Her hands were shaking as she uncorked her waterskin and took a mouthful.

"Please tell me you ain't serious." Her voice was as shaky as her hands.

"The trail is leading straight to it." He realized he was rubbing circles on her back. He stopped and gave her a matter-of-fact pat instead. "They don't just trade in kids," he said, pressing on but bracing himself for her reaction. How on earth did you tell a nun about this kind of thing? "They also trade in women."

"Women?"

"White women, Mexican women, Indian women: any woman unlucky enough to find herself hauled to *Hueco del Diablo*. There's a roaring trade in women in these parts."

"Fuck."

He'd heard her swear before, but not like this. She let loose with a string of the filthiest curses he'd ever heard. All of them aimed at the Georges.

At least while she was swearing, she didn't look like she was going to faint. And the shaking was subsiding. The more vigorously she cursed, the less she shook.

"I reckon they've earned that," he said dryly. His hand had started up rubbing circles on her back again.

"How far off?"

"Another two days." Now it was time to broach another difficult subject. "So we got the rest of today to work out where to put you and the others, while the boys and I go to Devil's Hollow."

Now the eruption came. "What in hell do you mean where to *put* me? I ain't being *put* anywhere. I'm coming with you."

"Didn't you listen to a word I just said? They trade in women, goddamn it, and last time I looked, you were a woman."

"I'm a *nun*."

"You think they'll care about that? Have you looked in the mirror lately? You're about the most gorgeous woman I've ever seen. You think they won't notice that? It takes all of four seconds to rip a black dress off a nun and make her a woman again!"

"You've clearly never tried to get one of these dresses off!" she snapped.

"Now ain't the time to be funny." He paused. "And thanks to you I *have* tried to get a damn dress off."

"We'll find somewhere to put Calla and Anna and Two Moon," she said stubbornly, ignoring his comment, "but I'm coming with you."

"No. You're not."

"Yes. I. Am."

"We're not discussing it."

"No," she agreed, kicking her animal into an out-and-out gallop, "we're not."

EMMA DIDN'T LIKE to admit it, but he was right. Not about much, but about the nun thing. A habit wouldn't stop anyone from raping her or hurting her or selling her at auction. No lowlife who sold people like they were horses (worse than horses, she thought sourly) gave a damn about God. This ugly black thing wouldn't protect her where they were going. It would only get in her way.

So the only thing to do was take it off.

Tom was going to have a conniption when he saw her. But he was going to have a conniption anyway. He and the boys had snuck off an hour after midnight, when they thought she was asleep. Two Moon was standing guard at the mouth of the cave, armed to the teeth. She let them go without protest but turned up the lantern the minute they'd ridden out of sight, filling the cave with light.

Their party had come to the scrubby ravine late in the day and had managed to back the wagon into one notch in the rock and set up camp in another. Tom had them move rocks and brush for a good two hours, screening the cave entrances. But Emma would be damned if she was being left behind in some dusty old cave. She wasn't about to sit here, safe, while Tom risked his life.

Calla and Anna didn't protest; in fact, Calla helped her get the nun gear off, and Anna packed her food and water.

"The little mite is going to need a woman," Anna said grimly, "and you've been through it yourself, so you'll know how to help her. If . . . she needs you to."

It. The great unsaid. They all feared that Winnie had been assaulted in some way. But there was still hope she hadn't been. With any luck, they could rescue her before anything happened.

"You shoot those bastards," Calla told her, passing her a hat.

Emma jammed it on her head. She was in her breeches and one of Tom's shirts, which they'd stolen from the saddlebags he'd left behind. The hat was Anna's. It was a broad-brimmed straw hat, her "gardening hat," she called it. Emma didn't have a simple hat of her own—her hats were all covered in feathers and bows and fancy silk flowers.

"Here." Two Moon held out her rifle.

"You'll need it," Emma said shortly. "You have to keep these two safe."

Two Moon held up her pistol. "I have others."

"I got one too," Anna held hers up.

"Me too." Calla held hers up.

"Tom gave them to us."

"Hell. Did he leave any guns for himself?"

"They have plenty. Black Horse took them from the ranch," Two Moon said with a quick grin. "A whole bag full. He was going to sell them."

Emma groaned. That was just about as bad as horse theft. Oh well. They might not even live to face the men coming after them from *de Gato*; there was no point in worrying about it now. And she figured Don Rey owed the three Indians more than a bunch of measly guns, for keeping them in "servitude" the way he had.

"Go get our girl," Anna said, wishing her luck.

"I will." She took the rifle. "And don't you forget to feed my starter."

It was a hot night, but that wasn't why she was sweating. She was sweating because she wasn't sure she could find Tom and the boys without getting lost. They only had a twenty-minute start on her, but a man could get a fair way in twenty minutes. She didn't think they'd be going faster than a walk, not in the pitch-darkness, but she was going mighty slow herself. And she wasn't entirely sure which way to go. East. That was about the long and the short of it.

Lucky it was a clear night and still. There wasn't a lick of wind. Noise carried on a night like this, and after a while, she heard a horse whicker. Then a soft word or two. Then the sound of hooves.

Please, let it be them. She didn't fancy spending the night following along after ghostly noises, only to find as dawn broke that she'd been following the wrong men.

She kept the rifle across her lap, ready to fire. The dark hours were long and grim. Her mind ran a well-worn track, imagining Winnie being snatched. If only Emma had gone up to check on her. If only one of them had stayed back from the dinner to keep watch over her. If only she'd seen the girl watching them from the gallery. If only Winnie had called out to her. *If only.*

Life was full of "if onlys," Emma thought tiredly. A woman carried a passel of them with her, every hour of every day. If only Pa had been able to handle his liquor; if only Ma hadn't died; if only Rory Baker had paid that goddamn hotel bill and not left her to the mercies of the inn keeper; if only Luke Slater had loved her like she'd thought she loved him; if only she'd never been a whore, had never been trussed up like a nun, had met Tom Slater simple like, woman to man . . .

"If onlys" were a heavy thing to carry with you. What's done was done. She couldn't take back the past. She couldn't go back to the ranch and sweep Winnie up in her arms and carry her back to bed, scolding her for running about in her nightgown; she couldn't tuck the little one up tight in bed and kiss her good night; she couldn't do anything except cock her weapon and try to right the wrong.

She was crying. It came on sudden, like a plains storm. One minute she wasn't, and then she was. And it was a big cry, the sort you only suffered once a year or so, when you couldn't get out of the way of the mudslide. She cried for Winnie out there alone, suffering God only knew what; she cried for herself and all those years of being poked; she cried for the whole sorry, sweaty indignity and pain of it all. The helplessness. The hopelessness. The never-ending *smallness* of it all.

Did men know what it did to a person to be treated like that?

They did. She knew they did. They didn't know it the way a woman knew it, they didn't picture it happening to them, but they knew it just the same. They knew what they were doing was a violence. They knew they were stomping on something, stomping and stomping until a body was barely a body anymore. But that was the thing. They *liked* stomping.

Not all of them. But enough of them to make it count.

Emma cried for the big, ugly truth of it. The pettiness of it and the pointlessness of it. She cried until she was swollen up and her head throbbed fit to burst. She cried until she couldn't cry no more.

And then she wiped herself down and faced the pale wash of a new day. Three riders emerged in silhouette against the pink-gray horizon. One of them was Tom Slater. She'd know those shoulders anywhere. She took a big drink of water and a deep breath of air. She'd had her cry. Now it was time to get down to business.

❧ 21 ❧

He pitched a fit, just as she expected, but it was nothing she couldn't handle.

"You're impossible!" he said finally, when he realized nothing he said was changing her mind.

"I am," she agreed. "And you'd best get it through your thick head, so we don't have to go through this nonsense again."

He lapsed into a sullen silence for a good long while. He looked tired. Could a man lose weight in just a few days? Because he looked thin too. When this whole sorry affair was done, she'd be sure to whip up a batch of biscuits for him. She had some jars of jelly in her luggage somewhere. She could bake him some jelly tarts. Maybe a cake too. Something with a fair whack of sugar in it to cheer him up. It would cheer Winnie up as well. Emma would be more than happy to cook cakes day and night if it would offer them even the smallest measure of comfort.

"How are we going about this, then?" she asked once she'd decided he'd been sullen long enough.

The look he gave her showed he wasn't done yet. She ignored it.

"Are we storming in, guns blazing? Or are we going to be sneaky about it, and act like we're here to buy some slaves, and then shoot them when they're not looking?"

He gave her an appalled look. "Neither."

"You could pretend that you're here to sell me."

"No."

"Or them." She nodded at the boys.

"No."

"Well, we cain't pretend to sell *you*," she said, exasperated. "No one wants an ornery ole white man."

"We ain't pretending to sell, or buy, *anyone*."

"I don't see why not."

"And that's exactly why I wanted you to stay back at the cave," he muttered.

"Are we going to steal in by the dead of night and slit their throats?"

He was pinching the bridge of his nose again. He only did that when his temper was sore.

"Well, what in hell *are* we going to do?"

"We're going to take stock."

"We're what?"

"We're going to find out the lay of the land before we go charging in with any harebrained plans."

"None of my plans are harebrained," she said, offended.

"Pretend to sell you," he muttered under his breath.

"That's a fine plan," she protested. "It would work perfectly."

"Until someone bought you."

"You wouldn't *actually* sell me."

"No? So when they offered me money, I'd just say 'Whoops, sorry, changed my mind'?"

She rolled her eyes. "Well, it sounds stupid when you say it like that, but of course that's not how you'd do it. You wouldn't get anywhere near that far. You'd see Winnie, and then the boys would snatch her and we'd all run away."

"That's a *much* better plan." He sounded disgusted.

"Better than *taking stock*."

"That's not the plan. That's the bit before we make the plan—the bit you seem to always leave out."

"Because it wastes time."

"A stitch in time," he said, sounding as pious as Calla when she was acting all nunnish. Although at least he was looking feistier now, which was good to see. Arguing pepped him up no end. Which was fine with her; she was happy to argue if that's what he wanted. It was kind of fun, in its way. Like playing catch.

"What do you know about stitching?" she carped, feeling zestier by the minute. "I bet you ain't stitched a thing in your life. I bet a man like you has no end of women offering to stitch things for him. If anyone knows about stitching time, it's me, and I'm telling you, *taking stock* ain't stitching anything but trouble."

They managed to keep tossing the ball back and forth for the rest of the day. By the time they camped, they were both in better spirits, although Black Horse and Spear Fisher were looking the worse for wear.

"You two are like a couple of bucks running head-to-head," Black Horse grumbled in his heavily accented English. It turned out he knew more English than he'd let on; the more he relaxed around them, the more he spoke. Complained anyway. He certainly seemed to like complaining about her to Tom. But he quit complaining quick enough when she served him his dinner. "This is good," he said. "How'd you manage this with salt beef?"

"I can manage anything," Emma said, not without smugness. "Cooking is what I do best." Outside of the bedroom anyway.

Tom ate his usual big helpings. She made sure to give him extra big ladlefuls, to combat his weight loss.

"Spear Fisher says his sisters were sold at *Hueco del Diablo*. He would like the chance to avenge them." Black Horse ran a finger around the rim of his bowl, to capture the last traces of dinner. "But his people are farmers more than warriors, so it's good you are with us." His gaze was sly as it darted over to Tom. "No one can stand against you, can they, White Wolf?"

Tom groaned.

"He's not White Wolf," Emma said quickly, before Tom could get his temper up. "Trust me, I've met him, and Tom ain't him."

"You called him Slater," Black Horse said with a shrug. "Tom Slater. Rides with Death. White Wolf. I'll call him whatever he wants to be called."

"Now, Black Horse, you listen to me—" Emma stopped dead as an idea hit her. "Oh . . ."

"No," Tom said, reading her mind. "No. No. *No.*"

"*Yes.* It's perfect! They wouldn't dare cross the Plague of the West!"

"They'd dare to shoot him, though!"

"Not with us at your side. We've got enough weapons to stock an army! They'll be so scared they'll drop arms and run."

He was nose pinching again. "You don't know these men."

"Everyone's scared of Deathrider," Black Horse said. "They'd be wary." He turned to his friend, and they spoke for a while. "Spear Fisher thinks it's a good idea too."

"It's *not*. It's *not* a good idea at all. It's the stupidest idea I ever heard."

"Stupider than dressing you as a woman?"

"Much stupider. By far."

"Let's do a deal," she said as she scraped the last dregs of dinner from the cook pot into his bowl. "I'll go along while you *take stock,* and after you take stock, we'll all put forward our plans. Then we'll vote on the best one."

"No."

She ignored him and turned to the boys. "What do you two think? Are you happy with that?"

They had a brief conversation. "Yes," Black Horse said.

"No," Tom repeated. *"No."*

"Sorry," she said cheerfully, "but you've been outvoted."

"Who said this was a democracy?"

"We the people. All three of us." She grinned at him. "And it's your turn to do the dishes."

THE WOMAN WAS going to be the stone-cold death of him. Tom felt like the full force of a stampede had hit him: it didn't matter how much he protested, she just went along like he hadn't said anything at all. Words bounced off her like rain off a cow's hide. They'd scouted Devil's Hollow this morning and had seen the Georges immediately. Creeping along the lip of the ravine, Tom had neatly downed the two guards who were standing lookout, whacking them upside the back of the head before they even heard him coming. Sister Emma had shown herself to be strangely proficient at tying them up and gagging them. He filed the knowledge away, along with a whole bunch of other bits and pieces that had him seriously doubting her nunhood.

They'd lain on their bellies on the canyon wall above *Hueco del Diablo*, passing Tom's telescope back and forth

between them. The camp in the canyon below was small
and shabby. There was a clump of women and a bunch of
Indian children. The women were separated out by race—
there were a handful of white women, a couple of black
women and half a dozen Indian women—all dusty and
thin and miserable looking. All of the children were Indian, except for Winnie. She was roped up to the white
women, right at the back of the group; she looked small and
heart-stoppingly vulnerable. Her nightgown was red with
dust, and her hair was a bird's nest of tangles. Tom felt his
rage reach the boiling point. The bastards who'd kidnapped
her were slouched against the rock wall, shooting the
breeze with the traders. English George spat a long stream
of tobacco juice onto the hard-packed dirt at his feet.

Tom's instinct was to pick them off from here. But what
if he missed? What if he got one down and the others used
the captives as shields? It was a narrow channel through the
rock. The bullets would ricochet. What if Winnie got hit?
Not just Winnie. Hell, some of the little ones down there
were barely hip high.

"Right. Everyone put your plans on the table," Sister
Emma demanded, once they'd wriggled away from the canyon edge and crept back to their horses.

"What table?" Black Horse asked.

"It's just an expression. It means tell us what you think."

"I think we should rescue the girl."

Spear Fisher said something to Black Horse, who translated. "He also thinks we should rescue the girl. But he insists that we should rescue the others too."

"That goes without saying."

Tom tried to say calm. She had a habit of just taking
over, like she was running things.

"The question is, Mr. Horse and Mr. Fisher, *how* are we to rescue them?"

The boys didn't have the slightest clue. And to be honest, Tom wasn't doing much better. Well, he did have one idea. But he was a measured man, and he wasn't about to rush into it without thinking it through. The problem was, while he was busy thinking, she went and hijacked the whole show. Before he knew it, she had the boys convinced he should pass himself off as a certain Indian, and the three of them were voting for him to ride on down there pretending to be Deathrider.

"He can't wear what he's wearing now," she kept arguing with Black Horse, as they hashed out the details without Tom's agreement. "He doesn't look the least bit like Deathrider in that. Don't you have any buckskins?"

"My people don't wear buckskins," Black Horse told her.

"They *must*."

"Why must they? Because you read it in a book? Not all Indians are the same. In my tribe, the men don't wear anything at all at this time of year."

"They don't?"

Tom couldn't believe it when she turned a calculating gaze on him. "Not on your life!" he snapped. "I am *not* going into *Hueco del Diablo* naked!"

"No, I suppose it's not very practical." She sounded regretful.

"Deathrider isn't *Taaqtam*. Why would he dress like us?" Black Horse squinted at Tom. "Just let him keep his white man clothes. Tom Slater dresses like that anyway."

"I *am* Tom Slater," Tom growled.

"I don't know why you keep denying it," Black Horse told Emma, "when he says straight out he's White Wolf."

"I didn't say that at all," Tom snapped. "I said I was Tom Slater. It's entirely different."

"But how will *they* know he's White Wolf?" Sister Emma had clearly given up any attempt to convince the boys he wasn't actually Deathrider. Which galled Tom no end.

"We will call him by his name," Black Horse said with a shrug.

"Listen, you *loco* idiots," he growled, "Irish George and English George are out *hunting* Deathrider right now. That's why they're *here*. And you want me to walk right up to them and say, 'Hi, boys, here I am'? Are you *insane*?"

"Oh." Emma deflated in front of his eyes. "I forgot about that."

"And *that* is why you take the time to *take stock.*"

She pulled a face. "What do *you* propose, then?"

He rubbed his face. Hell. He *hated* his plan. But only for selfish reasons. And they weren't reasons he could stand by. Not when Winnie was down there.

"Well?"

She sure hated not knowing things. He fixed her with a baleful look. "If you'd hold your horses and *listen,* I'll tell you."

"I'm listening, but you ain't *talking*."

"You don't give him much chance," Black Horse said mildly.

Ostentatiously, she pressed her lips together and didn't say another word. She held a hand up behind her ear, to illustrate how hard she was listening. Tom had a hard time not cracking a smile at that. She had enough spirit for *ten* women. If only she'd use her spirit to help him, instead of getting in his way.

"I reckon the simplest thing to do is to go down there and buy them."

Her mouth popped right open at that. "What?"

He shrugged. "They're hardly going to argue with a sale."

"But . . ."

"But what?"

"But . . ." She frowned at him so hard her eyebrows just about met in the middle of her forehead. "But that would cost a fortune! Wouldn't it?" She looked at the boys. "What would a slave cost?"

"Depends on the slave," Black Horse said with a shrug. "Fifty to one hundred dollars?"

"You haven't thought this through," she told him.

Tom shook his head. He had. He'd thought it through backward and forward and inside out. He was carrying a goddamn fortune on him; he'd just collected payment in San Francisco when he heard about the hunt and had gone tearing off to warn Deathrider. He didn't have enough money to pay one hundred dollars for every single captive, but if some of them went for less, he should have enough. And he planned to do some fierce haggling. He wasn't of a mind to give away more of his hard-earned cash than he absolutely had to.

"You're going to *buy* them?" she echoed, as though she couldn't quite believe it. Her tawny eyes were wide with astonishment.

"I don't see the point in fighting if we don't have to."

"But that's upward of two thousand dollars!"

It was. And he wasn't happy about it. But what in hell was he going to spend it on anyway? He had more money than he knew what to do with. He didn't have his own place

or his own family or his own much of anything. He didn't
even run his own cows. He bought them in Mexico and ran
them up to California and sold them on.

"You'd really spend that much to rescue those folks?"
Her eyes had gone all shiny. They twinkled with green light
and made his stomach flip.

"Does it get your vote?"

Silently, she nodded. For once, she didn't seem to have
anything to say.

❧ 22 ❧

"SHE'S A VIRGIN."

That was about when Emma almost lost her composure. Tom sensed it and moved to stand in front of her, to block her from the ferrety little trader. It gave her a moment to regroup.

There were three separate traders, responsible for three different lots of "stock." The whole setup turned Emma's stomach. Her trigger finger had started itching the minute they rode into the canyon. The Georges were still slouching in the shade but barely looked their way. They'd never seen Tom before; they'd only met him as Doña Elvira, so his appearance in *Hueco del Diablo* didn't startle them in the slightest. He was just another customer. Emma had Tom's serape wrapped around her and her hat pulled low over her face, hoping they wouldn't know her as the nun they'd seen back at *de Gato*.

Black Horse and Spear Fisher were perched on the canyon wall above, their rifles trained on the Georges. Emma doubted they were good shots, judging by the clumsy way they handled their weapons. She just hoped she wouldn't have to find out.

Tom and Emma had ridden in on a single horse. Even with the situation as grave as it was, Emma couldn't help but enjoy pressing up close against him. She wrapped her arms around his body, noting the hardness under her hands. His shirt was sweaty, but she didn't mind at all. Not one bit. He smelled like saddle leather and hot cotton.

"You leave the talking to me," he warned.

"Cross my heart and hope to die."

"Let's hope not."

She'd kept her promise so far, even though she'd had to watch the traders show off their "wares." She'd even stayed silent when the ferrety trader had pulled Winnie from the pack. Emma had been worried that the girl would give them away, but Winnie didn't even look up from her feet. Not once. Not when the trader turned her roughly this way and that, not when he rammed his fingers in her mouth to pull back her lips to show off her teeth, not even when he traced his fingers down her flat chest. The little girl stayed blank faced and staring at the ground. It killed Emma to see it.

"She's a virgin," the trader assured Tom.

That was when she lost her composure, and when Tom stepped in front of her to give her a minute to regain it.

"She's an obedient thing. A little thin, but as I said, still a virgin."

Emma rested her palms on Tom's back and bit her lips to keep silent. She wanted to shoot that man. It took every ounce of self-control she had not to reach for her gun.

"Virgins are rare in these parts," the trader said in his dusty voice. "So she comes at a price."

"What price?" Tom sounded calm as a still pond. Emma

didn't know how he did it. She knew he wasn't calm at all; she could feel the muscles in his back bunching tight under her hands.

"One hundred and fifty dollars, and she's a bargain at that."

"Bargain my boot. She ain't worth no hundred and fifty dollars."

"You're wrong about that, but I'll tell you what, mister, I'm open to a trade."

Emma froze. She had an instinct she wasn't going to like what the trader said next.

"You got a busty woman there behind you. Busty women fetch high prices round here; not virgin high, mind you, but close."

Emma felt the hostility coming off Tom in waves. She hoped the trader couldn't feel it too.

"I'll trade you your busty one for the girl here. I'll only charge you a difference of twenty dollars."

"This woman ain't for sale," Tom said tightly.

Damn straight, Emma thought. She was *done* with being bought and sold. She'd been done with it when *she* was the one doing the selling; she wasn't about to have this filthy little nobody claim the right. Or even the possibility.

"All women are for sale," the trader insisted.

Emma dug her fingers into Tom's back.

"Not this woman." His tone brooked no disagreement. "I'll keep the woman and give you one hundred dollars for the girl."

The trader gave a gritty laugh. "No deal. She's worth one hundred and thirty minimum."

Emma was painfully aware that their bartering had drawn the Georges' interest. Well, Irish George's interest. The man was too social by half. Emma could see he was just itching to join the conversation. If there was one thing that fat idiot liked it was the sound of his own voice.

"What if I buy the rest of them too?" Tom asked the ferret. "How much for the job lot?"

That sure shocked the hell out of the ferret. "You couldn't afford it." The trader cocked his head and then named an outrageous figure.

Irish George was creeping closer by the minute, drawn by the drama. He was gumming a plump cigar and looking far too perky for Emma's liking.

"Hey." One of the other traders had caught wind of what was going on. "If you want to be buying women, I got two fine black girls right here."

The third trader got involved at that. "Your pair don't hold a candle to my girls."

Emma watched as Tom deftly turned the traders against one another. Well, he *was* a cow trader, she supposed. And my, but he certainly did have some bargaining skills. Somehow, he had the three idiots undercutting one another, and before any of them knew what was happening, he'd bought every slave in the place at a cut rate.

He'd make a damn fine madam, Emma thought admiringly.

"That's some good deal you got there, my friend," Irish George called over as Tom rounded up the captives. Tom gave him a well-calculated absent-minded wave.

Please don't come over. Emma prayed their luck would hold and they could get out of here without the Georges getting suspicious. Luckily, Irish George had gone and pounced on the traders, jawing their ears off about how *he too* had once bought a bunch of slaves at cut price and then sold them on at enormous profit, all of which he'd spent on booze and whores in New Orleans. The traders didn't look happy to be listening to his nonsense.

"Don't so much as look twice at Winnie," Tom hissed at her as he pulled her into the saddle behind him. "English George is watching us. You don't want him thinking we've come specifically for her. He's sharp. Too sharp." Tom had tethered the captives' ropes to his saddle so they could lead them. They were all on foot. "We'll see to her once we're safely away."

Winnie. The poor baby. Emma kept her gaze fixed on the cotton between Tom's shoulder blades so she wouldn't look back at the girl.

"What do you need all these slaves for anyway?" one of the traders asked as they snaked by.

"Whores," Emma blurted. It was the first thing to pop into her head. She felt Tom flinch. But the trader just grinned. It made perfect sense to him.

"Anytime you need to restock, you come on by, you hear?" His gaze slid over Emma. "And if you ever want to make that trade, you come to me first. I sure do like the busty ones."

"I can't believe you kept your mouth shut," Tom said when they were well clear of the canyon. "I thought for sure you'd let him have it when he talked about your . . . body."

"I gave you my word."

He snorted. "You lie too much for me to trust your word."

"No," she disagreed, "I lie exactly the right amount. If I lied any less, you wouldn't be able to trust me at all."

"That doesn't make any sense."

"Only because you're thinking about it wrong."

Thank God for Tom Slater, she thought, pressing her

cheek to his hot back. Thank God for his steadiness, thank God for his planning, thank God for his ingenuity, thank God for his *money* and thank God for his ability to argue with her in the most trying of situations. She didn't know what she'd do without him.

Impulsively, she pressed a smacking great kiss on his cheek.

"What in hell was that for?"

He acted like he didn't like it, but she could feel his heart skip under her palm.

"It was just a thank-you kiss. Now hurry up and get us somewhere safe so I can see to Winnie."

❖ 23 ❖

EMMA HAD GIVEN it a lot of thought, and she couldn't in all good conscience let Tom pay for the folks they'd bought in Devil's Hollow. She felt guilty when she remembered how gracefully he'd suggested the plan and how he'd counted out his money into the traders' sweaty hands. *She* hadn't thought to buy Winnie's freedom, and she was carrying a fortune on her very person. He was a better person that she was. *His* plan had been carefully considered and peaceful. He'd been calm and he'd been controlled and he'd put everyone's welfare first.

He was just so *good,* she thought as she watched him trying to talk to the Serrano chief. The only language they had in common was Spanish, and the chief only had a patchy grasp of that, judging by all the miming Tom was doing. Black Horse had disappeared with Two Moon, and Spear Fisher had fallen asleep in the shade, leaving Tom to manage the discussion on his own. The few Serrano she could see were wary and whispering behind their hands as they sized up their strange guests. Black Horse hadn't been wrong; they weren't what you'd call overdressed. There was a lot of bare skin. Emma envied them, as the late-afternoon sun was fierce.

She fanned herself with Anna's gardening hat as she waited to talk to Tom. She had to keep to the shade of the junipers, or her fuzzy scalp would burn. She paced and fanned herself and waited. There wasn't much else to be done. Calla was fine on her own, soothing the untethered captives. Emma had done her share on the ride here. There was a lot of relieved weeping, some laughter, a touch of hysteria; they were a mixed bunch, with not much in common except they'd been taken captive. Emma had no idea what they were going to do with them all. They could hardly leave them out here in the wilderness, with no horses, no food, no water. The Serrano village itself, with its woven grass dwellings, was small, and she wasn't about to dump their problems on the tribe. They'd already imposed on them. There were only a handful of people in the village, and they didn't look pleased to see the white people. Black Horse said his people had suffered on the missions, and many had died of the pox plague when he was a boy, leaving the clans sparsely populated. Emma supposed that those who had survived the pox had then been forced to face the Californian indenture laws. She couldn't see too many young people around. She wondered how many of them were slaving away at *Gran Rancho de Gato*. That place certainly didn't seem so heavenly anymore.

The elder Serrano women had given Anna use of one of the huts, and she'd retreated into the willow-framed dwelling with Winnie. It was best to leave the two of them alone. Winnie trusted Anna, and Anna doted on the girl like she was her own. Emma was confident the child was in the best hands. Lord knew Emma hadn't been able to get a response out of her. The kid was like a turtle all gone back into its shell.

But now Emma was alone, with nothing to do. As a guest, she couldn't very well barrel in and start cooking. The Serrano had welcomed them with acorn soup, venison and flatbreads; it would be rude to cook straight after their hospitable meal. But cooking was the one thing that calmed Emma down. What she wouldn't give to get her hands into some dough and knead her feelings away. Instead, she was loitering here, waiting to catch Tom so she could pay him. As she waited, she practiced speeches. *Thank you for your gesture. It was noble. It was generous. Because of you, these women and children are free; they have a chance at a life; they won't have to face a future of toil and abuse.* She got herself a bit teary devising ornate ways to thank him. But when the time came to actually say the words, she botched it.

"Here," she blurted, thrusting the money at him.

She caught him as he left the chief, stepping in front of him and coughing the word up like a house cat coughing up a fur ball. Hell. What had happened to her grand speechifying? Why did he make her so nervous? Goddamn it, she'd known hundreds of men. She'd trekked thousands of miles across untamed land. She'd run businesses. She'd managed whores so contrary they could turn a blue sky red. Not to mention that she'd spent *weeks* with this man already; he was familiar to her. So why was she suddenly as awkward and tongue-tied as a green girl?

She didn't like it. In fact, she *hated* it. The only thing she hated worse than being tongue-tied was being *vulnerable*. And right now, she felt as vulnerable as a goose the day before Christmas. Damn it. And damn *him* for making her feel this way.

"What in hell is that?" He looked just about as cranky as she felt as he looked at her open hand and the dull shine of the nugget it held.

"What does it look like? It's gold."

"Real gold?"

"Of course real gold. Why would I offer you fake gold?"

"Why would you offer me *any* damn gold?" he growled, brushing past her.

"I'm paying you back!" She stalked after him.

"For what?" He looked genuinely confused.

She glanced over her shoulder at the captives and dropped her voice. "For *them.*"

"Look, Sister, I'm tired. I haven't slept more than an hour at a time for the last few days. I just want to go sleep. Can we talk about this tomorrow?"

Why in hell did her heart pinch when he called her "Sister"? What was *wrong* with her?

"We don't need to *talk* about it," she snapped. "Just take the gold and it's done. We're even."

"Even for *what*?" He'd reached his saddlebags and began unpacking his bedroll, moving to the shade beneath the junipers to escape the blazing afternoon sun.

"I can't let you pay for Winnie. Or the others." *Why* did it come out sounding so ungrateful when she felt anything but?

"I already did." He sat down on his bedroll with a tired groan. "I really want to take my boots off," he sighed, "but I don't dare. I know the minute I do, one of your posses will come through, looking to shoot me."

"*My* posses?" She felt like a bump on a log, standing here, holding out her gold. "What about *your* posse?"

"I don't have a posse," he said. "*Deathrider* has a posse." He considered his dusty boots. "Ah hell, who cares if they shoot me while I'm bootless? At least if I'm dead, I'll get some rest." He wrestled with his boots and then yanked his socks off too. He let out a groan of sheer pleasure as he wriggled his toes.

"I *want* to pay," she said. She chafed against a feeling of . . . she didn't even know what. "Please, let me pay."

"I can't take money from a nun." He squinted up at her.

Hell. She *wasn't* a nun. "I have more," she said defensively. "You won't be disadvantaging me. And . . . I feel ashamed." That was a touch too honest. To her horror, she found herself on the edge of tears.

He sighed. "This sounds like a big conversation, Sister. And I don't want to brush you off, but I'm cooked. I ain't got so much as a whimper left in me. Can I promise you we'll discuss all this when I wake up?"

The rejection made the tears multiply. It was appalling.

"Honey, I think you're as tired as I am." His green river-ice eyes were full of kindness.

Honey. For heaven's sake, since when did a single word have the power to undo her? The tears went tumbling down her cheeks. She dashed them away.

"You know what you should do?" he said. "You should sit down and take your boots off too. Have a rest." He pointed to the wagon. "Go get yourself a blanket, lie down and get some shut-eye. Everything looks better after a sleep. That's what my father used to say."

She did as he suggested, but only to give herself time to regain her equilibrium. She scrubbed the tears away angrily. Crying made you look weak, and she *wasn't* weak. But she was tired. He was right about that. She was heavy limbed and scratchy eyed and fuzzy-headed with it. But not so fuzzy-headed that she didn't make a plan. She'd store the gold nugget in Tom's saddlebags when he was asleep.

That's what she'd do. Then she'd tell him later. In the morning, if he was to be believed.

Tom was yawning when she got back. He looked plenty tired. Shattered, in fact. "I swear we'll talk tomorrow. But I ain't getting up till then." He stretched out full length on his bedroll and put his hat squarely over his face.

Emma stood there, feeling a weight of exhaustion land on her. She'd been a ball of nervous energy for weeks now. When he'd looked at her all kind and called her honey, he'd undone her. She had nothing left, she realized. Not one thing. She didn't feel capable of so much as unrolling a blanket. Oh God, there went the tears again. She didn't even have the energy to swipe them away anymore.

"Come on." Tom's voice was muffled by his hat. His hand patted the ground next to him heavily. "Stop thinking and get some rest."

The damn tears just kept leaking out of her as she unrolled the blanket on the ground next to him. She hadn't planned to sleep close to him, but he'd patted the ground like it was an invitation, and God help her, she craved his comfort right now. Just being next to him was soothing. He was so *solid*.

"Take your boots off." His muffled voice was thick with sleep. She had a feeling he wouldn't be talking for much longer.

She collapsed onto the blanket and picked at her bootlaces. They were crusted with dirt and solidly knotted. The tears that spattered on the leather made patterns in the filth.

Blindly, he reached out and gave her arm a pat. He must have heard her sniffle.

"Come on, honey."

Ah. Ouch. Why did his tenderness hurt? It was like he'd poked a deep black bruise. She ripped a nail getting the laces undone, but she got there. She couldn't believe the tears wouldn't just *stop*. Generally, she didn't cry. She just didn't. But the last two days, she'd been through storms and leaks and just general weepiness. It made a body tired.

She pulled the boots off, and he was right—it was a release. Once she was barefoot, she felt immeasurably better. Even though it was still hot, the air felt fresh against her sweaty feet. She sighed. His hand kept patting her heavily, slowing with each pat. She took a deep shuddery breath. He was right. Everything would feel better in the morning. And if it didn't, at least she'd have the energy to face that too.

EMMA DIDN'T REMEMBER the last time she'd slept so well. Her slumber had been deep and dreamless, and she woke slowly, feeling like she was swimming through water. It was only as she went to stretch that she registered the weight against her. For a minute, she couldn't remember where she was and her heart jolted. She thought she was back in the whorehouse, and she went hot and cold with horror. But then the weight squeezed her a little closer, and a familiar voice mumbled senseless sounds of reassurance.

Tom.

She went slack with relief. It was just Tom Slater.

Day hadn't yet broken, and everything was hushed and dim; the sky was growing pearly, but it was dark enough that the stars were still bright as diamond chips. There was only just enough light to see by; everything was shades of gray. She was on her back, and Tom Slater was pressed close against her, his arm thrown over her chest and his leg over her hips. His head was close by her ear. She could feel his breath on her skin.

They were *snuggling*.

She couldn't move. If she moved, *he* might move, and she didn't want that. She liked the weight of him. Damn that. Not just the weight of him; she liked *all* of it. She lay there, still as she could manage, her heart kicking up something fierce. He felt *good.* And was that . . . oh yes, it was. Against her hip, she could feel that he was enjoying this too. Very much. But then, men were prone to waking up happy, weren't they? It might not have anything at all to do with her.

She managed to turn her head slightly, so she could look at him. He felt her movement and gave a deep sigh. Lord, *look* at him. The man was just too astonishingly gorgeous to be true. In sleep, with the anger leached out of him, he was damn near *pretty,* he was so fine. His lashes were thick and black and curling, and he had the most beautifully arched black brows. She had *such* an urge to trace them with her fingertip. His beard had grown in while they were on the trail, and it accentuated his high cheekbones and angular jaw. And that mouth. His upper lip had a narrow but perfectly formed Cupid's bow, while his lower lip was plump and pouty. Even poutier in sleep than usual. As she watched him, he frowned. He looked like an abandoned little boy, on the verge of utter heartbreak. Her heart hurt for him. What was happening to him in his dreams?

She couldn't stand to see him look so sad. She put her hand over his, where it rested on her ribs. The touch seemed to soothe him. His face relaxed, and his hand turned over beneath her palm, his fingers twining with hers. He sighed again and burrowed closer, until his face was pressed against her neck. She felt a stupid stab of jealousy. Was he thinking about a woman? One who made him sad? Was he burrowing into her because he thought *she* was that woman? Was he making up with some other woman in his sleep? Was the other woman the reason for the hardness pressed against Emma's thigh?

What was she like, this other woman? Beautiful, obviously. Men like these Slaters could have any woman they wanted. They didn't need to settle for whores.

She scowled and pulled her hand away from his. He made a small sound of protest.

She'd be some sweet and pretty little town girl. Someone like his brother Matt's wife; Georgiana was about as fancy and pretty and proper as they came. But she also had wit and pluck. She bet Tom's girl had pluck too. She bet when Tom looked at her, he got that same dazed look Matt had when he looked at Georgiana.

Not like the way he looked at Emma. Half the time he looked at her like she was soft in the head, and the other half he looked at her like she was a rogue bull about to charge him. He might be attracted to her, but attracted wasn't the same as . . . as what he felt for that woman he was dreaming about. The one who made him heartbroken in his sleep, and then happy again, when he thought she'd come a-cuddling.

"Hey, Sleeping Beauty," she snapped, her ire at the imaginary woman getting the best of her, "you mind taking your morning glory elsewhere?"

He startled awake and, realizing he was draped all over her, jerked back like he'd been hugging a rattlesnake. That really pricked Emma's temper. So she wasn't good enough for him, was that it? Obviously, she didn't compare to whoever it was he was dreaming about.

She rose to her feet and brushed herself down, like she was offended by his touch and not secretly dying of shame that she didn't measure up to his dream woman. And why would she measure up? She was a goddamn bald *nun*.

"I'm sorry," he mumbled, blushing the shade of fine Spanish wine.

"Don't," she said shortly. She couldn't bear him apologizing for his distaste at finding her in his arms. It reminded her too much of the way Luke had apologized all those years ago. Only, at least Luke had just been a customer she'd fancied herself in love with, while Tom . . . Hell. She didn't even want to *think* about what Tom Slater was to her.

Nothing, she thought firmly, snatching her blanket and boots and stomping off to her wagon. He was *nothing* to her except a way to get safely to Mexico.

* 24 *

It took them eight days to get to San Diego. Tom felt like the Pied Piper as he slogged through the baking-hot days, a line of women and children snaking behind him, raising a cloud of dust into the silver-blue sky. Most of them were on foot. The smallest children sat in the wagon, along with one of the women, who was pregnant. Two Moon and Spear Fisher had stayed back at the village with Black Horse, even though neither of them was Serrano. They didn't fancy spending any more time with white people, and Tom didn't blame them. He hoped they managed to stay free of the Dons, and free of the authorities. As he walked away, he raised a hand in farewell. Only Two Moon waved back.

He'd given his horses to the exhausted captives, as had the nuns. They managed to get a woman and child on each horse and then established a rotation so everyone got a day riding and a rest from walking. Even so, it was a hell of a long way, more than a hundred miles, and it involved a thankless amount of walking.

"I don't see why you couldn't have picked somewhere

closer," Sister Emma griped at him on the seventh day. It had taken her the whole week to speak to him again. Tom just about shriveled with embarrassment every time he saw her. He couldn't believe he'd been grinding against a *nun* in his sleep.

Not that she'd looked like a nun at the time. She'd been wearing those riding breeches, which looked just about painted on and revealed the incredibly long, shapely legs that she normally hid under the drab black habit. He didn't know a body could even *have* legs that long. And then there was her rear, which was outlined in all its plump glory by the buckskin. Not to mention the fact that she'd been wearing *his* shirt. For some reason, the fact that his shirt was close against her skin turned him on no end. It was an old shirt of much-washed cotton and clung to her every swell and curve, and she sure did have some impressive swells and curves.

She even made a clipped head look sexy. It made her seem like a bobcat or a vixen, all pointed chin and big eyes. The sight of her standing over him, flushed and outraged, her impressive chest heaving, her tawny eyes snapping, was a constant memory, swirling to mind at the most inappropriate moments.

No wonder he'd been having such bewitching dreams. He didn't remember the details, but he sure did remember the sensations. He had a vague feeling he'd been dreaming about being back at *de Gato,* in that enormous cloud of a bed, as she sponge bathed him until he was hurting with wanting her.

Waking to find her in his arms, her hip rubbing deliciously against his hard cock, her breasts stretching his cotton shirt and filling his vision, was astounding.

He'd molested a *nun.* That was all he could think as he

watched her stomping away. He felt lower than a bug about it. She'd immediately changed back into her hideous black sack and then proceeded to cold-shoulder him for the next week. If she wanted to talk to him, she sent a message through Calla. When Calla threw a tantrum and said she didn't know when in hell she became the translator for everyone, Sister Emma simply switched to sending messages through Anna instead.

It had been a tiresome journey. Everyone was spent before they even started, and the trek was full of tears and spats and raw nerves. Tom had been just about pulling his hair out dealing with a mess of women all on his own. So he nearly melted with relief when Emma started talking to him again.

"I don't see why you couldn't have picked somewhere closer." She said it again, like he hadn't heard it the first time.

He still couldn't bring himself to look at her when he answered her, but he answered quickly, before she could change her mind and stonewall him again. "It's the *only* place close enough. We've nearly gone through all your provisions, so we need somewhere big enough to have well-stocked stores. Besides, I can't imagine what this lot would do in a speck of a town like Red Deer or Eulalia. We got to get them somewhere where they can make plans, where they can start over, or head home. Ships come and go from San Diego. It's the best place."

He darted a glance at her. She'd used her belt to hike the skirts of her habit higher, so she didn't trip over them as she walked. She was cooking alive in that thing. Her face was tomato colored, and she was dripping sweat. Tom was glad he wasn't wearing the señora's dress anymore. He'd rather take his chances with the posses; it was too hot to wear such a stupid getup. He sighed and looked over his shoulder at all the women suffering in their heavy dresses. Who knew women's clothing was so oppressive?

They did, I guess, he thought ruefully.

"Besides," he continued, "no posse will expect us to head for San Diego. They'll think we're off to Mexico. Or at the very least somewhere less . . . visible. It's like a double bluff."

She snorted at that. "Because they'll never find our trail?"

There was that. They were leaving a trail a blind man could follow.

"Not much I can do about that," he said. He darted another glance, only to find her staring at him. She jerked her gaze away. He flushed again. What on earth did she think of him? The first time they'd met, he'd been fall-down drunk; he'd gotten them lost and then vomited in the chaparral. Then she'd seen him dressed as a woman and shot; not to mention that she'd seen him spend his savings on slaves instead of handling it like a hero. A real man would have done violence to those bastards. Luke would have fought. So would Matt. Hell, neither of them would have let the girl get taken in the first place. If it had been Luke, he would have disarmed the Georges and there would have been no need to have gone to *Gran Rancho de Gato* in the first place. He would have handed the Georges over to the vaqueros, and they would have gone on their merry way. That's what Luke would have done.

Which was why women loved him.

Would Sister Emma love him too, if she met him?

Tom was surprised by the force of the jealousy he felt at the thought. It was stronger than the feeling he had when he thought about Luke and Alex.

Of course Emma would love Luke. *Every* woman loved Luke. The only woman he'd ever seen immune to him was Georgiana, and that was only because Georgiana couldn't tear her gaze away from Matt long enough to even look at another man.

Ah hell, what did it even matter? The woman was a *nun*. She'd chosen her husband, and He was God. He couldn't compete with that, and nor should he want to.

"At least you'll get to see the ocean," he sighed, as he slogged along, trying to push away his turbulent thoughts. "I know you always wanted to."

"Have you been to San Diego before?" Her curiosity was getting the best of her pique; she thawed a little at tell of the ocean.

"Yeah."

He heard a gusty sigh. "Well, come on, poet, what's it like?"

"Flat. Dusty. There aren't any trees."

"That ain't poetic. You can do better."

She still sounded a touch sour. He pulled a face. "It's on the bay, which ain't as pretty as the actual ocean. It's kind of flat too. And it ain't big. It kind of looks like a river. But on our way out we can go by the beach. We can mosey along the coast for a fair way, if you like the look of all that water."

"Fine. Don't do better." Now she sounded more than a touch sour.

He sighed. He knew exactly what she wanted. And he'd be an ass not to give it to her, considering the state of their relationship. He took a breath. "The beach is so long it seems to go on forever. If you were to follow it, you'd eventually reach sandstone cliffs that turn the color of butter in the evening sun, and when that sun sets into the sea, it's like the world is reflected on itself, all upside down and backward. And sometimes, when the light is just right, you can't tell where sky ends and the water begins. It all becomes one big watercolor. Sometimes it's the color of the shells that wash up on the shore, all pale pinks and purples, with a darker blush near the heart of it; other times it blazes red as a whore's best dress."

She arched an eyebrow at that, and he regretted the image. Who talked about whores to a nun? Especially after molesting her.

"Who says a whore's best dress is red?" she muttered as she dropped back. "Who says it wouldn't be *pink?*"

"I HATE THIS place."

"You hate everything lately," Calla said mildly. She wouldn't have said it so mildly twenty-four hours ago, but a lot could change in twenty-four hours. Emma guessed that listening to her bitch and moan as they kicked dust across California was a far sight more irritating than listening to her bitch while soaking in a tub in a nice little room in San Diego. Through the open window, they could smell salt on the breeze.

Emma had been disappointed in her first sight of the sea. It was flat, reflecting white sunlight like a blank mirror. It wasn't anything like she'd imagined. It looked so . . . *boring.*

"You won't feel so glum after a bath." Calla sighed happily as she leaned her head back and closed her eyes. On the table beside her, she had a glass of Mexican wine. The passel of freed women and children had been delivered to the U.S. Army barracks, which were housed in the old Spanish mission. The captain had been a bit bewildered by all the ex-captives but had pledged to do his best to help them. Especially after Tom had handed over Emma's gold nugget as a bribe. She'd spent the week hiding it in his saddlebags, only to find it reappear in her carpetbag every morning. When the captain had proven to be less than helpful, Emma had wordlessly passed Tom the nugget. He'd sighed and passed it along. And of course, with the weight of gold in his hand, the captain's concerns went away.

Then it was just the five of them again. Tom led them to a boardinghouse and ordered hot baths and food, and they'd all disappeared into their separate rooms. Emma doubted she'd see him again until they headed out in a couple of days. He'd all but run away from her just now.

"I ain't glum," Emma snapped at Calla as her friend lolled in the bath. "I'm . . . *irked*."

Calla cracked an eyelid. "Irked? Or *pent up?*"

"I don't know what you mean." Emma avoided her friend's gaze and poured herself a glass of wine from the jug. She moved to the window and took a healthy slug of it. There was no bay view here; their window looked out on a wall. There were chickens in the run between the two buildings. Emma could hear them brooding.

"You don't know what I mean?" Calla laughed. "I imagine our Mr. Slater don't know either, then."

Emma scowled at the wall.

"You two got more energy between you than a lightning storm. You just about make my hair stand on end."

"He thinks I'm a goddamn nun." Emma finished the wine and poured herself another.

"That's fixable."

"Is it?"

Calla opened both eyes now and wriggled upright. "You know very well it is. All you have to do is tell him that you're *not* a nun." She paused. "Which you're not," she reminded Emma.

"But Hec . . ."

Calla blew a raspberry. "Hec nothing. Hec won't be looking for you here. With any luck, he's been scalped by Apaches already. If not, he sure ain't looking for a bald woman in San Diego."

Emma rubbed her naked head.

"Hec's just an excuse," Calla said scornfully.

Emma sighed. "I know it." She collapsed on the bed and pouted at the floor. "I wish I weren't a whore."

"You ain't a whore."

"But I *was*. Most of my life I've been a whore. He's not going to want *me*."

Calla went all pinch mouthed at that. "How do you know? You ain't asked him."

Emma kicked her heels against the floorboards. "It ain't just the whore thing," she admitted.

The silence stretched out.

"Well, are you going to tell me, or are you going to make me guess?"

Emma grimaced. "I might have slept with his brother," she said with a wince.

Calla sat bolt upright at that. Water went sloshing in the tub. "You what?"

"I slept with his brother." She covered her face with her hands. Then split her fingers so she could peer out at Calla. "I fancied myself in love with him," Emma confessed, feeling hideously vulnerable as she did so.

"Ah." Calla winced in sympathy. "He was a customer?"

"Sometimes." Emma shrugged. "But sometimes it was something else. He would have called it a freebie, but to me it was . . . special."

Calla nodded. She understood. Things got complicated in bedrooms.

"How do I tell him *that*?" Emma asked despairingly.

"I don't know." Calla held out the wine jug. "But I'm glad it's you and not me."

"Thanks."

"Maybe you could *not* tell him?" Calla grinned. "Just enjoy it for what it is. I don't see why he has to know."

Emma took the jug. *Enjoy it for what it is.* There was the problem, wasn't it? *What it was.* Tom Slater could never take her home to his family. Even if he could get over the business about her being a whore, he'd never be able to get over Luke. And neither would Luke's wife, or anyone else in the family.

And who could blame them?

Emma stared into the ruby-colored wine. She'd been having silly fantasies this last week. Fantasies about Tom Slater and his magnificent body, yes, but also fantasies about . . . more than that. About his boots by her back step, his clothes in her cupboard, his head on her pillow. Not just for a night, or a bunch of nights, but for all time.

God help her, she'd been dreaming about *marriage* as she kicked through the Californian dust on the way to San Diego. *That* was what Tom Slater had brought her to.

"I'm going for a walk," she sighed, putting the wine aside. "I'm going to see if a sunset improves that flat bit of seaside." She struggled to put her cowl and veil back on, but she was good enough at it these days that she didn't need help.

"Emma?" Calla called as she went to leave. "Do you remember what you said to me the time I fancied myself in love with that Irishman?"

Emma paused in the doorway.

"You said, 'Enjoy it while you can.'" Calla gave her a

sympathetic smile. "'Save up the good times, for when times ain't so good.'"

Emma nodded, but she didn't feel cheered. She wasn't about to listen to *herself*. Her advice was a bunch of rubbish. She'd done nothing but make a mess of her life. And when it came to men, her choices were especially terrible.

She left Calla to her bath and wandered out into the street. San Diego wasn't anything like she imagined. She'd had an image in her head of an exotic Spanish-style town, but in actual fact it was just a bunch of rough buildings on a flat patch of land by the bay. It was just another dusty frontier town in Emma's eyes.

She wandered until she found a quiet spot by the water. It hardly even seemed to dignify the name *bay*, she thought sourly. It didn't look much different from a river. On the other side of the not-very-wide not-river was more flat land. Distantly, she could hear waves. But she couldn't *see* them. It was all just so disappointing, she thought, and she didn't really mean the view.

"The ocean proper is still a fair piece away."

She wasn't the only one out for a wander, it seemed. Her heart jumped to her throat at the sound of his voice. She turned to see Tom Slater standing behind her, his hands deep in his pockets as he squinted at the setting sun. Unlike her, he'd bathed. His dark hair was still damp. And he'd shaved, she thought witlessly, taking in the smooth planes of his face.

She was in trouble. Bad trouble. She didn't think she'd ever felt so acutely aware of a man before. Not even Luke Slater had made her witless like this. And with every day she spent in Tom's presence, the feeling only seemed to grow. Sometimes, when she caught his river-ice green eyes, the feeling in her stomach was so intense it was practically a pain.

"This is a funny little patch of water," he told her, still squinting at the sky. "It's got layers to it, with the water winding around spits of land. It's not wild, like the ocean. It's puts me in mind of a corral. I guess ships ain't too different from cows in that way."

She gave the water a dubious look. There weren't any ships there, and she didn't quite believe that any could fit in such a piddly bit of water.

Why was he here talking to her? He'd been ornerier than a bee-stung bear around her since the morning they'd woken in each other's arms. Why was he talking to her *now?*

Oh hell, she thought as an idea hit her: had *she* interrupted *him?* Had he been here before her, just trying to get a minute's peace? Had she come barreling in, imposing on him?

"I followed you," he blurted, not looking away from the sinking sun. The peachy light made his skin glow.

"What?" Emma thought she must have misheard him.

"I saw you leave from my window, and I followed you." He was looking all bee-stung again. "I thought we could make peace."

"We ain't at war."

"That's how I know we ain't at peace." He gave her a sheepish grin. "Our normal state is at war."

"I'm never at war," she objected reflexively. "I'm a woman of peace."

"A woman of tearing me to pieces."

He was teasing her. He hadn't done that in days. The way he was looking at her was playing havoc with her insides. How could a man look coiled and capable, but also careful and kind? It was a deadly combination.

"Thought I'd sit here and watch the sunset if you want to join me."

What was he playing at? Why was he being so nice to her?

Feeling like a green girl, Emma sat next to him. There was nothing to sit on but the ground, so they sat on the ground. Emma drew her knees up to her chest and rested her chin on top.

It was a pretty sunset. Much prettier than the puny little bay deserved. The sky was stacked with clouds, stained all kinds of orange and gold. The narrow stretch of water blazed as the sun slanted low across it. Tom wasn't a talker at the best of times, and he certainly didn't talk now. Emma had never met a man so comfortable with his own company before. She wished she could have an ounce of that kind of serenity. It was driving her nuts to sit here quietly. Her mind bounced from topic to topic, and she almost spoke a dozen times. But gradually, the silence sank in and she found herself calming down. Shafts of light speared through the clouds, catching the dust in the air and making it glitter.

She was intensely aware of him. The deep, slow rhythm of his breathing, the tangy smell of soap, the solidness of him at her side. She turned her head and rested her cheek on her knee, so she could watch him. She watched the wind blow a lock of hair over his eye. Absently, he flicked it away. As he did, he caught her staring. But this time she didn't look away; she didn't *want* to look away. Their gazes locked. The moment stretched out. The sound of the wind and the faint roar of waves receded; all Emma could hear was the rush of blood in her ears. He stared at her so intently, he didn't seem to blink. And the look in his eye . . . there was curiosity, fascination, bewilderment . . . but most of all, desire.

Oh, who cared, Emma thought in an impulsive burst. *Who cared* if she'd been a whore. Who cared if she was stone-cold terrified? Who cared if he wouldn't stay with her forever? That there might only be *now?* What did any of it matter when there was *this?*

Save up the good times, for when times ain't so good.

Maybe her advice wasn't all bad. Maybe she could work with it.

I choose good, she thought with a groan, giving up the battle. She lunged forward and kissed him. She'd wanted to kiss him since she first saw him, and if she wasn't wrong, he'd felt the urge too. She took him by surprise with her lunge, and he tumbled backward, his elbows giving out beneath him. She went with him, kissing him with every ounce of passion that she'd pushed down all these weeks.

He moaned and seized her by the arms. For a minute, she was afraid he'd push her away, but he didn't. He hauled her closer, rolling her over and pinning her to the ground. His mouth slanted hungrily over hers, his tongue plunging into her.

Nobody had ever kissed Emma like this in her entire life. And that was a shock to her. She didn't think she had any surprises left when it came to kisses and men, but it looked like Tom Slater was about to show her some new tricks.

He kissed like he lived: intensely, with immaculate attention to detail. His big hand cradled her head as he opened her mouth with his lips and tongue. His thumb rubbed a spot behind her ear that made her melt, while his other hand slid beneath her body, lifting her against him. She squirmed, wishing she could feel more of him, but the thick black habit got in the way. He felt her squirm and pulled her harder against him, until she could feel him settle between her legs. He was a divine weight. If she hadn't been trapped by the habit, she would have wrapped her legs around him and wriggled even closer. His tongue was driving her wild. And then he gave her lower lip a long, slow suck, and she just about lost her mind. She was trembling as she plunged her hands into his hair. It felt like silk between her fingers. She met him with her own tongue, sliding into the slick warmth of his mouth. The heat of it, the force . . . Emma couldn't do much more than hold on for dear life. It was like being in the middle of a storm.

Time lost all meaning. The kiss ebbed and flowed. They slowed to gentle teasing, then intensified again, then relaxed into a slow pulsing dance of tongues. By the time they surfaced, the sunset was long gone and they were in the languorous salt-scented darkness. Emma could hear his ragged breathing. It matched her own. She was liquid with desire. He gave a shaky laugh and pressed his forehead against hers. She felt the tickle of his eyelashes against her skin.

Then his laughter faded, and she felt the mood grow solemn.

"I shouldn't have done that," he said. He didn't sound regretful. Just sad it had to end.

"*I* was the one who did it," she disagreed.

"You certainly did." His breath was hot. Sweet, like boiled sugar. "But I got involved."

"You certainly did," she echoed, running her fingers through his hair.

He lifted his head and stared into her eyes. She felt it all the way to her toes. It was because when he looked at her, he *saw* her.

"I wish . . ." His voice was full of longing.

She knew what he wished. And it was a wish she could grant. If she had the courage. Or the foolhardiness.

She figured she had both in spades.

"Tom," she said shakily, "there's something I have to tell you . . ."

❧ 25 ❧

SHE WASN'T A nun.

Tom felt like he'd fallen off his horse. Into a cactus.

He should be furious at her lies. The woman was incorrigible. Every second thing she said seemed to be a red-hot falsehood. But the euphoric relief was too overwhelming to leave room for much else. And, to be honest, he'd already had his doubts. About her and Calla both.

He could have whooped up a storm, he was so happy. His conscience had been killing him. It was bad enough to have lustful thoughts about a nun, but even worse was the fact that what he felt for her was more than simple lust. She took up all the room in his thoughts. He heard her slow Tennessee drawl in his dreams, and the sight of her every morning sent his blood leaping, even when she was in that smothering black habit. He was aware of her movements every single moment of every single day. He knew her mood, her stride, her habits. He knew that her favorite time of day was when she got to bake. She fed her starter like it was a child, talking to it as she stirred in flour and water. She kneaded and shaped and baked and glazed and was constantly speckled with flour dust. She smelled like hot bread. And everything she made was the best thing he'd ever eaten.

When they reached the San Diego boardinghouse, after that torturous trek with the captives, he'd had a chance to think clearly for the first time in weeks. He felt like he'd walked through the desert for forty days. As he let the silence of his empty room fill him, his mind emptied. And it was only then that he realized he hadn't so much as thought of Alex in a long time. In fact, he could no longer quite remember exactly what it was that he'd felt for her. Whatever it was hadn't been *this*. This was like a wildfire; it tore through everything in its path, lighting up the world. Now that he was still, he found he no longer felt so wildly unhappy, so afraid of the sucking black emptiness that had been at the heart of him for so long. In fact, he felt anything but empty.

He felt exhausted. But *alive*.

As he sat in the bath, scrubbing off the trail dirt, he'd seen the scar on his hip was healing, and the sight of it brought that sinfully good sponge bath to mind. And once he started thinking about it, he couldn't stop. Before long, he was lusty as a bull. Sister Emma seemed to have that effect on him. Alex never had. Emma's sly tawny eyes and cheeky sharp-cornered grins sent him wild. As he sat in the tub, he felt a bolt of rage at fate, for giving him feelings for yet another woman he couldn't have. And if there was anything worse than fancying yourself in love with your brother's wife, it was falling head over heels for a *nun*.

But it turned out she wasn't a nun at all . . .

It was too good to be true. He didn't trust it.

But he also didn't want to jinx it. When she'd told him, all he could do was groan with relief and yank her closer.

They'd stayed in the dark, on the shore of the bay, kissing late into the night. Neither of them wanted to break the spell.

"How?" he'd sighed against her mouth. He was so drugged with her that he could barely find the words. "Why? Why are you a nun?" He didn't let her answer. He traced her lips with his tongue, until she melted and he could plunge into her.

She answered him word by word, between kisses. "Tomorrow," she whispered. "I'll tell you tomorrow."

That was fine last night. Last night he'd been happy to surrender to the maelstrom. They'd kissed like green youths. It hadn't gone further. Both of them had been oddly shy. There was something bewitching about kissing her. He didn't need more at that moment, and the kissing felt like fragile magic; he thought they were both afraid of shattering it, of letting reality back in.

Eventually, they slowed and lay in each other's arms, listening to the soft lap of the bay waters.

"I should go back before Calla sends a search party," she whispered.

He had a thousand questions. But he didn't ask a single one. They had plenty of time, he thought, feeling a spurt of joy. They had all the time it took to get down to Magdalena to get to know each other, lots of long September days in the mellow sun. There'd be hours in the saddle to talk, and even more hours late at night under the stars . . . his imagination fired at ways he could spend *that* time. He didn't want to spook her tonight, or push her to talk before she was ready. She might be a liar, but she'd always had an understandable reason for lying. She'd tell him when she was ready. He was more than happy to be patient, especially if he could spend the time waiting kissing her.

It had been hard to say good night. They'd stood in the hall outside her door, indulging in last kiss after last kiss. She tasted like red currants and spices, and went to his head like wine.

He thought he'd be too keyed up and lusty to sleep, but actually, he had the best night of sleep he'd had in years. He fell asleep with his pillow in his arms, smiling like a fool.

He'd never in his life been courting, but he figured this was exactly how it should feel. He felt like he was floating two inches off the ground. The next morning, he was up at cockcrow, hair brushed and teeth clean. He asked the landlady to deliver breakfast to the women, and then spent the early morning hours restocking their wagon.

"You did all this?" she asked, astonished, when she finally emerged into the daylight.

His heart jumped at the sight of her. She was fresh scrubbed and smelled soapy clean. She had flour dust on her dirty habit, he saw. He grinned, imagining her talking to her starter this morning and handing out batches of dough to the landlady.

"You got flour all over you," he told her, feeling shy. "The landlady said she can launder our clothes for a fee. If you don't mind being out of the habit . . . I know it ain't easy to wash." He had a flash of the room back at *de Gato*, of her naked shadow on the filmy dressing screen as she soaked her clothes in tub.

She flushed. She looked as bashful as he felt. "It is pretty dirty . . ." she admitted, brushing uselessly at the stains.

"If you're worried about being recognized," he hazarded (because why else would she be disguised as a nun?), "you can always wear my old señora disguise."

She brightened at that. "I can, can't I?" She grinned. "Forget asking the landlady to wash this, I might just toss it out! I'm pretty damn sick of being a nun. I ain't any good at it anyway. I'd make a much better señora. Wait here and I'll change."

Tom wasn't complaining about that decision. When she reemerged in the black dress, she just about took his breath away. The dress, which had originally belonged to Doña Maria's elderly mother, was terribly out of fashion. It had also been altered for Tom, so it wasn't quite able to accommodate Emma's substantial curves. The bodice stretched almost to the breaking point over her chest. It made his knees weak. The shape of the dress drew attention to the dramatic nip of her waist beneath her full breasts. He didn't imagine Doña Maria's mother had looked anything like *this* in that stuffy old dress. Emma made the ugly gown look so alluring that Tom was getting up a cold sweat.

She lifted the black lace veil and gave him a cheeky smile. "What do you think?"

"I don't think," Tom admitted. "I can't."

Her smile grew radiant. Goddamn, she was something. He'd not seen anyone so beautiful in all his life. When she smiled like that, she was like the sun breaking clear on a bleak January day.

"You'll have to call me Doña Elvira now," she teased.

"Why didn't you get me a black dress too, when we were back at the hacienda," Calla complained, yawning as she joined them in the yard behind the boardinghouse. "Now I'm the only one who has to wear one of these heavy things."

Emma cocked her head. "You know what, little Calida, why don't you just wear one of your own dresses. Hec ain't looking for *you*, and if there's a posse from *de Gato*, they'll be looking for nuns. So we probably shouldn't be nuns anymore." She looked down at herself. "Maybe I shouldn't wear this either. Guess I should have taken better stock, huh?"

Hec Boehm. Of course that's why she was dressed as a nun. He remembered the gold nugget she'd kept trying to foist on him, and it all made sense. She must have a gold claim. Hec Boehm had harried Tom's sister-in-law Georgiana out of a gold claim, and now he was trying to do the same to Emma. Tom felt a protective blaze of anger. He'd have to see what he could do about Boehm.

"I don't want to turn up in Magdalena as a nun anyway," Calla said happily, beaming at the thought of shucking her habit. "That would ruin everything!" She disappeared back into the house.

"I thought we'd take a couple of days here to rest," he said, still feeling bashful. "If you're interested, I thought I could take you to see the ocean today. The actual ocean, not the bay here. It's only a few miles away, and we can be there in an hour."

She lit up at that, and he felt absurdly pleased with himself. So much so he started to blush. If this was what courting felt like, he'd been missing out all these years. But then, he didn't think courting anyone else would be quite like courting Emma.

"We could take a picnic," he continued, feeling his blush deepen with every word, "and spend the day."

She let out a squeal and threw herself at him. She showered kisses on his face, eventually finding his lips and kissing him good and proper. His hands found her waist, and his eyes closed with pleasure as he pulled her in close. There was nothing but pure sensation. Warmth and pleasure flooded him. He could have stood there all day kissing her. And probably would have, if the landlady hadn't taken that moment to throw out her wash water, muttering disapprovingly at the sight of them.

"Go and get yourself ready," Tom said huskily, reluctantly releasing his grip on her. "I'll saddle the horses. Tell Calla and Anna not to wait up for us tonight."

She gave him a smile that made his toes curl and went skipping inside. He laughed. He felt rather like skipping himself.

❧ 26 ❧

EMMA WAS STUNNED. There wasn't enough poetry in existence to describe the vision before her. A stretch of white sand led to a vast landscape of water in shades of blue she'd never seen before in her life. She didn't even know what to call colors so pure. Foaming waves rolled in, breaking on the shore with a rushing sound that filled Emma with glee. The salty fresh breeze snapped at her veil, tearing it from her head and sending it sailing away down the beach. Emma laughed. The wind was welcome to the wretched thing!

"It's better than I ever could have imagined!" She turned to Tom, who was grinning at her pleasure. Lord, he looked fine when he smiled. The wind riffled his hair, making him seem even more boyish, and he was grinning ear to ear, showing off his heart-stopping dimples.

He dismounted and held his arms out to help her down. She almost giggled. Would have, if she didn't consider herself too old for giggling. She slid out of the saddle and into his arms. He lowered her slowly down his body, his green eyes growing hazy.

"Well," she prodded, "what are you waiting for? Ain't you going to kiss me?"

He was. And he did.

And then he led her down the beach. Emma threw out her arms and laughed out loud at the joy of it. Today might be her best day ever. *Save up the good times.* Oh, she would. She was squirreling away each little shining moment, packing them away for when times weren't so good. One day she'd look back on today and remember how it felt to be sun warmed and well kissed and happier than a body had any right to be.

By some unspoken agreement, they avoided talking about anything of consequence. Instead, they traded funny stories and teased and spoke of nothing much at all. They took their boots off and walked more than a mile on the beach, chasing each other through the tongues of water bubbling up the sand; they collected shells and skimmed stones, and ambled back to spread a rug and have a lazy picnic. There was a lot of kissing, and Emma smiled so much her cheeks were twitching. After lunch, Emma stretched out with her head on Tom's lap. She closed her eyes to the hard sparkle of the sun and almost purred as he stroked her head. Her hair was still just fuzz but it was better than being completely bald.

"Your hair's red in the sunlight," he observed, as he traced her hairline.

She smiled. Good. She liked being a redhead. She'd been worried it had darkened out to more of a brown, like her eyebrows.

He didn't ask why she'd shaved it. She would have told him, but she was glad to keep from solemn talk today. She rubbed her cheek against his thigh and enjoyed the heat of the sun and the feel of his touch. Enjoyed it rather a lot, enough to make her loose limbed and floaty in the stomach. Her nipples tightened as she felt that old lightning charge of theirs flicker to life. The air seemed to thicken around them. Emma heard his breath catch. And if she wasn't mistaken, something was stiffening up rather nicely under her ear.

She opened her eyes. Oh yes. He had that look. Like a lazy cat watching a bird. He wanted to pounce but hadn't quite made up his mind to do it. This kissing was all very well, Emma thought, cheekily rubbing the back of her head against his stiffening cock, but, despite feeling like a green girl, she *wasn't* one. She was a full-grown woman, who had the measure of her own body, and more than the measure of his. She was wet with wanting him and had been since their first kiss last night.

She gave him a sly look. She didn't want to play for pennies anymore. She wanted all in.

"Do you know how to swim?" she asked. Her question came out like a purr.

His hand shook, coming to rest mid-stroke on her forehead. "I do," he said thickly.

She sat up. "Shall we?"

That old cat was just about ready to pounce.

Not yet, cat. Emma planned to get the most out of this moment. After all, a girl could only experience it the first time with a man once. She might as well make a lasting impression.

He sat frozen, his burning green eyes trained on her. "What are you doing?"

She gave him a teasing smile. "Why, honey, I'm getting ready to swim." She stretched, giving him the chance to anticipate what she meant. Then she lifted her hands to the high neck of the ugly black dress. There was a line of buttons, which ran from her neck all the way down to her waist.

"Emma . . ."

He was worried. He thought she didn't know what she was doing. But, oh honey, she sure did.

"Hush," she told him firmly. One by one she undid those little black buttons. His gaze was riveted to her fingers. His color was high and his eyes glittered. He barely seemed to breathe as she peeled off the black dress. The wind whipped at her petticoats and threatened to blow the black dress clear away. Emma tossed it to him. He caught it and gripped it with white-knuckled hands.

"Wait," he said, when she went to undo the corset. "You can swim in that."

She laughed. "I can," she agreed. "But I won't." She unhooked the corset, taking her time. That always drove men wild. And this man looked no different. He was mesmerized. She dropped the corset to the sand.

"Don't forget to breathe, honey," she counseled. Startled, he glanced up at her face. When he saw her smile, he relaxed, all at once, and the smile he gave her in return made her stomach do a slow somersault. He looked wolfish. And sexy as all hell.

She fought the urge to rush. This was utter torture. But worth every slow, hellish minute.

His gaze had dropped to her chest. Her nipples were too pale for the color to show through the white cotton, but their shape was clearly visible. Her aureoles were large and swollen, her nipples pushing at the thin cotton. Emma slowly undid the ribbon that held her chemise together and pulled the garment open and down over her shoulders, revealing her breasts. She heard him groan. She peeled her undergarments off inch by tantalizing inch, tossing each item to him as she was free of it. When she was buck-naked, she gave him a wicked grin. "Last one in loses!" she sang, turning and dashing for the waves.

"That's cheating!"

She laughed as she plunged into the waves. They fizzed and bubbled around her. The water was warm, and she sank into it joyfully. She looked back at the shore to see Tom hastily shedding his clothes. When he ran toward her, she sure did enjoy the sight. The starkness of his tan lines—from his collar, and from where he wore his shirtsleeves rolled up his chiseled forearms—was sexy as hell.

He dove into the waves and had her in his arms in a heartbeat. Their wet bodies slipped against each other. His cock was hard against her stomach; her breasts were hard against his chest. He kissed her like he was a drowning man and she was air. Emma kissed him back, wrapping her legs around him and sliding her hand down his back until she cupped his buttock.

He made a sound of protest. She nipped his lower lip between his teeth.

"This is too quick," he groaned.

"We'll go slower next time," she promised. "Or maybe the time after that."

He surrendered, hauling her back toward shore and falling onto his back. She straddled him as the waves surged around them. His hands were everywhere at once: squeezing her breasts, pinching her nipples, sliding over the curves of her hips and buttocks. They rolled and thrust and bit and rode each other through the rising tide. When Emma came, she screamed. When he came, he yelled her name.

IT WAS ONLY later that Emma worried he might recognize her from that night at *La Noche*. Tall boots, a pink hat and some rouged nipples weren't much of a disguise. But as far as she could tell, Tom hadn't twigged. Or if he had, he kept quiet about it.

They swam and made love through the afternoon, and then crept back to their blanket to nap and dry off in the sun. She rested her head on his chest, lazily tracing the whorls of hair around his nipple. Her leg was thrown over his hips, and he had his arms wrapped tight around her. His left hand had found her breast, curling around it as he drifted in and out of sleep. The low light had turned buttery, causing the sand to glitter golden. She sighed, feeling bone-deep contentment. This might be the only time in her life she'd ever really been content.

If he *had* recognized her, she thought idly, she'd just have to tell him about the whoring. She hadn't planned to. After all, what did it matter? She wasn't a fool. She knew this wasn't forever. A man like Tom Slater didn't need to stoop to marrying a woman like her. He wasn't like that old prospector McGinty, happy to turn up a woman like Nora Paul. Tom Slater was a whole different kettle of fish. All of those Slaters were. Tom was the best-looking man she'd ever seen; he was a man with prospects. He could have any woman he wanted. Right now he had Emma, but he wasn't looking to marry her, was he? He was looking for some kissing and some love in the surf. Someone to keep him company in his bedroll on the ride down to Mexico. Emma knew he cared for her. She wasn't stupid. But caring and marrying were two completely different things.

So why spoil a beautiful interlude by bringing whoring into the conversation? If he didn't mention it, she wouldn't mention it either. She'd just save up these good times like a miser counting every penny.

"What are you thinking?" he asked sleepily, his right hand sliding up and down her spine.

"Nothing at all," she lied. She let her fingertips trail down the line of hair that ran between his sharply defined stomach muscles, all the way to his cock, which wasn't looking sleepy in the slightest. "What are you thinking?"

"Guess," he said thickly.

She did. And she guessed right.

❖ 27 ❖

THEY'D BEEN TRAVELING for almost two weeks and
weren't far out of Magdalena. Tom was getting itchy.
He and Emma had learned every last inch of each other's
bodies, but they hadn't got around to a single conversation
about anything important. She went skittish anytime he
tried. And she had treacherous techniques for distracting
him. His body was his own worst enemy at those times, and
afterward he was too content and sleepy to even remember
what he wanted to talk about.

The closer they got to Magdalena, the more excited
Calla got and the quieter Emma got. Calla chattered end-
lessly about home, circling one topic in particular. It didn't
take a genius to work out she was heading back for one reason, and that reason's name was Miguel Ángel Leon. Tom
knew the boy. Well, he wasn't such a boy anymore. He was
sure Calla wouldn't have any trouble catching his eye. Now
that she'd emerged from the habit, Calla was a striking girl.
She had masses of shining black hair, which she wore elab-
orately coiled on her head, and she had a string of fancy
dresses, which she wore even though there was no one out

here to admire her. It was amazing how those black habits had managed to disguise her looks, and Emma's. The two of them were beautiful by anyone's standards. Tom didn't think Ángel Leon had any idea what was about to hit him.

He knew the feeling. He wasn't quite sure what had hit *him*. Something had changed in him these last two weeks. Something he didn't want to change back. And it had everything to do with the bobcat over there in the black dress. They hadn't talked about what would happen when they got to Magdalena.

He needed to meet his men in Arizpe. He had business waiting. He wanted to ask her to come with him, but every time he tried to talk to her, she skittered away. And they were running out of time.

He was considering his next move with Emma when the trouble broke out. It was Winnie's fault. The girl had become a handful these last two weeks. Once she'd emerged from a state of shock, she'd grown sullen, and then downright angry. She was prone to tantrums and last week had even struck out at Anna. Tom had heard Emma talking quietly to Anna, counseling patience. And Anna had been patient. She had the patience of a saint, in Tom's opinion. But tonight Winnie must have pushed her too far, because she gave a shout and then exploded in tears. She ran off to the new tent they'd bought in San Diego and hid herself away, but they could still hear her sobbing.

"All right!" Emma's voice cracked across the camp. "That's enough."

Tom looked up from his whittling. He'd never heard Emma angry like that before. She fixed Winnie with a hard stare and was wiping dough off her hands with a cloth.

"You!" she ordered, pointing at the girl. "Come here."

Tom heard Anna gasp through the canvas, and then she came running from the tent. "Don't," she pleaded. "She didn't mean it."

Emma ignored her, staring at the child and crooking her finger for her to come. Dark eyes blazing, Winnie strutted over, oozing insolence.

"You best adjust your attitude, miss," Emma warned her.

"Or what?"

Emma's eyebrows went up.

"She doesn't know what she's saying," Anna protested, stepping between them.

"Yes, she does," Calla stepped up beside Emma, her hands on her hips. "She knows *exactly* what she's saying. And she's been a brat since we left San Diego."

"What do you expect?" Anna exploded. "She was kidnapped!"

Tom didn't know what to do with himself. He'd never been caught in a fight between women before. He felt like he should give them some privacy, but to be honest, he was kind of afraid to move, for fear he'd draw attention to himself and get dragged into it.

"That ain't no excuse, Anna, and you know it."

"She's just a baby," Anna wailed.

"No, she ain't," Emma said firmly.

Tom sat frozen as he watched Emma push Anna out of the way. He'd not seen her like this before. Her face was stern as she looked down at the girl. Tom felt an urge to step between them. He agreed with Anna. Surely, the girl deserved some time and care.

"You apologize to Anna," Emma said shortly.

"She don't need to." Anna was wringing her hands.

"I won't," Winnie said fiercely.

"Oh ho," Calla scoffed, "and why not? You think you're special? You think you don't have to act nice, like everyone else?"

Tom found himself rising to protect the girl. What in hell were they doing? Winnie was standing her ground, but even from here, Tom could see her chin was wobbling. Hadn't the kid been through enough?

"You stay where you are," Emma warned him, without even turning to look at him. "This doesn't concern you."

Tom stopped dead, half-standing, half-crouching.

"You think you're the only one who's had something bad happen to them?" Calla asked Winnie.

The girl had spirit, Tom gave her that; her look was mutinous as she glared at Calla.

"You ever bother to ask Anna why she ended up whoring? Or me? Or Emma here?"

What? Tom sat down with a thud. Emma glanced over at him, and he saw a shadow cross her face. But she stayed where she was.

Whore. The word rang in his head. And then he remembered the whore in *La Noche,* and he felt like he'd been punched. He remembered her posed at the head of the stairs, back arched, breasts bared. Hell, *everything* bared. The southern drawl. The long legs. The red hair . . .

Goddamn it. He was an idiot. How had he been so stupid?

But why in hell would he think she was a *whore?* Why would it even cross his mind?

Whore. The word turned his stomach. And then he remembered Deathrider throwing her over his shoulder and taking the stairs two at a time.

He felt sick. And following the cold wave of nausea came a hot flush of rage.

"You ask Anna about her husband, the one who just

about beat her to death," Calla was railing, "the one who sold her to his friends for liquor money." The words barely registered with Tom. It wasn't until he heard Emma's name that he looked up.

"You ask Emma who raped her when she was thirteen years old! That ain't much older than you are now, my girl. You ask her how many years she had to live through that. *All of us* have bad things happen to us, and it ain't no excuse. Not for *anything*. Emma taught me that."

"That's enough now." Emma put a hand on Calla's arm. "Why don't you go and look after Anna?"

Anna had gone quiet, Tom saw. She was weeping steadily, but she wasn't protesting anymore. Calla led her off to the tent. "You listen good to Emma, you hear?" she called back over her shoulder to Winnie.

Emma sighed and gave Tom one last glance. Then she seemed to dismiss him for the moment. Tom's head was spinning.

"You know how to make cinnamon rolls, Winnie?" Emma asked.

Cinnamon rolls? Tom watched in disbelief as she led the kid to the dough. He'd just found out she was a whore. That she'd been raped . . . at thirteen . . . and now she was making cinnamon rolls?

As though reading his mind, she gave him a sharp look. "You could do with making some rolls too," she suggested. "Get over here."

He didn't move. He wasn't about to make dessert. He felt like the whole world had just been turned upside down. "You're a whore," he said numbly.

"Was," she corrected. "I *was* a whore. I ain't been one for some time now." Her gaze was sharp as glass.

So Deathrider hadn't been a customer, then. Tom felt

like his horse had kicked him. It was bad enough to think she'd slept with Deathrider for money, but to think she'd done it for . . . because she . . .

Hell. He couldn't sit here anymore.

"You got raped?" Winnie still sounded sullen, but not quite so much as before.

He couldn't bring himself to leave before he heard the answer to that question.

"I did." Emma sounded appallingly matter-of-fact. She handed a hunk of dough to Winnie. "Here, roll some of this out." Emma tore off another hunk of dough and tossed it to Tom. Reflexively, he caught it.

She'd set three boards out for them to work on. She and Winnie sat on the ground by their boards, rolling out the dough.

"What happened?" Winnie asked softly.

Emma sighed. Tom saw a weight settle on her.

He didn't know who she was, he realized. An hour or so before, he'd been contemplating asking her to come with him back to Oregon. But what did he know about her, really? That she lied a lot. That she had a mole just behind her left ear. That she tasted of red currants and made the best bread he'd ever eaten in his life. That she was impulsive and argumentative and kind. That she made him laugh.

"This is a long story," she was saying to Winnie. "Are you sure you want to hear it? It ain't pretty."

Winnie nodded. Tom saw Emma close her eyes and take a deep breath. He edged closer and took the board she'd left for him; he moved a bit away from them, but he did sit down and start working the dough. Emma gave him a searching look, but he kept his gaze fixed on his hands.

"When I was twelve, my mother died. She was the one who taught me how to cook." Both Winnie and Tom listened, riveted, as she painted a picture of her childhood in Duck Creek, Tennessee. She described the farm, her brothers, the long winters. "It was the winter after my mother died that it first happened."

First happened. That meant it happened more than once. Tom kept his gaze on the dough.

"He saw me out in the bathhouse one morning, and after that . . . well, after that he was at me."

"Who?" Tom's voice cracked as he blurted the question. He thought he knew, but he hoped he was wrong. "Who was it?"

"My daddy," she said, as though it was the most natural thing in the world to talk about your daddy raping you.

"Your daddy did that to you?" Winnie was astounded.

"He did, honey. He'd come at me when he'd been drinking. All through that winter, and then the spring, and then through every season after that until I was fourteen."

Goddamn. That bastard had raped her for a year. The dough smooshed through Tom's fingers as he clenched his fists.

"Did it hurt?" Winnie asked.

"You bet it hurt." Emma leaned over the girl and helped her fashion her rolls. Tom watched their fingers mesh.

"It hurt so bad I used to have to bite down on my hand so I didn't yell out."

"Why didn't you want to yell out?"

"Because I didn't want to wake my little brothers."

"Jesus Christ." Tom got to his feet. He was too full of feeling to sit here and roll dough. He moved to the wagon and braced his arms against the tray.

"You feeling all right?" Emma asked him.

She was asking *him*. Tom's eyes pricked with tears. He screwed his eyes shut and wished he'd shot those bastards back in *Hueco del Diablo*. He'd never felt so ashamed of being a man before.

Anna and Calla had crept out of the tent to join them. Calla gave him a pat on the back as she passed. He flinched.

"I never got raped before I was whoring," Calla said. She took up with the dough Tom had left in such a mess. "But I certainly got raped plenty of times after. I got tricked into whoring by a man named La Trobe. He offered me a job as a cook on the goldfields. I was wanting to get away from home because . . . well, never mind the because. But as soon as we got far enough north that I couldn't get home easily, he started selling me. To vaqueros, to miners, to anyone who'd give him a coin. It didn't matter if I cried, if I begged, if I screamed, if I fought; they all took their time with me. They'd paid and they were going to get their money's worth. And then he sold me to a whorehouse in Moke Hill. And that's where I met Emma. She bought me."

"Like Tom bought me back in the bad place?"

Tom flinched to hear his name.

"Not quite. The thing about most whorehouses is they keep the girls in debt, so they can't leave. They charge you for every little thing: your room and board; cleaning the sheets; the broken furniture some of the men leave behind when they go. And you're permanently in debt, working to dig your way out, and just getting deeper and deeper in debt every night. But not Emma. Her place was different. She bought my freedom and then offered me the chance to make a whack of money—money that I could keep."

Tom rested his head against the back of his hand, which was still gripping the wagon tray with white knuckles. If he understood everything Calla was saying, Emma wasn't just a whore . . . she was a madam. A whoremonger.

He hadn't known the least thing about her. Not one bit.

It just about gave him vertigo, the gap between what he thought she was and what she actually was.

After Calla finished speaking, Anna started up. The things these women had survived beggared belief. They talked and talked, through baking rolls and cooking dinner and eating dinner; they talked until the stars had come out, and they kept talking until the moon had set. Tom didn't have an appetite and he didn't feel part of the conversation—didn't know how to even *begin* to be part of the conversation—so he took himself off to the edge of the camp, where he turned his head to watch the sky. He didn't say a word.

The long night of talking seemed to help Winnie. She watched the women avidly as they told stories, and she asked question after question. When the girl started yawning, Anna declared it was well past bedtime. Emma caught the kid by the hand as she passed. "Winnie," she said, her voice carrying clearly to Tom across the crackling fire, "what happened to you was a bad thing, but it wasn't as bad as it could have been, and it won't be the only bad thing that ever happens to you. You don't have to let it be the most important thing. There are good things ahead of you. We get back up and we get right on walking, right toward those good things. Don't forget that. And don't forget that no one expects you to walk alone. We'll be right here with you."

Tom had no doubt that Emma had got back up and got right on walking after her ordeal. He'd seen her do it. The woman had more grit than anyone he'd ever known. What he did doubt was that she'd entirely moved on from it. He suspected she'd dragged it with her all these years.

Once Calla left to join the others in the tent, Tom was finally alone with Emma. She stared at him warily over the cook fire. Tom couldn't bring himself to speak. He didn't know what in hell he'd say. When she didn't speak either, he rose to his feet and crossed the camp to join her on her side of the fire. He sat next to her, and they both stared into the flames.

"Hell of a way for you to find out," she sighed.

"Hell of a way," he agreed.

She took a shuddery breath.

"Is that it?" he asked, afraid of what the answer would be. "Is that all I need to know about you?"

"No," she admitted, and the tension in her voice made him freeze with trepidation. "No," she sighed, "there's one more thing." She sounded painfully sad and terribly tired. "And you're really not going to like this one."

❧ 28 ❧

MAGDALENA WAS NOTHING to write home about. If she'd had a home. Which she didn't. And she didn't have anyone to write to either. Especially now. *Stop it. Don't think about him.*

Too late.

Tom hadn't brought them to Magdalena himself. Instead, he'd changed his plans and taken them to Arizpe. It was where he was scheduled to meet his men, and after her revelation about Luke, he hadn't wanted to spend more time with her than he absolutely had to. Emma had known it was coming, but it didn't make it any easier to swallow. At least she'd had years of practice at staring humiliation in the face, she thought ruefully. She knew how to hold her head high when all she wanted to do was roll up into a ball and hide; she knew how to stay stone-faced and not cry, when inside there was a hot spring of tears; she knew how to stay still through the long, ashy nights, holding herself in suspension until the morning came, even though sleep was impossible. She knew how to walk tall and act calm and pretend nothing at all was wrong. It was a point of honor.

In Arizpe, they'd found Tom's men already waiting for him, and he wasted no time in off-loading the ex-nuns and getting on with his life. They'd barely watered the horses when a man named Emilio introduced himself and said he was going to be taking them on to Magdalena.

"As it's still early, señoritas, I thought we could leave within the hour. We should make Magdalena in three or four days, depending on the weather."

It took all of Emma's hard-won composure not to spit at that. So Tom didn't even want them around for another hour. No. Not them. *Her.* And he hadn't even had the common decency to tell her himself.

She could see him down the street. He'd remounted his paint horse and looked like he was about to ride out. Already.

"Where's he going?" she had asked, unable to help herself.

Emilio had followed her gaze. "Tom? Probably to his old homestead. José Flores runs it now; his wife, Rosie, used to be the cook back when it was the Slater place. She's known Tom since he was a boy. She'll give him a big feed, and then he'll buy the bulk of their cattle for us to run up north. Theirs are always the first stock he buys."

Her first thought was there was so much she didn't know about him. Her second was that he wasn't even going to say good-bye to her. Now, that boiled her blood. Even a customer usually had the common decency to say good-bye.

"Emma," Calla called after her as she started stalking toward him. "Are you sure that's a good idea?"

Yes. She was. She was going to make sure he at least looked her in the eye as he broke her goddamn heart. "Slater," she said, her voice like a whipcrack.

He turned his horse and squinted down at her.

"Your man Emilio says he's taking us on to Magdalena. Instead of you."

Tom nodded. He looked grim. "There's no need to pay him. I've already covered it."

Her chin went up. "I pay my own way."

He shrugged. "Suit yourself. I'm sure he won't complain if he gets paid twice."

Emma felt a lick of rage at him. At *men*.

What did he have to be angry about anyway? She hadn't even *known* him when she'd slept with Luke. And did he think she'd *enjoyed* whoring? Even if she had, what business was that of his? None of it, that's what. It was her body and her business and her life, and he should feel goddamn *honored* that she'd shared any of it with him.

"You know I don't even know your surname," he said flatly as he squinted down at her. He shrugged helplessly, as though that meant something. Then he turned his horse and without so much as a farewell headed out, and all she was left with was a view of his back as he rode away.

"I would have told you if you'd asked," she said to the empty street. "But you never asked."

Stop thinking about it. It does no good. That was good advice if she could take it. But her mind kept throwing up that image of him, riding out of her life. She scowled at Magdalena as they rode in. It was a dusty little patch of nowhere. It wasn't somewhere she ever thought she'd be.

"This is your home?" Winnie asked Calla, who was so excited she could barely sit her horse.

Emma couldn't see why Calla was so keen to return. The place was sleepy and scruffy, with dogs and chickens running wild in the streets. The mission was the prettiest thing about it, and even that was thick with dust.

"This is the town," Calla said, "but home is a bit farther out."

They said good-bye to Emilio in the town square. He was nervous about leaving them, but Calla assured him up, down and sideways that she'd take care of things from here. Shrugging, he tipped his hat and turned right back around to Arizpe. Emma figured he couldn't much see the point of staying a minute longer than he needed to in Magdalena.

She was being unkind. She knew it. But she *felt* unkind, and better she took the feeling out on a town than on the people she cared about. She tried to put on a pleasant face as Calla led them excitedly to her family's farm on the outskirts of town. Although *all* of it was outskirts in Emma's opinion. The center wasn't much more than a patch in front of the mission.

Her mood didn't improve over the next few days, as they were welcomed into the chaos of Calla's family home. If anything, it grew worse. She withdrew into herself, letting Calla take over. She watched as Calla passed herself off as a respectable woman, chattering merrily as her sisters eyed her beautiful clothes with plain envy.

"She's spinning as many tales as you do," Anna said dryly, joining Emma under the piñon tree in the yard. Winnie trailed along with her, as she always did. She didn't like to be out of Anna's reach.

"I guess she ain't likely to tell her parents she's been whoring all this time," Emma observed.

"No." Anna sighed and settled with her back against the tree trunk. Winnie curled up against her like a cat. They watched the chickens scratch and the breeze kick up dust. "So, miss," Anna said suddenly, "what are we doing now?"

"There ain't much *to* do," Emma said with a shrug. "I guess we could help shuck corn for supper."

"That ain't what I meant and you know it."

Emma stared resolutely at the chickens.

"I know you don't plan to stay here," Anna continued. "This place ain't your style." She took in the run-down yard and the dogs panting in the shade. "So what are we up to next?"

"I ain't got the faintest idea." And that was God's honest truth.

"Calla's fixing to go court herself a man," Anna said. "I'm curious as to how that'll play out, so I'm happy to stay for another week or so. But after that, I'll be asking again. I need to go get myself a job, for a start."

"Who's Calla courting?"

"Who do you think?" Anna snorted. "That fancy Ángel man she never stops talking about."

"He'll like her for sure," Winnie said loyally. "She looks pretty now she's not a nun."

"Does anyone here in Magdalena know about her past?" Emma asked sourly. "Because one hint of that and she can kiss her prince good-bye."

"He doesn't need to know," Anna said. "They all think she made her money as a cook in the goldfields."

Emma snorted. "And what's a cook doing with all those fancy clothes?"

"Try and be happy for her," Anna scolded.

But Emma didn't know if she had it in her to be happy for anyone. Or happy at all. Something seemed to have shriveled up in her on the journey from Arizpe to Magdalena. It was the memory of Tom's face that did it. The look in his eyes. She'd seen that look before. His brother had worn the same look; it was distaste. Worse than distaste: she repulsed him. It was hard to withstand a look like that and still find it in yourself to be happy.

Hell. What did she care? She'd faced worse. This wasn't the first time she'd been left. And at least this time she wasn't broke and alone. Or pregnant. She was *fine*. Tom Slater had been an interlude, and that was all. She'd enjoyed his body and his company, and she'd always known that it wasn't forever. So what if he'd been an ass at the end? Wasn't that a good thing? It made it easier to forget him and move on.

Only it didn't. And she couldn't seem to forget him, or move on.

She was played out, she thought tiredly, as she listened to Anna and Winnie talking. Even her dream of a little house on the bay no longer brought her joy. The thought of trekking all the way back to Northern California was exhausting. It used to thrill her, the idea of sitting in her own kitchen, alone, enjoying the silence. But now . . .

Hell. Now she felt like she had a hole right through the middle of her. All the good feelings just dribbled out through it. When she thought about her little house on the bay, all she could think of was that *he* wouldn't be in it. If she tried to imagine her kitchen, *he* wasn't there. When she tried to make bread, she was haunted by the fact he'd never eat it. When she caught her reflection and saw her hair was growing out, she realized he'd never see her with hair. He wouldn't know her.

And she cared. She didn't want to, but she did. She cared more than she could bear. At night, when everyone slept, she found herself weeping. She could keep the tears at bay all day, but in the furthest lonely reaches of the night, they overwhelmed her. And she all but drowned in them.

A FEW DAYS later, Calla and her family were invited to a feast at the Leon ranch. Calla had wrangled the invitation

by flirting madly with Ángel Leon at church on Sunday.
Emma hadn't gone to church herself, but she heard the
story later from Anna and Winnie. Calla had worn one of
her more modest dresses (which was still fancier than any
dress owned by the women of Magdalena); it was the color
of plum skin and buttoned to the neck with shiny ebony
buttons. She'd taken a black lace fan and a fancy parasol
and had caused a sensation when she'd arrived at the mission.

"It was like a fairy tale, wasn't it, Winnie?" Anna
gushed.

Emma was sitting in the yard shelling peas, listening
cynically and trying to pretend to be happy for her friend.
She wasn't doing a very good job of it. Her bitterness jutted
through like a broken bone.

"In she walked, and he stopped talking mid-sentence—"

"Like he'd been hit on the head!" Winnie added.

"His eyes got all big and starry, and he couldn't look
anywhere else for the whole service. And, oh, you would
have been proud of our girl. She played it to perfection.
Modest as a mouse. But glancing at him over her fan."
Anna mimed it, flapping her hand like a fan and giving
Emma quick darting glances with her eyes. "And wasn't he
hooked!"

He must have been, because the invitation came that
same afternoon, just hours after church. It threw the house
into a frenzy. Calla's mother was just about weeping, she
was so excited.

"It's like 'Cinderella,'" Winnie whispered to Emma, as
they watched the to-ing and fro-ing. "Only instead of nasty
stepsisters, there are nice ones."

It was true. The whole family got into the fun. Dresses
were freshened up, hair was washed and braided and coiled

and pinned, and the house was filled with excited chatter. Calla's father looked absolutely bewildered as his daughters ran about, trailing ribbons, planning fantasy weddings. And in the center of it all, glowing like a bride-to-be, was Calla.

"Imagine his face when he sees her in that," Anna clucked.

Calla was completely out of place in the adobe farmhouse. She was in a frothy cream dress, dripping with handmade lace, earbobs dangling from her ears. She was a picture of grace and charm, and her family regarded her with more than a little awe. It seemed inevitable that she would win the prince.

"I've loved him since I was this high!" Calla said when she came to show off her dress to Emma. She held a hand no higher than Winnie's shoulder. "He's so handsome and so strong and so kind and so *good*."

"This is a man we're talking about?" Emma grumbled.

Anna gave her a not-so-discreet kick.

"He sounds too good to be true." She meant it kindly, but it didn't come out that way.

Anna rolled her eyes. "He'll love you too," she reassured Calla. "He'd be mad not to."

Winnie nodded in enthusiastic agreement.

"Madre de Dios," Calla said, pressing her hands to her nervous stomach. "I can't do this."

"Yes, you can," Anna said cheerfully. "Can't she, Emma?"

"Don't make me lie to her," Emma said. "I'm done with lying. It's got me nothing but heartache."

"At least tell her how beautiful she looks. That's not a lie."

Emma's heart softened when Calla turned her big dark eyes on her. "You do look beautiful." And she did. She was a dream. "He doesn't stand a chance," Emma said grudgingly.

Calla threw her arms around Emma and just about squeezed the life out of her. "Thank you!" she said, giving her a smacking big kiss. "I'm so scared."

"Scared?"

"I want this so much. And nothing has ever worked out the way I wanted it to."

Emma's heart pinched as she saw the hope and fear in Calla's eyes. She took Calla's face in her hands and pressed a kiss to her cheek. "The best we can do is try. The rest is out of our hands. Right?"

Calla nodded. "Right."

"Good luck, Calida."

Emma followed Anna and Winnie onto the veranda to watch the family rattle off in their wagon. Calla gave them a wave, her smile a blend of joy and anxiety.

"For God's sake, have *fun*!" Emma called out impulsively.

Calla grinned.

Emma stood on the veranda, watching her go, envying her lightness and expectation, hoping at the very least Cinderella would have fun at the ball. And that the happy-for-now of tonight would be enough for her. Because Emma didn't trust princes; most of them were no good sons of bitches. And even the good ones were prone to breaking your heart.

IT WAS LATE when Calla and her family returned.

"Emma?" Calla came straight to the room Emma was sharing with Anna and Winnie. As she'd done a hundred times back at the whorehouse, she sat on the end of Emma's bed and wrapped her hand around Emma's blanketed foot.

Emma hadn't been sleeping. She found it impossible these days. That was something else to hold against Tom Slater.

Calla was solemn. "I told him," she said softly.

"You told him?" Emma frowned. Oh. She'd *told him*. Emma sat up.

Calla sighed. "He was treating me so respectfully, like a real lady. And I just got to thinking about it . . ."

Emma let the silence pull out, knowing Calla would resume when she was ready.

"I thought about you and Tom . . ."

Oh, that hurt. Emma blinked in shock.

"About what happened when Tom found out . . . and then I started imagining what would happen when Ángel found out. What would happen if I left it until I was so deep in love with him I couldn't get back out. And I thought I'd rather start clean than face that. To tell him the truth, and then if he loved me, he'd really love *me*." Calla gave a rueful smile. "Isn't that silly?"

No, Emma thought numbly. It was a damn sight more sensible than sitting here in the dark night after night with a sore heart.

"It was perfect tonight," Calla sighed dreamily. "He danced every dance with me, and the way he looked at me . . . I felt like a princess."

Emma knew that look, knew how intoxicating it was to be on the receiving end of it.

"But all I could think was that he wouldn't look at me like that if he *knew*." Her voice trembled. "And I was right. He didn't."

Calla wasn't upset. She just seemed truly, deeply sad.

"You were right," Calla said matter-of-factly. "No one

wants a whore. Not for anything but poking. And I'm done with being poked." She squeezed Emma's toe.

Even though she had been thinking the same grim thoughts, Emma felt like she'd been struck. She looked from Calla, sad in her beautiful dress, to little Winnie, who was sitting up in bed, watching every move they made and listening to every word they said.

"No," she blurted.

"Yes." Calla nodded. "I should have listened."

"No."

"I ain't good for anything but whoring. He made that quite clear."

"Fuck that!" The words burst out of her. They were the most honest thing she'd ever said. They felt good and strong and pure. Her exclamation woke Anna up, and she didn't look pleased to hear the language being thrown around.

Emma didn't care. This was a moment that warranted strong language. "And fuck *him*. Fuck him for a no-good toad. He ain't no prince."

"I ain't no princess, Emma," Calla wailed. Her composure broke, and she began to cry. "No story had a frog kissed into princedom by a *whore*."

"Well those stories are wrong, then. Fuck them too."

"Stop swearing in front of the child," Anna chided.

Emma was astonished. "No!" She met Winnie's big-eyed gaze. "This child has been orphaned, kidnapped and dragged across California without anyone asking her opinion on the matter at all. And now she has to sit here and watch Calla come back from courting with her heart all stomped on. She can cope with a little cursing. She's one of us, and I'll treat her like one of us."

"You should set a good example," Anna snapped.

Emma nodded vigorously. Yes. Yes, she *should*. She *should* set a good example. It was time to put aside dragging around like a goddamn victim. That kid was watching every move she made. And so was Calla. So yes. She *would*. She'd set the best fucking example anyone had ever seen.

"Get packed," she snapped at the three of them. "We've got plans to make."

❧ 29 ❧

*L*UKE. IT HAD to be Luke, didn't it? Of all the goddamn people in the world, she had to have been in love with Luke. Tom couldn't stop thinking about it as he drove the herds up to the goldfields. And he kept thinking about it as they went from town to town, selling the beeves. He might have been able to get past the whoring, he might be able to get past her sleeping with Deathrider, but he sure as hell couldn't get past the fact that she'd once whored for Luke. Not just whored for him but *loved* him.

What the hell was it about his brother that women loved so much? Luke was stubborn and bossy and high-handed . . . He left his dishes unwashed until there weren't any dishes left to use. He left goddamn horse tack every-where. He thought everyone should do what he wanted just because he wanted it. And he already had Alex. Why did he have to take Emma too?

Because he was *Luke*, that was why.

Tom knew in his heart of hearts that he was a poor shadow of his brother. Luke was taller, stronger, better looking. Women melted at his feet. No one melted at Tom's feet.

Had she been thinking of Luke every time she slept with Tom? Had she found Tom wanting in comparison?

Of course she had. He was *sure* she had. And the thought made him so furious he wanted to split things. Fortunately, he had a fair idea of what he could split to vent his anger.

Or rather who.

But there was no sign of Hec Boehm in Moke Hill.

"I reckon he's still off chasing that whore," the saloon-keeper told him. The people of Moke Hill were more than happy to gossip about Hec Boehm and the snappy red-headed whore who'd led him a merry chase across the gold-fields.

"I hear tell he went after her all the way to Frisco."

"The way I heard it, she went back east and he followed her trail."

"If anyone can outhunt that old dog, it's Seline."

Seline. It was the first time he'd heard the name, but he knew who they meant. He'd seen her, back in *La Noche*: tall, sassy as sin, with blazing red hair slapping at her naked behind. He heard the reverence in their voices when they talked about her, and he knew it was Emma. She had the same effect on him.

The last place he went was her old whorehouse. The spot was infamous throughout the goldfields. He was expecting it to look like a fancy wedding cake, like *La Noche,* but the Heart of Gold was something else entirely. It was a sprawling homely-looking place, the kind of place that made you want to settle right in and put your feet up. It smelled like baking and whiskey, rather than cheap perfume and stale beer. The place was all warm wood and lamplight, with plush chairs and couches and a great big Indian rug on the floor. When Tom walked in, it was too early for business to be humming—the miners were all off at their claims—but there was a black woman leaning at the bar, with a ledger in front of her, and a barkeep sorting through rows of bottles on the shelf.

"We're down two bottles of bourbon, Virge," the woman was complaining, "and the same thing happened last month."

"I don't know what to tell you, Justine. I tally up every empty bottle."

"One of those girls is drinking. I'd bet my ass on it."

Tom cleared his throat, and they both looked around.

"We're closed till this afternoon, sugar." The woman gave him a bright but absent smile. "The saloon across the way is open; they'll look after you. You're welcome back at four; that's when our girls are ready for visiting."

"I'm not here for a girl," Tom said gruffly. "I'm here for Hec Boehm."

They got wary at that.

"This ain't Hec's place," the woman told him coldly.

"I know. I'm just asking around. No one seems to know where he is."

"We don't neither," she said. She certainly wasn't smiling now. "And we don't much care."

"If he ever makes it back this way," Tom said, sliding a scrap of paper across the bar toward her, "you tell him I want to see him. You tell him the whore he's looking for is with me."

Her eyebrows went up at that. "She is?"

"Yes, ma'am, she is. And whoever wants to get to her has to go through me first."

"What's this?" She took the scrap of paper.

"Directions." Tom gave a tight smile and put his hat on.

"Wouldn't want him to get lost on the way." He nodded politely. "Have a nice day."

As he walked away, he heard her read the directions aloud. "If that don't beat all," she said. "Lucky Seline."

Something twanged in him like a pain at that. Some inner cord or tendon running from his heart. "Lucky" wasn't the word he'd use to describe her. Or him neither.

FROM MOKE HILL, he rode the Siskiyou Trail up to Oregon. He rode hard to beat the winter storms but didn't quite make it. He had a few horrible days fighting his way through heavy snow, but eventually, he got there. Matt's place was farther along the foothills than Luke's, but Tom headed there instead just the same. He couldn't bear the thought of living with Luke all winter. At least if he didn't see Luke, he had a better chance of blocking out thoughts of Emma.

He got to Matt's as the day was drawing in. The lamplight fell in pools on the snow outside the windows. His brother had made a beautiful home. It nestled in the forest like something out of a fairy tale, beckoning lost travelers in from the cold. He could hear the echoing *thwack* of woodchopping and turned the corner of the house to see his brother. He felt a surprising bolt of happiness. He'd been so miserable. It was nice to see family. Immediately, he felt less alone.

Matt looked horrified when he saw Tom riding in out of the snow. He stopped chopping, his breath forming billowy blue-white plumes in the winter air. It was only afternoon but already getting dark. "Are you insane, riding around in this weather?" He slung the ax over his shoulder and fixed Tom with his usual surly look. "Why in hell didn't you hole up in Utopia until the snow blew itself out?"

"Because it might not blow itself out until spring, and I didn't want to sit in town all winter."

"How'd you even know we'd have finished the house by now? We might have still been out at Luke's. What would you have done then?"

Tom had missed Matt's bearish grumpiness.

"Even you can finish a house in a year," Tom needled him, leading his horses into the barn. Matt followed along. "Stop fussing," Tom growled. "I can take care of myself."

"You wouldn't know it. Look at you. You look like an icicle."

He felt like an icicle. "I might not look so bad if you'd offer me some coffee."

"I ain't fetching for you like a maid. Get your own damn coffee."

Tom struggled with the saddle. Everything was iced up.

"You're late this year," Matt said. He set to work unloading Tom's packhorses.

Tom grunted.

"We're all fine, since you asked," Matt griped. "In fact, we've got some news for you. You're going to be an uncle again. Twice over."

"More twins?"

Matt swore at him. "God, I hope not. Don't wish that on me. It's just Alex is expecting too. Her and Georgiana are due round the same time."

Tom nodded grimly. "Congratulations." It looked like Luke was just piling up his blessings.

Matt sighed. "You still carrying that old torch? Don't you reckon it's time you put it down?"

"Drop it, Matt." Tom slung his saddlebags over his shoulders. "You got a room for me?"

"You know I do. You know Luke does too."

Tom ignored that and started slogging through the snow to the house. He heard Matt sigh.

"I'll water and feed your horses for you, shall I?" his little brother called after him. "You're welcome!"

Tom turned around. Snow gusted in his face. "You want to explain why you never told me Deathrider was going by *my name*?"

"Fine," Matt grumbled, "you don't have to say thank you."

"You going to ask how that went?"

Matt looked him up and down. "Well, you're in one piece, so I assume it went fine."

"You're an ass." He turned his back on his brother and fought through the snow to the house.

"Tell my wife that and she's liable to belt you one," Matt called after him.

Tom snorted. "She's liable to agree with me."

"Only after she's belted you." Matt's voice got whipped away by the wind.

Tom headed for the warm light falling through the windowpanes of the kitchen door. He could hear children's voices and the sound of breaking glass, followed by the indistinct sound of Georgiana yelling. He sighed. He didn't think it was going to be the most peaceful winter he'd ever spent.

HE WAS GOING out of his mind before it was even December. The winter was long, the snows were constant, the temperature was frigid and his mood was darker than the short, bleak days. He had too much time to think. And he didn't like the tenor of his thoughts.

He thought he might have made a terrible mistake. He warred with himself. And he thought about Emma constantly. Her childhood in Duck Creek, Tennessee; the way she carried her mother's sourdough starter with her, feeding it tenderly every day; the way she laughed loudly and often. The way she made sure everyone was comfortable and happy. The taste of her bread. The smell of her skin. The incredible shifting colors of her eyes: the tawny, bleached summer grass shades and the sparkles of oak-leaf green. Her sharp-cornered smile. The feel of her hands on his body.

She'd slept with his *brother*.

It turned his stomach.

"What's got you so sour?" Matt asked him on Christmas Eve, once everyone had gone to bed. The snows were too deep for them to get to Luke's, so they'd stayed in for Christmas. Tom was relieved. He knew he'd have to see his brother before he left again, but he wasn't ready. He was still too raw.

"Is this about Alex?"

Trust Matt to be blunt.

"Because I thought you'd dealt with that years ago."

"It's not Alex," Tom said shortly. He got up to stoke the fire so Matt couldn't see his face. Hell. He couldn't keep it all bottled up. But he also couldn't bear to tell Matt the full truth. "I met a woman," he admitted.

"A woman!" Matt sounded shocked. Pleased, but shocked. "Well, that's great."

"It ain't great," Tom sighed. "It's a mess."

"Yeah. That seems to be the natural way of it. But trust me, messes get worked out. Look at me and Georgiana. That was some mighty mess."

"This is different," Tom sighed.

Matt managed to be patient for all of about two minutes. "Why? Why is it different?"

Tom shook his head. "I can't tell you." How could he? It

was bad enough to be in love with a whore, let alone a whore who'd slept with your brother.

In love with . . . Hell. It was the first time he'd thought the words. But they were true. He loved her. So much it hurt.

Goddamn it. The feelings he felt for Emma made everything else he'd felt in his life seem puny by comparison.

"Look, I ain't the smartest man in the world," Matt said, "but I'm smart enough to know that love don't come along too often. If you really love this woman—whatever the damn mess is—you ought to go out there and get her."

Tom gave a brittle laugh. And then what? Bring her home to his family? *That* would be something to see, wouldn't it? It didn't bear thinking about.

But he did think about it. Every minute of every day until the spring thaw came.

❧ 30 ❧

IT SHOULD HAVE only taken three months to travel the sixteen hundred miles up to Tom's home in Oregon, but Emma had some errands to run first. The first stop had been to Frisco. Emma wanted to buy a second wagon and to stock up for their new life. She'd taken in the sprawl of buildings curving around the bay and the crowd of ships with their jutting masts and tried to imagine looking at that view for the rest of her life. She liked the bustle of San Francisco; she liked the salt air; she liked the sound of the sea and the blue glitter of the ocean. She liked the way the fog settled on the bay, and the way the winter sun made it glow. But, she thought, Tom Slater had been right. It was no more beautiful than other places. She didn't feel much of a pang when they left. Certainly not enough of one to stop her from pushing on and leaving her dream of a house by the bay behind. She wondered what she'd find beautiful about Oregon.

It would be a bit longer until she found out, because they had one more stop to make.

"I never thought we'd end up back here," Calla said mildly as they rolled into Moke Hill.

"Me neither." But it seemed appropriate.

"Seline!" Justine lit up at the sight of her. "You're the last person I expected to see."

The place was looking fine. Justine had given it a lick of paint and changed the curtains over; she didn't fancy pink as much as Emma did. The girls were looking plump and well; there were a lot of new faces that she didn't know. That was good. That meant the old girls had moved along, which made Emma's heart glad. Whoring wore a body and soul threadbare.

"Emma, not Seline," Emma reminded her with a smile. "The place looks great."

"Not Sister Emma anymore?"

Emma pulled a face.

"What in hell are you doing back here?" Jussy was looking at her like she was crazy.

"I'm looking to see Hec." More than looking to see him. She was looking to set that old hog straight once and for all. She was here to settle her accounts. No more running away.

"Hec?" Justine frowned. "Honey, he never came back from chasing you. Didn't you hear?"

No. She hadn't heard.

"There are a lot of rumors." Justine looked mighty puzzled. She peered over Emma's shoulder and seemed more puzzled by the minute. "That he got scalped. That he got caught up in a gunfight between Kennedy Voss and the Plague of the West. Even that he choked on a chicken bone and keeled over dead at the dinner table. But no one's seen hide or hair of him since he went chasing after you." Justine paused. "I must say, I'm surprised to see you. I thought you'd be in Oregon."

Emma was stunned. "How did you know we were headed for Oregon?"

"Your man came through a couple of months back."

"My man?"

"Tall, dark. Best-looking man I've ever seen. I thought you were one lucky woman, let me tell you."

Tom.

"Did you catch his name?" Emma was horrified to hear the quiver in her voice. Goddamn it. She wasn't supposed to be weak about that man anymore. She'd made her mind up about it. She was taking charge.

"No, but he left directions for Hec to come find him." Justine turned and reached for the ledger, which was wedged between a couple of whiskey bottles. "Here." She plucked a scrap of paper from between the pages. "I'm supposed to give it to Hec if he ever comes back."

Emma took the scrap of paper and sat down on one of the stools. She felt a bit wobbly. "Jussy, can you pour me a drink?"

Justine did. Emma tossed it back in one gulp and knocked the shot glass against the bar in a staccato beat. "Goddamn," she said, full of wonder. Tom Slater was trying to protect her. "Get me another. And for Calla and Anna too. And milk for the kid. What did he say exactly?"

Emma made Justine tell her about Tom's visit at least six times, prodding her to remember every word and expression. It was definitely Tom. How many Oregon-bound tall, dark, green-eyed cowboys could there be? Especially ones who came asking after Hec Boehm and saying they were traveling with Seline . . .

He still cared.

Well, of course he did! The man was in love with her. He was just too stupid to know it. And he needed time to digest her past. She'd make sure he'd have time for that. It was part of her plan. She wouldn't get to Oregon until springtime; by then he should be headed off on another cattle run. He wouldn't be back to Oregon until the following winter, which should give her plenty of time to get herself organized. She was under no illusions; she knew she'd need every spare scrap of time she had. She felt a bit queasy at the thought of not seeing him for another full year. What if he fell in love with someone else? What if he married someone? What if he got hurt? What if he never came back?

"I don't understand what you're doing here." Justine interrupted her thoughts. "He said you were with him."

"I was. For a bit."

Justine waited, but Emma wasn't forthcoming.

Once they all had a drink in hand, Emma proposed a toast. "To Hec goddamn Boehm," she said, holding her glass aloft. "Wherever he is, I hope the devil is pricking his ass with a pitchfork."

"Amen," Calla said.

"What's the plan now?" Anna asked as they followed Emma back out to the street.

"What makes you think I have a plan?" Emma grinned as she swung up into the saddle. She pushed her hat back at a rakish angle.

"Honey, you *always* have a plan."

Emma laughed. Yes, she did. And this plan was a *great* one. She was going to make sure nothing stood between her and Tom Slater. And that meant conquering his family, one by one.

MATT SLATER WAS the first to see the place. He swore and stopped dead in the street. The twins were right behind him and went barreling into him at full speed.

"What in hell?" Phin complained. "You almost made me drop my new slingshot slugs."

"Hush up." Matt didn't want to hear another word about those damn slingshot slugs. Especially since he'd be hearing enough about it from Georgiana when he got home.

"What are you gawking at?" Flip followed his gaze. "Oh."

It was Harlan's old place. He'd packed up and headed for the goldfields, like half a dozen other fools around here. Someone had painted Harlan's place pale pink, with bright white trim. There were pink velvet curtains visible at the windows, and white wrought iron furniture on the porch. There was a woman in a broad-brimmed hat planting rose-bushes in the newly dug garden beds out front. Matt bet they were pink roses. The owner of this place sure had a liking for pink.

What made Matt swear wasn't the pink paint or the white furniture or the woman planting bushes. What made him swear was the sign being hammered up on the shop. Dell Pritchard was up on the roof, pounding in the last nails. Blazing white letters spelled out a name Matt knew all too well.

"Seline?"

The woman planting roses turned and squinted up at him. Goddamn it. It was.

"Seline!" The twins all but bounced over to her.

"Nope. It's Emma." She looked them up and down. "Ain't you grown since I saw you last! You'll be taller than me in the blink of an eye."

"Hey, Seline, you got any of your pies about?" Phin craned his neck to check the white tables lined up along the porch.

"Emma," she corrected again. "And no, I don't. But I do have some fruit buns fresh out of the oven. Run along inside and tell Anna I said you could have one each."

"Just one?"

"Yes, just one, you greedy scamp." She stood up and dusted the dirt off her hands. "You push your luck like that again, and I'll make you share one between the two of you."

They bolted for the door before she could change her mind.

Hell, Matt thought. Georgiana would tar and feather him for this one. She'd always disapproved of the whore. "The sign up there says 'Seline's,'" he pointed out dryly. "Not 'Emma's.'"

"Well, that old whore paid for the place, so I figured the least I could do was name it after her."

Matt laughed. Then sobered up when he saw Mrs. McCauley spying from the front porch of the general store. "You know, I'm not sure there's much trade for a whorehouse in these parts," he advised quietly. "This is mostly a family place. Settlers and the like."

"Good thing this ain't a whorehouse, then," she said cheerfully.

"It ain't?" Matt sounded dubious as he regarded the pale pink exterior.

"Nope. It's a pâtisserie. Well, a bakery. But pâtisserie has a nicer ring to it, don't you think?"

"Why's it all pink like that if it ain't a whorehouse?" He squinted. "And how come you got those fancy curtains?"

"I like pink. And pâtisseries are fancy places, Matt Slater. I got some coffee on. Want to come in and see? You can have a whole fruit bun to yourself. I won't make you share."

Matt laughed. He'd always liked Seline.

"How's your brother?" she asked as she led him inside.

"Which one?"

She gave him a look.

"You mean Luke, I guess." She'd not met Tom. Besides, women always asked after Luke. And Seline and Luke had a history. Wait until he told his brother Seline was here. He almost grinned. He was going to be in so much trouble at home. Matt liked it when his bossy older brother got in trouble.

Matt wasn't sure where to sit in this place. He felt a bit like a bull in a china shop. It was a fine-looking place, and it smelled like heaven, but it wasn't for the likes of him. There were two rooms across the front of the store, one set up with tables and chairs, the other set up like a lounge room. Inside, it wasn't quite so pink. The walls were freshly painted white, and there were white lace tablecloths. The armchairs and lounges were sage green velvet or dark leather. There were woodburning stoves in the fireplaces, pots of ferns and flowers scattered about, and brass lamp fittings. It was fancier than anywhere else in Utopia. He considered one of the dainty chairs and grimaced. He reckoned he'd break the chairs and get the velvet dirty. Seline . . . uh . . . Emma watched him for a minute, looking amused, and then she rolled her eyes.

"Come through to the kitchen," she suggested.

Gratefully, he followed. He noticed the wood-paneled counter and rows of empty shelves and display tables. "How much pastry are you planning on selling?"

"Depends how much your boys leave me," she said wryly, as they entered the big, sunny kitchen at the back of the house to find the twins with a bun in each hand.

"She said we could!" Phin said defensively, gesturing to Anna. His cheeks were stuffed with pastry.

Matt stayed for a good hour. He had two cups of coffee and more than half a dozen buns. When he left, he took a bagful with him.

He didn't know it, but he'd given Emma the best start to her plan she could have hoped for.

MATT MUST HAVE told Luke she was in town, because the next day, he came ambling along, looking as ginger as an old tomcat. She'd half expected it and had dressed for the occasion. She wore her teal blue gown and topped it off with her peacock feather headdress. Her hair was still short, but the headdress helped disguise it. The getup made her feel better. Like wearing a trusty old suit of armor. Emma's heart was thumping fit to jump out of her chest as she watched him amble up. She hadn't seen him in years, and she remembered keenly what she'd used to feel for him.

He was the same old Luke. Tall, dark and handsome. But not as handsome as his brother, she saw as he got closer. He was too solid. Too glib. He lacked Tom's intensity and Tom's stillness. His eyes were the wrong color. They were midnight black, with none of the nerve-tingling beauty of Tom's river-ice green eyes. His mouth was all wrong too. It didn't have that thin top lip, with its sharp Cupid's bow, or the plump lower lip that always looked boyishly pouty. He didn't have Tom's shyness, or his mix of puzzlement and wonder. And, to be blunt, there was nothing even remotely poetic about Luke Slater.

Emma was thrilled to realize that she didn't feel the slightest trace of her old feelings for him. Not one little spark. She was so thrilled she beamed from ear to ear. She hadn't realized how anxious she'd been about it.

"Why, look who the cat dragged in," she said happily. "If it ain't Luke Slater!" She could breathe easy now, she thought, as she put her hands on her hips and sized him up. "You look real good."

But not as good as your little brother. Not even close.

"Howdy, Seline," he said. He looked as uncomfortable as all hell. "I won't come in." He took his hat off.

"You sure? I got coffee on."

"My wife would skin me alive if I took you up on that." He gave a quick grin, and she saw a flash of his old charm. "She ain't happy to see you've set up in Utopia."

Emma frowned. "You told her about our history? That was dumb." Why would he do that? Had she meant more to him than she'd realized? Her stomach dropped. Why else would he tell his wife? Oh God, she hoped he didn't have feelings for her. The thought made her feel ill. She didn't fancy having *that* conversation.

"She saw us in Independence. You saw her too."

Emma frowned. Who exactly had he married?

Luke waved a hand. "It doesn't matter. It's a long story, and it's not what I came to say." He cleared his throat. "I've come to ask you to leave, Seline."

Of course he had. Emma flushed. How stupid could she be, thinking he'd had feelings for her? A whore. She was thicker than clotted cream. Her chin went up. "It's Emma," she said stiffly. *Remember the plan*, she counseled herself. *You expected this. Stick with the plan.*

He glanced at the sign but nodded. "Emma. Look, I'm happy to cover the costs."

"I beg your pardon?"

"For you to relocate. I'll pay whatever you need."

He wanted to *pay* her to leave? That really got her riled, but she kept her composure. "I don't want to relocate," she said.

"You can't stay."

She pursed her lips. "And why not?"

"My wife . . ."

"Did you tell your wife you were a virgin when she married you?" Emma asked bluntly.

"Well, no."

"Did she think for a second you were?"

"No," he said stiffly.

"Have you got any plans to renew our relationship?" Which would happen when hell froze over, but she wasn't going to deign to tell *him* that.

"No!"

The horror on his face made her feel ill again. She forced down the old feelings of shame. She remembered Calla sitting on the bed down in Magdalena, her hopes all stomped on. Well, Calla had nothing to be ashamed of, and neither did she. And she'd be damned if she'd let anyone make her feel otherwise.

"Well, honey, if she knew you weren't a virgin, and you got no interest in me now," she drawled, "I don't see what the problem is." She crossed her arms. "This seems like a matter between you and your wife. I'd appreciate it if you'd leave me out of it."

He flushed. "I mean it, Seline."

"You mean what? You want to buy me off? You want to bully me out of town because your wife doesn't like the fact you dipped your wick before you married her? You go home and tell her I'm retired. You hear me? I don't take money from men like you anymore. And, honey, I wouldn't sleep with you without payment if you were the last man on earth."

That was mean. But it sure felt good to say.

Luke blanched.

Emma sighed. "Ah, hell, why'd you have to go and prick my temper? You know I've got a bad temper." She wanted to stay mad at him, she really did. But Luke had been good to her. He'd been kind when she'd needed some kindness in her life. He was acting like a fool right now, but she didn't have to be mean about it. And she needed Tom's family to accept her. *Tom* would need it.

"You were nice to me back in Independence, Luke," she said. She descended the porch stairs and stood in front of him. "It meant an awful lot to me. And I thank you for it. But you were an equal partner in our past, and you got no right punishing me for it. You're the one who paid *me* for sex, not the other way round. I ain't here to chase you or any of these other men. Go tell your wife that. I got no interest in you, Luke. And you got no interest in me. People have pasts, and they shouldn't be punished for them."

"I ain't meaning to punish you," he sighed. He ran a hand through his hair. He was clearly wrestling with thoughts.

"Congratulations on getting married, by the way," she said, giving him a nudge. "Who'd have thought it? Luke Slater married. She must be quite a woman."

"She is."

Emma didn't feel the slightest bit of jealousy. "I'm happy for you," she said. And she meant it.

He nodded. "Thank you." His old gentleness was back, that sweetness that had been a shaft of sunlight in her life. "You look good, Seline."

"Emma," she corrected. "My name's Emma."

"Emma." He shook his head. "This is going to make my life a pure misery."

"I'm right sorry about that. But you can't change what you did before you met her."

"You sure I can't convince you to leave?"

"No. I got my heart set on this place."

"Can I ask why?"

"You can, but I ain't going to answer. Not today."

"I don't suppose you've gone and got yourself married too? Because that sure would help my case."

She laughed. "Not yet. But give me time."

"I can't say I'm thrilled about it . . ." He held out his hand. "But I guess this is welcome to town."

"Thanks." She shook his hand. "You want to buy some pastry?"

He grimaced. "You trying to sign my death warrant? I can't be taking your pastry home. I can't be visiting you again either."

She laughed as she watched him leave. Over the way, she saw a clump of women standing and gawking at them. She waved gaily, and they turned away. She bet Luke's wife would be getting a string of visitors in the next little while. Emma bet Mrs. Luke would get her dander up about today. With any luck, she'd come to hash it out with Emma, and then Emma could get to work on her too.

It would take time, but she had time. It was only spring.

❖ 31 ❖

THE PEOPLE OF Utopia weren't keen to let a lady move on from her past. Summer passed and fall fell. The leaves started to turn, and in the mornings, there was frost on the windowpanes. Emma wanted Winnie in school and marched her on down to the schoolhouse behind the church, counseling her to keep her head high as people stared. Calla had come along on the off chance of seeing the preacher, who had pricked her interest. Between them, they jollied Winnie along. Emma hadn't let Anna come; she kept weeping about Winnie going off to school. It just made the kid nervy. There was a new schoolteacher in town, a girl who didn't look old enough to be out of pinafores, but she was sweet enough, and while she blushed when she spoke to Emma and could barely meet her eye, she was kind to Winnie. And that was really all that mattered.

The children themselves sure as hell weren't always kind, and neither were their parents.

"You sure you don't want to find another town?" Anna sighed one night, as they sat upstairs after another fallow day. The four of them lived above the store, in two rooms they'd cozied up into a fine little home. "These people are about as friendly as a den of grizzlies."

"I'm sure." Emma was sewing a new dress. Well, she was turning an old dress into a new one, and Calla was helping her. She wanted to look her best. Just in case Tom turned up early.

"You know she ain't going anywhere until she's seen him." Calla giggled. "She hasn't gone to all this effort just to toss it in now."

Anna clucked. "Well, I hope he hurries up, because you sure can't afford to keep losing money like this."

"Sure I can. My money situation is just fine," Emma said. "Those old cats will get used to us eventually. Once they taste our baking, they'll be doomed."

"And I ain't leaving the preacher," Calla added.

"He ain't even spoken to you yet." Anna couldn't quite keep the exasperation from her voice.

"Sure he has. He shakes my hand and wishes me a good day every Sunday as I leave the church. I'm making headway. I can tell." Calla looked satisfied. She didn't have to worry about this one finding out about her past—the whole town already knew.

"And what if it don't work out with Tom?" Anna asked, turning her attention back to Emma.

Emma grinned at her. "Are you doubting me? I'm so confident I'm even buying a house here."

She'd found a property east of town. It was a pretty little farmhouse, with a view over the valley, where she could see the smoke curling above the treetops from the Kalapuya camp. From the front porch, you could see the whole town laid out, smoke puffing from the chimneys, with the mountains rising in the background. It had a nice big kitchen, and the bedroom windows looked out on the same view as the porch. She fancied lying in bed and looking out at all that prettiness. At this time of year, the leaves were singed red and gold, like burning embers. And the back of the house looked out on a whole ocean of trees. When the wind blew, it sounded just like the sound of the surf rolling into the shore.

"You liked the house, then?" Anna asked.

"It's perfect."

Anna didn't agree it was perfect at all when she finally saw it. "It's not even finished!" she complained. It was true. The man Emma had bought it from had caught gold fever before the house was done. It was missing a couple of walls and most of the stairs. As well as all of the fittings. But she had money; she could pay someone to get it done. Dell Pritchard was always hanging about like a bad smell; she might as well put him to work.

"This way I can have everything exactly the way I want it," she told Anna cheerfully. "I can buy the stove I want, and have more windows put in. I'm going to get a bathtub with a view, just like we talked about at the hacienda. I'll put it round the back of the house, so I can look out at that big old forest. I'll put double doors in the bathroom, and they'll open onto a balcony, and I'll be able to throw them open in summer and bathe naked to the world!"

Calla applauded with glee.

"Can I live there too?" Winnie asked.

"No, pet, but you can visit. You and Anna are going to have the store all to yourselves." She hadn't told Anna yet, but she was going to give her the deed to the place. She'd keep shares in it, because she was sure one day it would turn a profit, but Anna would have her own little nest egg. And a home in which to raise Winnie.

"And where am I going to live?" Calla asked.

"With the pastor, I assume. Once he gets up the nerve to actually talk to you."

All of Emma's plans were just about in place. She figured Tom would ramble into town sometime around late fall. By then, she needed to be established. That was part of the plan. For that to happen, she needed those damn townspeople to stop being so stuck-up and to come and buy a pastry or two.

It was Georgiana Slater who finally broke the drought. It was Sunday after church, and Emma and Anna were sitting on the porch, finishing a pot of tea and waiting for the crowds to pass. Emma was hoping one of these days the smell of fresh pastry and hot coffee would draw someone other than Dell Pritchard or Josh Masters, who were het up by the idea that she and Calla used to be whores. They tended to trail Calla back from church and follow her inside, flirting madly as she tied her apron on and stood behind the counter, waiting for customers who never came. Calla didn't pay them no mind. She'd got firm ideas in her head about that preacher.

"He's just adorable," she sighed, when they saw him skittering by every day, blushing bright red at just the sight of Seline's place.

Emma didn't see the appeal of him herself, but she was glad to see Calla moving on from that mess down in Mexico. And if she had to set her cap for someone, a bashful preacher seemed like a safe enough choice. The poor preacher had to pass their place on just about a daily basis, and you could see it pained him no end.

Emma liked to torture him. "Pastor Sparrow!" she'd call out cheerfully, whenever she saw his bent head and pink ears. "You remember what I said: preachers get free coffee in our establishment. I'll throw in a cinnamon roll for your first visit too." He ran along like a little old rabbit. It was actually kind of sweet.

"If you boys are going to hang around like flies round a pigpen, you can buy a bag of pastries each," Emma called inside as Dell and Josh traipsed after Calla on this particular Sunday. They'd been open for months and had done next to no business. She sure did hate to see her baking go to waste. There was only so much pastry the four of them could eat themselves.

"How was the service, honey?" she asked Winnie, as the girl plodded up the stairs. Winnie liked to go along with Calla on Sundays. She liked the stories and the singing, and seeing the other children. Not that they played with her, the little beasts. But Winnie did keep trying. The kid had grit.

"The preacher was telling about Abraham and Sarah and their maid. Hagar isn't a very pretty name."

"No, it sure ain't," Emma agreed, passing Winnie a custard tart. The girl shook her head. That's what things had come to, Emma thought in disgust. The kid had been eating leftovers for so long that now she couldn't even stomach the fresh stuff.

From the street, they heard the sound of a braying horse. Only it wasn't a horse. It was a little girl, decked out in her Sunday best. She had a clump of friends who giggled behind their hands.

"What in hell is wrong with that child?" Emma asked.

"Nothing," Winnie mumbled.

The girl whinnied again, and the other children squealed with glee. Oh hell. Emma got to her feet, and the children ran off laughing.

"Susannah Bee Blunt, you get here this instant!"

It was the first time Emma had seen Georgiana since she'd got to town. Matt's wife had just delivered a baby when Emma had arrived and hadn't been into town all summer.

Emma watched, amused, as Georgiana marched down the street. She looked like a queen. A little one, but fierce. Susannah had stopped dead and was watching her mother approach with a look of pure dread.

"What on earth do you think you're doing, torturing that child?"

Georgiana hadn't changed a lick, Emma thought. She was still the perfect little lady, dressed to demure perfection in deep blue. Her bell skirt was enormous, and she glided along without it swinging in the slightest. But all that class hid a spark that Emma admired.

"She wasn't one of them," Emma called down from the porch. She hadn't even realized Susannah was there. The girl was across the way with a knot of older girls, casting glances at the boys slouching over at the general store. Susannah looked absolutely mortified that the boys were watching her being dressed down by her mother in the middle of Main Street.

Georgiana wasn't mollified. "You get here right now and apologize," she said imperiously.

Susannah flushed. "But I didn't do anything!"

"You certainly didn't do anything to stop it, did you? And after all Seline did for us on the trail."

Well, she'd certainly changed her tune. Georgiana had been scandalized by Seline on the trail. She wouldn't even eat the food Emma cooked. But then, she'd been half-mad with grief at the time, and jealous to boot. Which was ridiculous, as Matt had never so much as looked twice at Emma. But there was no accounting for jealousy. Some people got bit hard by it.

"Get up there and apologize to Seline and her girl."

"Emma," Emma corrected. "My name's Emma. Seline was the whore."

Georgiana blinked at the baldness of her statement. But then she remembered who she was talking to and gave an imperceptible shrug. Emma saw Matt coming to see what the trouble was, baby in arms and the boys trailing behind.

"I'm very sorry," Susannah muttered, shamefaced, after climbing the porch stairs to stand beside Winnie. "I should have spoken up for you."

Winnie had gone pink. Emma couldn't tell if she was equally mortified, or pleased.

"And you will next time," Georgiana insisted.

"And I will next time," Susannah repeated. She swallowed hard. "I really am very sorry." She sounded absolutely genuine. And when she looked at Emma, her cornflower blue eyes were swimming with tears. "I'm sorry, Seline."

"It's Emma, honey, and I know you are." Susannah had always been a sweet girl, and Emma had a soft spot for her. And she was just about Winnie's age, so this might work out very well indeed. "Here, why don't you take these to your friends?" She held out the plate of custard tarts.

Susannah looked to her mother for approval.

"You can take them, but you can also take—Winnie, is it?—you can take Winnie with you and introduce her to your friends. If those little ones are going to be horrid to her, you older girls can take her under your wing. She's your responsibility, you hear?"

"Yes, Mama." Susannah took the custard tarts, and Winnie, and headed back to her friends.

Winnie looked back over her shoulder with wide excited eyes, and Emma winked at her.

"I'd like to pay you for the tarts," Georgiana said. Ignoring the horrified looks of the townspeople clustering by the general store, she climbed the porch steps. "I hear you've had a hellish reception?"

"It's not the worst I've ever had." Emma grinned. "But it's close."

"Are we stopping for coffee?" Matt called up from the street.

"Indeed we are," Georgiana said, loud enough for the whole street to hear. "And tarts too. Seline is the best baker this side of the country."

"Emma," she corrected cheerfully. This was going better than she could have imagined.

"Sorry. I'm just so used to you as Seline."

"You'll get used to me as Emma."

"I've been meaning to come," she said, "but the baby had colic, and I swear I haven't slept for months! It was just impossible."

Emma felt something loosen inside her as Matt and Georgiana and the children settled in on the porch for a visit. She could feel all the eyes watching her as she and Anna served them coffee and pastries. She practically heard them gasp when Georgiana let her cuddle the baby. Not that she had him long before Anna stole him.

"Another boy," Matt said, "but at least it's not twins."

Emma laughed.

"Do you sell your bread too?" Georgiana asked.

"Of course."

"We'll take a dozen loaves, if you have that many. You won't believe how much bread those boys can eat. Let alone Matt. In fact, make it a standing order. We'll come by every Sunday and collect."

"Can we get tarts every Sunday too?" Phin called over

from where he and his twin were doing backflips off the porch railing.

Georgiana told them off for it, but Emma didn't mind. Railings could be repainted. She liked her porch lively.

"Matt told me you were the one who made the pie for our honeymoon," Georgiana said abruptly. "That you were the one to organize everything: the picnic, the tent, the flowers, the blackberry wine."

Emma rolled her eyes at Matt. "You were supposed to take credit it for it, you dunce."

He shrugged. He had his arm around the back of Georgiana's chair and looked about as relaxed and content as a man could look.

"I never thanked you for it," Georgiana said. "That moment brought me back after Wilby . . ." she trailed off.

"You don't need to thank me."

"I do and I shall." Georgiana smiled at her. "And I also want to ask you for the recipe for the pie."

"That you shall never have." Emma laughed. "But you can buy one."

"Make it a standing order too. We'll take one every Sunday."

When they finally left, they were weighed down with bread and pastries, tarts and cupcakes, and even a fat pork pie for supper. Emma waved cheerfully as they rattled by in their wagon.

"We'll see you next week!" Georgiana called.

"That," Emma announced with satisfaction, "is the beginning of our good times, my friends."

SHE FOUND SHE was looking forward to seeing Georgiana again the following week. But she didn't even have to wait a week. Emma was out at her farmhouse the next day, boss-ing Dell and Josh around, when she saw a wagon rattling up the dusty path. She'd been standing at the upstairs win-dow when she saw them coming. Two bonnets. Women. Coming to visit her. In her gut, she knew who it was. Her plan was working! She dashed down the unfinished stairs, past Josh, who was trying to finish them, and out onto the porch to watch her guests approach.

She straightened her dress. She didn't want to make a poor showing in front of Luke's wife.

But when she saw who was sitting in the wagon next to Georgiana, her mouth popped open in astonishment. "I know you!" She racked her brain to think how she knew the woman. She was a looker. She had big gray eyes and a stub-born little cleft chin.

She gave Emma a look of pure, unadulterated dislike.

For some reason, Emma kept thinking of whorehouses. *How* did she know the woman? Surely, she wasn't a whore . . .

"I don't think you've met before." Georgiana was frown-ing at her. She glanced back and forth between the two of them. "Emma, this is Luke's wife, Alex. I thought the first time you met should be somewhere private, and not in the theater of the Main Street. That didn't seem fair to either of you."

"We *have* met," the woman said shortly.

And just like that, Emma knew how she knew her. "You're Dolly's cousin!" She'd only met the woman once, in the whorehouse in Independence, but she remembered how furious she'd been. "I think I tried to rip your hair out . . ."

"You did," Luke's wife said flatly.

Emma tried to remember the details. "You were giving him a freebie—it boiled my blood." She laughed. "He was supposed to meet me, and I was enraged to find you giving it away." It was such a long time ago. It felt like it had happened to a different person.

"I most certainly was *not*," Mrs. Luke said coldly. "You made an assumption."

"Based on the fact that you were in your underwear and you were kissing him." It was all coming back to her now. Oh, how jealous she'd been. It seemed ridiculous now.

"I'm only here because Georgiana all but kidnapped me," Mrs. Luke said through gritted teeth.

Georgiana cleared her throat. "Is that Dell Pritchard up there?" She was looking up at the upstairs window.

"Yep," Emma said. "He and Josh are helping me finish the place. I want to be in by winter, if I can." She had plans for winter, plans that needed privacy.

"It might be best not to have ears listening to this conversation," Georgiana suggested tactfully. "Perhaps you could come for a drive?"

"Sure." This was exactly what she wanted: a chance to soften up the last holdout in the Slater family. In order to do that, she'd have to stop needling her and play nice.

"Josh," Emma called into the house, "I'm just heading out for a bit." She paused, taking in the stony set of Mrs. Luke's features. "I might be gone awhile."

She climbed up into the wagon tray behind the bench, where she had a view of Mrs. Luke's set shoulders.

"We can't be gone long, as the babies are back at the house waiting for us," Georgiana said nervously.

"Babies?"

"Alex and Luke just had another little girl. Born three days before our Henry."

That explained why she hadn't seen Mrs. Luke all summer either, then.

"Congratulations," Emma said cheerfully. She was about the only cheerful one in the wagon. That, she hoped, would change. She had a plan to soften Mrs. Luke up. And it was right simple. She was going to tell the *truth*. It all its raw, unvarnished glory. It was novel for her, but she wasn't shy to try new things. She was going to tell these ladies about her childhood, her whoredom, her lost babies, her need for kindness when she got fooled into thinking she loved Luke, and most of all, about how she'd earned herself a new life. She had her own money, her own plans, her own little makeshift family. And she'd fallen like a sack of rocks for their brother-in-law.

This time, she wasn't going to disguise *anything*. She was going to strip herself naked in the only way she never had before. She was going to show them who she really was.

And if Mrs. Luke didn't thaw then, she probably never would.

That would be unpleasant, but Emma had lived through unpleasantness before. And nothing, especially not something as trivial as a bit of unpleasantness, was going to stop her from getting what she wanted. And what she wanted was Tom Slater.

❧ 32 ❧

SHE WASN'T IN Magdalena. Tom didn't know what he expected—that she was pining away for him in an adobe hut?—but he was stunned to find her gone. He'd been fixated on Magdalena all spring. He'd pictured riding in and sweeping her up and taking her home. Wherever she wanted home to be.

But she wasn't there. The only thing he swept up was a face full of dust when the devil winds blew.

He went to Frisco next, expecting to find her there. But again, there was no trace. There was plenty of gossip about the hunt for Deathrider: rumors he'd been killed in a dozen different ways—but no proof. And there was gossip about a certain redheaded whore, running loose with the Plague of the West. In those stories, he wasn't dead at all, and the two of them, the outlaw and the whore, were leading the hunters a merry chase across the west. Was it true? Had Deathrider been the one she cared for all along? Or was she only gallivanting about with him because Tom had left her? If he hadn't left her, would she care about Deathrider at all?

He thought the last months had been hell, but as he rode out of Frisco, he began to realize that he barely knew what suffering was. What if he never saw her again?

He was an idiot. Worse than an idiot. Why had he waited so long? Why had he left her in the first place?

So he'd been hurt. So what? That woman had been through hurts worse than he could imagine. And she hadn't run off. Not like he had.

It had been the worst year of Tom's life. And he'd had bad years before, so he knew what he was talking about. But now that he knew she was gone from his life, all the color seemed to leach out of the world. He plodded north, headed for another winter alone, feeling like the last man on earth.

He paused on the trail outside Utopia. He didn't know if he had it in him to winter in either of his brothers' houses. He couldn't face the happy chaos of children and families; he couldn't face being the odd one out for one more year. Maybe it was time to board somewhere in town instead. Luke and Matt might not like it, but they'd understand. He could visit. And then retreat to a quiet room inside a quiet boardinghouse, where he could be alone with his thoughts, with his memories. Where his glumness wouldn't impinge on anyone else.

Yes, he decided. That would be for the best. And maybe, if this winter was as wretched as the last, he might think about moving south permanently. Somewhere where he could see the sea.

He rode through the fringes of the winter forest, the fallen leaves soggy under his horse's hooves. Everything was charcoal, gray and brown, as drab as he felt. Main Street was churned-up mud. Until the snow came, everything was ugly and cold. A bitter wind blew, rattling the windows. Tom saw the church spire at the end of the street, and it occurred to him he could stay with Alex's brother, Stephen. He had a little whitewashed house next to the church, and there was only him in the place. He had plenty of spare space, and he was a quiet sort. He wasn't likely to bother Tom out of his glumness.

Goddamn, he thought, as he slowly trekked down Main Street. What in hell had Harlan done to his store? It was *pink*. But then he got closer, and he realized that it wasn't Harlan's anymore. His mind went blank. He couldn't quite register what he was seeing. He stopped his horse.

Seline's.

The sign rattled in the bitter winter wind.

A feeling so enormous, so overwhelming, rose up in him. His throat felt tight. His eyes burned and prickled. It couldn't be.

But he knew it was. There was all the pink, for a start. And then there was the yeasty smell of hot bread seeping out. And that sign.

There were other signs too. Fancy painted signs swung from the porch. One said, "We got pie!" and the other read, "Cheap Tarts!" Tom was startled into a laugh. And once he started, he found it hard to stop. He laughed so hard he started to cry.

THE DAMN FOOL man was just *sitting* there. In the middle of the street. Staring at her shop. Why didn't he come in? He had his hat pulled low, so she couldn't see his face. Damn it. This wasn't the plan. She'd always pictured him storming in. Or riding off. Or *doing something*. Not just sitting there like a bump on a log.

And now it was starting to snow. It was the perfect sign he should come inside. But the idiot didn't seem to see it that way. Not even when the snow gusted in flurries on the brisk wind.

"You should just go out to *him*," Calla suggested. She, Anna and Winnie were plastered to the windows, waiting to see what he'd do.

"Why do I have to do *all* the work?" Emma grumbled, as she reached for her shawl.

"Don't put that on," Calla complained, snatching it off her. "It ruins the look of your dress!"

"I'll freeze without it."

"No, you won't. You'll just shiver a bit. With any luck, he'll take the hint and sweep you up in his arms." Calla gave her a shove toward the door. "Go on, hurry up before he rides off."

Emma took her advice and stepped out onto the porch, her heart louder than a prairie thunderstorm. Snow was flying through the blue afternoon.

Oh my, it was good to see him.

"You're here," he said gruffly.

"So are you." She tapped her foot. "Are you going to come up here, or are you going to make me shout across the street at you?"

Silently, he swung down from the saddle. "You got somewhere I can stable my horse?"

"Not yet," she said. "You might need your horse yet."

He'd definitely be needing it. She planned to take him up to see their house. It wasn't quite finished yet, but it was private. And she could hardly ravish him *here,* with everybody looking on.

He tethered his horses to the hitching post, looking wary. She stood at the top of the porch steps, so she was looking down on him. Her memory hadn't done him justice. His gaze cut through her like a hot iron through ice.

"My surname is Palmer," she said, apropos of nothing. "My middle name is Jane. My mother used to call me Emmy, but no one's called me that since she died. I don't mind if you want to call me sugar or honey or just about anything at all." He looked like he'd just fallen down a gully. Good. He deserved it. "You didn't ask me my surname," she said primly. "But I still told you."

He took the point and nodded, a touch sadly. "I guess we didn't talk much, did we? Not about anything important. The important stuff I only know because I heard you talking to the kid."

The air got all charged up as they remembered what they *had* been doing instead of talking.

"You know a far sight more about me than I know about you," she said.

"You know I got a brother." There was some of his old bite. Good. She liked him biting.

"I know you got two." This was more like it. She'd practiced this snap and patter in her dreams.

"I went down to Magdalena to find you."

"What?" That wasn't in her plan. "You what?"

"I went to find you. I went to beg forgiveness." He searched her face. "I went to tell you I love you."

Emma felt winded, like a horse had just kicked her in the stomach. She hadn't planned this. She didn't know what to do with it.

I love you. He'd said *I love you.*

She'd been expecting a fight . . . or something . . .

Suddenly, Emma knew what she'd been expecting. And the realization was so painful she had to hold on to the rail.

She'd thought she'd have to *talk him into* loving her. That she'd have to *convince him.* That she'd have to argue and beg and cajole and charm and tease and *perform*. She'd thought she'd have to *earn it*.

She'd never expected him to arrive already convinced.

She'd spent months fixing everything. Removing his reasons to protest . . . Only, he wasn't protesting.

"Goddamn it, Emma. I've been sad my whole life. And I didn't even know it until I met you. I've been walking around with a great big hole sucking away inside me, like a tornado. But I ain't sad when I'm with you. When I'm with you . . ." He struggled to find the words. "When I'm with you, I'm . . . I don't . . ." He seemed to gather himself up. "I don't see the darkness. All I see is the stars."

"But I was a whore," she said numbly.

"I love *you*. Everything about you, even the hard stuff. I know how much pain it holds for you. I know what it means that you made your fortune the way you did. I'm not going to stand here and say it was easy to hear, or easy to think about, but *hell* . . . I'm sorry I shamed you for it. I never should have done that, and it's been eating me up inside. I never want to cause you pain."

"But your brother . . ." Her head was spinning. This wasn't going the way she'd pictured. People didn't talk like this, not to her.

"I can't say I like it," he said. He climbed the stairs until they were eye to eye. He reached out and touched her cheek gently with his fingertips. It was only as his thumb swiped away a tear that she realized she was crying. "But that was before me. You can't change the past."

"No," she agreed, "you can't."

"I don't know that I'd want to, even if I could," he said. "I reckon you love me as much as I love you. If that's so, who cares about the past? We got the whole future."

"I bought us a house," she blurted.

"Us?" His voice shook. "You bought *us* a house?"

"Come here." She took him by the hand and led him out to the corner of the porch. "Look up there." She pointed. "That place up there?"

He nodded.

"That's ours."

"Ours?" He sounded dumbfounded.

"Yes, you idiot. Ours. You think I'd move to a town like this if it weren't for you?"

"I thought you wanted a hacienda like *de Gato,* but by the sea."

She wrinkled her nose. "It lost its appeal after I met Two Moon and the boys." She leaned against the porch railing and watched fluffy snowflakes fall. They were as fat as duck feathers now. "Besides, I think I like it here."

"Here." It finally hit him where she was. "My family . . ."

She waved a hand. "It's all worked out. They've got standing bread orders."

"I don't . . ."

"Don't think about it now. I'll tell you about it later."

"But *here?* You wanted the ocean." He sounded uncertain.

She wasn't uncertain at all.

"You said it was the most beautiful thing you'd ever seen," he prodded.

"This is beautiful too," she said, and she meant it. "You told me once that everywhere has its own beauty. Nowhere's *more* beautiful. It's just different. I think your home is beautiful. The sound of the wind in the forest is like the sound of an inland sea."

"Home." His jaw clenched. He seemed to be in the grip

of a strong emotion. "You know, this place never felt entirely like home to me." He leaned his head forward and pressed his forehead to hers. He only ever did that when he was overcome. "But with you here . . . it does."

"It's going to feel a damn sight more like home once we fix that place up. Right now its draftier than a whore's drawers."

He laughed.

"But before we do that, I have a plan."

He groaned. "Of course you do."

"Yes," she said happily, "and it's an *excellent* one."

And when she took him up to the house and showed him what it was, using her mouth and tongue and hands, he had to agree. It was an *excellent* plan.

"I love you," he said, as they lay in each other's arms in the drafty house, listening to the sound of wind in the trees, like the rush of an inland sea.

"I know you do," she said, giving him a pat.

"And?"

"And that was all part of my plan." She gave him a cheeky smile.

He rolled her over, and she squealed. "You haven't told me that you love me yet . . ."

"Haven't I?"

He pressed kisses along her collarbones.

"You ain't so bad," she sighed, enjoying the feel of his hot mouth.

"I bet I can make you scream it," he threatened, trailing kisses down her body.

That was a bet Emma was happy to lose. And she did lose it. Over and over and over again.

AUTHOR'S NOTE

There's a gap between fiction and history, and as a novelist, it's difficult to manage that gap. The stories I tell are larger-than-life and more in the vein of an old screwball comedy or a Technicolor musical than pure history. That comedic tone can be hard to keep when writing about the west, because while the frontier was full of adventure and ideals and freedom, and the hope for a new world where people could build lives for themselves and not be trapped by existing class systems, it was also a place of violence and oppression and theft, particularly the theft of land and the violence against and oppression of the First Nations people. I want to acknowledge the First Nations people of California, where most of *Bound for Temptation* is set, particularly the Serrano, Miwok and Cahuilla people (the tribes I mention in the book). I would also like to acknowledge the First Nations of Oregon, in particular the Kalapuya of the Willamette Valley, where the Slater brothers settle.

Turn the page for an excerpt from
the first Frontiers of the Heart novel

BOUND FOR EDEN

Available now from Jove

Grady's Point, Mississippi, 1843

ALEXANDRA BARRATT WASN'T a violent woman. Most times she couldn't even crush a house spider. But Silas Grady was no spider. Silas Grady was a blackhearted, lily-livered, weak-kneed swamp rat. If anything, death was too good for him.

She couldn't believe the nerve of him, knocking on her door like nothing had happened. He was swaying on his feet and there was still dried blood stuck to his neck.

"It's your only hope," he said thickly. "Marry me, Alex."

If Sheriff Deveraux hadn't been standing right there, she might have forgotten she wasn't a violent woman and reached for the ax. But Sheriff Deveraux *was* standing right there.

"Marry me, Alex. I can keep you safe."

"Safe!" White fury licked at her. He was mighty lucky that ax was out of arm's reach. "And who will keep me safe from *you*?"

"Alex—"

"It's Miss Barratt to you, and how *dare* you come here after what you did today?"

"What I did . . .?" He swayed, confused.

Alex said a silent prayer. With any luck she could carry this off and get out of here before Gideon showed up. Silas was a lecherous, scheming idiot, but his brother was something much, much worse. "You arrest him," Alex demanded, turning to the sheriff.

The fat old man looked startled. He made a gruff *harrumphing* noise and hiked his pants up. "Now, Miss Barratt, you know I can't do that."

"I know no such thing. Every week since Ma and Pa died I've come to you with a complaint about this man." She pointed a fierce finger at Silas's face. "He and his brothers have terrorized us. They've tried to starve us out. And you've done nothing!"

The sheriff grew red-faced, but didn't manage more than a mutter. It was all Alex expected from him, bloated excuse for a lawman that he was. "If you won't do anything, I'll send for a federal marshal."

"Now, really, Miss Barratt, this isn't the frontier."

"It might as well be, for all the law there is around here." She lifted her nose in the air and tried to look imperious, which wasn't easy considering her rising panic. She had to get out of here before Gideon came. He'd probably made it home by now and found the mess she'd left . . . Oh glory, the thought was almost her undoing. Gideon was a maniac. Who knew what he'd do to her if he caught her?

"If you aren't going to arrest him, I don't see what choice you leave me." She kept brazening her way through it. Thank the Lord Silas was still concussed from that blow to the head. If he had half a brain, he'd be demanding that the sheriff arrest *her*. He had fair cause: over the course of the afternoon she'd knocked him out cold, stolen his brother's property and assaulted his evil witch of a mother.

And it was entirely his own fault, she thought, fixing him with a black glare. He flinched and fingered the wound on the back of his head.

"I've told you at least twenty times in no uncertain terms that I won't marry you," she snapped at him. "But you won't take no for an answer, will you? Well, I didn't say yes when you starved us, and I won't say yes now. So get off my property! It *is* still my property, you know." She turned her black glare on the sheriff, who at least had the good grace to look shamefaced. "If you won't arrest him, you could at the very least escort him off my land! Trespassing *is* still illegal, isn't it?"

"Come on, Grady," Sheriff Deveraux mumbled. "You'd best try your luck another day." He took Silas by the elbow.

"I'm your last hope," Silas said miserably. "He won't hurt you if you're my wife."

"Get out!" The edge of hysteria in her voice was quite real. She slammed the door behind them and yanked up the trapdoor to the root cellar, where her foster siblings were hiding. "Up!" she ordered. "Quick!"

"Give the gold back," her foster sister moaned as she struggled up the ladder. "Now, while the sheriff is still here."

"Are you mad?" Alex raced through the small house, throwing what precious little they still had into a sheet and tying it into a bundle. She tossed it to her foster brother, who was sitting on the lip of the cellar, looking despondent. "Don't worry, Adam," she soothed, running her fingers through his tousled hair.

"*You're* the mad one!" Victoria snapped. "Gideon will kill you if you don't give that gold back."

"He'll kill me anyway," Alex said grimly.

They heard a shot and Victoria screamed. Alex ran for the front window.

It was too late. Gideon was here. Poor, fat Sheriff Deveraux lay on the squashed dogwood blossoms, slain by Gideon's shotgun. As Alex watched, Gideon took a swing at Silas with the still-smoking gun. Silas managed to duck, but slipped on the fleshy blossoms and fell on his behind. Gideon kicked him.

"This is your fault, Spineless," he snarled. "If you hadn't kept sniffing after that bitch, none of this would have happened." The look on his narrow, ferrety face made the hair rise on the back of Alex's neck. It wasn't the anger that was frightening, it was the glint of barely suppressed glee. Gideon wasn't just going to hurt her, he was going to *enjoy* hurting her.

He looked up and saw her standing in the window. "Evenin', Miss Barratt," he called. Like they were meeting down at the store, or at one of Dyson's dances. She'd be damned before she'd show him fear. Alex yanked the blind down. It was a relief not to look at him, but a little scrap of cloth wasn't going to protect her from him. She bolted the door.

"Well, that ain't a neighborly way to behave," he called. God help them, the bastard was enjoying himself already. "Ain't ya going to ask us in for tea?" He laughed and Victoria started to cry.

"What are we going to do?" Vicky whined. "We don't even have a gun."

No. And the ax was still buried in the block out on the porch. Alex grabbed a couple of kitchen knives. They looked puny in her hands. "Here." She gave one to each of her siblings. "We'll go out the bedroom window. Go!" She grabbed a fire iron for herself.

Victoria looked down at the knife in horror. "What do you expect me to do with this?"

"Be careful," Adam said. "Ma said to be careful with knives. They cut."

Alex closed her eyes. What was she thinking? What good would a knife do Adam? He couldn't hurt anyone. *You were touched by God,* Ma used to tell him when the town children had laughed at him and called him names. The Sparrows had taken him in when no one else would have him. *You're one of His special children.* He was eighteen now, the same age as Vicky, but he was still a child. He would always be a child, and she had no right asking him to wield a knife.

"Don't touch knives," he said firmly as he looked down at the blade in his hand. "Don't touch the stove, it burns; don't touch the fire, it burns."

There was a knock at the door. "Last chance to be neighborly, Miss Barratt!"

"Go to hell!"

"Alex!" Alex heard the raw terror in her sister's voice at the exact moment she smelled the smoke. Victoria had opened the bedroom door to reveal a slow rolling cloud of smoke and the lick of orange flames. The bastard had set fire to the house!

"Oh, little pigs!" Gideon called, his voice bright with laughter. "Open up or I'll huff and I'll puff and I'll blow your house in!"

"We're going to die!" The knife fell from Victoria's fingers and clattered to the floor.

"No, we're not." Alex shoved Victoria and Adam toward the ladder to the loft where Adam slept. "Climb," she snapped. The smoke was rising and they coughed as they scurried upward. As soon as they reached the narrow loft,

Alex threw open the window. There was a big old black cherry tree growing close to the house.

"You can't expect us to climb down that!" Victoria gasped.

"Why not? We did it all the time when we were children. Out you go, Adam. Be careful. When you get to the bottom, run for cover in the woods. If we get separated, we'll meet at the old fishing spot." She turned back to Victoria as Adam disappeared down the tree. "Did you hear me?"

"The old fishing spot, I heard." Victoria coughed. "If I die climbing down that tree, I'll never forgive you."

"Fair enough."

"Alex?"

"What?"

"What if Bert and Travis are out there too? They might have circled the house."

It *had* occurred to Alex that there were still two Grady brothers unaccounted for. But what choice did they have? They could hardly stay here and burn, could they? And walking straight into Gideon's arms wasn't an option. "I saw them heading into town earlier. They'll be out drinking all night," she reassured Victoria, although she wasn't sure it was true. Gideon might have fetched them home after all the kerfuffle.

She heard the crackle of wood and winced. "Hurry, before the whole house goes up." The two of them scrambled into the tree. Alex heard Victoria's shallow breathing. "Don't look down," she counseled. By the time they reached the bottom the house was an orange blaze.

"Oh, little pigs!" Gideon was coming around the house, his mad voice high and clear, even over the crackling of the fire.

Alex grabbed Victoria and they went belting toward the woods. And ran smack bang into Silas. Victoria screamed.

"Shut up," he growled, covering her mouth with his hand.

"You let her go!" Alex shrieked, clawing at him.

"Shut up the both of you, or he'll find us." Silas's eyes widened suddenly and he went very still.

"Adam!"

Her brother still had his knife, the tip of which was pricking Silas in the kidney. "Knives are sharp," he said, "knives cut."

"Spineless?" Gideon's voice was coming closer. "Have you caught a little pig?"

"Let her go," Alex hissed at Silas.

"Let me help you," he begged.

"You?" she scoffed. "I'd sooner trust an alligator than a Grady." Alex took the knife off Adam.

Silas regarded it with disdain. "That won't be any match for his shotgun."

"Run, Victoria. Take Adam and run."

"Where?" Victoria was wild-eyed with panic. "And what about you?"

"If we leave him, he'll only come after us. Get away. I'll meet you at that place I mentioned." She shooed them with her hand. "Go!"

She couldn't risk looking away from Silas. She was afraid he'd make a lunge for her. She could hear the crunch of bracken under her siblings' feet as they ran, and then they were gone and she was alone with Silas Grady.

"What are you going to do now?" He sounded smug. He had her. She couldn't run; he would throw her to the ground the minute she turned her back.

"I'll tell you where the gold is if you promise to let me go."

He shrugged. "Gideon will make you tell us where the gold is anyway."

"Spineless!"

She jumped. Gideon was so close.

"I can protect you, Alex," Silas whispered. "Your brother and sister are free. They can stay free. I can keep you safe."

Like hell. Alex's fingers tightened around both the knife and the fire iron. She would rather die than give herself to Silas Grady. But she couldn't die, she thought desperately. Victoria and Adam would never survive without her. They needed her.

"You promise you can keep me safe from Gideon?" She crept closer to him, playing for time. The longer she kept him occupied, the better the chance of Victoria and Adam getting away safe. The hilt of the knife was slippery in her sweaty palm. Did she have it in her to use it?

"I'd do anything for you," he said. It was hard to see his face in the falling darkness, and the glow from her burning home backlit him, rimming him with orange light. It was a mercy not to see his expression. She didn't want to see his stupid look of adoration, or the uncompromising lust in his eyes. She shuddered.

"Anything?" She crept closer, until they were almost touching. One thrust would send the knife sinking into his belly. Her fingers tightened around the hilt.

She broke out in a cold sweat and the knife trembled in her hand. She couldn't do it. She just didn't have it in her to murder a man. She pictured Vicky and Adam waiting for her at the fishing hole, huddling together in the darkness as the bullfrogs sang and the mosquitoes whined. If she didn't kill him now, she would have to sacrifice herself. She clenched her teeth. One thrust and it would be over . . .

No. She couldn't. The knife fell from her fingers and she tasted ash. "You win," she said softly.

"Oh, Alex." Silas's foul mouth crushed down on hers and his disgusting tongue jabbed at her lips. The minute she felt that thick, hot slug of a tongue she came to her senses. Revolted, she spun around and struck out. The fire iron whistled through the air and came down hard on the back of his head. Silas made a grunting sound and then slumped to the ground.

She heard Gideon closing in, still mocking her with a sound like a squealing pig. Panicked, she ran. Behind her, the black cherry tree had caught and blazed like a roman candle, and there was an almighty crunching noise as the house collapsed in on itself. Sparks flew skyward into the night. There went home.

Alex ran like the devil himself was after her. She had to find Adam and Victoria and get out of Grady's Point before Gideon caught up to them. She heard a gunshot echoing through the firelit woods. Never mind getting out of Grady's Point, they had to get out of the state, maybe even the south. She wouldn't rest safe until she'd put a thousand miles between herself and Gideon Grady.